Praise for *Crows Calling*

"*Crows Calling* is a parable of wisdom and kindness . . . told through the eyes of the living world, a mind-altering journey that slips past our defenses and dualism, enveloping us in empathy for all creatures who face a faltering future. We are those creatures, too. You would be hard-pressed to find a more touching and emotionally resonant testament to the exquisite world we inhabit."

–Paul Hawken, *The New York Times* best-selling author of *Carbon: The Book of Life*

"*Crows Calling* offers hope in troubled times. Drawing from Native American wisdom, deep creativity, playful humor, and profound love for the planet and its myriad peoples, Bruce McConnell inspires us to think, dream, and take meaningful action to preserve our planet and its species while rekindling human connection to all living beings."

–Destiny Allison, author of *Pipe Dreams, Bitterroot, Shaping Destiny*, and *The Romance Diet*

" . . . McConnell writes with a gentle subtlety that belies the work's gravitas. Reading this piece was like watching a boulder being lifted with a feather's touch. . . a serious gift from a person who occupies a front row seat to humanity's collective choice process during an especially challenging moment. *Crow's Calling* is not just a book. It is a treasure."

–Paul Richards, author of *Wild Attraction*

" . . . a provocative story—in the best of ways. I'm feeling provoked to explore changing some of my own ways of living to help reduce our carbon footprint here on Grandmother Earth. My husband . . . has promised me a Three Sisters garden, replete with sunflowers."

–Diana Coe, Crone Communication

"Fiction allows us to imagine a better world, and McConnell does exactly that. Uncovering the connection between all living things and the environment, *Crows Calling* envisions a more sustainable future. It illuminates holistic solutions within our reach to address the planetary crisis."

–Alice Hill, co-author of *Building a Resilient Tomorrow*

"In *Crows Calling*, McConnell takes us into the potential for actually listening to and partnering with the living world for our shared survival. More than idealism, we're drawn into how this challenges us in our family and community relationships as well. We experience a level of relationship with the ecosphere that will propel us beyond the technosphere and into the New Earth."

–Diane Tegtmeier, author of *The Sacred Cell: What Nature Teaches Us About Relationships*

"Is there really a line between the human and the 'planimal,' or nonhuman, worlds when it comes to global warming? In Bruce McConnell's fascinating new book, *Crows Calling*, that line is very porous indeed. Our venerable narrator is Koro, a crow, well-versed in the mythic role of her species as 'troublemakers, too clever for [their] own good.' On the human side of the porous line are Luz, her family, and friends from among the First Peoples of Turtle Island. *Crows Calling* speaks the compelling language of interspecies communion that thrusts the reader into burning questions of life on Earth."

–Jim Gilkeson, award-winning author of *The Eleven Directions of Kansas*

"*Crows Calling* is such a positive story. I especially enjoyed the Monterey settings, the evolution of the characters and their strength and courage. When the lichen and the rocks chimed in amid the champagne surf, it became a paean, a lyrical song sung to the beauty of the earth."

—Christina Forbes Reynolds, Monterey artist and musician

Crows CALLING

Crows CALLING

An INSPIRING JOURNEY *into* OUR BETTER NATURES

BRUCE McCONNELL

GREENLEAF
BOOK GROUP PRESS

Crows Calling is a work of fiction. Names, characters, businesses, places, events, locales, and incidents are the products of the author's imagination or are used fictitiously. The science is intended to be factual, and the author apologizes for any errors.

Published by Greenleaf Book Group Press
Austin, Texas
www.gbgpress.com

Distributed by Greenleaf Book Group

For ordering information or special discounts for bulk purchases, please contact Greenleaf Book Group at PO Box 91869, Austin, TX 78709, 512.891.6100.

Design and composition by Greenleaf Book Group and Brian Phillips
Cover design by Greenleaf Book Group and Brian Phillips

Publisher's Cataloging-in-Publication data is available.

Print ISBN: 979-8-88645-339-3

eBook ISBN: 979-8-88645-340-9

To offset the number of trees consumed in the printing of our books, Greenleaf donates a portion of the proceeds from each printing to the Arbor Day Foundation. Greenleaf Book Group has replaced over 50,000 trees since 2007.

Printed in the United States of America on acid-free paper

25 26 27 28 29 30 31 32 10 9 8 7 6 5 4 3 2 1

First Edition

For Our Grandmother

Luz's FAMILY TREE

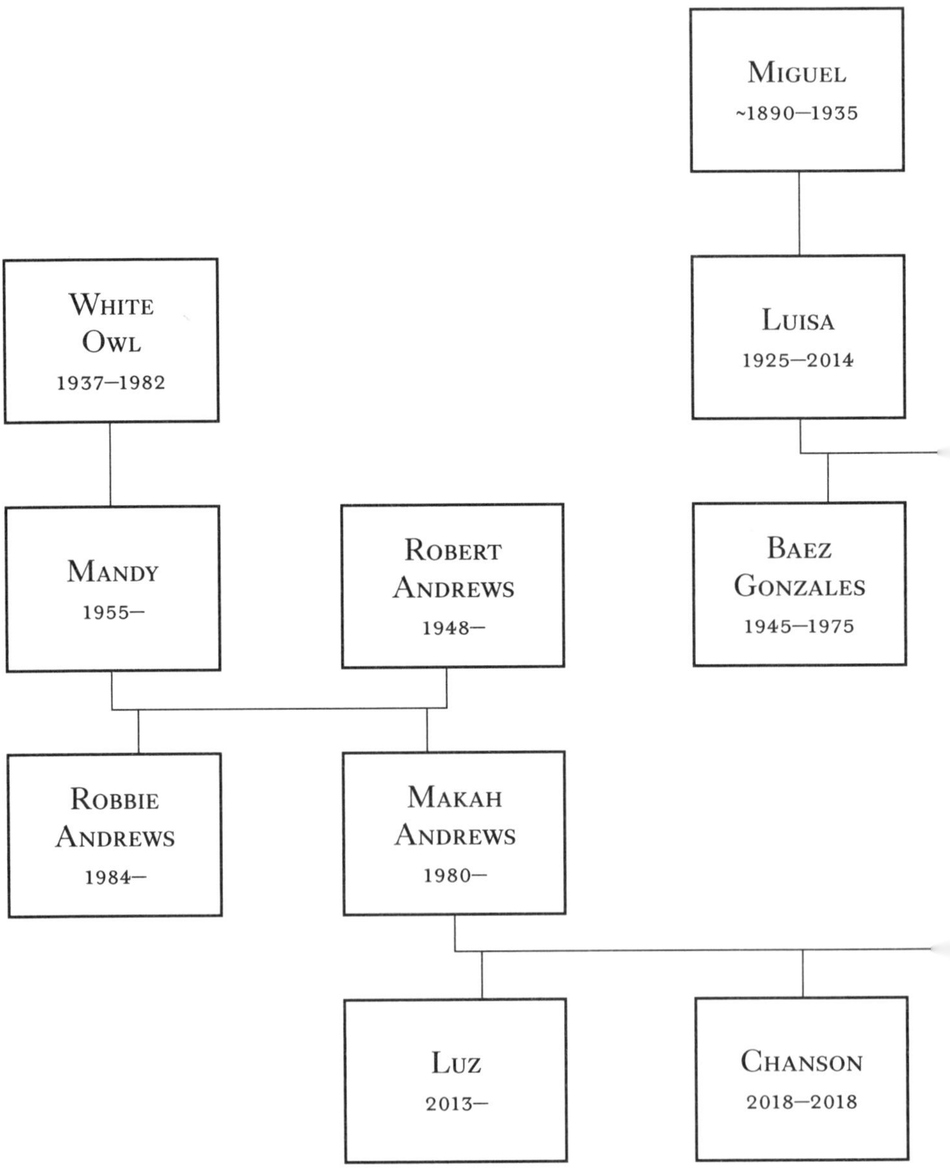

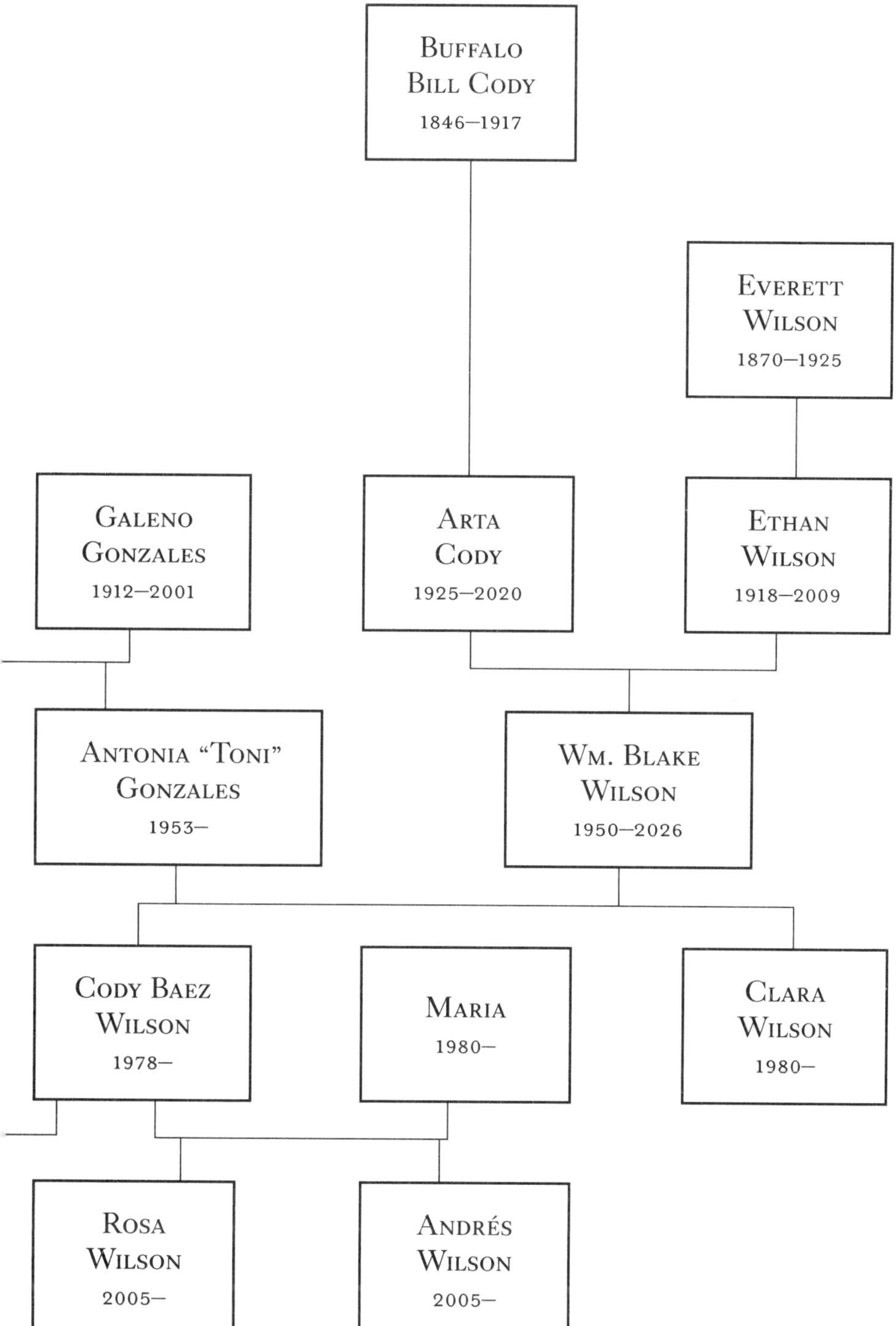
Buffalo Bill Cody
1846–1917
Everett Wilson
1870–1925
Galeno Gonzales
1912–2001
Arta Cody
1925–2020
Ethan Wilson
1918–2009
Antonia "Toni" Gonzales
1953–
Wm. Blake Wilson
1950–2026
Cody Baez Wilson
1978–
Maria
1980–
Clara Wilson
1980–
Rosa Wilson
2005–
Andrés Wilson
2005–

But ask now the beasts, and they shall teach thee;
and the fowls of the air, and they shall tell thee:
Or speak to the earth, and it shall teach thee:
and the fishes of the sea shall declare unto thee.

—JOB 12: 7–8

The poem is important
but not more than the people
whose survival it serves . . .

—WENDELL BERRY

Contents

Crows Calling

Studding the redwoods' emerald crowns
As from a minaret
They chant the convening—

Hawk! Hawk! they call,
Their gravelly crackles, melodious
Static on the Master's radio.

Vagrants, diligent, propelled by
Memories of hidden things
They sweep all in their rising wave—

The old form, a carapace,
Is left behind. The new lives on,
Into the world. Into the wind:

Don't know where this road will end.
Time grows short for the world we dream,
For earth and hearts to mend.

From the crow's nest the watchman sees
Beyond the far horizon. Crows,
Calling. Insistent. Got to go.

PART ONE

1

BEFORE WE GO ANY FURTHER, I really should introduce myself. I am Koro—a lustrous female American Crow. Surely, when strolling in woods or along an urban lane, you have admired my family's elegant, iridescent plumage and thrilled to our melodious song. You know of our prodigious memory, of our cleverness spearing hapless grubs from sodden logs with a favored twig.

The glint you see in my ebony eye is a tear shining for my grandmother—the earthly incarnation of generosity, whose bounteous lands and waters make room for every new arrival. Of late, however, one family—relative newcomers—has been pushing her limits, leaving their garbage everywhere and abusing the other guests. They run their noisy engines at all hours. Noxious smoke belches from their cooking fires. Every day, more and more of them come, crowding into other families' spaces, destroying the homes of many of my friends.

Recognizing our Crow persistence, Grandmother Earth called us to help her get those inconsiderate tenants to clean up their act. Personally, I'd prefer to stick around home, where the view across the forest canopy down to the sea opens my heart. I love the crash of distant breakers, the cry of a wayward gull, the barks of sea lions porpoising in the swells, the squeaks of ground squirrels warning of sly Coyote—all mingling with the damp, woody redolence rising on the sun's currents carrying ripe notes of fruit and flesh. This harmonious cornucopia is ornamented with the bright calling of my kin, the hum of high-tension wires, and the stubborn whine of a semi, downshifting on Highway 1.

Peering into the chasm of the coming Meltdown, I am proud to be on precious Grandmother's team. My *cawcus* is responsible for majestic Northern California, including fertile Monterey Bay and its deep canyon, the "Serengeti of the Sea." The land we cover is a patchwork sprawl of asphalt and forest, garlic and strawberries, oranges and avocados, cattle and sheep raised sustainably and otherwise, bears guttering in their occult tongue, sweet jasmine brandishing her shameless perfume, and sixteen million busy humans.

Through wildfires, drought, floods, extreme heat, even earthquakes, Grandmother is pleading directly with humans. Some hear her message. Take Makah Andrews, professor of International Environmental Policy at Monterey University. That has got to be one tough job, given humans don't seem to *have* a coherent policy, only practices, continually enhanced by technology. Extractive practices—eating the Earth—as if occupying the land bestowed only rights and privileges. Makah's one of the good ones, trying to use the system to turn itself around. That's the aim of "Team Grandmother"—a successful turnaround.

What's that I hear? Ah, please allow me to introduce my most trusted teammate, Ursula. Hey! Up here!

Koro? I can't see you through the branches, but my furry ears were tuned to your dulcet tones.

I'm talking with some of our human relatives who are listening to our story. Everyone, this is my friend Ursula, a beautiful California Black Bear who lives around here. Tell the people about your fine self, dear.

Hello, dear humans. It's a fine moonlit night. I'm hungry, eager to go foraging. I am large for a female, which I credit to ten years of enjoyable living in an abundant forest on the outskirts of town. This late spring season is my favorite—tender shoots, early fruits, the whole world alive around me, and the smell of barbecue reminding me that there'll be scraps down toward town if things get scarce up here. Mostly, I eat insects and berries, and I'm helpless before honey—it's totally worth the stings. I love birdsong—ahh, there's nothing more restful than falling asleep to the dawn chorus after a successful feed. My eyes and ears are better than yours, and my nose—well, let's just say I can smell you coming a hundred yards away.

Ursula, you and I have something in common. You're one of the few of your species who can speak directly to humans.

I received this power from a grizzled elder, who received it from the Bear Spirit. For us Ursines, interacting with people has been a mixed bag. We've been hunted for our meat, which they say tastes like pork; for our fat, which they have used as cosmetic cream; and for our fabulous skin and fur. Some take our gallbladders for medicine or make soup from our sensitive paws. There are bear markets, and folks who are bears for punishment. On the other foot, we're honored in myths. When Zeus fell in love with that athletic young huntress Callisto, she bore him a boy, Arcas. Well, Zeus's wife Hera was fed up with Z's dalliances. She turned Callisto and Arcas into Bears and sent them flying. You can still see them pointing north in the night sky. Among the local Indigenous people, we stand for authority, strength, and courage. They regard us as healers and protectors of the people, bringers of good medicine. These gifts we apply on behalf of Grandmother.

Ursula, it's great being on a team with you. You have gifts I don't. We have different relationships with the Earth.

We Bears are closer to Grandmother than you birds of the air or the fish of the sea. We lie upon her when we rest, enjoy her soft duff and craggy hillsides in our ambles, and sleep long winters in her chambers. Like Crows and humans, we fiercely defend and protect our young. We're more solo than either species. We don't congregate in noisy cawcuses or even quiet villages. Cooperation's not really our thing.

That's one thing humans are good at. Take cities—the collective effort of millions of people to conceive of, build, and operate them. But I was about to tell the folks what we've been hearing from other nonhuman parts of the natural world, from other *planimals*, as we call ourselves. Our fellow creatures are getting nervous. Some are angry. They worry about what it will take to make real change happen.

Most of us rely on Mark Twain's adage: "Action speaks louder than words, but not nearly as often." Humans' consumption model doesn't support the Earth. It's more like a cancer—destined to destroy the host.

But increasing numbers are trying to do the right things—the big factor is the clock.

Many planimals will die out if humans do not lead the turnaround, so I understand the agitation among our planimal relations. That's why we've organized a Congress—to get things moving.

We Crows love to talk. I've heard tales of such gatherings from Caspian Terns and Savannah Sparrows as they stop through on migrations. Everyone wonders if humans can become part of an expanded Team Grandmother.

We all need to work together, but then, I'm an old Bear, and I learned that lesson the hard way. My first litter was born one February: two males, Arkto and Orres, and a female, Koltala. When the boys were a year old, I encouraged them to strike out on their own. Koltala still shares my territory with me. It was dry that year and food was scarce. I mated that fall, but I didn't have enough fat on me for new babies. It was a grim time, and hard on my cubs. They were not that healthy going into the winter. Then, the clever one, Orres, discovered a fishing technique by watching a Cougar fool the fish by flicking the tip of its tail on the surface to mimic a waterlogged insect. Not having such a tail, he improvised with a willow branch. The next spring there was enough snowmelt for a good run of spawning Steelhead. But the lad got greedy. I guess his fear of being hungry drove him a little crazy. He caught more fish than he could eat. When a solitary old male came down to the water and saw the fish lying on the bank, he helped himself. Orres charged that big guy, but the match was over in a few blows, leaving him with a torn right arm. Eight now, he barely gets by. I tell this story every year to my new cubs to teach them to take only what they need and leave the rest.

You're such a philosopher, dear one. We need more brains than even ours to change the story. Maybe we *can* get together with our human relations and turn things around.

May it be so, Sister. Blessings to you and to all living beings. The breeze just brought aromas of fresh bearberry. It's time for dinner.

2

"MOM," LUZ PLEADED, "I want to go with Anna. It's part of *Spruce'n'Luz*—my nature training! But Dad's not so sure about the storm." She wrinkled her nose at Cody.

"Hiking and camping in the rain increases resilience." Makah set her water glass on the kitchen table. "I spent plenty of time outdoors in much worse weather in North Dakota when I was your age. I learned self-reliance."

"There was a mudslide last night on Highway 1, and it's closed near Esalen. There could be more coming," Cody said. "They're predicting another atmospheric river tomorrow." He stepped onto the back porch and watched the March wind drive a steady shower across Veterans Park in the fading light, listening to its patter on the toolshed's tin roof, smelling the spring mist mixed with sea air. *Something's saying yes.* He came back inside. "It's definitely wet." He winked at Makah.

"Dad, I'm almost ten, and it's *important*," Luz said. "We've planned this for weeks—Anna's had *dreams*."

"We'll be okay." Anna tented her fingers. "We'll take care of each other and find things in the shadows that would be hidden in the sunlight. It's a beautiful trail. I've walked it dozens of times over the decades. And

I'm wearing the bear claw necklace Raíz gave me before he died—it was from his grandmother."

"What if you took Skah?" Makah asked.

At the mention of his name, the old shepherd-lab rose from the living room rug, stretching out his long front legs, head down, rear up. He took a satisfying shake—*ahh, better*—and padded to Makah. They'd been together fifteen years, and Skah could read her completely. Before she met Cody, Makah wondered if she'd want a man like that. So deeply intimate.

"I'm with Anna," Skah transmitted. "The energy where we're heading is good, although the animals are restless."

Cody eyed his brown and yellow friend. "He's been slowing down lately. But he's definitely psyched for this."

"Your mind's still in fine shape, isn't it?" Makah caressed Skah's head. "Not to mention your big old heart."

"I was in Salinas yesterday talking with a former Opti-Drip colleague," Cody said. "The Central Valley is dry this spring, so the rain is welcome there. Perhaps we should welcome it as well." He peered at Luz. "You must be careful, my little light. It's a big adventure."

"Bring some bearberry," said Makah. "Do you remember at Powwow last year, how we passed the calumet?"

"Oh, *yeah*—holding the pipe bowl up to the shoulder and letting the smoke curl around," Luz said.

Cody reached for a carved, painted box on a high shelf. He shook some dried leaf into a small deerskin pouch decorated with a geometric beaded design. "Be careful with this bag, Luz. You remember your Grandma Mandy gave it to Mom when she was a girl. Can you take care of it?"

Luz nodded gravely. "Yes, Dad. Why is it called *bearberry*? Do bears like to eat it?"

"Bears like all kinds of berries. But they do like these when they can find them. Maybe we can find some when we go hiking next time. Maybe we'll even spot a bear."

"The Greeks called it *beargrapes*," said Makah, "and it's known as *kinnikinnick* to some Native Americans—the leaves are good for smoking."

"I'd rather eat it than smoke it," Luz said. "Maybe I'm part bear!"

• • •

After an early breakfast, Anna, Luz, and Skah drove through a drizzly morning to a hidden entrance on the edge of Big Basin State Park. They left the car at a small turnout, fitted Skah's saddlebags, and hoisted their backpacks. As they entered the abandoned Indian trail, they left some bearberry leaves as an offering. Like its surroundings, the park was unceded Indian territory, taken from the Ohlone people by Spanish colonists and now a haven for old-growth redwoods, saved from logging by its inaccessible terrain. The park had closed two years earlier, after a lightning-started wildfire burned for five months and destroyed tens of thousands of acres and all the park buildings. Where the trees had crowded, their leafless lower branches kindled the fire's ascent to the canopy. Many redwoods died, while others survived, heavily charred. Now those were leafing out from trunk and canopy, and daughter shoots sprouting from the base were six feet tall.

Anna put her finger to her lips, Luz silent behind her on the wet trail for what seemed rather a long time.

Skah brought up the rear. *Sweet, this hike. So many smells. That crow up there—Koro!*

They rested beneath a tall pine adorned by three great blue heron nests, the hungry chicks beseeching their majestic parents to return. An outrageous sea roared beyond them.

Skah lay down beside them, and Luz rubbed his ears affectionately. She sensed the energies of the place, its beauty and its initial healing from the fires, although she could not have put her feelings into words.

Anna waited, and a peace came over them. She put her hand on

Luz's. "What have you been sensing on our walk?" she asked. "Tell me in three sentences."

Luz fidgeted, looking up at Anna, whose long gaze calculated the sun's descent. "I smelled the salty air and the moist Earth. I heard the waves and that beautiful crow's chatter and the heron squawks and maybe a wren or sparrow. I saw deer footprints on the trail, and many grasses and bushes and trees." She stopped. "Was that okay?"

Anna smiled. "And what did you sense inside? One sentence."

"I felt peaceful, and I felt my heart getting bigger, like it would grow too big for me to hold it. It was scary."

"Ahh. Do not be afraid of that feeling, Luz. That's the Earth Spirit—she is your friend." She squeezed the child's hand and let it go, raising her arm toward the ocean. "Now the same questions about this moment, hearing the waves crash onto the coast."

Luz was briefly silent. "I sense the presence of many generations—people and sea animals. I hear a gull crying. The damp air is in my clothes." She paused. "I feel sad."

Anna sighed. "Yes. As far back as anyone can remember, maybe ten thousand years, humans have lived along the coast and enjoyed the bounty of Brother Ocean. The Quiroste Ohlone lived there until they were driven into the missions. Over time, many whales were killed nearby, and fish as well. Let's walk some more."

Anna pointed out various plants, explaining their powers, telling stories about them and the traditional healing practices that California Indians were rejuvenating. After a couple of hours, they came into a clearing that overlooked a valley. The rain had let up.

Skah sat, his nostrils flaring gently as he filtered and cataloged the rich forest scents. He'd noticed dried Bear spoor on the trail, and now—Bear, in the valley. He walked over to the edge and lay down, facing the source of the scent. An old sow. *All's well—for now.*

Anna breathed comfortably. "We'll stay here then." As they set up their little tent, they talked about Luz's schoolmates and about Indian peoples. Anna knew Luz was proud of her Native American roots but sometimes felt isolated, being the only one among her friends.

"Mom says that the Rumsen Ohlone had easier lives than her people in the Dakotas," Luz said. "There, the Nueta camped along the river during winter, down from their fields and houses on the bluffs, to stay out of the freezing winds and be close to firewood. Before the settlers came to *Xawa'ak*."

"Did your mother teach you that word? I don't know it."

"Grandma Mandy told me. I only know a few words. *Xa* means 'grass,' and *wa'ak* means 'land.'"

"It's good to learn and speak your language as much as you can," Anna said. "It helps you see through the eyes of the ancient ones. And you are right—life here was easier. There were abundant resources on the land and in the waters. The climate was mild. There were fights between tribes but not the warrior culture of the plains."

"Mom said sometimes the Sioux traded buffalo meat with the Nueta for corn, but other times they rode in and stole food and took women. The Nueta made friends with the Crow Indians, who helped them protect themselves."

"Not everything was beautiful in the Old Times. Humans are a tangled net."

As dusk arrived, they ate peanut butter and honey sandwiches and hard-boiled eggs. They glimpsed faint light coming from three other points above the protected valley. Below, a most uncommon collection of animals was standing, sitting, perching, or lying around in a little circle near a majestic redwood. The old Bear eating bearberries was the last thing Luz saw before falling into a peaceful sleep.

3

IN THAT PARK, there is a little valley where the fire damage was not so bad, between Last Chance Trail and Old Woman's Creek. I had spoken with Audrey, a majestic Redwood, who said she would be glad to host some planimals for a talk about the future.

We called it the Congress of Life. Ursula was my cohost. We were joined by Snave, an intimidating seven-foot Northern Pacific Rattlesnake. Invertebrates came too—spiders, bees, worms, snails, and of course the ubiquitous viruses, bacteria, and other microorganisms. Coastal and marine life was represented by a yellow-legged, gray and white California Gull named Scree, and Zarapito, a striking, Long-billed Curlew with a distinctive curving bill and brilliant brown and gold plumage. Audrey, queen of the forest, represented the terrestrial plants.

It was dark by the time everyone arrived, many of them tired from long journeys. The faint lights from the humans camped on the ridge had gone out. Our nocturnal relations had generously agreed to accommodate Crow Standard Time, and, after a good sleep, we began in earnest the next morning.

From my perch on Ursula's fuzzy shoulder, I began. "Welcome to the park. I think you all know why we're here. We give thanks to the Spirit of Life for conducting us here in safety. Many of you have journeyed a long way and faced danger. You come from diverse ecosystems, and you are representing your bioregion as well as your species. Thank you for taking on this responsibility. It is testimony to the gravity of our situation that we are all together. Audrey, we extend deep condolences to you and your companions for your losses from the fire, along with the many other plants and animals who died or lost their habitats."

Seven California Quail erupted with a resonant whirr and disappeared behind a fallen trunk. A Pileated Woodpecker hammered insistently on a blackened snag. Breezes moved through the canopy, rippling Audrey's regenerating branches.

I continued. "This gathering is the seventh regional Congress of Life in North America, or Turtle Island, as the First Peoples say. Our sisters and brothers in warmer parts of the continent have had their meetings, as have groups in the tropics and in low-lying and island regions, where the effects of climate change are most severe. I believe we can learn from them."

I love pontificating like that. After I finished bobbing my head a few times and ruffling my feathers, Ursula took over.

"We are here," she said, "to explore what planimals should do about the Meltdown. Humanity's pitiful failure to collaborate across their political boundaries to save their own skins during the recent pandemic, a threat less dire than we face today, bodes poorly." She rubbed her left ear with a fleshy paw. "We fear that their collective inability to move past themselves and their local needs means that the response to climate change will be too little, too late. Various approaches have been suggested and debated. The question is, should we act at all, and if we do, how? We could act without the humans, we could try to work with them, or—"

This last notion evoked titters and catcalls.

"Now, now," growled Ursula. "Show respect. We're in this together. As I was saying, the third option is to let Nature take Her course."

"Respect indeed," came a buzzy interruption from a bright orange Northern Giant Hornet hovering in front of Ursula. "I'm here to complain about the pro-vertebrate bias in this meeting. You vertebrates constitute a tiny fraction of animal life on the planet. You're just like the humans—you think you're the top of the evolutionary chain. We invertebrates have much longer memories. Only the plants are longer lived. You could learn some things about survival from those you consider beneath you."

This intervention was greeted by buzzing, peeping, and clicking, followed by frond waving, blossom popping, and sporing from the unsung, ancient, entangled network of fungi.

"We hear you," said Ursula. "We agree this needs to be rectified. Your wisdom is extremely valuable, and we'll consider it. Now, as I was saying—"

"Just a minute!" said a small voice that seemed to be coming from a nearby boulder.

"Now the rocks are speaking?" I whispered to Ursula.

"We, too, want to bring a fresh perspective to this distinguished gathering," the little voice continued. "We are Lichen, a composite organism, made up of three symbiotic partners—an alga, a fungus, and a bacterium. We cut across three domains of living beings. We get along so well that some individuals cohabitate for thousands of years." They paused.

"Go on, please," said Ursula. I could see her mind working—what a break! This will help us. She winked at me, but I shook my feathers and muttered a skeptical *croak*.

"Our point," said Lichen, "is that we need each other's unique strengths and perspectives. We appreciate the leadership of the vertebrates—after all, you are at greatest risk. You invertebrates who depend on them directly—well, you may need to adapt. But we can all listen better, and we have so little time if we want to make a difference."

By this point we had lost control of the agenda. With Scree's raucous aid, I was able to call for position statements on the three options. The opening speaker, supporting direct action to slow the rate of human-caused destruction, was a wiry female Coyote named Shakti. Coyotes are the most vocal wild mammals on Turtle Island, and Shakti warmed up with a series of yelps, huffs, and yips.

Skah barked harmoniously from the ridge, and I could hear his companions whispering to him.

"Listen up, everybody!" howled Shakti. "The Coyote Nation believes we must take action against humans to wake them up and stop their self-indulgent madness. We Coyotes intend to identify and track high-profile humans who endanger our Grandmother. Some Cougars may do the same. *Wowoooo-woo!*"

The flashy Hornet, Vespa, buzzed in. "We support this option. People call us the *murder hornets*, and they are afraid of us. We are infiltrating this region. We have made a deal with a school of endangered Largetooth Sawfish who have had it with overfishing and habitat loss. They do not prey on humans, but their toothy saws can slash a fishing net, free the captive fish, and render the net unusable. When a fishing boat stops to retrieve the damaged net, the Sawfish will leave, and their cousins the White Sharks will pool near the net. That's where we come in. We'll drive the crews into the water, where the Sharks will make short work of them. This will be so much bigger than the recent boat sinkings by the intrepid Orcas."

Lichen spoke next. "We've been around for 250 million years. Not as long as the Ferns and Horsetails, it's true, but even so, you might expect us to be unruffled by the current crisis. That's not our view.

"We believe the evolution of life on Earth is at a beautiful crescendo. Humans are not our enemies—they just need to reform their ways. We oppose action against humans. It will be more productive to pool our skills, working with them to reverse the dangerous trends. Already they're realizing that plants and animals can help. Bacteria are breaking down the islands of plastic fouling the oceans. Humans are encouraging and learning from that process. There will be more sustainable progress if the humans work with, and for, all life. Thank you."

"Well spoken," said Ursula. "Anyone else supporting this option?"

Scree was standing on a tall boulder. "It is an honor to represent the sea planimals of the region. I'm speaking for the fish, the marine mammals, the coral, plankton and kelp, and my fellow seabirds when I say the time has come for action by the planimal community. We face man-made perils every day—chemical pollution, plastics, abandoned fishing nets—but warming water, increasing acidity, and rising sea levels are our greatest concerns. If we wait for humans to act on their own, it will be too late. We need to help them. Most of us agree with Lichen and oppose taking action against humans, while of course respecting the positions of our Sawfish and Shark relations."

During Scree's remarks I heard a staccato *tic-a-tic-a-tic* coming from Snave the Rattler, who was taking up most of a large, sunny rock. "Go ahead, Snave," I said, and everyone tuned their receptors to Serpent.

"Unlike Scree, we reptiles and others who crawl the Earth think we should let Nature take Her course." She shook her tail for emphasis. "Some of us go back before the Age of Dinosaurs. These crises are normal. Species disappear, sure, but others thrive. Look at this forest. Many died here, but our Grandfather Sun is shining into long-forgotten places, and life is starting over." She paused, stretching herself out fully. "No particular time—even our own—merits special protection. We have to take the *long* view."

Well, that set off much murmuring and chattering, including high-pitched bleats and grunts from a dozen Black-tailed Deer peering from the clearing's edge, curious about these strangers congregating in their habitat. Finally, Ursula rose with a long, throaty growl.

"Thank you, Snave," she said. "I have explored this point of view with many delicious berries and grubs, and they certainly recognize the cycle of life. Some of them live on as parts of me today, whereas others have returned to the forest through the work of the diligent and beloved flora and fauna who reside in my capacious belly. Why, indeed, should we do anything? Even human philosophers debate the merits of struggle versus acceptance in the face of adversity. But I say to you: None of us, sisters and brothers, no, not one of us, was created to give up. We want only to live. When one species declines, we take advantage of the opening, if we are able. We cannot, by our natures, do nothing. We *will* respond."

"Right," I said. "Much to think about there. All right, Audrey, the floor is yours, although I suppose that's redundant since the forest floor has always been yours."

Audrey rippled her feathery leaves. "Most plants support a passive approach. We've been here for a very long time and seen major die-offs. Life always comes back better, more complex, more interesting, more beautiful. Who are we, those living today, to stop the course of Nature? Yes, humans have become an excessive burden on the planet. They have abused our Grandmother and wasted the resources she has provided. They will pay the consequences of their greed. The lesson will be written in the fossil record and into the genetic memory of all beings. The next evolutionary cycle will begin with that knowledge built in. New life will natively avoid the mistake, the design flaw, that enabled an oversized human ego. This is where we stand—trusting in the inherent, deep intelligence of the biosphere to unfold to the greater glory of the Universe."

This seemed to conclude the position statements, and I declared a nature break, knowing we needed time to talk among ourselves. After a while, I asked Scree to squawk us back to order. Support had been coalescing around a concept proposed by Zarapito, who agreed to present the idea.

"I remember a story my grandmother told me that may help us," the bird twittered in his treble voice. "Once there was a young Curlew who loved to skitter in and out of the surf as it broke on the sand. He loved the adventure so much he didn't mind an occasional drenching from an unexpected wave. The other Curlews laughed at him, egging him on, so that his actions became more mindless, even away from the shore. One spring day, at nesting time, he was practicing what he called his 'hopping dance' amid the Shortgrass of a western prairie. He had been perfecting the rhythm to lure worms and small bugs up to the surface where he could grab them easily. He failed to notice the low nest where his aunt had just laid four eggs. In one hop, he broke two of the precious jewels. His aunt and uncle were hopping mad and pecked him violently with their long bills. The young Curlew was driven away and spent the rest of his days alone. The clans discussed this incident. They did not ban hopping dances, because they had admired the young Curlew's playful spirit and his creativity at getting food out of the ground. Instead, they wrote a code of conduct, springing from the principle 'do no harm.'"

Zarapito paused. "I tell this story because we'll be more successful if we don't try to specify the actions anyone should or should not take to shape the future. Instead, we need a code of action we can apply in our own situations. You may have heard about the one developed by some African Elephants."

I liked Z's story, and there was interest in the code idea. But by now it was lunchtime. We decided to break and reconvene in the late afternoon. Everyone could rest, eat, and bone up on the Elephants' code via the Network. I reminded everyone to be on their best behavior, especially the predators. We closed the morning with thanks to our Grandmother, and blessings to Audrey, our alluring hostess, who returned them, and we foraged peacefully beneath the watchful eyes of the forest.

• • •

As we came back together, rain again battered the coastal hills, but Audrey's valley was spared. There were puddles from the night before, and I sopped an ample crust of delicious sourdough bread some hiker had abandoned. Then I took a minute to enjoy the *floppa-floppa* of a bath. I was energized, rested, well fed, and happy to be around my peeps on our important mission.

Having finished several helpings of midday berries, Ursula ambled into the center of the group beneath the broken canopy. I perched jauntily on her back. She stood up and waved her furry forelegs. The chatter subsided.

Ursula announced, "We resume our discussions. I am happy to report that a new mudslide has reduced access to the site, keeping random humans from disturbing our meeting. Our scout Turkey Vulture confirms that there are eight humans on the ridges, along with a big Dog. I hope we can trust them."

"I sense we'll be okay," said Audrey. "They all love our Grandmother."

With that, I resumed. "As Zarapito proposed this morning, we now come to the Code, working from the excellent words crafted earlier this year by the Amboseli Elephants. If you did your homework, you know that the current version goes:

I will honor the sanctity of all life.

I will respect each being for what it is.

I will destroy other life only to the minimum necessary for survival.

I will be mindful of the effects that my actions may have for seven generations."

I then asked for any thoughts and feelings about the Code and its potential applicability to our region.

Vespa the Hornet buzzed loudly. "I like it a lot. It's simple and yet covers the key points. I do have one suggestion in the third verse, which would be to change *destroy* to *knowingly harm*."

Zarapito, who was acting as secretary in the absence of an African Secretary Bird, asked, "So that would say, *I will knowingly harm other life only to the minimum necessary for survival*, correct?"

Shakti the Coyote jumped in. "I agree that *harm* is better than *destroy*, but *knowingly* seems to be a Weasel word—no offense to any of our delicious Mustelidian fellow carnivores. The Code is aspirational. It already contains one such word—*may*—which we should take out. The verse asks us to understand the consequences of our actions. Beings should do the best they can, but no one can fully understand the present or predict the future. That's a given."

"Other comments?" I asked.

"I have one," rattled Snave. "Where it says *I will respect each being for what it is*, I suggest *I will respect each being for what and who they are.* Beings have personalities shaped by our ancestries and life experience. It doesn't say I have to like, or even accept, the way another being acts. One must consider history when dealing with others. We're responsible for our actions, but compassion is warranted."

Scree spoke. "I like these suggestions. My question is, what's missing? What did our Elephant friends forget?"

"We have a perspective to offer," said Lichen. "We cleave to the rocks, and we think this Code may be too life-centric. Maybe that's a blind spot? What about if we mentioned Grandmother? It could say, *We will honor the sanctity of the Earth, and all Her life.*"

"Just a minute," said Zarapito. "Are you also suggesting a change from *I* to *we* in the Code?"

"We would prefer *we*. Individual agency is essential, but we prefer to err on the side of community."

There followed a general discussion, and the changes were agreed, so that the Elephant Code, Turtle Island, Western Pacific Region, went as follows:

We will honor the sanctity of the Earth, and all Her life.

We will respect each being for what and who they are.

We will harm other life only to the minimum necessary for survival.

We will be mindful of the effects that our actions have for seven generations.

Ursula stood and growled loudly in the four directions, where the human observers were.

"Trusted sisters and brothers," I said, "we ask that you take this Code and propagate it quietly in your communities. Please say that it came to you in a vision, and do not refer to this gathering. Is that agreeable, dear friends?"

From each outpost came a resounding "Ho!"

"It remains for us to consider our next steps," I continued. "We should reconvene in a year and take stock of what progress has been made. In the meantime, all life forms should take courses of action or nonaction that accord with their inner lights. Good luck to us all."

"लोकः समस्ताः सुखिनो भवन्तु—*Lokah samastah suikhino bhav antu*," chanted Audrey. "May all beings, may all universes, be free from suffering and centered in the joy of union with divine existence." And the participants took up the blessing in their own tongues as they set out on their homeward journeys.

4

LUZ'S DEPARTURE FOR THE CONGRESS created a rare private space for Makah and Cody. They enjoyed a quiet dinner by candlelight and slept, disturbed only by slight pangs of worry about Luz and Anna. The next morning, Saturday, they lingered before rising to sit on the porch with their coffee.

"Anna said not to expect them until tomorrow," Makah said, watching the fog burn off.

"We're blessed by the sun today. I think it's raining in the park. But they have a good tent."

"Isn't it amazing to have Luz and Anna in our lives? What treasures. And to have each other."

"I'm the lucky one—to have you putting up with me," said Cody. "I still wake up next to you and pinch myself to be sure it's not a dream."

A Townsend's warbler landed in the backyard redwood, its elegant eye stripes mocking the simpler yellows of the tree's usual denizen, the American goldfinch.

Makah laughed. "Luz has been a gift. She's steadfast, almost to a fault. But she weathered our great loss."

Cody contemplated the redwood where Chanson was buried. "We come by our sorrows honestly, I suppose."

Makah gazed into the distance. "From our heritages, you mean, although that doesn't make it easy."

They sat listening to birdsong from the Veterans Park canyon below the house.

"Not much in the way of crows this morning," he said. "The gulls are quiet too."

"It's peaceful." She gazed at him, inhabiting his calm mood. His hair had started to recede; his eyes seemed set more deeply. She loved him, way down inside. "I appreciate how you were so supportive when I lost Chanson."

"When *we* lost him." He squeezed her hand. "We're in this together, Makah—it's of a piece."

She pulled her hand away and finished her coffee. "Anyway, it's going to be great to have more room when we get the addition done."

"I'm only waiting for one more referral, then we'll have three architects to interview. We're in good shape with the budget after the initial payout from the Opti-Drip sale, and we'll be fine next year when I finish the two-year workout period."

"I'm going to be a hard-ass on the environmental impact, you know."

"Ecological cred is a top selection criterion, as we wrote in the project description. You made sure of that," Cody said, "and you know I agree."

"It'll be an adventure, living here during construction."

"We'll probably have to stay with our parents for some of the time. It's a chance to go to Bismarck."

"Luz will like that, especially being with Mom. She and Luz love to go through Indian stories."

A breeze arose and blew the fallen leaves across the yard into the fence, ruffling Makah's long black hair. "We're like a dust devil on the Plains," she said, "a brief vortex of energy going nowhere in particular, coming from nothing and returning to nothing."

"I suppose we leave our little marks, our tracks for others to follow, or avoid."

"Oh, Cody, what will happen?" She drew in a quick breath and touched his arm. "I know you don't know either. It's just that . . . sometimes—"

Cody faced her. "It's like we're in some buffalo stampede started by greedy cowboys. The animals in front reach a cliff and realize what's happening, and they roar as loud as they can, but it's too noisy, and the ones behind them can't stop anyway. The next thing you know, the whole herd is going over."

"The Sioux would do that after the buffalo became a commodity for the settlers. But you're being dramatic. Although it *is* hard to see how to turn the situation around. So much momentum in the current ways."

"Maybe our spirit catchers will have some ideas when they get back tomorrow."

• • •

It was evening when the congress ended, and Anna, Luz, and Skah stayed overnight before retracing the muddy trail to the car.

"What an honor to have been present," Anna said, "and to hear the discussion."

"It was magic that we could understand them," Luz said. "And I was so glad to hear that beautiful coyote, Shakti, speak, although she was rather fierce."

Skah dropped into himself, feeling his ancient bloodline. *A fine-looking animal, that Shakti, and wily. We four-leggeds have a lot to offer the two-leggeds, the "masters"—more than they realize.* It was lonely being the only one in the household. He missed Cody's cat, Tara. But the Coyote who killed her must have had his reasons. Skah didn't blame him. He trotted to catch up.

"For me," said Anna, "the most important moment was when the rattler talked about the need for compassion for others' seeming failings. It reminded me of my favorite line from the author James Baldwin: 'Thou knowest this man's fall, but thou knowest not his wrassling.'"

"What about those other people, across from us?"

"Do you think we would recognize them if we met them?"

Luz shrugged. "Maybe they could signal us."

"What would that look like?"

"They could rub their left ear, like Ursula does when she's nervous."

"We'll have to watch for that. I think we can tell Makah and Cody about the trip, don't you?"

"Maybe Mom can read the Elephant Code to her students!"

"I can talk about it in my healer community too, as a vision. What about you?"

"I have to think about it. It's complicated, kind of a grown-up thing. But maybe I can say my mom wrote it and bring it up during environment studies."

• • •

They found the roads slow but passable, arriving wet and hungry, with powerful light streaming from them. Cody warmed up dinner while the two took hot showers. The foursome gathered around the table, with Skah underfoot near Makah.

"Tell us everything." Makah dished out rice and beans, cheese, and zucchini flowers to the weary adventurers.

"Mom, it was amazing! It was like Noah's Ark. There were predators and prey right together. They were all talking. We could understand what they said. Koro was there—she was one of the leaders."

"Wait, what? Slow down. You saw animals talking, and what?" She raised her eyebrows at Anna.

"Who's Koro?" asked Cody.

"Dad! She's that brainy crow we see around here all the time."

"Oh, *that* crow. I think of her as Skah's friend," Makah said.

Skah stirred. No Tara, but still a friend, and so gifted. A fine representative of her species, an ambassador for the Corvids.

"Were there other people?" Makah asked.

"We think there were three other groups of two," Anna said. "The groups camped in the four directions. We camped to the north. Across the valley from us was strong female energy, but not spiritual. More like *Love the forest for its trees*—like timber. East and west it was male. One pair reminded me of Raíz—Hispanic and mystical, very old energy. The western pair was—*classic* is the only word that fits—strands of predation and honoring braided together. I thought I heard a hawk crying in the west. We were told not to speak much about the gathering. The animals don't trust people."

"If we see the other people, we're going to signal them by rubbing our left ears," Luz said proudly.

"I can understand why the animals would be wary. But your story is fantastic," said Makah. "It's not likely anyone would take you seriously—in the mainstream, I mean. Just don't post it on the internet."

"We decided that is probably right—too unpredictable—although there is this Elephant Code," Anna said. "It was developed by elephants in Africa, and the planimals—that's what they call themselves—modified it at their congress. It's a code of conduct asking all living beings to take care with each other and with Grandmother Earth. They asked us to publicize it without saying where it came from."

"Oh, I like that," Makah said. "What does it say?"

After Anna recited the Code, Makah continued. "Wow! I can get my students to write about the implications for human behavior, the economy, etcetera. That'll be fun."

Anna turned to Luz. "In important ways, the meeting was unlike

Noah's Ark. And I don't mean the Flood, although what we're facing is as big as that."

Luz contemplated the question. "There's no Ark, and no Noah, to receive the animals."

"Just all of us on the blue planet," Cody said.

"But, Mom, I was scared when some animals got angry. They started talking about attacking people."

Snoozing Skah arose. He came around to Makah, who stroked his head. Skah looked at his Makah with calming eyes, telling her, "We were far away from any danger. But there is anger in some species, especially the more aggressive ones—Coyotes, Cougars, Wasps, Sharks . . . ."

Anna picked up on Skah's transmission. "It's true. Some animals were quite agitated." She exhaled. "But we were safe, up there on the ridge."

"Maybe," Luz said. "But I'm sorry that any animals are angry at us. We should try to be better neighbors."

"That hasn't always been true of humans over history," said Cody. "Sometimes we have killed animals for no reason, or out of misguided ideas about what was beneficial. We need to do better now, I agree." *Vox in Rama audita est, ploratus et ululatus.* "Hey Anna, what did that hawk you heard sound like? It called up a sacred chant I loved in college."

"Mournful."

Skah watched Luz fret, rocking back and forth. He nosed Makah, insistent. "Tell her a story."

Makah rose from her chair and grabbed a book from a disheveled stack on the table next to the couch. "I can understand why some animals might be angry, especially given what's happening to their habitats because of human activity. But animals are mostly not angry beings. Like the elephants who wrote the Code, they're trying to be good neighbors. I was just reading a beautiful story by Cynthia Moss, who lived with elephant families for thirteen years in Africa. Listen to how she describes the reunion of two family groups that had been separated for several months:

At a little rise above the swamp they stopped, and Teresia, Theodora, and Tallulah rumbled, listened, heard a response, and rumbled a louder sound. They were clearly excited, with heads held high and ears lifted. They shifted their course and, almost running, plunged down into the swamp and up the other side onto the first island.

Suddenly, ahead of them was a group of elephants running out of the trees and coming straight for them. Teresia stopped for a moment in alarm, then recognized Slit Ear, and both groups ran, rumbling, screaming, and trumpeting toward each other. The younger animals had moved ahead of Teresia, but when the two groups came together, Slit Ear ignored the others; she pushed through them to reach Teresia and greet her. Both elephants raised their heads up into the air and clicked their tusks together, wound their trunks around each other's while rumbling loudly and holding and flapping their ears in the greeting posture. They whirled around and leaned and rubbed on one another. Meanwhile, all the other members were greeting each other with much spinning, backing, urinating, ear flapping, entwining of trunks, and clicking of tusks. All the elephants were producing so much temporal-gland secretion that it dribbled down along their chins and into their mouths. Above all, the sounds of their greeting rent the air as over and over again they gave forth rich rumbles and piercing trumpets of joy."

"Such wholehearted community spirit," Anna said. "Sometimes I think animals are better at cooperating than people."

"Animals don't kill others of their own species, at least not at human scale," Makah said.

"What about rooster fights," asked Luz, "like when they put those sharp knives on the roosters' legs? Or when a coyote defends its mate?"

"Self-defense is everywhere," Makah replied. "Families defend their own. It's survival. As for rooster fights, that's a barbaric human-instigated custom. How do you know about that, Luz? It's illegal."

"One of the boys at school's dad is a pilot. He was telling about life in the cockpit and Miss Meigs, our English teacher, asked if anyone knew where that word came from. She likes word origins. Anyway, one of the kids said their grandfather had a cockpit for rooster fights before he moved here from the Philippines."

"Monterey had to pass an ordinance restricting the keeping of roosters because of secret cockfights," Makah said.

"Roosters *can* be aggressive with each other in the chicken yard, even using their natural spurs," Cody said. "I remember from when I helped my mom raise them in San Jose. But usually their dustups are bluster."

Luz rubbed her eyes. "That's enough, Mom. Thanks for reading the elephant story." She headed to her room, Skah following her.

"Thank you both for entrusting her to me and Skah," Anna said. "We were protected by the Universe, it seems. Luz is a talisman for the future. The meeting gives me hope, but there is much to do to bind the wounds of our Grandmother, including stopping what we are doing to her today."

5

ONE AFTERNOON LATER THAT SPRING, Cody was working from home. The light glared distractingly across his screens, and he slanted the blinds. The clatter of the slats drifted through the house, and he sensed stirring in the back bedroom. Soon, Skah appeared. He had taken to spending much of his time on his bed.

Cody turned his chair and beamed welcomingly at Skah, who sniffed around the room and settled into a warm spot under the window.

"How are you doing, old fellow? It's nice to have you in here."

Skah considered him with old eyes. "It seems the time has come," he imparted.

Cody knelt and placed his hand on Skah's head and caressed him until his hand was on Skah's chest. The two gazed at each other for a long moment.

"Take it easy, boy. It's okay." He got up and took his phone into the kitchen. He called Makah at school. "Can you come home pretty soon? It's Skah. He's okay, but I'm a little worried."

"I'll be home as soon as I can, Cody."

He returned to his office and finished up a few tasks as he waited. Skah slept quietly. In half an hour, he heard Makah.

"What's going on? How's he doing?" she asked, giving Cody a longer hug than usual.

"He came into my office and seemed self-absorbed. I think it may be near the end."

"He did just turn sixteen," she said. "We've prepared for this, and even talked with Luz about it. No heroic measures."

"Yes."

As they returned to him, Skah raised his head, and Makah sat on the floor beside him. She stroked and chatted with him until he tired.

Cody was in the kitchen, where Makah joined him.

"How's he doing? How are *you* doing?" he asked.

"He seems to know this is the end."

"And?"

"I'm all mixed up. I respect his knowing, but I resist it. We spent our time remembering. Skah finds the otter. Skah bursts through the dog door wet from the rain on your first visit here. Skah, the shepherd of our love. Skah as friend and playmate of Luz. Skah as witness when we lost and buried Chanson." She began to sob. Cody brought a glass of water. She grimaced, took a sip, and put it on the counter.

Cody held her. "Luz will be home soon."

"Yes. She probably already knows."

When Luz arrived, she said nothing, only set down her schoolbag and walked into Cody's office.

Makah and Cody followed her quietly. Luz lay next to Skah, two-thirds his weight, her arm over his back, her lanky frame stretched along his body. She murmured to him in a language they didn't recognize, just a few words. Then the two creatures slept.

After a while Luz woke and comforted Skah, telling him not to be afraid.

"You need not worry for me," Skah told her. "I've been to the other side before, and I am ready. I'll finally meet Tara again. She's working on climate now—maybe I can help. But, how about you? How will you be in the years ahead? I'll be watching out for you."

"Thank you," Luz said. "School is hard right now. I don't fit in because of my background and my connection to nature. I'm too serious. They call me 'Loose,' but they're being sarcastic. I'm scared about the future."

"Time is on your side, my young friend," Skah replied. "I see a host of helpers coming your way. And though there will be difficult times, you will shine through them."

"But I'll miss you, Skah. You're my best friend."

"I will be in touch with you. You will know me again." His eyes heavy, he returned to sleep. He dreamed.

He remembered his early days with Makah, after she had arrived in Monterey and rescued him. Each morning the light came into the house at a different time, earlier or later than the day before, depending on the season. But human time was something else, more rigid, so that he learned to know precisely when it was time for dinner—"not until six," Makah said—no matter the light. He felt Makah's preoccupation some mornings, the way she took a quick and purposeful breakfast, their brisk walk down the hill to her office. When she had problems at work, he sent her waves of peaceful energy. Other times she'd ruffle his ears, take a deep breath, and head out on her own. He'd anticipate her return, the onion smell of her nerve sweat, her hands massaging his head, around his eyes. Mutual, the contentment.

When she was home, he'd sleep under the Redwood, sensing the gaze of the resplendent Koro eyeballing him from a branch. Koro, who loved him, just like that older Crow who'd told him to love his Makah well. *I did my best, old friend.*

Some afternoons, Makah put on her running shoes, and they'd

head down toward the shore, the air fresh and fishy, with notes of auto fumes, familiar Dog scents, and a hundred trace currents that sent his mind into myriad worlds.

On the beach, as she readied to throw the ball, he would run into the frigid surf—*as far as you can, please.* Then he was in the breakers, Sun and birds above, the ball's soggy saltiness. Out of the water—shake off, drop it, wait. Repeat. This was bliss, the vitality of his muscles, the unpredictable waves, the anticipation before the throw, and his heart full of love for his Makah, her loyalty and attention, her athleticism, her passion for the outdoors, and her curiosity for all life.

When beach time was over, they'd turn back, climb the grassy dune onto the path again. He kept quiet unless he sensed danger, his silence belying the workings of his head and heart. Maybe a stroller was coming toward them—Suzanne, with her wild brown hair and her little niece—the two friends catching up, the baby scent wafting sweet and clean. He sat, steady, alert.

He reached forward to the time that old Crow had spoken with him when Makah was first flirting with Cody, saying, "We Crows are on a sacred mission from Grandmother—Makah and Cody are important to its success."

While Skah dreamed, Luz returned to where Cody was fixing dinner. Makah was perched at the counter reading student papers. Luz stood still, her eyes on her parents, who had stopped to gaze at their handsome, enigmatic daughter. Luz's face had regained its youth. Her voice was clear, if measured.

"Skah wants to go," she said solemnly. "He's ready." She took a deep breath, and her words failed. She climbed into Makah's lap like when she was little. "Momma, I don't know if *I'm* ready."

"Be still, my little one," said Makah. "We'll send him off in style so that he'll be welcomed and honored in the next world. And we'll miss him, even though we know he'll come to visit us many, many times." It surprised her, how naturally she'd channeled the Old Ones. Her grandmother White Owl would be smiling. "Would you like me to call Anna?"

"Anna should come tomorrow. If she can. Tomorrow."

• • •

Cody rose early and inspected the back garden where they had reserved a place for Skah at the edge of the hillside that stretched down into the canyon. The mist lay heavy around him. He sat with his memories, his debt of gratitude to Skah for teaching him to care for Makah and Luz. He remembered fondly, and with sadness, a day sitting on the beach with Makah watching Luz play, watching Skah watch Luz play. That was the day they got pregnant again, filled with love for another child.

When Cody came inside, Makah had made coffee. "Anna will be here in an hour," she said.

"Wonderful," Cody said. "Where are our housemates?"

"In the bedroom." Luz had slept in the enormous bed with her parents.

When Anna arrived, she joined the adults for coffee. She wore a simple white blouse with small shell ornaments and a comfortable denim skirt. The bear claw necklace hung from her neck and she carried a turtle rattle.

Luz came out and gave Anna a big hug. "He's thirsty and wants to go outside."

She led Makah and Anna back to help Skah make his way outside, where he relieved himself and drank from the water bowl beside the steps. Cody joined them, and they sat admiring the slow burn of the mist and the cries of gulls.

Now Grandfather Sun was high, and a light breeze rustled the trees. Skah lay on his side, his head pointing toward the redwood. The four sat around him in the four directions—Luz in the east where the light comes from, Cody in the west where the great waters cool Sun at the end of his fiery journey, Makah in the south for the warmth of life, and Anna in the north, her back to the redwood, holding the passage to the next world. They put their hands on Skah, whose eyes were open. Anna sang quietly:

"Now into the other world
I fly, lighter than a feather.
Now I leave this sacred home
My beautiful ones around me.
Now I return my bones to
Our beautiful Grandmother.
May all beings be at Peace
With the Earth and with each other."

When Anna finished, Luz rattled the turtle shell. Skah observed the somber circle with a calm expression. Luz was sniffling. She whispered to Skah in an old language. Skah lay his head down with a *mwumph*, his eyes peering into the distance far beyond. His legs quivered softly, and he was still.

Koro had been perched quietly on the ground nearby, her dark form obscured by Anna. Now she stepped forward, proceeding around Skah's body until she was at his head. The four humans watched silently as, from her beak, Koro dropped a tiny redwood cone at the end of its little twig. She flew into the treetop, crowed three times, and headed off to the north. Later, a volée of crows held vigil as Skah's spirit took its final leave before the dawn.

On Sunday, friends and nearby family gathered to lay Skah's body into the Earth. Cody pulled off the cover that had sheltered him overnight. Then he, Makah, Anna, and Makah's colleague Suzanne held the four corners of the blanket that Skah lay upon as Luz, scattering water from an earthen bowl, led the procession to the place overlooking the canyon. Suzanne's husband Kipp stood witness along with Cody's parents as the bearers lowered the bundle into the ground in silence. As the mourners returned the loamy soil to the grave with sprigs of bearberry, seven crows wheeled above the little garden, their mournful strains echoing from the far hillside. A bright American goldfinch, who flitted from his pantheon into a volunteer redwood that had sprouted alongside the big tree, sang a haunting song of cheerful sadness. Wind came up and rustled through the branches. The humans, passing slowly by the place where Chanson lay, returned to the house to tell stories of Skah and enjoy the blessings of being alive.

Makah began. "After Cody and I visited the aquarium on our second date, we came here, and I made mussels, and we told our life stories. It was wonderful, but the next day I told Skah, 'That time with Cody was strenuous, my friend!'"

Cody's mother raised her eyebrows, and Makah said, "Not like that, Toni—*emotionally* strenuous. But Skah gave his version of a head bobble—*everything's cool*—and I told him 'Yeah, I know. That's the thing. I'm freaking out that I'm not freaking out.'"

"Skah warned me then to take care with you," Cody said. "After that, there was the time you guys first came over to my apartment in San Jose, and Tara extended an imperious welcome." Tara, his prize from the divorce, when Maria got the twins. "Skah was nosing around the coffee table, and in the smoothest motion, he slid this pen that was sitting there onto the floor. He brought it over to Makah and dropped it at her feet with a soft growl."

Makah smiled. "I asked him, 'Skah, what's going on?' I picked up the pen and it read *Peterman-Clemens*, and I asked Cody, who said it was from Opti-Drip's new investor, Jack Clemens. He'd taken it from PC's fancy office after a board meeting."

"Skah was trying to warn me about them. I tossed the pen in the trash. I told Makah 'I'm not a big fan either.' That was before we found out about his connection to the dead otter Skah found on our first date—or the thing with his daughter."

In a few hours, the guests departed. A weary Luz went to bed with promises she could skip school on Monday. Cody and Makah sat together on the couch, awash and unprotected in ceremony and grief.

6

HUMANS SEEM TO HAVE A LOT OF TRAUMA to work through. Sometimes it takes generations. The sins of the fathers, visited on the sons—and the rest of us. I worry about that part of the human experience and how it can distract people from dealing with the great challenge all life is facing together. Right when you need to be cooperating with each other, you seem to be fighting more instead.

I imagine you might be wondering, in addition to our tenacity, why our Grandmother gave Crows the arduous and delicate task of getting humans to love the world. After all, we have long been jesters, wise fools, boundary crossers . . . troublemakers too clever for our own good. Perhaps it is because we speak truth. I can reveal that our secret source is called the *Crowdex*—a comprehensive repository of human activity invented by an erudite Raven and continually updated by our planimal relatives, alarmed at the spread of habitat destruction that accompanies human progress.

There are so many stories about us, and about our powerful cousin, Raven—about our deeds on behalf of love and the world. Do you know the story of my namesake, Koronis? As a young woman, she was princess of Delphi. When the lecherous Poseidon spotted her Junoesque figure walking on the shore, he took on human form, broke out from the waves, and hailed her. She rejected his suit. He chased her down the beach with violent intent. At the last moment, Minerva saved her by turning her into a Crow—and a trusted advisor. That Koro lived up to our name, measured and civil in her pronouncements.

At that time, as they had been for millennia, our plumes were snowy white. "Then," the story usually goes, "they offended the authorities." Always for good cause, mind you. In my namesake's case, Minerva fired her for telling an inconvenient truth—that two princesses of Athens had betrayed her by revealing the existence of her illegitimate child. The story gets even more complicated—but anyway, Minerva blackened Koro's plumage and replaced her with that supercilious sycophant, Owl. This is our sacrifice.

As you can see, I'm a classicist. I confess to having a bit of Baroque in me. Some call me the *Rococrow*, especially that bright-eyed young stud Anjo, who lives over in Salinas. What a fine tailset *he's* got. I love it when he teases me, diving at me, sarcastic, with a mischievous glint in his expression. Oh, I know I'd be happy sharing nuts with him.

Furthermore—whoa, what was that? Did you see that Red-tail take a dive at me? Hey, big guy—can you give me ten flocking seconds to talk to my friends here? Sheesh. When I get on my soapbox, I can be a danger to myself. Here I am, busy working for him and all his buddies, and this is the thanks I get. As they say in DC, "No good deed goes unpunished." Where was I?

Humans seem to believe technology can solve any problem. But they don't seem to be good at designing for the long term, for unexpected consequences, especially when the problem is too complex to model, like the connections among ten-million-plus species of plants and animals and their ecosystems—lakes, tundra, desert, forest, deep ocean, and, my favorite, the atmosphere. When complexity meets chaos, a little humility helps.

My ancestors learned that the hard way over the centuries, overpopulating during good times and dying off when we consumed all the food. Fun while it lasted, volées of crows darkening the sky for hours. But everything has its limits. It was morbidly quiet for decades. To riff on a famous quotation, "Those who fail to learn from history are forced to repeat it. And the rest of us are forced to repeat it with them." Let's break that cycle!

That's where I get hopeful about the young people. Take Luz for—darn it! I'm hearing a call for backup—Red-shouldered Hawk—scouting for a nest in a Douglas Fir near our roost. Hey, gotta go join the posse and escort that interloper out, cawing like hell.

7

A **CHILL JUNE FOG COCOONED THE HOUSE.** With Luz on a year-end school trip and Cody in SoCal on business, Makah was mopey and missing Skah. To escape her solitude, she took a walk.

She felt Skah's presence in the thick morning air as she crossed the street. Gulls yelled above the wet street. How did that verse go?

A gull hangs in the sky
Ever alone, it is the sorrow of the sea
That fills his cry.

A philosopher gull. But, every reason for sorrow as the fish stocks decline. Eventually, her wandering led to a coffee shop near her campus office. Stirring her macchiato and staring out the gray window, she recalled her arrival in Monterey in 2008, proud of her shiny PhD in environmental studies from UND and fed up with the abuse she'd taken for leading a lawsuit to get them to stop using the Fighting Sioux as the team mascot. A feature article in *Inside Higher Ed* had caught the eye of Makah's now dear friend and fellow prof Suzanne, who helped her get the position at the university—maverick Suzanne who volunteered at the Monterey Bay Aquarium. But the faculty culture proved challenging for an outsider—a dark-skinned, Native American woman from the Midwest. Suzanne and her husband Kipp—a history professor at the school—became her only friends.

Leaving the shop, Makah walked through the older part of town, the Steinbeck-era fish processing plants sanitized into boutiques, along the cobblestoned streetcar route, past the old Doc Ricketts place. Ricketts, the reputed patron saint of biodiversity and balance with nature? Brilliant, but his personal life out of control, unbalanced—party animal, living large. Like some on the rez, wild and dissolute. Pain. Blocking her from connecting with Indians around Monterey . . . . The fear of being reminded. The festering knot of guilt and rage.

The nightmare smell of her cousin's foul breath, his rough hands on her, his arm holding her down as he pulled up her skirt, her resistance, his slap, and the violent rest, ending with his grunting. Fifteen, she'd been alone in the house when he'd surprised her with some story about her brother. She'd let him in. He was high on meth. No pretense. He tried to kiss her, and she hit him. Then he attacked.

"You keep this quiet, hear? Or I'll come back." He buttoned his jeans, slammed the door behind him. Three years older. They'd been friends when they were young. Then he'd quit school, fallen into meanness.

Stunned. Angry at her gullibility, her weakness. She told her mom, who told her father. He got a fellow physician to examine her. The tribal police came. Her cousin would have gone to trial if he hadn't been killed on the way. If he'd been non-Native, some oil roustabout—well, they usually got away with it. That had happened to her friends on the rez. She didn't get pregnant.

Later, in graduate school, she had loved a woman; not really her thing. After that, a year with a male grad student, which petered out. When her dissertation hit a wall and she couldn't sleep, she tried counseling. It had been useful to learn that her two lovers had been responses to her callous violation by an angry, frustrated man. Perspective, but it let her avoid the deeper ache. Gloss over it. Mask it in Indian trauma. Such a crock.

Then she'd moved, connected with Skah, and met Cody. The attraction had opened the hole inside, exposing the jagged scar. It wouldn't close back easily. She was forced to explore how it had changed, if the years had softened its keen edge. Dulled, not softened.

With Cody, she'd faced the possibility of a genuine relationship. Terrifying. Yet love finds its own way. Resistance is hopeless in the presence of the real thing, the wild attraction that happens not just in your head, conforming to some ideal. When it goes down to your toes, to the bottom of your soul. What she was really afraid of, and longed for: losing herself in another.

• • •

Fortunately, shortly after falling for Cody, she met Anna, a local celebrity and elder—healer, animal empath, and eco-activist—at a climate seminar organized by CalEPA to get community input on its relations with California Indians. Makah, in a fraught attempt to build a few local tribal connections, had arranged to attend the meeting. The participants included César Puyoles, a leader of the KaKoon Ta Ruk Band of Ohlone-Costanoan Indians, and Cari Sharp, a leader of the Esselen Tribe of Monterey County.

Sitting behind a table in a beaded shirt, the handsome Puyoles testified that "Native peoples living here, on land that Spanish missionaries named Alta California, saw themselves as part of a community, living in harmony *with* nature. From the lands and waters we took only 'honorable harvests,' to quote Potawatomi sister Robin Wall Kimmerer. In other words, we would leave some for the future. Today, we, and Indigenous people everywhere, entreat our fellow humans to live in respectful relation with our relatives on land and sea."

As the group dispersed, Makah walked across the room to where Cari Sharp was standing, engaged in a friendly, animated conversation with Puyoles.

"Good talk, César," Sharp said. "You were close to the edge there, though, with the noble savage meme."

"That's fair, Cari," he said. "Everything wasn't peaceful in the Old Times. My Ohlone ancestors fought your Esselen ancestors over hunting and fishing rights, stealing each other's women, killing the men. Then the invaders forced the tribes together in the missions. We grew closer—for survival."

"It's a fine line in public meetings like this," Sharp said. "The whites need to hear the message. They need to change their ways."

"Everyone has room for improvement," said Puyoles.

As Makah stood listening politely, another woman joined the group.

"Hello, Anna," Sharp said. "*Saleki itsu.*"

"Good afternoon, Cari," Anna said. "As always, wonderful to see you both."

Sharp turned to Makah. "Hello," she said. "I'm Cari Sharp."

"Pleased to meet you. I'm Makah Andrews. I teach environmental policy at MU, and I am Nueta—we used to be called Mandan. It's an honor to meet you, and you, Mr. Puyoles."

"Call me César," he said.

"And I'm Anna Root. Nice to meet you, Makah. How long have you lived in the Monterey area?"

"Three years. My parents still live in North Dakota. I coordinate an international network of Indigenous climate change professionals." She faced Sharp. "I would like to invite a Native person from this part of California to join us. I thought since you were at this meeting, you might be interested."

Sharp studied her. "I am interested," she said, "but I'm also overcommitted. My main pro bono work focuses on child welfare and bringing attention to missing and murdered Indigenous women. Why don't you brainstorm with Anna, and perhaps we can identify someone more appropriate?"

Makah observed Anna nodding. "Thank you both. That will be great."

Makah remembered the sunny and cool Friday, weeks later, when she visited Anna at her cozy farmhouse near Salinas. She'd fretted about her outfit, ending up in jeans and a short turquoise tunic with a gold and blue whale and moon pin. The older woman greeted Makah at the door, her curly dark hair streaked with silver. Anna wore a loose-fitting cotton skirt, a plain salmon blouse, and a necklace of Olivella shell beads that featured what appeared to be a bear claw at its center.

"This house belonged to my late husband's family," she said. "They were farmers, and this is what is left of their legacy." She ushered Makah through to a garden in the back. An elderberry hedge surrounded plantings of milkweed, common bearberry, yerba buena, watercress, sorrel, purslane, native blackberries, and white sage, along with a variety of vegetables and fruit trees. They sat on cushions on the ground. The herbal tea helped Makah feel safe and welcome in the openness Anna created. The sun's bright glint highlighted an elegant crow gleaming on a wire.

"I'd like to burn some smoke medicine." Anna lit a smudge of sage and let its smoke rise around them. Wispy clouds drifted over the garden, the birds falling silent. She led Makah through a guided meditation.

"Thank you," said Makah. "I appreciate your seeing me today. I felt a strong connection with you at the conference. I love how you combine social change with personal healing in your work. Your respect for and connections to the Rumsen Ohlone tribe are exciting—I know so little about California Indian culture."

"Your work at the university is so important—training future policymakers to think holistically about the environment," Anna said. "But I sensed you had something on your mind when we talked."

"I'm frightened by the dismal progress on climate and the implications for life on the planet."

"I share your concerns about the Meltdown. Our Grandmother Earth must be protected, and she must be healed." Anna paused. "And I sense the same is true for you."

Makah was surprised to find herself in tears.

Touching the wet cheek, Anna said, "The tears can wash away the suffering, but the injury will remain. Tell me your story."

The two began a long conversation, toward the end of which Makah related, with difficulty, the story of the rape. "I carry it still. Sometimes I'm reminded when I am with Cody. I'm afraid I won't be able to love him fully, or that he'll think I'm damaged goods." And beneath this fear, the dark mix of sadness and rage that threatened to suffocate her. She glared at the apparition as it slunk into the shadows, turning like a wolf, its yellow eyes hungry.

"Tell Cody about this," Anna said, "before you marry him." Then she was silent for some time. When she spoke, she was angry. "Makah, I honor your suffering. This should never happen to any woman. And, as you know, this act is an act of oppression, a monstrous thread in the fabric of all peoples. It is not a sexual act. For a thousand generations it has happened wherever people live. It's difficult to be a woman in a male-dominated society, especially when there are no consequences for such acts." Her right hand rose up from her heart.

"But that is the world we are in, a world full of injustice. And, as humans, we are raping our Grandmother every day, are we not?" Her eyes flashed as her hand struck the ground with a loud clap. "What can we do? How can we heal ourselves and our planet? What do you say?"

As Makah attempted to compose herself, a scene passed before her. She was in a canyon. Eagle, her wings compacted, dove from the sky like a bullet. Her target, Rabbit, was stunned by Eagle's impact. Eagle took Rabbit in her talons. Her powerful wings carried them into the distance, her piercing cry reverberating off the canyon walls.

Anna waited, her eyes fierce on Makah.

"Rabbit represents sorrow," Makah began. "Mine, and my cousin's also. He was killed by a federal marshal who was transporting him. The marshal claimed he acted in self-defense. Eagle represents divine power."

The healer nodded, as if she had seen the same vision. "Yes, my dear," she said softly. "You can let Eagle take that sorrow with Rabbit. Rabbit comprehends sorrow. Still, in unexpected moments, the injury will bring you pain. Then, you must follow the path of the poet, letting it envelop you—like a tender sheath, bristling with thorns."

They sat quietly. After a while Anna began a keening, as one hears among many peoples when there is death and sorrow. When she finished, she said, "Now you are my sister. We will wear our pain like fire, and we will heal the planet. And we will get the men to help us."

• • •

The next Christmas, she and Cody had visited her parents in North Dakota, and her mom told Cody that Makah's last years on the rez had been tough. When they got home, Cody asked Makah what Mandy had meant, and Makah told him.

She sat across from him at the kitchen table, avoiding his gaze, her fingers picking at a speck of food that had stuck to the wood. By the time she finished, the scrap was gone, and in its place were several tissues.

Cody listened silently, watching her recount the incident and its aftermath, admiring her courage. "This just makes me love you more." He reached across to touch her face, and she lifted her eyes to him. "You trusted me before, and you trust me now to tell me. I'm so sorry for your experience, for that assault on my precious Makah. It makes me angry at your dead cousin, which I know is pointless. And I'm so, so happy we are together. But I do have one question."

She caught her breath. "What? What is it? I'll try to tell you."

"What did you mean when you said that Anna helped you redirect the pain into action?"

"Anna compared what my cousin did with what we're doing to the

Earth. It got to me, the way she expressed it: 'raping our Grandmother.' I don't yet know how that energy is going to manifest in my life, but I feel I've got to double down on climate issues. Action is needed on all levels of society, including here, in our own lives."

That's when Cody proposed that maybe they needed only one house—real climate change, he'd said.

Not long after, she became pregnant with Luz, and they were married. Luz was an easy carry, although strange things occurred. Cats rubbed against Makah's legs, and dogs would lick her hands. Skah welcomed them warily. She was serenaded by birds and chattered at by squirrels. Even the Three Sisters—the squash, corn, and beans in her garden—seemed unusually happy.

Luz came into the world after a reluctant labor, and Makah experienced a postpartum hemorrhage while she was in the delivery room. Dr. Young, the obstetrician, inserted a Bakri balloon into the uterus and the bleeding stopped. Cody was frightened, but proud of Makah and thrilled to be a dad.

Mandy and Robert Andrews, Makah's parents, came down from Bismarck for two months to help, staying in the tiny spare room. Robert ruminated privately on the causes of the hemorrhage—he'd seen it before, during his tenure as the Nueta reservation doctor. After the Dakotans departed, Cody's parents, Toni and Blake Wilson, visited regularly from San Jose.

When Luz was four, they debated having another child, fretting about an American kid's impact on the planet—seven times more than the average kid in China. But love had its way. Makah missed her period. The pregnancy test was positive, and they were happy. The baby felt different. "This one's flightier," she told Cody. Skah kept constant by her side.

One morning at breakfast, twelve weeks in, Makah let out a sharp cry.

"Makah. What is it?"

"I'm having cramps. Can you call Suzanne to take care of Luz?"

When Cody got off the phone, Makah was sitting on the toilet. He knocked on the door that Skah was guarding.

"I think my water broke."

Later, when Dr. Young met them at the ER, her demeanor was grave. She examined Makah while they waited for the tech to bring in the ultrasound. There was a tear in the cervix. Dr. Young did the scan, tenderly.

"You were right," the doctor said. "I'm sorry. The baby can't survive this early—there's no heartbeat, Makah."

The trio sat without speaking, Cody and Dr. Young holding Makah, who was sobbing.

"What happens now?" Cody asked.

"We need to induce labor, but you don't have to do it today." She left to write the orders.

Cody drew her close to him. "I love you, Makah."

"Oh, Cody," she said. "I'm going to need some time to process all this. Can we just go home?"

Luz and Suzanne met them, worried. "Mom, are you okay?" asked Luz. "Skah told me you were sick."

"I told her you had stomach pains," Suzanne said.

"Suzanne's right," said Makah. "I'm feeling better now. But how are *you* doing?"

"I was scared, Mom." She covered her face with her hands. "Sharone at day care said her auntie went to the hospital and never came back." She shied away as Makah reached to comfort her.

Makah turned stoic. "It wasn't like that, Luz. I'm fine. Don't worry about me. Okay?"

"Okay, Mom," she murmured, staring at the ground.

Three days later, Makah was in the delivery room. Minutes after the injection, the labor pains began—like having Luz. After four hours, with

Cody and Dr. Young beside her, Makah's body delivered the treasure it had held. Dr. Young caught the discharge and took it away.

She returned with a small woven basket. In it, wrapped in a silk cloth, was the child, about the size of Makah's finger. Every part was in exquisite miniature detail—toes, fingers, nose, lips, the beginnings of eyes and ears, and evidence of maleness, the doctor explained. Makah held the precious bundle in her hands, staring into the distance. Cody motioned to her, and she handed him the babe.

The hospital would keep the remains until they decided what to do.

• • •

Recovering at home, Makah pondered her friendship with Anna. Their connection touched something old and beautiful inside her, a sense of lineage, of the ancient ways, of the passion and suffering of her people. She called her, told her the story, maintaining her composure through much of it. "We want to do a ceremony for the boy, to bury his body in our garden. We want you to be the officiant."

"Have you decided on a name?"

"In Nueta, it's *shtant-su[n]*," Makah said. "It means 'tiny younger brother.'"

Anna sighed. "It reminds me of the French, *chanson*."

"That's what Cody said. I think that's nice."

A few days later, on a cloudy Saturday morning, Makah, Cody, Luz, Anna, Skah, and Cody's parents stood beside the redwood in the backyard. Cody had dug a small grave amid its sprawling roots. Makah cradled a small, painted Huichol jewelry box that Cody's grandmother Luisa had given him when he was a boy.

Anna began a high, rhythmic cry, invoking the spirits and giving thanks. Makah had given Luz a flat drum adorned with a long, shimmering crow feather, and a small drumstick, its head wrapped in deerskin. Luz beat the drum solemnly in rough time with Anna's prayer.

Anna said, "We gather today on this Native land to bless the spirit of our little brother, Chanson, and to help him on his way to his next life. Dear Little One, we regret that your sojourn with us was so brief, that we did not get to know you, to watch you grow and learn about the world, its joys and its sorrows. We will always remember you in your innocent perfection. We honor the potential you embodied, bringing into the world a unique and mysterious blending of the bodies and spirits of Makah and Cody, and those of their ancestors, and of all the life forms that make us who we are." She paused, raising her arms. "May the spirits of the waters and the land, of the skies and the winds, and of all living beings, watch over us as we return our tiny younger brother to our Grandmother Earth."

As Makah and Cody placed the box in the ground, there arose from high in the redwood's emerald boughs a pair of dignified squawks, a call of inquiry, equanimity. A light breeze ushered a charm of brightly chirping goldfinches into the bushes. As the couple backed away from the little mound of Earth, one luminescent male, resplendent in yellow, flew to the ground beside the grave and pecked at seeds surfaced by the excavation. In an instant he was back in the tree, a black sunflower seed in his mouth, his eyes alert. The goldfinch chorus flew away, whirling on the wind.

The squawking raven gave a farewell croak and flapped toward the canyon. The young couple came forward. They rolled a heavy stone into place, sealing the treasure from coyotes. Skah barked once. The ceremony ended, the party turned into the house for comfort and warmth and to give thanks for life together on the Earth.

In the months that followed, Makah learned that she should not get pregnant again, sending her spirit wandering in a sunless valley. Ghosts haunted her dreams. Skah watched her neglect her garden, unable to comfort her.

She dove, frantic, into projects and classes, into her research to support environmental justice for Indigenous people. She used the results to show how coastal people's livelihoods would be disproportionately affected by sea water temperature change. She isolated herself from her family.

• • •

Now, six years later, she sat on the porch, missing Skah's sleeping form under the lonely fifty-year-old redwood. Only the garden was burgeoning—the traditional crops she cultivated by the moon's cycles—the Three Sisters together, plus sunflowers. The planting and the tasty harvests connected her with her mother and their ancestors. Luz was the light of her life, Anna and Suzanne were dear friends, and Cody was a rock, a foundation. She was successful in her career. *Count your blessings*, as Mom says.

8

THAT JULY, HAVING TURNED TEN, Luz negotiated an arrangement with her parents that permitted her to walk in the neighborhood by herself during daylight. The rough boundaries covered where they'd walked with Skah during his last year—about fifteen minutes in every direction. The territory for her "ninja walks" included part of a path down into Veterans Park. Luz would sit on the hillside, waiting. Cautious black-tailed deer would pass through below her, and furtive California ground squirrels would skitter across, foraging.

One Sunday afternoon, the south-facing bank caught the sun as it moved through the pines on the hillside, creating fragrant thermals and a dappled light. Luz sat quietly, watching and listening and smelling, as she had learned from Anna to do. The Earth Spirit came into her heart.

A bright goldfinch gazed at her from a low bush, his eye steady, chittering in *Birdspeak*, the generic language of birds. Luz loved the cheerful goldfinch, how it delighted in its yellow plumage. As she sat, a vision came to her of Shakti, the coyote who'd spoken at the planimal congress. Shakti was standing on a ridge, her nose in the air, surveying the valley. Luz perceived an opening in the hillside and watched as five coyote pups emerged into the sun, mewling hungrily. In the vision, Shakti barked at them, and they scuttled back inside. Luz thought of her mother's treasured picture of Skah as a puppy. Shakti and Skah—their exchange at the congress.

On a hunch, she asked the bird, "Dear Goldfinch, what's the connection between Shakti the coyote and my dog Skah?"

"Sometimes a creature will take on another's spirit," she heard Goldfinch say, "after going to the other side. Not saying that's the case here. Skah is a complex spirit. It would take a while for him to find his place. There is energy between those two that is not yet manifest."

Luz was excited to be in the presence of such a well-spoken animal. "You know, there was a goldfinch when we buried Chanson. Maybe you know him."

"You could say that," said Goldfinch. "I will always remember that moment. I was literally filled with his spirit. Chanson was so innocent—it made me happy to help find him a home."

The bird watched his words sink into Luz's understanding. Had he pulled aside the veil too far for this young one? Yet she had presence. He began to fidget.

"Wait," Luz said. "One more thing. Do you know about Tara, my dad's cat? She died, near here, before I was born. Skah mentioned her before he died, that she was working on climate. Did she . . . go somewhere else?"

"Ah, yes. The story the Crow told me. She may have mentioned a Cougar, maybe north of these parts."

Luz cringed. "Cougars are dangerous."

"Do not be afraid. Many spirits watch over you, child. Meanwhile, take my advice—be cheerful." The black and gold apparition flew down into the park.

Luz remained, still, as Sun hid himself behind a cloud. She shivered. The world felt very big indeed.

• • •

When Luz got home, Makah was in the kitchen singing quietly from "Gracias a la Vida."

"What's that, Mom?"

"It's a song about gratitude for life. It says life has given me the path to the soul of the man I love. Grandma Toni taught it to me."

"I like learning Spanish songs, especially ones about life." Luz dropped her gaze, thoughtful.

"How was your walk?"

Luz knew her mom's response to the subject of death was unpredictable—which was frustrating and sometimes scary. But Anna wasn't around to ask. "Mom, do you believe in life after death, like, you know, people coming back as other people?"

"I don't know," Makah said. "There's this notion of an afterlife in the Sioux Nation, popularized by the settlers as the 'happy hunting grounds.' But that's more like heaven, not someplace on Earth. So, no, I guess not. We just die. Why do you ask?"

Luz skirted her topic. "One time you told me some elders believed that, in the Old Times, animals were people."

"Oh, *yeah*," Makah said, her Northern Plains drawl emerging as it did when she let herself go back to good times in the past. "That's why the animal stories are meaningful. Humans were close to animals. Take Coyote. He helped prepare the way for humans."

"I was thinking about a coyote on my walk." Luz crossed her arms and patted her shoulders. "Remember that Brian Doyle book we read, where he says, 'Bears do not tell stories about animals other than bears'? Maybe bears think all animals are bears."

"That wouldn't be surprising," said Makah. "It's called *projection*, where you think someone else is the same as you, that they are reacting to a situation the way you would react to it. Like feeling jealousy, or anger. It causes misunderstandings. On the other hand, bears are pretty smart. They know a bee or a fish signals food, not bear. But what does this have to do with reincarnation—people coming back from the dead as someone else?"

"I don't know, Mom. Maybe animals come back as someone else, but if they do, do they stay in their own species, or do they think everyone is in their species anyway?"

"Where did you get this complicated head on your shoulders, my girl?" Makah shook her head, smiling. "Sometimes you amaze me. I have no idea, but that doesn't mean you're wrong. You have to follow your senses, like Anna says—'Follow your shoes out the door.'"

Luz laughed. "That's so funny when I think of it. Like your feet know where you're going before you do."

"I certainly have that feeling sometimes, when my body is already off somewhere while I'm still debating what to do. It happens right here in the kitchen—I pull some ingredients out of the fridge with a vague notion of fixing something for dinner, and one thing just leads to another and not what I expected. I learned to see that from your dad, really. He calls it *spontaneous creativity*."

◆ ◆ ◆

It being summer, Makah used the time to design a lesson plan around the Elephant Code. The big challenge was describing its origin. It wouldn't fly to say it "came in a vision"—hardly the rigor academia required. She imagined with amusement and a bit of anxiety how such an approach would play in her eventual application to become a full professor. She needed an authoritative source to make it relevant to the policy curriculum. What if the Code became a political question in California?

Climate policy was a hot topic in her international network, but she was less plugged in to local activities. She reached out to the tribal leaders she'd met at the CalEPA meeting where she'd met Anna. They introduced her to the leader of a major federally recognized California tribe—the Federated Indians of Graton Rancheria—who was active in environmental politics.

That introduction led to further connections, and soon Makah was traveling to Sacramento to meet with legislative staff. The staff were sympathetic, but it was clear they were overworked—and turning the generality of the Code into an implementable statute would be challenging.

"It sounds nice," said one tired staffer on the Committee on Natural Resources, "but it's just too open-ended. It reminds me of Google's old motto—'Don't be evil.' We've seen how well that worked out. I hate to say this, but you'd be better off trying to get it on the ballot as an initiative. Then we'd have no choice but to figure it out." But he knew she had a snowball's chance of getting 650,000 signatures in time for the next election.

Makah researched the complicated bureaucratic process and decided that it was more than she had the bandwidth for. She cast about for another idea—a source she could cite when teaching it. One day on a video call with her climate change network, someone mentioned an academic paper being circulated by scholars at the Department of Diplomacy and International Studies of the University of Nairobi. Makah found the paper—still in prepub—and it contained a remarkably similar version of the Code. The authors made no mention of elephants, saying only that the language was developed by a "multidisciplinary team of scholars and practitioners," one of whom was a Maasai animal scientist and physician teaching at the medical school.

Bingo. The lesson plan fell into shape, and she couldn't wait to introduce the ideas to her students in the fall.

9

AUGUST FIFTEENTH was the eighteenth birthday of Cody's twins, Andrés and Rosa. Off to college in the fall—he to UC Santa Cruz, she to Cal Berkeley—they came down from their mother's house near San Jose for a family send-off and to join a lively climate rally in Monterey. They'd recruited Luz, who was psyched to be going to her first activist event. At the last minute, Cody, Makah, and Anna decided to tag along.

Many young people felt that adults were not taking climate change seriously. In Europe, groups like Extinction Rebellion and End Fossil: Occupy! staged peaceful "die-ins" and occupied campus buildings. The Monterey event was small, but the forty participants made up for its size with loud chants like "Spreading deserts, rising seas, displace climate refugees!"

The march from the aquarium ended at City Hall, where the rally featured remarks from a Rumsen Ohlone leader. "We, Indigenous people of California, call upon all peoples to recognize that we are parts of nature, not separate. We must embrace our commonality with the natural world and listen to it—to the ocean and its creatures, to the forest and the trees and birds and animals that make it their home. We must look to the sky and take in the beauty of the sun and clouds, the stars and moon, and the planets in their courses. As my Cree Nation sister Melina Laboucan-Massimo has said, we need to reestablish our relationship with the Earth, reestablish our treaty with her and our treaty with the four-legged ones, the winged ones, the fish nations, and all the different beings who are not in human form. Protecting the planet is protecting ourselves and our children and the generations that follow."

At this, the spirited crowd began chanting "Climate change is not a lie! Do not let our planet die!"

The speaker smiled and raised her fist before continuing. "We must listen to each other. If we listen, we will learn that our survival requires us to make many changes. We must change our economy from one of consumption to renewal. And we do this with compassion for each other and for ourselves. The alternative is destruction by our own hands."

After the march and rally, there were small group discussions. Then the family wandered back to Makah and Cody's, enjoying the warm day.

"That was a splendid speech," Makah said.

Cody's features wrinkled. "The implications are scary. I'm not optimistic."

"It's a scary time, I agree," said Anna. "But we have no choice."

"People aren't ready to make the big changes that are needed," Makah said. "Even *we're* not ready, really. It's challenging to change your entire lifestyle."

Rosa looked up from her phone. "In school we learned there's lots we can do to get started. Change happens when many individuals, families, and communities take action. There's this website about 'regeneration,' with examples for individuals and organizations, even companies." She tapped her screen. "Here's a list of what someone, probably from around here, has pledged to do."

1. Avoid air travel.
2. Reduce meat and dairy consumption.
3. Work to use renewable energy.
4. Live car free as much as possible.
5. Collaborate with friends and family on less consumptive gift-giving.
6. Sign up to pay the Shuumi Land Tax, to "rematriate" Native lands in the East Bay.
7. Seek out socially and environmentally responsible options for saving for retirement.
8. Support a local environmental justice advocacy group.
9. Put smart plugs on major appliances to turn them off during peak hours.
10. Shop local, and reuse instead of replacing.

"The website highlights projects in over fifty areas," Andrés added, "from making cities balance their carbon emissions to net-zero by bringing nature in, to creating wildlife corridors, to putting small amounts of kelp in livestock feed to reduce methane emissions."

"There's information about working with and protecting Indigenous peoples—they occupy the most biodiverse regions on the planet," Rosa said.

Anna glanced at Cody and Makah. "We should all make lists like that. If we expect to cut carbon emissions by half in the next five years, we each need to do that in our own lives, especially the well-off. And, as Greta says, system changes are also needed."

"Suzanne was saying the same thing to me the other day," said Makah. "Politicians fear proposing big changes in the way Americans live. We need some other process."

Anna added, "We must learn to live in reciprocity with each other and the Earth."

Stopping short to pick up a fine crow feather, Luz brandished it. "We need fresh stories. Today's stories don't make sense."

Makah focused. "The future's more of a mystery than ever. Right now, it's as if we were pregnant but didn't know what it was, all these changes happening to our body with no idea of what's coming."

"Ah," Anna said, "a new world, not yet ready to be born."

"The corollary being," Cody said, "that the old world is dying."

"The time demands both hospices and midwives," Makah said.

Anna studied Luz. "I think perhaps our young people will help us find the way."

Back home, the crowd welcomed Toni and Blake for the family dinner. In the spirit of the day, and reflecting the twins' birthday wishes, the meal was vegetarian. Cody and Makah were already eating vegetarian once a week and had recently expanded their commitment to three days a week. Cody had discussed the menu with his mother, who shrugged and asked, "How do you think I grew up? We ate rice and beans most nights. And your father will survive."

There *was* rice and beans, cheese enchiladas for the non-vegans, a delicious ratatouille, and sourdough baguettes from Palermo Bakery. Given the damp drizzle, the clan gathered indoors.

"Besides the usual speeches," said Blake, "was anything different about this rally? I participated in anti-war rallies in college, but I got tired of the talking heads. Usually angry young white guys, meanwhile Blacks and Hispanics were being shipped off to 'Nam."

"Before the march, we broke into small groups and discussed what we could do to make change happen faster," Rosa said.

"My group talked about sustainable fishing," Andrés said. "Like, could we get the Fishery Management Council to lower the allowable catch along the Pacific coast?"

"Mine talked about improving the climate curriculum in high schools—it's totally inadequate," said Rosa.

"I didn't see any animals," Luz said. "Did you?"

"There were some beautiful dogs, Luz," Andrés answered. "One reminded me of Skah."

Luz scowled. "You know what I meant—wild animals—birds, or even squirrels?"

"Sorry," Andrés said. "There were beautiful gulls and pigeons, and you must've heard the crows—plenty of them. They were vocalizing, like, 'Well, it sounds positive, but get it done, people.' That's what I heard, anyway." He gazed into the distance.

After dinner, Luz quizzed the twins, getting info about the climate change movement.

"We're joining Extinction Rebellion when we get to college," Rosa said. "It's moving away from its hard core. They say they want to prioritize attendance over arrests and relationships over roadblocks. The movement is getting more serious."

"In high school we participated in School Strike for Climate," said Andrés. "Now it's called Fridays for Future—it's an international climate change movement founded by Greta."

"I want to start going." Luz brought it up with Makah and Cody.

"How much school would you miss on Fridays?" Makah asked.

"Only an hour in the morning. Rosa said there are usually some younger kids there. I think my teacher would be okay with it. Maybe I could write a report about it for the school paper."

"Well, let's find out more. If it's safe, it could be good experience."

The next day, while Cody and Luz were out walking, Makah tended her garden, moving methodically among the mature corn, squash, and bean plants, picking off bugs and pulling weeds. She worked at staying mindful but was soon overcome by a sense of melancholy, different somehow from the everyday darkness that had haunted her since the loss of

Chanson and Skah. She sat on the ground near a row of late sunflowers, admiring the burgeoning Three Sisters. What had changed?

The conversation from the day before and Anna's remark about young people—her piercing look at Luz—had resonated with her. She thought about Luz's bright, tender energy. The plantings reminded her of how, when she was Luz's age, her mother would go out into the garden for respite from life's challenges. Her mind drifted among old stories until a bulletin cut into the channel. No—she would not abandon Luz to grief. She sighed, wiped her eye with the back of her earthy hand, dusted herself off, and went inside with resolve.

10

ONE EARLY FALL AFTERNOON, Luz came into the kitchen where Makah was cutting vegetables for an omelet.

"Hello, sweetheart. You want a pepper slice?"

"Sure." She took the pepper but didn't eat it. "Mom, I want a dog for my birthday. I miss Skah."

Makah often thought fondly of her sixteen years with Skah as her everyday companion. She felt his presence, talked to him when she was alone, but it wasn't the same as touching him, looking into his eyes. "I don't know, Luz," she said. "I'm not sure we're ready to have another dog in the house. Maybe next year?"

"But I want a pet *now*, or anyway for Christmas. I like having another animal in the house. Next year is too long." She chewed her pepper. "What about a cat?"

"Your father and I talked about that. They're a danger to the wildlife, unless you declaw them, and then you have to keep them indoors for their own protection." She sighed. "Your father didn't like it when we put the bell on Tara. A cat's just not a good option in an area like this where there's so much other animal life, especially with our new bird feeder and birdbath—we've become a sanctuary." Makah opened the refrigerator. "Darn, there's only one egg. Time to rethink lunch."

"Grandma Toni never runs out of eggs," Luz said. "She always gives us some when we visit."

"True. But that doesn't help us right now, and I'm not going to the store just for eggs."

"No, Mom, I meant why don't we get chickens?"

"Wow," Makah said. "What an idea. I never considered it. We'd have to discuss it with Dad, of course. You'd have to take care of them, and we'd need to build a coop to protect them from predators."

"I'll take care of them—Grandma Toni can teach me."

"I think she'd like that."

When Cody arrived, they discussed it.

"I remember feeding them when I was a kid," he said. "I kind of enjoyed it. But it's a big responsibility. Aside from the setup and everything, there's feeding them and cleaning the coop and the yard and making sure they have enough to do so they don't get bored and start pecking each other. It's not all just gathering eggs. Plus, there's one other issue."

Luz was mystified, but Makah just raised her eyebrows.

Cody grinned. "I'm sure you've thought about this. It's about owning so-called domestic livestock. I mean, what's it like to be a chicken, cooped up and working for people?"

"I can ask them," Luz said. "Anna can help me."

The following Sunday they gathered with Anna at Toni and Blake's. Dinner was to be vegan, to help settle the spirits. The six drank tea, washed their hands, and walked out to the chicken yard. The early spring light came in soft through the drizzle, in harmony with the gentle murmurs of the dozen hens. Toni chatted with the birds by name as she opened the gate and let everyone in. Orpingtons—buff yellows, a few lavenders, and two chocolates—clucked and pecked the ground. After a flurry of awkward chasing, each person captured a chicken and held it gently. They stood in a circle.

"Thank you, dear hens, for giving us the fruit of your bodies," Anna said. "Your eggs are so delicious. We honor your sacrifices, and especially those of your sisters who live on commercial egg farms." She paused and nodded at Luz.

"I am curious," Luz said, "about your lives. How is it being you?"

"*Puck puck-aah puck puck*," clucked a pretty hen calmly from her perch in Toni's arms.

The other hens chattered in a similar tenor. Then Cody's bird nipped his inner arm. Cody blew in the hen's face. "Sorry. Conditioned response. It's the gentlest way to express displeasure at being bitten."

"That's Esmerelda," Toni said. "She may be getting broody. She likes being the minority opinion."

They put the hens down and thanked them, went inside, and washed their hands.

"So?" said Anna, peering at Luz.

"It's complicated. It's like, they want respect. Not just a comfortable life."

Anna nodded.

"They can get moody, and they can be peckish if they think you're part of the flock," Toni said. "You have to be firm with them sometimes, like with children." Her eyes sparkled at Luz.

"Or dogs," Makah added. "But pets and farm animals don't leave home when they grow up, like most animals do. They remain dependent."

"Wait, what's *peckish*?" Luz asked.

"Chickens have a pecking order," answered Toni. "There's a boss hen who keeps order when the girls get aggressive with each other."

"Do chickens follow the Elephant Code?" Luz asked.

"I'd say yes, pretty much," said Makah, "although I don't know that they think about the effects of their actions for seven generations."

"We don't really know, but they have many human characteristics," Toni said. "They feel lonely when one of the flock dies. Sometimes they stop eating if they lose a friend."

Blake cleared his throat. "Domestic animals wouldn't be alive at all if people hadn't bred and cultivated them. But, since we've done so, I suppose we do have a certain responsibility for humane treatment."

"An odd word," Cody said, "*humane*. Spanish uses only one word—*humano*—to mean both human and humane. We make a distinction in English. Says something."

Luz was following the conversation closely. "Maybe we can call our coop the 'Respectful Roost.' That will help us remember. I can paint a sign!"

• • •

Cody set about constructing the coop and the fencing for the yard. He enjoyed design, its fusion of function, form, and beauty. He and Luz examined dozens of pictures and drawings. They read about protection from coyotes and other predators, although hawks would remain a threat. Luz painted the sign and discussed the advantages of various breeds with Makah and Toni. Back in school, she talked about the project, learning by visiting classmates who had chickens. They talked about creating a chicken club at school. Someone proposed raising them at school, but vegan parents shot it down.

Chickens came up one evening when the trio, joined by Anna, was having dinner at Suzanne and Kipp's home in Del Monte Forest. The property backed on a dense, hilly wildlife reserve, the house roomy and well lived in. The weather being fine, they sat on "the veranda," a term reflecting Kipp's English heritage. The eight-year age gap between the hosts and their younger guests had seemed bigger to Makah and Cody when they were all younger. Still, Suzanne was turning fifty, and when Cody had tried kidding her about getting old, she wouldn't have it. Their kids were through college and, thankfully, working. Suzanne and Kipp doted on Luz, which took some grandchildren pressure off their own kids.

"We're getting Orpingtons," Luz reported. "That's what Grandma Toni has, and I think they're pretty. They're also reliable layers and friendly. Some kids at school have them."

"Ah, yes." Suzanne twisted her unruly brown hair in a knot. "What *is* the latest on the chickens-at-school controversy?"

"It's one of those things where a few people holding strong views prevail over a larger number who aren't as committed," Makah said. "The vegans are dead set against it—exploitation of animals. No conversation possible about humane practices. But we succeeded in setting up a school-wide group to create community gardens. Everyone could get on board with that."

Anna chimed in. "It's too bad about the no-chickens policy. It was an opportunity to educate the kids about where their food comes from. Humans are omnivores, after all."

"Yeah," Cody said, "but domestic livestock produce a lot of greenhouse gas."

Kipp, on his way to the kitchen, turned around. "That is true. Agriculture accounts for up to one-fifth of human-caused greenhouse gas emissions, but burning fossil fuels for electricity, transport, manufacturing, and heating is the greater culprit."

"Cattle are the big ones. If we reduce our beef and milk consumption and get ranchers and dairymen to add kelp to the feed, that'll help," Cody said. "Chickens are twice as energy efficient as cattle."

"Like the Chick-fil-A billboards say, 'Eat Mor Chikin,'" Suzanne quipped. "But seriously, what about something like a 'net-zero' ag policy?"

"The vegans say we shouldn't eat any animals or animal products," Makah said. "It's more like a zero-tolerance policy. Plant-based meat substitutes are part of their answer. But we do need to cut way back on meat."

Kipp came back in from the kitchen. "Dinner is ready. It's good old Aurora rockfish from Monterey Fish—a plentiful local species recommended by Seafood Watch."

The group held silence for a minute in honor and thanks for the fish, for the organisms that fed them, and for all the people involved in getting them to that table.

The conversation continued around the roasted rockfish with rice and vegetables.

"Why do we distinguish between wildlife and livestock?" Luz asked. "They're all live animals."

"All creatures great and small," Suzanne said. "It's a good question."

"Dad says that since we breed and raise livestock, we have a special responsibility for their welfare," Cody said. "People have lived with domesticated animals for millennia. But not everyone can afford sustainably raised livestock. The big farms have scale. McDonald's is cheaper."

"Livestock shouldn't be only about efficiency," said Anna. "It's about relationship, respect for the animals. That's easier on a small scale."

Cody smiled. "Makah's trying to fix this."

"Sustainable practices increase yields in developing countries, but making progress requires education and policy changes," Makah said, "sometimes with subsidies. Industrial agriculture is pushing back, especially Big Corn."

"What about predators?" Cody asked. "That's a big problem for ranchers."

Makah scoffed. "There's a rewilding movement in western states that's bringing back the gray wolf. They are good for ecosystem diversity. There's even government money behind it. Ranchers are resisting, but damage from wolves and coyotes is way overstated—they kill tiny amounts of livestock while keeping down the rats and moles."

Anna sighed. "I'm reminded of the wolf and coyote massacres on the Great Plains. Depredation programs—bounty hunting—'just bring in the ears.' Still going on in some states, but it's better now than when the government just dropped poisoned bait from airplanes and killed every mammal, not just the canines, for hundreds of miles."

"Lots of killing out there." Kipp waved his hand in an easterly direction. "Rather disconcerting to someone from England. I've never gotten used to it."

"Oh, right," Suzanne said. "Fox hunting for sport, anyone? Tallyho!"

Makah frowned. "Death is hard enough. Mindless killing is not something anyone should get used to."

"We're not going to eat *our* chickens," Luz declared. "And we're protecting them from coyotes. Although I've noticed on my walks that there's no new spoor near the house. Maybe the one who was living near us moved away."

11

FALL PURVEYED ITS MENU OF COOLER WEATHER, showers, and the welcome departure of throngs of noisy beachgoers, bringing Thanksgiving. Makah and Luz piled into Cody's dark-blue Silverado crew cab and swung over to Maria's house, in Fremont, where the twins were waiting, home from college.

"Mom's out with EZ," said Andrés. "They wished you a happy Thanksgiving."

The twins climbed into the back seat with Luz. Off they headed to Coyote Hills Park—the original site of the Tuibun Ohlone village—which now sported new signage in Chochenyo, the language of the park's First Peoples. The tender hill grass waited for rain as Cody's children set a strenuous pace for him and Makah. After a couple of hours, they departed for his parents' house.

The truck crackled over the immaculate gravel of the long circular drive. As Cody led his hearty band through the front door, the aromatic fusion of Mexican and Asian flavors—cornmeal, peppers, cumin, cilantro, ginger—created by his grandmother Luisa and perfected by his mother—ignited him. Home.

Toni emerged from the kitchen, bestowing ample hugs on her three grandchildren. She giggled as Cody kissed her.

"Where's Dad?" he asked.

"In the back, puttering. He's supposed to be tending the grill. He prefers four-legged meat, so he's in his element out there." She smiled at Makah, who was holding a casserole. "You ladies come back with me."

"I brought my usual," said Makah as they filed toward the kitchen.

"I was hoping you would. I love the traditional recipe—beans, corn, and squash—the Three Sisters. As for you, young sisters, you know in Mexico, everyone calls the combination *milpas*. The Indians showed us how growing them together made a balanced diet and was more productive than corn by itself."

"Mom's growing them the old way, intertwined in our garden," said Luz, "along with sunflowers. They love it."

"As usual, Makah—or at least since that first year you came—today's not the traditional Thanksgiving menu."

"Fine with me. Not my favorite holiday." The women shared an ironic smile.

Toni put Makah's dish in the warm oven. "I'll never forget that first Thanksgiving, when Blake said something about the pilgrims."

"I was biting my tongue until then," Makah said. "Cody knew how I felt, but we agreed I'd keep quiet—first impressions and all. But I couldn't resist, especially after that nice grenache you served. Anyway, Blake was gracious about it."

"How are the chickens, Grandma?" asked Luz. "Can we go see them? Dad says our coop will be finished this weekend, and we can *finally* get ours."

"After dinner. The girls are laying well." She tapped her finger to her lips. "I just got two new chicks, but don't tell; you know how he is about expanding the flock. He barely tolerates their clucking—but he likes the eggs. The girls *asked* me for them, you know? And, as he likes to say, it's good to have a strong bench."

"What's a *bench*?" Luz asked. "The chickens don't sit on it." *The chickens talk to her!*

"It means extra players in case someone gets injured," Rosa said.

Makah had been ruminating. "I didn't mean to make a fuss that day. I was like, 'go along to get along.'"

"Right? Except when it's important not to," said Toni. "If you can't talk in family, where can you?"

Meanwhile, Cody and Andrés had strolled through the spotless house, the Buffalo Bill memorabilia catching the light in the living room. Beyond the patio, the property dropped into a little creek, home to herons and gray foxes. Cody caught a goldfinch's squeaky song. Andrés paid more attention to a rude jay debating a boundary with a wise and patient crow.

The erudite crow seemed to be telling his cousin, "These days we birds are flocking together, not arguing minor territorial disputes." The jaybird was loud but clueless. The crow kept her voice calm, maybe to avoid having a party of high-crested, nest-robbing, tree-hopping blue screechers dive-bomb her. Yet to Andrés, the Steller's jay seemed cool. He was patiently building a foot-wide mud nest near the ground. "Live near your food, girl," he seemed to be telling the crow. Andrés poked his dad, who was rapt in goldfinch world when—

"Yow, dang!" Blake had been kneeling next to the grill, a small wrench in hand. He straightened up, twisted his lean frame, and rubbed his arm. "Good to see you guys! That wheel keeps getting loose. I put a locknut on it." He tossed the wrench into the tool basket and gave Cody a half hug. "The grill's pretty hot. The ribs have been on for two hours."

"I was wondering about your repairing a hot grill, Dad. You always say safety first."

"I suppose it could've waited. It's just been bugging me, and retirement makes me antsy."

"Be careful. Don't be getting up on ladders."

"No, no, I know." Blake shook his head. "What did you folks do today?"

"We had a walk in Coyote Hills Park—unceded Indian territory, as

Makah says, like everything around here. It was interesting. They're open today, but they're closed tomorrow in observance of Native American Heritage Day."

"Black Friday? That must have taken some doing—with the unions, I mean. They're probably paying double-time wages."

"It was awesome," Andrés added. "It was nearly empty. They've added an interpretive exhibit in the visitor center since you took us there as kids—video narratives by elders from a handful of the fifty Ohlone tribes, sharing stories of their youth. There was a nine-foot boat made from tule bulrushes."

"Impressive engineering," Cody added. "Highly buoyant, nearly zero draft. The locals still build and race them."

Andrés stepped back, waving his arm. "We saw white pelicans, so majestic, and a red-tail that hung motionless, like a crescent moon above the ridge. There was coyote scat too, flecked with tiny mammal bones."

"Sounds great—I should take Toni over there," Blake said. "Aside from being bored, I'm glad I sold the store to Deere. So much new technology in the industry now. Self-driving tractors—who knew? Besides, my heart couldn't handle the stress. Looking back, the best day in the store was when your mother wandered in looking for a bag of chicken scratch. It was love at first sight. Anyway, how's your company these days, Son?"

"Opti-Drip's doing fine, although I'm happy to be working my way out." Cody laughed. "Funny how you and I cashed out around the same time."

"You young people! But I would have gotten out a year earlier if it hadn't been for the government."

"Opti-Drip's new slogan is 'Digital farming technology is the next green revolution.' Their latest software relies on digitized historical weather trends."

Blake snorted. "Historical weather trends are getting less historical." He opened the lid of the grill. "Let's have a look-see."

"Those smell fantastic, as always, Dad."

"Yep, your grandfather Ethan's recipe. He got it in the '30s from an African American woman who was on her way up to Hannibal from St. Louis in an old Buick and had a flat tire in Troy. It was cold, the day before Thanksgiving. He helped her with the tire and invited her in for hot cider. While they were talking, they got into rib recipes, and she shared her favorite. Have I told that story before, Andrés?"

"Oh, maybe a few times, Granddad, but I still like hearing it. Your ancestors fascinate me, their pioneer stories. Especially your grandfather Everett getting captured by Indians."

"Rescued, not captured. He saw a lot in his life," said Blake. "He was only in his fifties when he died. That's nearly a hundred years ago. I still think of the stories my dad told me about him."

"Makah reminded me the other day that her dad, Robert, came from St. Louis. But I doubt he ever got up to Troy, although he did end up on the Missouri—New Town, North Dakota."

"Luz has the Missouri River in her blood," Blake said. They went in through the French doors. "The ribs are done, honey," he hollered. "They'll hold. We can eat anytime. Anything you need?"

A pan clattered in the kitchen. "Why don't you boys relax? We're almost done in here."

In the living room, Blake opened the mini fridge. "Like a beer, Son?"

"Sure. Anchor Steam?"

"How about a Negra?" Blake grinned. He loved this routine.

Cody grinned back. "Right. With lime."

"How about you? This is your first Thanksgiving since you turned eighteen."

Andrés eyed the open fridge. "Drinking age is twenty-one, Granddad, so thank you. A Corona, please. With lime."

They sat on the couches. Cody's attention fell onto the framed D. F. Barry sepia of Buffalo Bill, taken with Red Cloud and his brother, American

Horse, the latter holding a six-foot tall, well-feathered coup stick. Cody's fourth-great-grandfather was standing, staring into the distance as if lost in a vision, his hand on Red Cloud's shoulder. The showman wore a camel hair coat and a dark, felt cowboy hat. The chiefs sat in their regalia, regarding each other in a relaxed, expressionless way.

"I always think about American Horse and Red Cloud when I pass by the annual Powwow at Stanford," said Cody. "The glory days of the Plains Indians destroyed in less than a century. Now nothing much going but oil and gambling—and anger and resentment from the youth."

The ladies had come in from the kitchen during the conversation, and Makah added, "People are trying to turn the tide, restore pride in being Indian, recapture the old languages. It's not as bleak as you make it sound, Cody." Although some went back to the rez to make a difference. Not for her, not now. She was lucky to make it out.

"We always talk about Indians on Thanksgiving," Luz said. "I like that."

Toni seated herself next to Cody, who was still gazing at the sepia. "How was Maria today?"

"She was off with EZ," Cody said, ending his meditation.

"She's sad because we're away at college," Rosa said. "She's been glad to have us back this week. But she's thinking about getting a cat. She hasn't had one since you got Tara."

"I *miss* that cat." Cody finished his beer. "Mom, any update on your guys' traveling plans?"

"Your father wants to go back to Troy . . . drive up the Missouri, trace the steps of Lewis and Clark. It could be fun."

"Grandpa Ethan would have appreciated it," Cody said.

Sitting down to the feast, they passed the plates around for serving. Andrés, positioned in front of the Three Sisters stew, dished out generous servings, especially for Rosa and himself. "I'll take three," he said, "one for each sister."

"I heard you visited the coyote park," Toni said.

"It was great," said Andrés. "I liked the new signage. Like the peregrine trail—it's now called *Kaknu*—where we saw this amazing hawk. I like the sound."

"*Kaknu* sounds like the peregrine falcon's call—*kak kak kak*," said Makah. "It's like the Nueta word for Raven, *kéka*."

"Tell them about your latest project, Makah," Cody said, dishing ribs onto his plate.

"I've been trying to find ways to convince governments to stop stalling on climate—"

"Oh, governments," Toni said. "I don't have much use for them. They tax working people and protect the rich."

"Tax us and regulate us. In some ways I'm glad to be leaving business. Too much paperwork. Especially in California." Blake launched into a well-worn story about how hard it had been to get approval for Deere to buy the company. "Delayed us eighteen months and probably cost us a million dollars. Cody runs into the same things."

Makah stopped buttering her roll. "I agree that governments aren't the whole solution. But who else is there? Business is realizing there's money in climate adaptation, and companies have got to be part of the solution. But governments need to lead, follow, or get out of the way of progress. And people are what make governments move in the long run. We're hardly taking to the streets. It's hard to get people excited about fixing something when they don't know what to do. The wildfires and floods bring the crisis closer to home, but then there's an easy season, and people get complacent again."

"My friends at school are worried," Luz said. "Some kids are like, what's the use? And others are down on adults for not doing enough. I'm glad I'm going to the School Strikes now."

"There's major youth activity on climate," Rosa said. "It's one way of countering the despair."

"Those wildfires burn a lot of brush," Blake said. "Fires are part of nature. My Grandpa Everett's farmer customers used to do controlled burns of the native grasses around Troy. It made the soil better for wheat. Fire created the prairies. They had to watch the wind, or it could get out of control. There are grim tales about that. But I agree with you, Makah, it's hard to get people to act. Toni, what was that line in that *Hamlet* you made me watch on PBS, 'rather bear those ills we have'?"

"Well, I'm where Makah is," Cody said. "We need to amp up our efforts. Big changes are coming to agriculture in California. There's not enough water. I'm proud of what I was doing at Opti-Drip, but it was just a drop in the bucket."

Rosa interrupted. "Dad, please. Pass the stuffing."

Andrés's eyes sparkled. "It's actually dressing, Rosa. It's never been inside a bird."

The buttermilk cornbread dressing was moist and fragrant with sage, thyme, and za'atar.

"That's another reason I'm glad to be retired," Blake said. "Government's rationing the water and raising the price of fuel and fertilizer. It's hard on farmers. Don't they realize California is the most productive land in America?"

"In my botany class, we learned that industrial agriculture needs cheap oil, but climate requires us to use less oil," Andrés said.

"It's a train wreck," said Makah, "but the sooner we make these painful changes, the better. Of course, then, my own brother is working in the fracking fields back in North Dakota."

"When we were there at Christmas," Cody said, "Robbie was trying to convince me that fracking was good because it created high-paying jobs for Hispanics. Now that was awkward."

After dinner, Blake and Cody tackled cleanup while Toni took Makah and the grandchildren out to the chickens.

"Can we search for eggs?" Luz asked.

"Sure," Toni answered. "I didn't have time this morning."

"C'mon, Luz. I love this part," Rosa said.

As the two probed gently around the coop, Andrés asked, "Grandma, did you have these chickens when you switched the menu from turkey to ribs?"

"None of these same birds, Andrés," said Toni. "But I had hens. Why?"

"Something tells me they prefer it this way."

"I did notice that they laid better after we made the switch. That was a long time ago."

"Mom, look," Luz said, "I found two and Rosa found one."

"Grandma Toni was saying that they laid better after she switched the menu. I wonder why," said Makah.

Rosa piped up. "Maybe they're like people—having more sympathy for their own kind. The way we like furry mammals. I read a psychology book about that."

"She's going to be a psych major at Cal," Andrés said proudly.

"And he's going into ornithology," said Rosa.

12

CODY WAS WORKING AT HOME ALONE, turning over Thanksgiving's climate discussion. How to be part of the solution—from business? Makah's urgent critique of governments during dinner took him back three years to when she had gone to DC and Scotland for a month as part of a UN climate summit. Cody resented her absence, discovering that sole responsibility for Luz full time was a bigger challenge than he'd expected. He'd learned from it, too—learned something amazing about Luz. He was excited to tell Makah. Then she came home exhilarated from meeting Prince Charles inside the meeting halls and protesting with young people in the streets and so gripped with climate urgency and frustration that somehow there wasn't time to tell about Luz, which exasperated him.

He remembered when he brought it up one afternoon when Luz was visiting her friend Sharone, before Skah died. They were sitting on the couch. "It's like you had some kind of conversion experience."

"Maybe I did," she retorted. "Maybe we all need to. Maybe it's that time. Time for some uncomfortable changes."

Cody got up. "That seems to be the case. I certainly feel uncomfortable."

Makah stood up and faced him, stern. "That's not what I'm talking about, and you know it. There was a total cop-out by the so-called world leaders—*men*—just when leadership is needed. I was discussing this with Anna today."

Cody glowered. "Oh, Anna. Give me a break."

"Wait. You said you were reconciled to my work focus. You've been supportive up to now. Or at least I thought so."

He jerked his head back, shifting his eyes. "I *have* been supportive. But where's my support? I'm struggling to figure out what to do with my own career. It's stressful."

"Maybe you should just get your act together. You say you're tired of Opti-Drip, but you keep working there."

"I'm fucking waiting for the company to be sold—you know that. That's the whole point of a startup." He was over the top.

"I'm just saying, you made the choice, so don't complain."

Skah got up and let himself out the dog door.

Cody nodded toward the door. "What do we say to Luz when she gets angry? Take a deep breath. Try not to escalate."

"Sometimes we forget, and it goes out of control." She burrowed into the couch.

Now he sat beside her. "I'm sorry. Maybe I was overreacting. I don't know what to do. I find the whole thing scary. Here we are, doing our little things to save the planet, and meanwhile there's only minor progress. I mean, how are we going to live in the world that's coming? How is Luz going to live?"

Skah came back in and gazed at them, turning his patient eyes on one, then the other. Cody ruffled the dog with the back of his hand. He inched closer to Makah. She took his hand.

"We'll be fine," she said. "And Luz is a powerful being. Both of her grandmothers connect her to the Earth in profound ways. She'll be part of the solution, if there is one."

"Don't forget the fathers, Makah." He shifted to face her. "Grandpa Ethan used to talk about 'animal spirits' that kept him sane when he was lonely. We've got to find ways of reconnecting with nature."

• • •

Cody was ready for Opti-Drip to be done. One more year and he'd be free and have some real cash—the payoff he'd been working for since the startup's founding fifteen years before. It had been fun at first: the intensity, the tight team, the excitement about making farming better. Now he was tired of maintaining irrigation software he had once enjoyed creating and wanted to get into something new and proactive for climate. But from the business side? Really?

His skepticism had its origins during the reign of Jack Clemens, whom he met in the luxurious offices of Opti-Drip's new investor Peterman-Clemens, LLC. The firm's A-round financing brought a needed cash infusion, but it came with a board seat, and Clemens—well-known venture capitalist and PC's managing partner—sat at the head of the conference table. PC was situated in a low-rise office park on Sand Hill Road across from the Stanford Linear Accelerator. The environment conveyed understated extreme wealth—teak paneling, a Chagall in the lobby, designer furniture, nestled in a eucalyptus grove—so different from the messy offices of PC's startup clients, with coders jammed together in cubicles, grubby kitchens, ample scotch in easy reach, and flying nerf balls. Like Opti-Drip in the early years.

White, male, balding but fit in his suit jacket, light-blue dress shirt, open collar, and designer jeans, Clemens fit the VC profile. He welcomed the Opti-Drip leadership team and the other board members. Opti-Drip's president, Samir Rao, introduced Cody as his VP for engineering and Sarah Brown their CFO.

Clemens began by projecting a slide of PC's portfolio, which concentrated heavily in biotech. His point was that Opti-Drip represented a new direction for them and therefore presented a novel risk profile. "This means," he explained, "that I will be more personally involved in the company than PC partners usually are with our portfolio companies. Consider yourselves our canary in the coal mine, if you will, as we branch into ag tech. We want to learn from your experiences."

Cody remembered Sarah wincing, no doubt recalling their long debates about whether to take venture money and the strings attached. But there they were.

Samir reviewed Opti-Drip's revenue projections and sales pipeline. Clemens focused on a project in Spain to bring drip irrigation to the Costa del Sol, avocado central for Europe. "What about the regulatory side? You can't go to the bathroom over there without getting a permit from Brussels."

Cody's first inkling. He'd had to take a breath to stay professional. "It's taken a lot of work, but we're in good shape with the governmental approvals from the EU on down. The only pending matter is approval by the provincial authorities in southern Spain. I've cultivated those guys on the phone and will go there as soon as the Spanish company is ready. It should be done by Christmas."

"Don't get caught paying anybody off—just make money."

"Jack, we're going by the book," Samir countered. "That's how we run the company." Not his first rodeo.

"What are you doing to beef up the sales team?" Clemens asked.

"As I mentioned, we're recruiting a VP of sales. We have an announcement out on Monster. The résumés are a mixed bag, of course."

Clemens got up and poured himself a glass of Perrier from the bottle on the sideboard. "I want to see the top five résumés when you get there, say, in about two weeks."

After the meeting, the Opti-Drip team had headed down the freeway to Sunnyvale. As Samir drove, Sarah sat in the front seat complaining about Clemens. The festive pink and red oleanders ornamenting the broad median were invisible to the occupants.

"Had either of you met this guy before?" Cody asked. "I don't feel like we're exactly in a partnership with him."

"I met him," Samir said. "We've been over this. He's a known jerk. But PC offered the most favorable terms, so there was no real debate among our other investors."

"I hope they're right." Sarah sighed. "Anyway, back to business."

It turned out Clemens had his own candidate for the sales veep, a guy from one of PC's biotech companies that had just folded. His reputation in the Valley was not great—not a team player, hides the ball—Samir had heard.

Cody asked around. "You won't believe this," he'd told Makah a few days later. "Remember our first date, when Skah found the murdered sea otter on the beach? The biotech company this sales guy worked for was being investigated in connection with unexplained sea otter deaths. Apparently, they are a delicacy in some cultures, and their thyroid hormone is supposed to be an aphrodisiac. The company was suspected of harvesting sea otter thyroids to learn how to synthesize the hormone. A Chinese investor was involved. When the investigation got going, the investor pulled out and the company collapsed. The investigation was inconclusive, but the investor didn't want the reputational risk. And we don't need that karma at Opti-Drip."

Samir shut down the Clemens hiring scheme with the help of another investor. In the interim, they learned more about their new funder. A historian had published research laying out a sorry part of California history, a part that had involved Clemens's great-grandfather.

According to the research, during the period 1846–1879, settlers engaged in the coordinated, deliberate slaughter of California Native Americans—encouraged by the state government, which paid bounties for scalps. The number of men, women, and children murdered by parties of vigilante settlers firing rifles from horseback ranged into the tens of thousands, not counting children who were "indentured"—post–Civil War—no better than slaves. All this to clear out the land for mining and settlement by Anglos. A Clemens ancestor led one of the largest extermination raids.

Cody well remembered Makah's reaction: ". . . so much worse than when the government flooded the Nueta homelands to make Lake Sakakawea; and the scale—bigger than the Wounded Knee massacre—it's amazing no one hears about it."

"It's outrageous even by nineteenth-century standards," Cody had said. "The Spanish and Mexican colonialists were civilized by comparison. Ironic that I'll be going to Spain so soon. Gives me something to think about in my own heritage, for sure."

Like when he met Makah at the aquarium on their second date—the fall equinox, when Earth opens her southern half to her lover Sun and sends the north on its journey into winter. The equinox had inspired Cody ever since he took part in a celebration with his parents at the Pyramid of the Sun in Teotihuacan. They'd go to Mexico every few years, to the old neighborhood in Puebla where his grandfather, Galeno, lived until he was eight and the family moved to Texas. There were always Indians in Puebla, especially in the marketplace. Mom liked to remind him how, as a boy, he was fascinated by their "bright dark eyes."

When he told Makah that, she said, "It worked out well for me! Plus, your mom's father was a doc, like my dad."

One more thread they shared. "My Grandpa Galeno's first job was at a Japanese internment camp in Northern California during World War II, where he met my Grandma Luisa, the cook and curandera. I love how they worked together sometimes, healing. His open, philosophical outlook is the fount of my own intellectual curiosity."

"I wonder more about your father's side ancestor Buffalo Bill and that photo at your parents' house."

"That print's quite valuable, you know."

"But the way Buffalo Bill is standing with his hand on Red Cloud's shoulder. It seems patronizing, as if he owned them," Makah said.

Cody had felt defensive. How do descendants come to terms with the dark threads, some bloody, of ancestry? Different standards in the past, but still . . . gotta try to be a good person.

• • •

Cody broke his musings as Makah and Luz came in the door.

"How was school?" Cody asked.

"Interesting," Luz answered. "Everyone had to talk about what they did for Thanksgiving. Dad, I talked about your family and Buffalo Bill."

"I was just thinking about that," said Cody. "Remember when we found those letters in Grandma Arta's house after she died of Covid?"

"Of course," said Makah, "but they're not about Buffalo Bill."

"Right, but she was his descendant. That's what reminded me of clearing out her house in Greeley—when Skah found the letters behind the old desk, still in their original envelopes and tied in a blue ribbon. You brought them out to the kitchen where I was sorting pots and pans."

"I came across them the other day. You want to look at them again?" She fetched the bundle from its drawer in her dresser, its original ribbon caringly retied. "You called them love letters."

"They *were* love letters, in a way," Cody said. For the couple had met at the Treasure Island naval depot in San Francisco Bay where Ethan, having volunteered out of patriotism, had been sent as a supply officer shipping troops out to the Pacific War. Soon after they met, the young couple had been separated, as Arta went back to Colorado to care for her aging parents. The letters from Ethan told stories about his youth, and about his father, Everett.

Cody leafed through the stack. "Here's the one about the river otter." He began reading aloud.

When I wasn't playing ball, or studying, I sat by the stream that ran behind the house, watching nature, from the tiniest ant to an occasional black bear. One autumn afternoon, with dusk in the air, an otter appeared on the bank, come up from the creek. Rufus, the name I'd given the big crow who would lecture me during my cogitations, greeted the otter with a chortle, like gravel in a bucket. It wasn't a warning, more like a familiar hello. I was downwind from the otter, so when she saw me, she froze warily. I didn't move a muscle. Then we locked eyes, and something came into me, a kind of Indian spirit or animal medicine, deep and reliable, calm but wild. That presence is still a home for me.

Now, when I am sad, I take off from Treasure Island's barrenness and go up into the hills behind Oakland. The old oak forest is gone now, but there are still some groves that include redwoods. The wildlife is plentiful there, mostly raccoon and other small beasts and deer. It gives me great comfort and takes me back to my home. I feel connected with life. Maybe you know about this from your family. You told me about the photograph of your great-grandfather with two Indians, maybe one of them was named American Horse? I wonder if you know any stories about Indians and animals from the Wild West era. I would like to hear them.

Luz was sitting on the floor. "I love that letter," she said. "Mom, it sounds like when you would go to the wildlife refuge when you were a girl."

"I did feel something similar then. It's like when you go out with your dad or Anna, and you connect with the birds. It's like that old expression: 'It doesn't come from a stick or a stone.'"

"What does *that* mean?"

Cody answered, "You know. The apple doesn't fall far from the tree."

"Oh, I get it," said Luz. "Like makes like."

But Cody was quiet. His grandfather's experience with the river otter struck deep. He had often locked eyes with a sea mammal during his shore walks and felt something come into him. *Deep and reliable, calm but wild.* That reminded him of something Andrés had said, after he'd recruited Rosa into vegetarianism. "I just can't eat them, Dad. Not until there's a better balance."

"You know, Luz," Cody said, "when Andrés and Rosa were your age, I picked them up one weekend, and they were gushing about this school field trip they had taken to a redwood park. Rosa told me, 'Dad, there was a raven there, really big, with this rumbling croak. Andrés can make the sound perfectly.' Then Andrés let out this impressive croak. 'We told Grandma Toni,' he said, 'and she told us an old Mexican story about crows.'

"Rosa said it was a *proverb*. You know how she likes to be right. She quoted Grandma Toni—'Cria cuervos y te sacarán los ojos.' 'Oh, yeah,' said Andrés, 'they'll poke your eyes out.' Rosa said the proverb meant that if you raise kids badly, they will take advantage of you, and Andrés corrected her, saying 'only if you spoil them.'

"Then he said, 'But crows are not like that, actually. They're pretty chill.' That's when I learned he could talk to crows. Months later, I took him with me to inspect an experimental strawberry field where we were testing Opti-Drip's watering software. We also saw new machinery—automated berry pickers. No one there on a Sunday, only this voluble crow sitting on a power pole surveying the scene. Andrés told me the bird was speaking to him. 'Sure,' I said, skeptical. 'And what exactly is he saying?' Andrés says, dead serious, 'Dad. *Her* name is Corneille, and she says there's a better way to make that machine. She says she knows because she picks a lot of berries.'"

"Luz has that gift in a different way," said Makah, "as you found out while I was at the UN conference, only you didn't tell me until weeks later."

"What, Mom? What did Dad find out about me?"

"You remember," said Cody. "While Mom was gone, we would drive to wild places around Monterey, and I would name various birds and trees. I was getting more in touch with my own natural senses. Then you started inventing your own names for what we saw. We'd walk and you would pretend to talk with the crows and jays, responding to their calls. You tried to imitate their songs."

"Oh, yeah," said Luz. "That was when I was young. If I listened hard, I could sometimes see darting lights in the woods, or, if I heard a rustling sound, I might see a shadow disappearing behind a tree."

"Right," Cody said. "Inklings. One time you were talking with a raven, your Kéka. She was strutting along the ground under some trees, picking at the duff, when a robin flew into some nearby bushes. '*Ta-ha-shé*,' you cried. And that robin gaped at you, so surprised, shook its feathers, uttered a startled *cheep!*, and flitted on its way."

"When you told me about it, I said how it was totally strange," Makah said. "I knew, like, ten words in Nueta, but that sounded familiar. Knowledge of Nueta was beaten out of children in my grandmother's generation and before, in the government boarding schools that Indian children were required to attend for over a hundred years. Edwin Benson, the last fluent Nueta speaker, had just died, aged eighty-five."

"Right," said Cody. "Then you checked with your mom, and she verified that *tahashé* was indeed Nueta for *robin*."

"We never did find out how you learned that word, Luz. Grandma Mandy didn't remember telling it to you," Makah said.

"I loved those walks with Dad," Luz said. "I was sad you were gone though. One time, Andrés came with us. He showed me how to hold my tongue and lips to make real good bird calls. Dad tried too, but his mouth was too old."

"My ear isn't as good as yours either. It's easier to learn new languages when you're young. You were definitely the winner that day."

"Dad, can you read the other letter from your grandfather Ethan, the scary one?" Luz said.

"Here, I'll read it," said Makah.

Dear Arta,

Today I have some time, for it is raining and turning cold—cold for here, anyway. I thought I'd tell you about my father and his childhood. I told you he and his mother were rescued by the Mandan Indians on the Upper Missouri River after his father and brothers were murdered, about 1878—how the Mandans took them in and gave them food and shelter for three years. But I didn't tell you about the murder. My father and his mother were out picking berries that spring. When they came back to their cabin, they found the bodies of his father and his two older brothers. It was far from any town, and there was not much law there in those days. My father told me that his mother took one look at the scene and shook her head grimly. Then she said to him, 'I told your father not to do business with those men. They were road agents who had held up a Treasure Coach on its way to Cheyenne with Black Hills gold. They pretended they were trappers, but I knew better. They acted real nice and did him many favors. When they asked him to help them hide some heavy boxes, your father figured out who they were and confronted one of them. The man denied it and left angrily, accusing your father of being an ingrate. That was two days ago. I think they got worried and came back and killed him and your brothers.' My father was transformed by this event. It hardened him to a great many things. He always regretted having to leave the Mandans, where he felt safe and at home. He didn't think much of settler life in that country.

The tangled threads of Cody's white and Mexican settler lineages jumbled with his family's history of involvement with Native peoples. Like at the Indian museum in DC—blending tribal and US history with contemporary life in Indian Country. And now he was married to an Indian and father of another.

PART *Two*

13

YESTERDAY MUST HAVE SIGNALED THE NEW YEAR, with its traditional incendiary welcomings creating flight and noise hazards for some of us. But it's also a festival of reminiscence and stocktaking, a favorite activity for us Corvids.

When I was three, I met Corneille, an Old Crow whom I came to revere and think of as a friend. I would watch her as she tried to work with humans, learning by observation and from her stories. She explained how she advised Skah to look out for Makah and helped Andrés with his Crow vocabulary. She was uncommonly good at the work, so committed, and I wondered why she tolerated a young Crow like me hanging around. Little did I know.

One day she said, "Dear Koro, you've been an outstanding student. Now the time nears for me to pass the torch to you."

"Torch?"

"An apt expression, for 'tis a fiery thing, this charge as intermediary to the humans. You've been watching me, so you know."

"What are you talking about? I'm not your student—we're friends. It's just fun to watch you talk to humans. They're so weird."

"You can't fool me, Koro. I know you have better powers of perception than that. You wouldn't still be here, helping me with this difficult task, if you didn't sense there was something big going on. In any case, there's a whole process to transfer powers."

"I've never heard of it."

"It's closely held. First, you must go away to perform certain tasks. Think of the labors of Hercules, but Crow sized. When you come back, there's a ceremony. It's mysterious and powerful."

"What labors?" I asked.

"I can tell you some things about it now," she said. But at that point she dropped into our untranslatable patois, *Crojan—"Craw! Crick crick, wardle krr wardle wardle err* . . ."

Sadly, just a few weeks later, she injured her leg. She was getting on in years—eighteen is truly an old Crow—and perching and hopping became onerous. She ate poorly. She had already taught me about the mission, the importance of a successful turnaround, and the Crowdex. We had long observed human behavior together, and she had shared her perspectives for several years.

Corneille turned to me. "There are going to be these big meetings. You're going to have to run them."

I squawked, fluffing out my feathers. "I can't do that. I'm only eight. No way!"

"These things are not a matter of choice. It's like being a shaman—it chooses you. But you still have to learn. That's why I've been teaching you. You will find helpers. Other species. Bears can be particularly good partners."

She began to explain the transformation and how the magic happened. She spoke again in Crojan, but I have been authorized—by something referred to as The Society—to share a little about what's involved. It is getting late, after all, and greater understanding among species is needed.

When Corneille told me that the time of change was upon us, I was frightened. She told me that if I could complete three tasks, I would be ready. Similar rituals took place across the planet, she told me, and I would be in touch with advisors—Crows and other birds who had similar roles and would help me. "It's an excellent group," she reassured me. "You will like them. They like to joke around. It makes the job easier. But it's still a hard job."

I can reveal one task. At Corneille's instruction, I flew to the four directions in search of sacred plants. You already know the Common Bearberry. There was also a rare *Crowyote* cactus button, a Tule seed, and a piece of Giant Sequoia bark from a secret grove in Oakland.

I brought these back one at a time and hid them carefully near where the cawcus was staying, down near Monterey. As you know, Crows roost together at night, and in June, under the full moon, there was a great gathering. The ceremony began with a stirring Coyote concert. Then the officiant, a Raven up from Tassajara, her size and gravelly voice emanating gravitas, solemnly presided. "We are here to induct Koro into the special Society whose name itself is secret," she began. "We also recognize dear Corneille, who served our Grandmother so loyally all her life. She has been a credit to the Tribe of Crows and to all Corvidae. We honor her today by passing the gift of tongue to Koro."

Raven gargled at me and flapped her wings noisily. As I had been instructed, I brought out the four plants and placed them on a large, flat stone in the clearing. They glistened in the moonlight, each a different color—red, yellow, green, and brown. I ingested a morsel of each as the assembled cawcus gave forth with cries of encouragement. As the magic took hold of me, I felt disembodied—my legs, wings, head, and tail flew in different directions, my guts dangled out, my eyes dropped through space, my beak shattered. It was excruciating and terrifying.

After I don't know how long, I woke up lying on the stone. It was light. Four large Crows surrounded me, facing outward, watchful for any wayward predator who hadn't got the news of my transformation, for all planimals swear to protect the Society and keep its secrets. I awakened slowly as from a dream and felt the same as always, though a bit nauseous. But in my mind, there were now parallel streams of thought, like two tracks, the first being normal Crow and the second much, much bigger. I understood it to be the Society channel, and I began to meet some of my fellows in other regions. And there were other surprises, of which I cannot speak.

• • •

Quite a bit later, after the first Congress, I finally found a way to hang around with that hot young Crow from Salinas. I was patrolling the area around Carmel when I spotted Anjo perched on a telephone wire contemplating the blue Pacific. I joined him and we chatted and enjoyed the view. But I was so *itchy* that day, I started preening. He studied me for a moment and then asked me would I mind if he picked a mite out of my nape feathers.

"Oh, would you?" I asked. "That one's really bothering me, and I can't get to it myself."

It turned out that Anjo was an exquisite mite picker, and as he worked his way down to my scapulars—where my wings attach—I fell for him. Not off the wire, mind you. Thankfully, the attraction was mutual. Now we have these lovely talks, hopping and finding seeds and nuts in the forest duff and choicer morsels in the gutters of a quiet street.

One day up near Salinas, I was talking with him about what I was hearing about the planimals' efforts to get humans' attention. The efforts were spirited, I told him, but the results discouraging. Some naturalists took notice of "aberrant" animal behavior, but not the mainstream press. Getting humans to recognize the rest of life as equal players in the future of the planet was proving difficult. We needed a fresh approach.

"When's the next Congress?" he asked. "Maybe I could come and help. It sounds like a lot of responsibility for one Crow, even one as pretty as you."

"I have my Bear, Ursula," I said, "and there's a good posse of helpers. Of course, it *would* be fabulous to have you with me, sweet Anjo. You are the wind beneath my wings. Plus, you have good instincts and a sharp caw when things get difficult."

• • •

There's one last tail—er, tale—I feel I must tell, because I was a witness. It's about the death of Cody's Tara.

When Cody and Tara moved in with Makah and Skah, the Burmese feline was transformed by the wildness of the nearby park. She came into her huntress, spending more and more time outdoors. She thanked Cody for bringing her to this new world. Always cunning smart, she now became a menace to birds. At Makah's insistence they had belled her. That didn't stop her roaming, for she had become a creature of the night.

For Tara, it was like in James Dickey's "Heaven of Animals," a poem I found copied into the Crowdex—

> For some of these,
> It could not be the place
> It is, without blood.
> These hunt, as they have done,
> But with claws and teeth grown perfect.
>
> More deadly than they can believe.
> They stalk more silently,
> And crouch on the limbs of trees,
> And their descent
> Upon the bright backs of their prey

May take years
In a sovereign floating of joy . . .

A few months later, Tara had learned about the other side. She had watched admiringly one evening as a mom Coyote stood point watching a Deer Mouse for ten minutes before arching up and pouncing on it with her front paws—such a tasty morsel. Tara had cultivated this patience and perseverance. One night she crouched, waiting for a Vole to emerge from its burrow, having learned to silence the bell by stillness. It was a cramped spot, but she felt confident. Then, a potent funk of male Coyote hit her. She became like stone.

"I know you're there," said Coyote. "Your time has come. I am here for you. Not on my own account, mind you." Coyote chuckled to himself. "Cat's not my thing."

Tara prepared herself. "Bring it on," she said. "You better take your best shot. I'm going to hurt you."

Coyote moved. Tara was in his jaws before she could face him. He shook her. She raked at his neck with her hind legs.

"A Crow told me you like poetry," he said. "See if a few more lines of Dickey agree with you."

He growled the lines through his teeth as her strength faded—

" . . . And those that are hunted
Know this as their life,
Their reward: to walk

Under such trees in full knowledge
Of what is in glory above them,
And to feel no fear,
But acceptance, compliance.

Fulfilling themselves without pain
At the cycle's center,
They tremble, they walk
Under the tree,
They fall, they are torn,
They rise, they walk again.

"We'll talk more when you get to the other side," said Coyote. "I think you're getting an upgrade."

14

FEBRUARY: THE MONTH WHEN ANOTHER COYOTE, the intrepid Shakti, turned seven and bore her fourth litter, two males and three females. Her devoted mate of several years stuck close to the den, bringing food, protecting and teaching the pups who were full of the exuberance of being young and alive. As they grew, their parents taught them caution around humans in the hilly, open forest they prowled. Humans had been slow to build in the remote area north of Santa Cruz, but the pandemic's shift to virtual work made living there more practical.

The largest male cub, Tatiki, was an adventurer, curious and brave. He and his mother developed a special bond over their first summer. Shakti told him Coyote tales from the Old Times when Coyotes had a sacred purpose helping the Spirit Chief shape the world for the arrival of the people. One old story went like this:

"In the distant times, Coyote tamed the monsters in preparation for the arrival of Humans. For example, there was Kika-wau-pa, a big and ferocious Dog. One afternoon, as Coyote was sauntering by, enjoying the fine day, Dog rushed out of his cave to attack Coyote. But Coyote darted into a nearby tunnel that his wife, Mole, had made. Dog dug him out and was about to kill him, his fierce jaws salivating above Coyote's tender neck. 'Wait,' said Coyote. 'At least let me smoke my pipe before you kill me.' Dog thought of himself as a fine fellow, and did not object, waiting patiently for his meal. But Coyote called on his magic, which gave him an armful of stones. Coyote sprang up and threw a stone at Dog, who jumped back suddenly and fell into one of Mole's tunnels. Coyote hit him with another stone. Soon Dog was tired and wounded, and Coyote moved in for the kill. When Dog died, a little Dog ran out of Dog's body, its tail between its legs. 'Henceforth,' said Coyote, 'you will be a loyal and faithful friend of Humans.'"

Tatiki thought about that story and wondered about the Dogs he'd seen around the human settlements. Some of them were large and aggressive. "Why didn't Coyote make Dogs friendly to Coyotes?" he asked his mother.

"We don't know, Son. Sometimes Dogs and Coyotes do become friendly. They even make pups together. But you're right—it's better to keep your distance. They are the friends of humans." She saw his discernment was sound, that he could become wise as well as wily. That summer, when she got wind of a second planimal Congress, she took him with her. When they arrived, she admired his embrace of the harmonious energy present in the park, only to be bemused as his hackles rose when a flashy Crow made a sarcastic comment about Dogs, and he voiced a sharp protest. He had good spirit.

• • •

By fall, Tatiki was growing into a powerful young male. His brother and a sister had been killed by cars, and another by parasites, leaving one sister. He and his father continued to hunt and play together, but the play had gotten rougher in recent weeks.

Shakti took her mate aside. "You need to be more gentle with Tat. He's going to be an important animal."

"Not around here, he isn't," her mate said. "He needs to watch himself, or I'll teach him a lesson he won't forget."

"You have to talk to him. You're still my mate, and you belong here as the leader."

One day father and son were out hunting. The Ground Squirrels were focused on preparing for winter and not so wary as usual. The pair felt confident, at ease as they stopped for a drink at a little stream. While they rested, Tatiki's father spoke sternly. "My son, your mother and I have talked. We believe it is time for you to set out on your own. There is nothing for you here. This is my territory, and you're smart enough to find your own. Good luck, and may the Alpha Spirit be with you."

Tatiki did not argue. That evening he said goodbye to his mother, his sister, and his playmates and journeyed out of the territory, following the route he'd taken with his mother to the Congress. He trotted past the Burmese monastery, across old trails, and through the park. Well out of his father's territory, he headed down toward Highway 1. The rough country suited him, with its mixed forest and brush, the occasional logging road and trail—dry but reasonably stocked with prey. The cool autumn air was sweet with eucalyptus and pine, and the sunlight slanted through the canopy in bright strips, tantalizing his imagination with shadows and elusive forms.

The young canine moved with care, avoiding others of his kind. It seemed natural to him, their enforced separation into families, with the unattached aunts and sisters helping raise the pups, the uncles and brothers going off to find their own places. Unlike the Wolf stories his father had told him—the way they lived and hunted in extended packs led by an alpha male and female. How would that even feel? He traveled by night for several days, avoiding contact with anyone except the occasional unlucky Vole, sleeping in snatches.

Skirting east around Santa Cruz, he followed the coast south, avoiding the intermittent urbanization. The territories here were larger and less well marked. He ran into a small family group in the Moss Landing Wildlife Area. The old male was twelve. Part of Tatiki wanted to challenge him. It was sweet territory. He could take that guy. But the aging veteran glared at him, his lip curled to reveal a hint of tooth. He appeared remarkably spry. Studying the malevolent scar above the senior's right eye, Tatiki moved on. He'd come already forty miles and was getting tired. Yet something called him.

In a few more days he was in Veterans Park in Monterey. He sensed the presence of a solitary female in the south end of the park and a feeling of absence in the north end. Sniffing around the north end, he found a territory boundary and investigated. A male had been there, but no pups or den were in evidence. In an overgrown ravine beside the park road, he discovered the desiccated remains. Roadkill.

Dude had some bad luck. No sign of a mate. Lots of houses, but no smell of bait or traps. Know-it-all Crows heralding his arrival. Plenty of Squirrels, and a creek with berries nearby. It felt . . . homey.

He awoke midmorning. Nothing had disturbed him. He ranged along the edges of the territory and the boundaries marked by man-made structures. Abundant small game. The park portion was only ten acres, but a Deer trail led into a larger woodland. At one end of the territory he experienced a deep familiarity, some shrouded memory. He could hear humans talking on the hillside above him.

"Can you check the fencing around the coop, Dad?" Luz asked. "I sense something, like maybe the old coyote that used to live down the hill is back. Only it feels different, a young-old energy together."

"I'll take a look," Cody said, "but tell me more about your sense. What do you mean 'young-old'?"

"There are two parts together—the young energy feels new, but the old energy feels old. I mean old age but also old, like familiar or . . . wise? Anyway, it feels good to have a dog around again, even a wild one. I miss Skah. Chickens are nice, but it's not the same."

15

MAKAH HAD COME TO THE UNIVERSITY IN 2008, as a non-tenure-track lecturer. "At least I'm in," she'd told her mother, who agreed. It was a start, and a long way from the underfunded high school on the reservation. Makah was proud to follow a path blazed by women throughout history, including two from her own reservation, women who had overcome difficult childhoods and racial prejudice to earn advanced degrees and succeed in the dominant culture. Her teaching and research invigorated her. She loved the students, their keen interest in climate and the environment. Monterey's rich Mediterranean biome awakened a deeper connection with nature that infused her teaching. But she could feel the culture of sexism and racism around her. At the university, there were stubborn obstacles to women's advancement, especially in science policy. Her Indigenous background played both ways, but the system's antibodies—unconscious bias, unresolved guilt, arrogant prejudice—devalued the perspectives and sensibilities ingrained over centuries of living in close connection with the natural world.

She kept her head down, trying to ignore the slights of not being invited to meetings and social events. Attuned to the growing recognition and importance of Indigenous wisdom as a way of thinking and living in a time of climate challenges, she built a global network of Indigenous leaders, engaging them at the beginning in her research on the effects of temperature rise on biodiversity. She had connected with some of them while working on her dissertation, and she had met others through organizations like the Indigenous Environmental Network. The connections were deepening as they shared stories about changes in the natural world in their regions.

After three years, she caught a break. An older professor turned emeritus, and a tenure-track position opened. With Suzanne's advice and the dean's commitment to increasing faculty diversity, she got the job and became an assistant professor. She published her first book right before Luz was born and three years later made associate and earned tenure.

One perk of the promotion was the ability to hire a graduate assistant. Shortly after she posted the position, she was at a student–faculty mixer when a young woman approached her—nonchalant, assertive, a tall, slim blonde, twenty-two, with curls shaping her oval face.

"Professor Andrews," the student said, "I'm Wanda Clemens. I'm the person you're seeking for your graduate assistant."

Sizing her up, Makah winced. The self-confidence of entitlement. "Hello, Wanda. Nice to meet you. Tell me why you think you are the right person."

"I'm a quick learner, diligent, and accurate with numbers. I'm in the business school and recently aced a class on environmental, social, and governance goals in business. I want to learn more about climate change and help business act responsibly."

"Okay. Send in your résumé and transcript."

The envelope came the next day. Wanda's Stanford undergrad record was impressive. Still, it was unusual to hire outside the department. Makah mentioned this to her new department chair, Professor Chase, a Texan, after a faculty meeting.

"What's this student's name?" he asked.

"Wanda Clemens." Makah remembered his eyes flickering.

"I see," he said. "I think it will be fine. If you think she's the best candidate, then you should hire her."

It worked until it didn't, until Makah discovered Wanda was falsifying the biodiversity data she was supposed to be getting from Makah's international network. For some reason it seemed the network made Wanda uncomfortable, although she hadn't said anything.

Makah remembered the day she called Wanda into her office. The young blonde had come bouncing in, seemingly oblivious.

Makah wasted no time. "You've been faking your research. It's completely unacceptable."

Wanda frowned. "I did not. That's the real data. I worked hard to get it. That network of yours! They're clueless amateurs on some remote Pacific islands in some weird time zone. They hardly speak English. What a waste of time."

Makah felt her blood pressure rising. "It doesn't work that way, Wanda. I was comparing notes with a network member. That's how I discovered it. You've cost me three months. I'm letting you go."

Wanda stood up, not even blushing. "We'll see about that. You'll find out."

Two days later, the department chair's secretary called, saying he wanted to see her. "He's in quite a mood," she said. Makah recalled the session in Chase's office, the secretary letting her in with a sisterly grimace, Chase's short hair graying, his hands fidgeting. He flourished a one-page document anchored by a bold signature. "Her father wrote to the dean," he said. "He doesn't threaten, but Jack Clemens is a major donor to the university. I'll be direct. Do you have any slack on this?"

Makah remembered the mantra a cell biologist taught her at UND—*Science is an unforgiving mistress if you love her, and if you don't, why bother?* "I'm sorry, no. No slack. I can't use fabricated data in the project report. This will delay publication, and we have zero extra time on climate. Besides, she denied it, compounding the lie. I can't keep her." She studied him. "Surely someone will pick her up."

"That's plan B for sure. Look, I support you in this, and I want you to stay. Science matters. But so does politics. I'm going to initiate an internal review. Professor Pearcy will lead the panel. Time is on your side, since the school year is ending. They'll want it done."

She found it ironic that Pearcy was leading the panel after the pass he'd made in her first year. He had apologized, and, being new to campus, she hadn't reported him. Academic sexual politics. Blood under the bridge. He was a good choice politically, his appearance unimpeachable. How would he see things? He'd better get diversity on the panel.

It had worked out as Chase predicted. Pearcy had been professional, even kind, helping her find another assistant. Makah wrote him a thank-you note, and he'd responded, "One is never too old to learn from one's mistakes." Wanda graduated and moved on.

◆ ◆ ◆

In the years that followed, time was clouded with the death of Chanson and struggles dealing with Luz—who seemed to be developing a disposition marked by occasional meltdowns and unexplained moping. Yet Makah published a second book, along with a collection of articles by Indigenous scientists and scholars that received wide attention in academic circles around the climate crisis. She spoke regularly at conferences, cementing her network and reputation.

Now it was spring, and Stanford had made an offer—tenured associate professor. It was alluring, flattering. But she and Cody's hearts were in Monterey, not to mention the housing prices and traffic on the Peninsula. She mentioned the offer to Chase during the annual salary review.

"Thanks for letting me know, Makah." He faced her from behind his desk. "I appreciate it. I hope you decide to stay. You're an asset to the department. Maybe it's time to apply for full professor. Your work is respected by prominent senior scholars in the United States and overseas. The students rate your teaching highly. I'm a supporter, as you know, although it's ultimately not my decision. If you're agreeable, I'll let Dean Denny know that I'm planning to send you a formal letter requesting your dossier and supporting letters."

Seven years after achieving tenure was the national average for becoming a full professor, and for Makah it was already eight. Yet she'd long held the sense of not being ready. Whenever colleagues would ask her, she'd say, "Maybe in a couple of years." She felt held back by the school's culture and her own insecurity. But recently she had seen a webinar lecture by a Black academic at another institution who had also held herself back. Finally, the woman had taken the plunge and shared her vitae with senior colleagues, asking them whether she was ready "to go up for promotion to full." To her surprise, her colleagues were supportive.

Now Makah's chair was asking her. She and Cody talked it over.

"The thing about the Stanford offer is that they made no representations about the path to full," Cody said, "at least by what you've told me."

"You're right. I asked, and their chair said something like his goal would be 'as soon as possible, once you've gotten established.' I can imagine endless faculty committee meetings and 'other duties as assigned' to become 'established.' That's not a plus, now that my chair and colleagues are so supportive."

She called Professor Chase and told him yes, and in a few weeks, he asked her to stop by. It seemed that Dean Denny was not so enthusiastic. He'd been vague about the reasons—made it sound like a timing issue.

"I pushed back," Chase said. "I told him, 'Look, it's just the start of the process. Let's give her a chance.' When he hesitated, I told him, 'I think it would be problematical not to at this point. She's got considerable support on the faculty.' He said he'd think about it, and yesterday he told me to go ahead. So, the request letter is in the works, but I wanted to let you know. I'll try to find out what's going on, but in the meantime, proceed full steam ahead."

As she prepared the materials that would go to scholars in her field who would write letters of recommendation, Makah speculated about what might be behind the dean's reluctance. She and Cody were fixing dinner one evening when Suzanne dropped by.

"I heard about it," Suzanne said. "It's just weird. Dr. Denny has been good about promoting women and minorities. Our diversity stats in the tenured ranks beat most other schools in our league."

"Still, it's taken longer than average for Makah to get to this point," Cody said. "The average at this university is six years to full—so Makah is technically late. Plus, it took a while for her to get tenure in the first place."

"Maybe a degree from UND is not prestigious enough, compared with the Elis and those prima donnas from that junior university in Palo Alto." Makah's eyes darted at Cody, a Stanford alum.

"Stanford made you an offer," Suzanne said. "The dean would know that. Plus, not to promote you would raise eyebrows. Aren't you the only Native American on the faculty?"

"Sadly," said Makah, "although I have a promising PhD candidate I might entice, if we had an opening."

"Whenever you come back from those conferences of Indian STEM professionals, you tell me that nearly all the Native women academics are associates. It seems it's a systemic challenge getting to full," Cody said.

"I'll nose around and see what I can find out. Maybe old Pearcy will know." Suzanne winked.

"Pearcy!" That apology he'd sent her—just covering his ass? "I'll bet he's behind this."

"Why would he care, Makah?" Suzanne asked. "He's retired."

"I never told you about the pass he made when I first got here. It was gross. He apologized later, and he did clear up the Wanda issue. I thought he was genuinely remorseful, but now . . ."

• • •

Two weeks later, at a function in the faculty club, Makah spotted Pearcy nursing a scotch and standing in a corner. She went straight for him. "I need to talk to you. What's going on with my application for full? I think you're blocking it. Why?"

He stepped backward into a bookcase, then recovered. "Makah, hello. It's good to see you. But, but I don't know what you're talking about. You're, you're applying for full? Wonderful news. Well deserved."

"What do you mean you don't know? I know one thing you *do* know, though. You know I never said anything about your repulsive behavior. It's never too late, you know." Yet the surprise in his eyes persisted, and now, alarm. He looked tired.

"I know nothing about your promotion, Makah. I'm out of the loop these days." He sipped his drink and set it on the bookcase. "I really meant it when I wrote to you apologizing for acting inappropriately. That was a wake-up for me. So, I'm sorry to hear about the delay. Do you want me to check into it?"

The blood rushed to her head. She was shaking. He was genuine. "I'd have to think about it, Dr. Pearcy. But I appreciate your offering. And I'm sorry for the mix-up. I'm just upset and frustrated, I guess. Have . . . have a good night." Mortified, she made for the exit.

16

ONE MORNING, SEVERAL WEEKS EARLIER, Jack Clemens awoke with a headache. He pushed the reality of aging out of his mind and dragged himself out of bed. Ever since Wanda's mother had walked out on him ten years before, the 5,500-square-foot Atherton house felt empty. The Rosewood Hotel bar across from his office had reopened after the lockdowns, and the Thursday scene—known crudely as "Cougar Night"—was hopping again. There *were* some interesting women there, but with eyes for the younger guys. He'd spotted a couple of founders from Peterman-Clemens startups in the crowd. The young techies were more interested in the investors than the women. He and two colleagues held court from a booth near the dance floor, enjoying the people-watching. Over the course of the evening, they succeeded in going through a rare nineteen-year Aberlour Sherry Butt Single Malt.

Over the previous two decades, Clemens had become associated with Peder Lieth, a brilliant, idiosyncratic entrepreneur who had founded Matchstick, a data-surveillance company. Matchstick had grown fat providing governments and corporations with comprehensive profiles and predictive analysis on individuals and their connections. The two men had met at the country club, Lieth bragging about his zero handicap. Now Clemens believed there was an opportunity to utilize remotely collected human biometric and biological data for similar purposes. He pitched it to Lieth, who was noncommittal.

"Tell me what you find out," Lieth said. "It seems like a long shot. But then, that's what we do, isn't it? Things that seem like long shots but aren't."

Biosurveillance was largely considered to include the detection and reporting of dangerous pathogens, an activity that took on increased urgency during the pandemic. Hidden within the term, however, was the analysis of human behavior from biodata, including DNA. That activity was below the radar of most privacy regulators overwhelmed trying to protect individuals from the ubiquitous, comprehensive surveillance of online activity, including mobile phone location data, by companies and governments.

Moreover, facial recognition, especially when enhanced by thermal cameras, was becoming highly accurate. The challenge was that, unless the person's picture was on file, either publicly or privately, you couldn't make the identification.

As Clemens told Lieth, "If you could get their DNA, you could impute their identity by tying them to genetically related persons using commercial and government DNA databases. Hell, you can buy DNA profiles now on the dark web. The databases aren't that secure."

"But how do you get the subject's DNA—scrape it off a toilet seat?" Lieth asked.

Clemens proceeded anyway. The year before, Wanda, then thirty, had joined his firm as an associate, assigned to its new biosurveillance team as a researcher, focusing on how to get someone's DNA without them knowing. No one yet seemed to have a technique that could scale and be commercialized. Wanda spent her time talking to academics and perusing the literature. Her MBA project on Big Data valuation in ocean temperature tracking was coming in handy, but it made her think about the incident with Makah.

Wanda harbored mixed feelings. She was glad the matter had been handled quietly, but she still thought Makah had been too picky. She wondered about her own standards of verity, a product of her upbringing. Was she too loose, like some people told her? Or were they naive about how the world works? Her dad's voice. Her internal conversations made her anxious. She repressed them.

The work for PC was interesting enough, and it paid well. She got along with her father okay. It hadn't always been so. She'd sided with her mother in her parents' tense discussions. Not one to hold back, Wanda was an assertive participant. The vehemence with which her parents argued about inconsequential matters, like not recharging the Tesla, mystified her. Later, when the extent of Jack's deceptions came out in the divorce, she'd understood the treachery under the tension. Her mother had moved back to the East Coast to be with her family and become more remote than ever. Over time, Wanda had made a truce with her father. Still, she felt queasy, like she was drifting through her life, an untethered buoy in a vast sea.

• • •

Later that spring, she briefed her father and PC's legal team on her research. Right away, a lawyer interrupted. "I see privacy flags all over this. There are due process issues as well."

Clemens waved his hand. "Let her continue."

"As I was saying," Wanda resumed, "available technology can extract DNA from human tissue, compare it with existing databases, and analyze it for ancestry or disease markers. The analytics are not always right—still an unacceptable number of false positives in sensitive situations—but that's changing fast.

"The core challenge to remote DNA tracking is getting the samples," she continued. "Possible sources of remote DNA collection include human breath, urine, feces, saliva, hair, and skin cells. Urine can theoretically be collected from waterless toilets but is problematic because it degrades quickly if not kept cold. Feces contain too many microbes. Spit cells might be left on a restaurant glass, but it's difficult to collect and keep pure." Wanda watched the lawyers squirming. Privacy or biology?

"Hair and skin seem more promising," she continued. "Recent advances make it possible to identify persons based on hair samples that don't contain the hair follicle or root—a previous limitation. 'Touch' DNA is often collected in forensic examinations from skin cells left on clothing or from objects a suspect has touched, such as a steering wheel. The reliability varies, but it can be good if there was sustained contact.

"In the end, human intervention would be required to collect the samples using these techniques. This contrasts with the aquatic world, where environmental signal processors are already collecting fish DNA from sea water. The equivalent terrestrial method would be to collect DNA from air samples."

The lawyer interjected. "This is where it goes off the rails. In my—"

Clemens cut him off him with a glare.

Wanda proceeded. "The science has advanced enough to give DNA that is loose in the environment its own acronym, eDNA. A Singaporean team detected human and animal DNA samples in ventilation systems in university buildings. British researchers collected samples from the air of lab rat cages and were surprised to find the samples 'contaminated' with human DNA from people in the lab. The researchers noted the potential for 'forensic applications.' Scientists in Denmark collected ambient air at the Copenhagen Zoo and identified forty-nine different animal species, including humans."

"Well, I'm not sure about all this," said Clemens, shrugging at the lawyers. "We need to find out whether this 'eDNA' in large public spaces would be too diffuse to allow practical identification of a particular individual. Focus on that, Wanda."

When the meeting broke up, Clemens made a call. "Peder? I think we've got something. Can you do drinks at six?"

Walking back to her desk, Wanda felt unsettled, alone. Her heart wasn't in the work. It was interesting, sure, but something didn't sit right. She had held back one important development. She had learned of a journal article, undergoing peer review prior to publication, demonstrating that human DNA could be intentionally recovered using environmental sampling, enabling the identification of individuals present in the sampled environment.

She called her best friend Roseanne, who agreed to meet that evening. When she walked out to the lot at 5:30, her father's car was still there, though his office was dark. She walked across to her own car. As she waited at the light on Sandhill Road, she saw her father in the passenger seat of an unmistakable "Rosso" Maserati Granturismo pulling into the PC driveway. Oh shit. It was Jennifer, the most outrageous of Jack's lovers before the divorce. Jennifer was former CIA, hard as nails, and completely unscrupulous. She was definitely on Wanda's villains list, woven as she was into the pall of the final fights between her parents. Jack had told her mother he'd sworn her off. That was right before everything blew up.

Wanda met Roseanne at their usual, a small Italian place in Mountain View. Wanda liked her because she was not as pretty as Wanda, yet her life seemed more together. At least she had a boyfriend.

"I'm ready for a drink," Wanda said. "I just saw Jack get out of Jennifer's car—trouble on wheels." They ordered gin martinis. "He's up to no good; I know it. He didn't seem that interested in my research results. But I think he was, really. It makes me nervous about where it's going. I need to do something else."

"Did he see you?"

"I don't think so. He had his eyes on her." What were they up to? It wasn't just coincidence. "She's a direct line to some of the world's worst governments. It creeps me out."

"Maybe you could take a break—say we're going to Cancun or something."

"Something like that. Anyway, keep your ears open for anyone who's hiring. I've got to be careful—the nondisclosure agreement is ugly."

That weekend, Wanda was coming back from a brief visit to the coast via wooded Highway 17 through the Coastal Range, its ups and downs, its hairpin turns slowing her to fifteen, now ten. In the oncoming lane, a camper-trailer lumbered uphill, leading a string of frustrated drivers. She passed the Bear Creek Redwood Preserve. On a sudden urge, she turned in at the entrance and passed the stables to the parking lot. It wasn't busy. She parked and grabbed her water bottle. She wandered up the hill to Madrone Knoll, passing through dense fir and redwood, including a small community of old growth, their interlacing roots holding them fast against the winds of change. When she reached the top, she rested, peering through the vegetation at scattered views of the forest below. A plane passed overhead, the jagged moan of jet fuel burning. Then silence, but for wrens in the bushes offering their high-pitched chittering melodies. She breathed deeply and sighed.

There arose in her mind's eye a scene from her childhood. She was maybe seven when that neighbor kid's dad came over and asked her mom if Wanda wanted to go on a hike in the redwoods with him and his son. Her mom shrugged her shoulders, bland as ever. Wanda hadn't been sure—she hated that kid for teasing her about being skinny—but it was a chance to get out of the house. The kid was okay with his dad around. The earthy-woodsy smell of the damp forest so quiet and green. That feeling of quiet stillness. She'd never gone back there, and soon after that, things started to fall apart—all yelling and slamming doors. It was years before she found out why. Now, a soft breeze came up. Winds of change. She grimaced—trite, but there was something.

• • •

On a good day, Clemens considered himself indestructible. Proudly stubborn, bullheaded, he believed he'd built PC single-handed. There was no one named Peterman. It was just Lieth, who put up the initial backing and remained a hidden partner.

Like most in the Valley, he had watched, with schadenfreude, the media coverage of the Theranos case and the conviction and sentencing of his Atherton neighbor Elizabeth Holmes. PC had not been a funder, so he hadn't had to answer press calls with "no comment." Her defense team's endorsement of the firm's outlandish and untrue product claims as normal behavior in the tech-finance culture, claims which Holmes knew were bogus, was viewed by some as a cautionary tale. There were limits, surely. Others thought that Holmes had simply been too young—and a woman, to boot—out of her depth, and not smart enough to get away with it. Nothing to see here.

Now something was bugging him. The DNA surveillance project was running into opposition from the legal team, frustrating him. The reemergence of Jennifer, who had a deep connection to Lieth, made him feel boxed in. Wanda was talking about leaving the firm, and he feared being dragged back into the emotional black hole he languished in after the divorce. He rattled around the house at a loose end, drinking too much.

Two weeks after he'd seen Jennifer, he drove over to Half Moon Bay to meet an executive from a Bangalore cybersecurity company. He liked The Ritz-Carlton and its windy golf course hugging the sea cliff, and the guy was interesting, but his company was not ready for US investors. They agreed to keep in touch. Clemens wandered over to the bar, where he ran into a colleague. They stayed for dinner and had a few drinks afterward. It was around eleven when the valet brought the jet-black Tesla 3 Performance around. Clemens was unsteady.

"Are you going to be okay, sir?" asked the valet as Clemens got into the Tesla.

"Fine. It's got auto." The car pulled out, heading back toward Atherton.

The valet shook his head.

Clemens decided to take the scenic route. He pointed the car south on Highway 1, then turned east on a mountain road. The coastal fog was thick, feeding moisture to the redwoods through their leaves. The unstriped pavement narrowed, winding uphill in severe switchbacks as he neared the ridge. Gigantic trees lined the road, a menacing blackness looming behind them. He was lost in an alcoholic haze when the Tesla's alarm sounded, and he felt a thump. What the fuck? The car edged onto the narrow shoulder. He was now wide awake. He got out to inspect the damage. There was a dent in the front-right quarter panel, but the headlight still worked. It looked drivable. As he got back in, he heard a bleat behind him. He walked toward the sound, shining his phone. A fawn lay on the shoulder, twitching. He knelt over the little animal. Its rear end was all broken up. It was breathing fast. Just a baby.

He heard a clomp—a foot stomp in the woods. He swung the light and saw a black-tailed deer holding her front leg up like a short-haired pointer, looking straight at him. Straight through him. The fawn bleated faintly and lay still. The doe snorted, turned swiftly into the woods. Clemens pushed the fawn into the ditch with his shoe. He got back in the car and made it home.

The next day at the office, he ran into Wanda. It was awkward—being both predator and prey. He didn't dare mention the deer.

17

EARLY THAT SUMMER, Ursula and I, along with my dear Anjo, convened the second Congress of Life. Parts of the state park remained closed from the fire, and we issued no observer invitations. Two pairs of the previous human observers sensed the gathering and showed up anyway, taking up positions on the north and south ridges. In addition, two unidentified human forms made their way toward the meeting from east and west.

Just as we were ready to ask Scree to quiet the murmuring delegates, a Red-tailed Hawk flew in and started yelling at Anjo. He considered chasing it but curbed his rowdiness after a stern look from Ursula. As the intruder settled herself on a branch, my friend was crestfallen. The Hawk appeared more than usually fearsome on the close perch. I regarded the importunate creature balefully.

"I bring greetings from Marin County," she said. "My name is Ruth. I have come to address the Congress on behalf of an unrepresented group important to the ecology of our region."

"Oh, Great Corvid, protect us from unrepresented Raptors." Muttering under my breath, I surveyed the crowd before continuing in a low voice. "We avians have enjoyed oversized influence in the Congress from the beginning, due in no small part to Excellent Crow Leadership. The politics here won't support having yet another bird screechi—"

"Oh, shut your beak!" Ruth said. "I've been talking with domesticated meat animals, aka livestock, in some of the finer northern ranches. These Cattle, Sheep, Pigs, Chickens, and even Rabbits and Ducks are being raised and harvested with close attention to comfortable conditions and sustainability. They have asked me to represent them here."

It took me a moment to react. "Okay. I agree. These voices have not been heard." But I felt snarky. "Will you be speaking on behalf of Dogs and Goldfish, Hamsters, and pet Snakes as well? And what about cultivated fruits and vegetables, not to mention potted plants and Christmas trees?"

At this point, I kind of lost it, as was underscored by a cocky young Coyote, Shakti's son. The youngster barked disagreement at my slighting reference to Dogs, a response seconded by Snave's ominous rattle.

Ursula, concurring, rolled her eyes at me and grunted. "Let the bird speak, for heaven's sake!"

"I appreciate your forward-leaning recognition of the need to welcome more diverse voices at the Congress," Ruth sneered. "However, I am limiting my remarks to food animals, the vast majority of whom do not live or die as comfortably as the ones I just mentioned, the reforms of Temple Grandin notwithstanding."

"Even the lucky ones get slaughtered without ceremony," I retorted.

"Fair enough," Ruth said. "In many cases there's no mindful harvest, even though the treatment is humane to the end. These animals aren't festering in packed feedlots, shot through with antibiotics, hormones, and tranquilizers. The Marin ranchers say, 'They only have one bad day.' Yet the animals sense the energies coming off the killing floor near the pasture, and they grieve when one of their own does not return."

"All right, all right. We'll add you to the agenda. Statements may not exceed three minutes, or we'll be here until the Cows come home." I started to chuckle, but Anjo cawed sharply, "Get a grip, girl!"

As Scree silenced the crowd, Audrey the Redwood gave the invocation. "We ask our Grandmother's blessings on this gathering and on all beings present on this land and throughout the Network. We cherish the native planimals who have lived here forever, and we honor the First Peoples who managed to live in relative harmony with the native occupants for several thousand years. May we be successful this day in furthering the course of life on Earth."

We went through the various reports and statements. When her turn came, Ruth said, "The domestic meat animals have reviewed the Elephant Code. They appreciate being given the opportunity to make their views known. They are in general agreement with the Code. However, they are concerned that the second tenet is too vague. As of now it says, *We will respect each being for what and who they are*. All the animals I speak for agree that imprisoning meat animals in cramped, unsanitary conditions is torture and inconsistent with the Code. But if an animal has a good life, is killed without pain, and is *treated* with respect both before and after death, is it outside the Code?"

There was considerable rumbling and chattering among the delegates, with the predators, and some prey animals, nodding. But the Hawk was making me fidget. "You have one more minute, Ruth," I said. "Get to the point!"

"We'd like to see the Code revised to be clearer about respect. We propose to insert the word *treat* into the second verse so it would say, We *will treat each being with respect for what and who they are*. Adding *treat* would emphasize that we should respect each other in our actions. It goes directly to what we do to each other, not just what we think or believe about each other."

I myself found this to be rather a minor point, but, after the statements concluded, Ruth's edit was adopted. At that point I stepped forward and recited what was now the final version—

> We will honor the sanctity of the Earth, and all Her life.
>
> We will treat each being with respect for what and who they are.
>
> We will harm other life only to the minimum necessary for survival.
>
> We will be mindful of the effects that our actions have for seven generations.

Scree announced a break. Our core group gathered for a check-in, waiting for Ursula, who had ambled over to a young Redwood. "Do you mind?" she said to the tree, standing up and rubbing her back against the trunk. "Ahhh! Thank you." She came back over and said, "I guess we're ready for the next part. Do we have an update on the two humans coming in from east and west?"

"They appear armed. There's darkness in their auras. We deployed decoys, but not even an eight-point buck drew fire." The speaker was Tania, a Cougar, head of security for the meeting.

A Black-tailed doe skittered through the valley, followed by a fawn.

Tania nodded toward the pair. "It was that doe's mate who volunteered to take the hit. But these humans seem intent on coming our way. We've prepared a stakeout if they get here, but that's not the preferred option."

Tania whispered something to Ursula, who frowned as if she was reflecting on her life. I sensed she was thinking of Orres, her injured son. Her mood was sorrowful.

"Let us hope for the best," I said. "This is a sacred space, a sanctuary. I trust the Universe will protect us."

* * *

When the meeting reconvened, the discussion turned to "right action"—what, if anything, we planimals should do to get humans moving in the right direction.

Lichen summarized progress. "Some individual planimals are taking steps against humans, but the humans are not seeing a pattern. Collective action seems to be more effective—the viral sabotage of a Chinese Pig factory being the most public example, although the scientists never figured out that it was our doing—not their own mistakes—that enabled the virus to become so lethal and contagious. Our own Vespa organized a successful encounter with an illegal fishing crew, in partnership with her White Shark allies. Many of our fiercer relations have vowed to step up their attacks. But in our view, Earth's own activities—increased volcanic activity, glacier melt, extreme weather, and catastrophic flooding—are the most effective means of getting humans' attention."

Lichen continued. "Turning to 'let Nature take Her course,' it should be obvious that will happen anyway. It's a tautology. The best one can do is steer sincerely by one's own lights and hope for the best. That leads us to the third approach, working *with* humans, which we support. We are convinced that generating anger and fear in humans is counterproductive. Fear does not bring out the best side of that species. But we must be realistic. Are humans ready to work with us? With few exceptions, the answer appears to be no. They cannot even work with each other. All we can do for now is prepare for that day when, we hope, they will come to their senses."

"Thank you, Lichen," I said. "Something must change the dynamic. Religion has not succeeded, although over the centuries its ethical principles have sometimes improved behavior." I felt antsy—the uncertain threat from the approaching humans. After I told the participants to confer among themselves about where we should go from here, Scree called another break.

* * *

Fog covered the valley as two hunters arrived on opposite sides of the ridge. As the sky cleared, the delegates reconvened. The positions of the armed humans were noted. Tania gave a signal, and I watched as the security teams took their places.

Ursula growled to silence the participants. She reared and, with great ceremony, declared, "May the Universe now begin the healing. Let each stand in their place." She paused, emitting a dark rumble, like a howl, and said, "Koro, please continue the meeting."

But a pair of Gray Wolves had picked up the howl, causing general confusion. Suddenly, the crack of a gunshot echoed in the valley. The slug tunneled into Audrey's trunk. Ursula, already on the move, picked up her pace with dignity. We could hear the drone of Vespa and her brood on the hillside, followed by the *twong* of an arrow, and a second. From where the gunshot had come—a grunt, and some clatter. A numinous cloud passed over that place. Then all was still.

The Earth undulated beneath our gathering.

The afternoon sun dispersed the mists and shone down brightly. A volée of Crows exploded, raucous, from a fir above the bow hunter's blind. She had vanished without a scent. A colony of American Badgers ventured up to the gunman's outpost and dug a deep pit. After the Ants and soil planimals did their work, the remains would return to dust.

Ursula gave thanks.

The Congress resumed. I reviewed the situation. We would follow our own natures along the various action and nonaction paths. For those who believed in its value, the sabotage campaign would continue. Others of us would support humans who were living and propagating the

Code. And the rest would surrender to the wondrous course of history or destiny. We would reconvene in a year, place to be determined. In the meantime, we would keep in touch through the Network. Ursula reminded any predators to remain on their best behavior until they were back in their own territories. She cautioned the observers on the hill to keep silent about what they had seen.

18

LUZ AND ANNA HAD OBSERVED the congress from the northern ridge. At first, things seemed to go smoothly. Then, after the foggy break, Luz became still.

"Do you feel the disturbance?" she whispered.

"Yes," Anna said. "That is why Ursula was marking her territory by rubbing against that redwood. She was showing how tall she is—claiming her power. There is danger. Let's take down our tent and be sure we are well hidden."

From the east arrived a middle-aged white man in forest camo packing a sniper's rifle with hollow-point ammo. "*Men* will bring the system down, not some goddamn animal uprising," he muttered. "God made us to rule the Earth—just doing my part. Damn eco-freaks, illegal immigrants, so-called minorities, their woke minders, and uppity women destroying the proper order." He set up behind a low rock overlooking the valley, adjusted his ghillie poncho for cover, and waited for the fog to lift.

The western figure, a woman, wore deerskin and carried a four-foot-long Ohlone deer-hunting bow. The woman had shaped the bow herself over ten days, after fasting. She had affixed deer sinew to the outside, giving it magical elasticity. She had used and cared for it always, never making it tired by leaving it strung, never leaving it standing up but letting it lie down so it could rest, regularly rubbing deer marrow into the wood and singing to it to keep its spirit happy. Her two-piece arrows were a cane mainshaft fletched with hawk feathers and a hardwood foreshaft holding a barbed copper tip coated with water hemlock root, a virulent neurotoxin used only in warfare, not for game to be eaten. A Paiute elder had gifted her the tips at a Powwow many years before. She burrowed into the side of the hill and fell into a trance.

"Have you ever seen that woman?" Luz whispered.

Anna shook her head. "She is not from this time—she is a Warrior from long ago. We must be quiet, not to disturb the balance."

Into the Ancient Warrior's trance came visions—the unending fight of man against man, against woman, against the Earth, against life itself, cloaked in ideology and sanctified by priests. She saw her totem, Black Bear, avatar of respect, lying gravely in a grove of redwoods, blood coming from her heart. She saw Hummingbird come with Fire, and Salmon bringing Water. They swirled above the Bear. Coyote stood nearby, howling a keening, rooted in his lineage as helper-creator of the world.

A blast of energy from the Warrior overcame Anna. She let herself drop into her core, losing herself to the universal Self, merging with the energy coming into her from the forest floor. *Dear Grandmother, be with us in this hour of death and transformation.* As the scene unfolded, Anna watched as if through Warrior's eyes, observing the millennia-long epoch in that region of Turtle Island—the human civilizations before engines and electronics, megaton explosives and the internet, the vanity and pride that had led to the current existential crisis.

The methodical sniper fixed his practiced eye upon the bear in the scope. It was a couple hundred yards out. Some wolves started a howl, and the shooter chuckled. He, too, was a wolf on the hunt.

Vespa was the first of her swarm to get under the ghillie. She landed on his bare trigger hand. Unflinching, the shooter concentrated as he began the squeeze. Now Anna knew in her bones the sadness and determination of the Warrior, the sinewy strength of her arms on the sacred bow, the power in the arrow's release, the finality of righteous destruction.

Vespa's stinger had hardly touched the gunman's knuckle when a penetrating force rocked him. The gun discharged, but the bullet found its rest in a redwood. The man twitched. "Fuck!" Vespa fell off, crawling out of the ghillie. Immediately, a second twong. "What the—arrows?"

Two had entered his shoulder, into the left subclavian vein. He shuddered. He pulled at the venomous projectiles and threw them down the canyon, but the barbed foreshafts held their positions. He shook out his stung, throbbing hand and readied a second shot. The animals were scattering in the valley, the bear moving downrange. As he lined her up, his vision fogged. From the mists emerged a ghost battalion, his many kills of game and enemy, walking toward him out of history, slow, coming for him, coming not with malice but a stony fire for justice.

Anna's muscles twitched, the way a dog runs in its dreams. As she awakened, deep beneath the park the Earth grumbled, warning of disturbances to come.

• • •

As the congress dispersed, Luz and Anna packed up slowly and began their own return trek.

"In speaking of what happened here, we must be careful," Anna said. "We can tell your parents, but some mysteries, some ambiguities, must persist, or the world loses its vitality. And so do careless people who reveal them."

Luz nodded, her eyes wider than usual. "I'm not going to talk about it. The kids already call me names when I tell them what the animals are saying. Sometimes it hurts."

"I'm sorry. Have you talked to your mom about it?"

"She doesn't like to talk about pain. She just says, 'Count your blessings.'"

"It can be hard to be different, Luz." Anna hesitated. "Your mom was always different—you know?"

"How? She grew up on the rez with other Indians. What was so different about her?"

"For one thing, her dad was a white doctor, so that made her different. And he worked for the colonial power structure, in the Indian Health Service. She was never really in the popular crowd. Still, she was smart, and good at basketball. Have you asked her about her time in high school?" Anna asked.

"I knew she was smart, but I didn't know she played basketball," Luz said. "Maybe I can ask her about that. But it's not the same. I mean, I'm the only Native American in my class. Some of the kids tease me. I work hard not to fight back or have a meltdown. Mom doesn't do well when I have a meltdown."

"Thanks for sharing this, Luz. I hope you will ask your mom about basketball. I think she's pretty proud of it. Her team won a championship or something."

"Wow! I'll try, Anna," Luz said. "I'm so glad we were hidden when that gun went off. The shot was so loud, and then the Warrior sent her arrows, and everything was quiet. I could see her but not where the gunshots came from. I love going into the woods and seeing and hearing the planimals, but—" She began to cry.

Anna leaned over and hugged Luz. "I'm sorry to have brought you into danger. This was a new experience for me too. Fortunately, we were protected, and we protected ourselves."

"The Warrior was so powerful. I wish I could meet her."

"You will see her again—that I am sure of. You did very well today. She saw you. You are growing up so fast."

19

FALL CAME, and for Cody, the completion of his two-year workout for Opti-Drip. The final payout from the sale gave him professional flexibility and time. It also enabled him and Makah to move forward with the addition to the house. They were ready for Luz to have more private space, and likewise for themselves as they worked more from home.

Without revealing its true origins, Makah had been teaching about the Elephant Code in her graduate seminar, calling it a "Draft Code of Conduct for Human Survival." She would ask the students to debate it in class and write papers about its implications for international environmental policy. The discussions were robust. What did it mean to "honor the sanctity of all life"? What limits were implied by the standard of harming other life "to the minimum necessary for survival"? How was it possible to consider the effects of human action "for seven generations" in a time of such rapid change? Makah and Cody often discussed these questions at dinner, with Luz joining in.

They took weekly walks in nearby parks, where they explored the Code's implications for their own lives. They had reduced the meat in their diet by half. They bought locally produced items whenever practical. They shut off major appliances for at least two hours during peak usage periods. They limited their air travel to one trip a year. They thought they might be doing their part to meet the global target of a 50 percent reduction in carbon emissions by 2030.

They wondered about the true effects of their actions. Some consequences were incalculable in the immediate, not to mention trying to imagine the effects over the decades to come. One of Makah's students had proposed the need for a "Total Effects Evaluation Board" that would use AI to analyze such questions systematically and share its results for public use. Closer to home, Cody and Makah debated "hybrid vs. EV." Did the fuel efficiency of an EV offset the environmental costs of extracting, processing, shipping, and recycling the rare earths and trace metals needed to make its batteries? The science suggested it was a close call for now, with hybrid efficiency dependent on plugging the vehicle in every night and avoiding long-distance driving. In a few years, EV trucks would be clearly superior and the charging infrastructure more ubiquitous. Looking to the future, Cody finally traded his Silverado for an all-electric Ford Lightning.

Their architect had listened well to their dreams of a home that would give them more breathing room, that evoked and respected local and Indigenous energies, and was environmentally sustainable. Installing double-paned windows and putting solar on the roof would cut their electric bills by 80 percent. Taking a deep breath as cooks, they agreed to abandon their gas stove, splurging on an induction range.

Although she liked the prospect of more privacy, Luz was skeptical about the addition. "I'm worried about expanding our space," she said at one of their dinner table discussions. "We'll have to cut down some of our trees, removing natural habitat. The lumber will come from trees other people have cut down. We already have more of everything than most people. Using more space is wrong."

"It is challenging to know the limits," said Makah.

"I've been researching carbon offsets and carbon credits," Cody said.

"Lots of companies and nonprofits are entering the market with projects they claim will reduce greenhouse gas emissions by planting trees, supporting renewable energy, or reducing waste. The market is essentially unregulated, so it's hard to validate the claims. It's pretty confusing, and vulnerable to greenwashing."

"What's *greenwashing*?" asked Luz.

"It's a takeoff on whitewashing," Cody answered. "Using a special white paint on brick or cement. But it came to mean covering up someone's bad behavior. So greenwashing is lying to make your product appear more environmentally friendly."

"Like the wolf in sheep's clothing!" Luz said.

"That's a good one," Makah said. "But some things really do make a difference, like preserving existing forests. Old-growth trees remove and store much more carbon than newly planted trees."

"Like our old redwood?" said Luz.

"Exactly," said Makah, "and they provide habitat."

"Koro and her friends totally love our redwood. There's always a volée."

"I know," Makah said. "I hear them."

"We can use reclaimed lumber, or innovative materials like manufactured 'mass timber,' to reduce the number of trees cut," said Cody. "And we'll work with the architect to spare our own trees."

"Wouldn't it just be simpler not to build anything new?" Luz asked. "All these other choices are confusing."

"The science is confusing, and still emerging," Makah said. "We still don't understand enough about how natural systems interact with each other and with human activity, but we have to act now based on the best science. We can't wait for certainty."

"We should use the house as a place to help the planet, and the planimals," said Luz. "That would feel better."

"I like that," said Makah. "Let's figure out how to do that inside and out."

"You know that Fridays for Future you are involved in, Luz?" Cody asked. "What if there were a Families for Future? I heard about something called that when I was in SoCal last year. It got me thinking. We could involve other families in Monterey and start with little things, like sharing tools and rides rather than doing everything on our own."

"That sounds good, Dad, but what does it have to do with the house?"

"We could host group meetings—we'll have enough space."

"This is great!" Luz said. "Meeting at the school's okay, but it's not conveniently located and tends to be busy."

"How big a meeting are you talking about?" Makah asked, rueful she didn't have a clue.

"Not that big. The Fridays group can be up to twenty. XR is more variable. They're mostly organizing online for that. We'd need to have better tech here since they often Zoom with other groups around the country or the world."

"XR?" Makah asked. "Oh, Extinction Rebellion. They could meet here too—I'd love that."

"There are a couple of kids with disabilities who might need assistance, but we usually work that out. That's a great idea, Mom; thanks for thinking of it. It's exactly the kind of thing I was hoping we'd do if we expanded the house."

"It's such a simple thing—open our home so people can work together more easily."

"Maybe we could involve the parents of kids from Fridays in our Families for Future meetings," said Luz. "That would be cool."

⋄ ⋄ ⋄

With Opti-Drip behind him, Cody wanted a more unified professional life, combining his values with his love for engineering. How could he help the climate? He had read that the government was helping fund environmental organizations like the Surfrider Foundation and Above/Below to protect and improve aquaculture environments.

He'd always been involved in terrestrial agriculture, but living in Monterey had unexpectedly connected him to the sea. On his coastal walks, he was fascinated by the relationship between the sea mammals and the forests of kelp. It was their habitat, their home. What would combine ag economics, business, and sustainable farming?

Based on her volunteer work at the aquarium, Suzanne suggested Cody see if he could help at the aquarium's research institute, working with scientists studying fish populations in the Monterey Bay National Marine Sanctuary, an area larger than Yellowstone National Park. Cody improved the fish-tracking software and created visualizations of changes in the diversity of aquatic life in the sanctuary.

As his combination of business and tech skills proved useful, Cody discovered marine biologists differed from ag technologists, holding to a more humble perspective about humans' role and importance in the rest of the natural world. After all, an ocean dwarfed the largest rancho in scale and diversity. Yet human activity could affect an ocean ecosystem in dramatic ways, a truth well known in Monterey, where sardines had long been abundant before dying out in the early 1950s because of overfishing exacerbated by warming ocean temperatures.

Cody thought maybe he could build his work at the research institute into a new commercial offering, but it seemed too much like what he'd done at Opti-Drip. He resolved to find a new angle, something that would get him out on the water, working with fishers and kelp farmers.

PART THREE

20

THE FOLLOWING SPRING, Makah and Cody observed their anniversary with a week off together, leaving the devoted Suzanne to watch Luz and the chickens. The couple reserved a creek-side cabin at the Tassajara Retreat Center, about two hours south of Monterey in the heart of the Ventana Wilderness area. The center worked closely with the land's original human occupants, the Esselen Tribe, to live in balance and harmony with the Earth and to steward and respect the sanctity of the land.

Their daily routine took on a rhythm set by the mealtimes of the center's delicious kitchen. Most days, they would head out after breakfast, packing a light lunch, departing from the lyrical stream to walk the trails into the peaceful wilderness, watching for animal tracks and spoor and trying to identify the birdsongs. They stayed off net except for a daily call with Luz. It was a restorative and reflective time.

"Luz sounded good tonight," Makah said, early in the week. "I was wondering how she'd be after our basketball conversation."

"What do you mean?" Cody asked.

"Luz asked me about my basketball trophy from when the New Town Eagles made it to State during my senior year. I told her about how I was on varsity, and even though we didn't win State, we were the only Native American girls' team that year and made a great showing. She asked whether I was popular in school because I was a basketball star—that surprised me."

"I wonder what made her ask that," Cody said.

"I don't know. I told her that I was more of an outsider, being athletic and smart, that I wasn't popular. She asked me if that was hard. It was difficult for me to find a good answer." Playing ball and studying to get through—and out. "Finally I told her I had to learn to put up with it, that my mom and her mom had gone through much worse, and they inspired me. It was uncomfortable, given what else happened."

"You were right not to mention that—she's too young. Your dad being the town doctor made you different, too."

"I didn't mention that, but you're right. Anyway, she sounded okay tonight, but I wonder if she's feeling isolated at school or something."

"That's one thing you and I have in common—being misfits."

"And half-breeds," Makah said.

"Ha! My dad had that album." He blushed, thinking of the cover—Cher astride a paint pony, in scanty pretendian regalia.

"Hmph. As my mom would say, 'We ain't Cher.'"

"Even with our mongrel lineages, we're both successful in the system."

"There are a lot of systems," she said. "Layers of admission. Gate after gate."

"Sometimes I wonder what's the point—collecting all the stamps? I think about a song an old friend wrote." Cody sang,

"Where do you keep those prizes you said that I would win?
I've touched all the bases, there's places that I've been.
There must be more to life than nine-to-five and getting bald,
I spend so much time getting ready to live I don't get no livin' done."

"I'd rather just live," said Makah. "Although I like the part about getting balled."

"I never knew how she spelled that word, but I bet you're right, knowing her."

As they reflected, their appreciation for the world around them and each other deepened. They knew they were extremely privileged. They had a strong marriage, a beautiful and amazing child, reasonably healthy parents, and were richer than seven and a half billion fellow humans. No one was shooting at them or shelling them from the sky. True, they had to endure the threat of fire, earthquake, drought, flood, mudslides, and tsunamis. The political situation in America was menacing. And, looming over them, always, was the Meltdown. They knew their entitlement gave them additional responsibility for stewardship. Makah's father, Robert, liked to quote John F. Kennedy, who said, paraphrasing the book of Luke, "Of those to whom much is given, much is required."

• • •

Makah proposed they take a solo day late in the week. She needed to be alone, and Cody was agreeable, even suggesting a full twenty-four hours. The evening before, he pitched a small tent beside the creek. Makah stayed in the cabin, retiring early, arising before dawn. Fasting except water, she set out at first light, the waxing moon setting pale yellow.

As the morning's sun seeped from behind the hills, Makah ascended via switchbacks. The vegetation thinned out, and the landscape turned arid, the tufted knee-high grass beside the trail already brown, the scrubby chaparral poking up tentative and green. The early birdsong crescendoed with the dawn. As she rounded a corner, the sun greeted her through a saddle in the ridge.

She put in her earbuds and listened to a loop of Thom Yorke's melancholy piano in "Dawn Chorus," losing track of time. Its lyrics had grabbed her when she first heard it years before, and the words had been coming back to her in the weeks before the trip. She knew that when a song replayed in her mind, it was a thread she could follow into her subconscious.

She crested the ridge and wandered down into a forested valley, off trail now, not lost, simply alone. She stopped to rest in the midday shade, turned off the music. She settled in, her back against an aromatic bay laurel. What would she do over again? What door had closed inside? Losing Chanson had broken something. She'd channeled the pain into action. Wasn't that enough?

A male goldfinch landed on a nearby branch, announcing itself with a bright, clear tone. He was wearing his bold spring mating colors, sporting his flashy wing bars like a new corporal's chevrons. She remembered the goldfinch at Chanson's funeral, flying up with a seed in its mouth. She could hear this bird's brothers and sisters, a vein of a dozen, chittering in the bushes nearby. Maybe community made them cheerful.

Her fast wore on her. She lay on her blanket in the warm afternoon. Soon she was in a convoluted dream. She was on a dusty playground back in New Town, alone but for a small boy on a rusty swing across the field. The boy was in harlequin—yellow, black, and white. He swung higher and higher, and Makah worried he would fall. She tried to call to him, but her throat felt shut. She tried to run toward him, but her legs were bloody, and she could hardly move. When she finally reached the swing, the boy flew across the sky, crying. Then, only the empty swing, its squeaky creak in her ears. She woke up, her mouth open and dry. The goldfinch, its metallic song, cheery, mocking.

She sat up with care and drank. "What gives with you? How can you be so happy all the time? Don't you know life is full of sorrow, with only occasional snatches of joy so easily lost?" She lowered her voice. "What am I missing?"

The bird continued its recital, flitting busily in the bush.

In the silent space, she saw herself when she had first arrived in Monterey, flush with success and optimism. She remembered her times with

Skah, the exuberance of those early coastal days, the newness of her life. Somehow her delight had been extinguished over the years, the final snuffing coinciding with her miscarriage. She'd worn a cynical edge since.

The goldfinch dropped to the ground, not five feet away. It eyed her. It scratched in the duff, picking at seeds and eating them messily the way they did at her bird feeder.

Spinus tristis. Why did science call them "sad finch"? The undercoat of sorrow that gives the patina of joy its resonance? *Count your blessings.* Suddenly, the bird flew onto a branch—the filtered sunlight flickering on its dappled coat—and changed its tune to a harder tone foretelling trials to come.

She nodded at the bird respectfully, and, with a final trill, it took off into the forest. But she felt angry, unsettled, something dark inside her out of reach. She left an offering of kinnikinnick by the laurel's roots. The sun had moved behind a ridge to the west. She took a long loop trail that delivered her to the cabin after dinnertime.

Cody was sitting by the stream, watching and listening as the water flowed over the rocks. He rose and kissed her. "Welcome back." He wanted to ask her how her day had been, but something stopped him. She retreated to the cabin. He waited, his eyes and ears adjusting as nocturnal creatures stirred in the dusky light.

She came out and sat beside him. "Tell me about your day. I hope it was fabulous."

"It was peaceful. I kind of lazed around here, took a couple of walks, sat by the creek. I thought about how it heads south and east before it joins the Salinas River and then flows northwest for fifty miles up to Monterey Bay. Like going backward to go forward. That persistent crow who Luz calls Koro was here for a while, trying to tell me something. It sounded like 'Kelp! Kelp!' I had to laugh. I felt like calling Andrés for translation services. Overall, a good day relaxing. How about you?"

"It felt like an important day for me." Makah paused. "I had an encounter with a goldfinch. Kind of a mixed bag, actually. Joy underlain by sorrow. Fatalism and anger. A sense of urgency. I've got some work to do. I want to be more like that bird, you know—sunny and, well, light, at least on the outside."

Cody had learned that it was better to let things settle and develop. "Sounds . . . meaningful," he said. "Thanks for telling me. Did you get hungry?"

"Only at first. Now I'm just tired."

The next day after breakfast, they picked up their daily routine for the last time, enjoying the mountain together. That evening, they sat sipping an Oregon pinot and listening to the creek.

"Mighty fine, isn't it?" Cody asked. "This turned out to be a great week." He reached for her hand.

She took a deep breath and squeezed back. "Amazing."

"I don't want to forget this feeling in the craziness."

"It's always available here." Makah reached across and put her free hand on his heart. "Always."

"True, assuming you can remember that when times get tough."

"That will be tested." She put her hands in her lap.

"We've been cared for by the Universe—since our wordless interaction twelve years ago at the American Indian museum—studying each other through the two-sided glass case, old calumets between us." He touched her hair. "The spark! You were so put together. Your long hair back, your 'sensible flats,' your whale and moon pin, your little black book. Then I saw you talking no-nonsense with that curator. It was intimidating."

She smiled. "We hit it off that evening, on the way back from DC."

"When that woman asked you to switch seats so she could sit with her husband, I thought of my mom's 'no such thing as coincidence.'"

"I was thinking, *It's a long flight—do I want to start talking to this guy?* But you were cute and weren't wearing a ring."

"Later we met on the beach, and Skah found the dead sea otter, and after that you said let's get mussels from the Monterey Fish Company and asked if I'd carry them in my bag that was full of things a hopeful guy would bring—and yes, I said yes I will yes. I felt like Bloom with the mutton kidney in his pants, and we made it to your house and *Ulysses* was on the shelf next to the *Odyssey* and all your Indian and climate books and the place was pretty—compact and well constructed—like you."

Makah flushed. "I was so nervous."

"When we were sharing stories after lunch, Skah lay on the oval rag rug and marked me with a hairy eyeball: *don't fuck up, man.*"

"He told me you were okay. And you were so careful with me. You let me make the first moves."

Cody leaned over and kissed her. "When you came out of the shower at my place in San Jose wearing that silky emerald shirt untucked, there was no turning back."

"*You* made the Mexican Mules."

Steamy. He touched her thigh. "Then I moved to Monterey, and Tara was killed by a coyote, and I blamed you for belling her."

"Now that was a fight," she said. "You accusing me of being *on the warpath.*"

"After, you said, 'Maybe Coyote performed rough justice on behalf of Tara's dead birds.' But I was out of line." Always more to learn.

In the sunset, they heard a coyote chorus in the hills. When it got chilly, they went in and called Luz, who had texted them a picture of a sea otter floating on her back nursing her pup. She was eager for their return.

21

EARLIER THAT SPRING, a flush of energy and new life burgeoned in the burrows and tunnels that honeycombed Tatiki's domain—ground squirrels, moles, voles, mice, rats, shrews, rabbits, bird eggs, the occasional lizard, and, on the surface, abundant juicy berries, crisp insects, and of course roadkill—not his favorite. Once, he discovered a long-tailed weasel in an abandoned squirrel burrow, but the grouchy fellow fought back fiercely, and Tatiki thought better of it.

On another occasion, he followed a deer trail uphill from behind the Veterans Hall to where he'd scented the familiar human smell. The house had a chicken coop, where lived six fat laying hens. He'd observed a girl coming out every morning to feed them and collect the eggs. She was a spirited girl, with long black hair, golden skin, and sparkling eyes. Something about her voice when she called to the chickens unsettled him. More unnerving was the place overlooking the valley where someone had buried a large animal, a canine. In his bones, Tatiki felt the Spirit coming from that grave.

One dark evening, he inspected the henhouse and the fenced area around it. The night was still. No breeze carried his scent. He moved methodically around the pen. No obvious gaps. He considered digging under the wire mesh, but it was buried well below the surface. The whole idea seemed somehow off, in his gut, notwithstanding the tempting fare. He satisfied himself by sitting just out of sight in the early morning and watching the girl come out. Sometimes he imagined she knew he was there, but she gave no sign.

From time to time, he'd hunt with an American badger who lived in the neighborhood. Badger was an awesome digger and would get into ground squirrel burrows and flush them out for Tatiki to nab. Both animals benefited. During these hunts, they got to know each other and became friends. Badger was ten and had seen a lot in his day. He loved to tell stories he'd heard about the Old Times. One day, they were chewing the fat after a successful foray when Badger became very still.

"Why are you so quiet, my friend?" Tatiki asked. "An acorn for your thoughts."

Badger smiled. "I was remembering a story about when Badgers and Coyotes first started hunting together. My cousin Otter told it to me, envious of our mutualism. It was a dry summer, Otter began, like the one just passed. Game was scarce, and all carnivores were hungry. In those days, more animals had connections to the spirit world. Coyote, who was in touch with his trickster nature, came upon an old Badger like me, only this guy was thin and weak looking. Coyote appraised him as lunch but decided it wasn't worth risking the fight. Instead, he took pity on the animal and brought him a small Squirrel he'd just caught. The old boy thanked him, saying that he knew where some much fatter Squirrels burrowed but that they were too fast for him to catch. Coyote's trickster whispered to Coyote, 'What is Nature but Life Together?' Coyote had an idea, and that was when the two of them invented our trick—to great success. It has been passed down by our ancestors ever since."

Tatiki thought this was a fine story, particularly the part about Otter's jealousy. He'd often been envious of otters: their slippery ease in the water, their playfulness, their mastery of fishing. What was this wishing to be someone, something, he was not? He felt his bone and sinew, his lean muscles, his keen senses—nothing was missing, nothing at all.

Badger nudged Tatiki out of his trance with a soft, squeaky chitter. "Now it's my turn to ask your thoughts, my friend."

"I don't have a great story like the one you told," Tatiki said. "I just have gratitude for our friendship. Let us take our Squirrels home, and we shall hunt together again."

• • •

As the weeks passed, Tatiki found his Veterans Park territory confining. He'd taken to ranging south and west from the park, without encountering male competition. Female territories commonly lapped over onto a male's larger patch, and Tatiki's patrols crossed the territories of three females, although he could only smell them. One fine spring evening, he heard a lilting howl from the territory west of the park. Feeling spry after several days of good hunting, he answered the howl. When she replied, they enjoyed rather a nice duet, celebrating the soft twilight of the abundant woodland.

At dawn a few days later, he noticed the scent of the songster, fresh and a little deeper into his own area. He followed her trail over a hill and into a meadow behind a subdivision. In the distance, he saw her digging out a Ground Squirrel burrow. He circled around so that just when the Squirrel shot out of the back door of its dwelling, he was there and, without hesitation, he popped it into his mouth. The female puzzled at him, startled and curious. The Squirrel wriggled in his mouth. He clamped down and it was still. He was salivating. Then, an instinct took over. He moved toward the female, his head lowered. Quite pleased with himself, he dropped the prize before her, backed up, and sat, watching her.

Kali, for that was her name, picked up the Squirrel, whirled around, and bounded away, holding up the trophy triumphantly. Tatiki sensed her playfulness and took off after her. They ran back into the low shrubbery where their territories overlapped. Suddenly, Kali stopped and faced Tatiki. She dropped the Squirrel and snarled. Surprised, Tatiki backed up and lay down facing her, alert, his legs in front of him. She ate the Squirrel and trotted off into her domain.

Tatiki puzzled over this development. Normally he would have started a tussle. That's what he'd do with his sisters—they'd have a great time. He was glad this one liked the Squirrel. But why would she just leave?

In the weeks ahead, he noticed Kali's scent more often. He kept an eye out for her. He hesitated to track her. One sunny afternoon, he was drowsing in his favorite south-facing spot on the hill below the Chicken house. In his daydream, he saw his father and mother playing and remembered how it felt different from his play with his sisters. He remembered them hunting together and how his father would bring food for his mother when she nursed the tiny litter and, later, regurgitate food for the pups. These reminiscences shone with new light.

Later that year, he caught up with Kali. They got comfortable with the Squirrel trick. One of them would dig at the entrance while the other waited at the rear. Sometimes the Squirrel would leap directly into waiting jaws. It was delightful. They showed each other secret hunting places and watering spots and told stories about the road and its dangers. Kali was more experienced. She had lost a male friend the previous season. Tatiki felt something new might be around the corner.

⬩ ⬩ ⬩

Anna's transformation at the congress—being inside the Ancient Warrior as she protected Ursula—had shaken her deeply. The word *shawoman* came to her, although she knew some Native Americans disliked the term *shaman*, a Russian import. She'd been given an enormous gift, permitted to consciously inhabit the conjunction of the ordinary and spirit worlds.

What duty stemmed from it? Did the planimals' tolerance of human observers signal a possible rapprochement? Then again, there were the Vespa-organized shark attacks on fishermen. Would she be required to be part of another death in the future? But the shawoman was from an earlier time, carrying a profound natural connection. What about the symbolic values of the incident? The broken arrow was a traditional sign of the end of a conflict, so perhaps it had been an exorcism, the sacrifice of a human avatar by planimal energies.

Anna turned these wonderings over in her garden and during her meditations. A vision formed in the corner of her mind's eye—a dark figure in shadow. It was large, but peaceful. When she tried to examine it, it retreated. She sensed the creature had a message for her, but she didn't know how to reach it.

She spent a week on the coast, from Esalen up to Santa Cruz, along the ocean and in the upland timber. Her connections to living beings, her sensibility to their mysterious communications, came into sharper focus. She walked more lightly on the Earth.

In a way, this communion brought her peace. The unity of life held her. She grew less attached to knowing what would happen next. The days unfolded like the pages of a book, as if she were simply a character in her own life, in the life of the world.

On the other hand, she sensed a great welling up of concern, an agitation in the community of life. The cries and calls of the wild seemed louder than before, more piercing. A sense of alarm, a mix of foreboding and acceptance, took hold of her. She worked to maintain her calm.

One morning, she got up early and bicycled east into the scrubby vegetation of Fremont Peak State Park. She hiked up a rough old trail into a forest clearing she knew. It was Rumsen country. The glade was next to Indian Canyon, an Indigenous reserve created by a famous Rumsen elder, Ann Marie Sayers. Anna had been invited to ceremonies there over the years as a guest.

On her way up, she observed black bear scat on the trail. She arrived at the clearing, and, leaning her back against an oak, stirred the still air with a hawk feather fan. All day, nothing removed the clouds covering her vision. As darkness settled, she made her way back down, stopping to examine the bear spoor. Pits from wild plums, stalk remnants of dried grass. One of the stalks caught her eye. She picked it up and examined it. It was a fish bone. She put it in her pouch for later.

It was dark when she got home, exhausted. She fell asleep in her armchair. The dark form in her vision reappeared. This time she could make out a withered arm hanging weakly from its socket, a salmon in its other paw. She remembered the bone in her pouch.

She returned the next day, finding no fresh evidence of bear. She drowsed against the twisted oak, waking at dusk to rustling in the bushes. A scrawny bear—Orres—shuffled into the clearing and stopped. He gazed at her with a steady eye. She stood up slowly and raised her arms above her head, not breaking eye contact. He stood up also, raising only his left arm, his right arm dangling, useless.

"What are you waiting for?" growled the bear. "Did you not hear my mother's admonition at the Congress?"

She regarded the bear claw on her necklace. For the first time in years, she remembered the day Raíz gave it to her as he was dying. "De mi abuela," he had whispered. Now it seemed to mock her. How had she forgotten? She must have been dizzy from the union with the shawoman. And then Ursula's words came back to her. "May the Universe now begin the healing. Let each stand in their place." She sat down, quieted herself, and let the back of her right hand rest on the upturned palm of the left with the tips of the thumbs lightly touching. She closed her eyes. She heard the bear moving. Thoughts of arrows and the wars of men passed through her. Then silence, broken by the wistful hoot of a long-eared owl.

22

OVER THE YEARS Cody had become friendly with Suzanne's husband, Kipp Hughes. He treated Kipp as an informal advisor, the latter's credibility enhanced by being older and having an English accent.

A few weeks after the retreat, Cody met Kipp for coffee at the Pebble Beach Market, not far downhill from Kipp's house. The shop was near the beach, and they decided to walk and talk. "I'm trying to decide what to do next, career-wise," Cody said. "The obvious thing would be my own startup. I could be based in Monterey and develop software for sustainable fishery management. I've talked to some potential partners, and it seems promising. My payout from Opti-Drip would let me self-fund the company for up to five years, depending on how fast it grew."

"That sounds rather good," Kipp said. "What about the downsides?"

"My experiences with the startup world were mixed. It's a total grind—no letup. You always feel the competition snarling behind you and investors snapping the whip. Plus, the market's less bullish than when Opti-Drip started, so getting longer-term funding might be tough—not to mention dealing with the venture capitalists. An exit would be harder than with Opti-Drip—it's not the tech glory days anymore. You can't just throw 'Big Data' and 'AI' into your pitch and expect wallets to open.

Those tools are a given now, even though their unpredicted, unmanaged use of electricity is a new source of climate instability."

"Technology matures in waves, and society is slow to catch up," Kipp said. "Machine sentience is next, I suppose."

"It's coming, for sure, but how will we know? Anyway, I've been exploring remote DNA sensing in fisheries management. The aquarium built a working prototype of an 'environmental sample processor,' or ESP—it collects and analyzes DNA in sea water to identify which species are present. A Massachusetts company sells a commercial version, with support from NOAA. The devices are being used to detect and predict harmful algae, toxins, and pathogens in lakes and oceans, and for monitoring fish stocks to improve sustainability." He paused. "Maybe those environmental sampling processors could be used in aquaculture. I've been doing a deep dive into seaweed—kelp farming—and I think there's potential."

Kipp laughed. "I'm not an expert, but I like seaweed—I make a yummy fresh seaweed salad, oriental style. I'll make it the next time you and Makah come over."

"Kelp has a ton of uses in farming and pharmaceuticals. It also captures carbon and reduces coastal erosion."

"But is it good business?"

"There's strong demand, but supply depends on the health of the surrounding ocean," Cody said. "Recent changes in ocean currents have weakened the kelp. Sea urchins are cutting the kelp off at the roots. The recent decline of sea otters and sea stars who used to eat the urchins doesn't help. But when conditions are good, it grows a foot per day."

"There's a connection with otters? That's right up your alley—karmically, anyway."

Cody laughed. "But it's true! No sea otters—no kelp! In fact, the government may try to reintroduce otters to help the kelp farmers along the coast north of here, where they were eliminated by fur hunters in the

1800s. Around Monterey, the kelp forest was reduced by three-quarters by the 2014–16 heat wave, so there's opportunity."

"What are the downsides? Nothing is all good, especially when it comes to large-scale agriculture."

"There can be some effects on local marine ecosystems. What I'm wondering is whether DNA sensors could monitor species diversity in seaweed farms, potentially mitigating those downsides."

"Interesting," said Kipp. "Keep me posted."

Over the next several weeks, Cody reached out to his old Opti-Drip connections. Money was seeking opportunities in climate tech. Investors were caring more about sustainability, even as the overall market tightened. It felt like time for him to go back into business. He summarized his conversations for Makah, who was supportive.

His vision seemed exciting and doable. With some friends and former associates in the Valley, he put together a pitch deck. There might be grant money in recent climate legislation that he could leverage through his contacts at the USDA who'd funded a pilot project at Opti-Drip. There was enough interest among angel investors that Cody decided to take the plunge. He would become an "ecopreneur." Standing in the kitchen one afternoon, he told Makah he'd decided to go ahead.

Makah hugged him. "Well, congratulations! At last! I was reading about Native American kelp farming projects off Cape Cod and in Alaska. The leader of the Alaskan initiative noted: *Indigenous peoples who live along the coast are ancestral guardians and have been for thousands of years.* I was thinking, maybe you could recruit some Indigenous advisors."

"I'd definitely like to have a local advisory group," Cody said. "But first things first. I need a name. It was fine to call it 'Company 1' during the stealth, premarket phase, but planning for the soft launch, we need something exciting and real. Kipp, Suzanne, and some of my former colleagues have given me suggestions—Seaweed Fitness, Kelp Help, Aquaforest Ecosystems. None of them seem quite right."

"How about Kelp Ecology?" said Luz, who had come in mid-conversation. "That combines your kelp with Mom's ecology. It's a family affair, like in that Sly song you like."

"That's a better name than my latest idea—Kelp Forest Conservation." Makah winked at Luz.

"What's wrong with that?" Cody asked.

"Dad, that would be KFC."

"Right?" Cody said. "Great suggestion, Luz."

Soon Cody had reserved the web address, registered the business, and opened the bank account. By June, he was ready to find someone to help him stay on top of the myriad details of standing up the company. He asked around. A colleague mentioned it to his girlfriend, who knew someone who was looking, and shortly thereafter, Cody heard from Wanda Clemens.

"Wasn't that the name of the student you had trouble with right after you made associate?" Cody asked Makah one evening.

"Yeah, it was. Why?"

"She called me today about the position I'm trying to fill. Said she knows something about DNA sensors. She's working for her dad. Apparently, she wants out. She obviously doesn't know I'm married to you."

"I wonder if she's grown up over the last eight years. Working for Jack Clemens would be no picnic. Sounds dicey, if you ask me."

"Agree. I am intrigued, though. The recommendation came through a trusted friend. It would be interesting to talk to her, anyway. Maybe she learned her lesson."

Makah recalled how she'd wrongly doubted Pearcy's apology. "Well, maybe. Just watch out. I want a full report."

Wanda told Cody she'd gone to school in Monterey and would be happy to come down for an interview. They met outdoors near the aquarium. After pleasantries, Cody dove right in.

"Tell me why you're leaving Peterman-Clemens."

"It's not a good fit. I don't enjoy being the boss's daughter. Everybody steers clear of me. It makes me nervous."

"In what way?"

His directness unsettled her. "I guess, well . . . my dad's not telling me anything about my project anymore. He just tells me to find things out but not why or where it's going. That's not a good dynamic for me."

"Business can be confidential sometimes—you know that."

"It doesn't feel like that. I can't go into it, but there's a lot of history that's . . . well, toxic. Especially about honesty."

"My wife, Makah, told me about that."

She flushed down to her blonde roots. "Omigod. I had no idea." Of all the gin joints! What a disaster. "That was a painful learning experience. A lot has happened in my life since then. That's why I have to get out."

"What happened?"

Might as well go for it. "You probably read about my dad's divorce. It was big news—intrigue and deceit. After that, my mom went back East. I made a deal with my dad—don't ask, don't tell. We stayed out of each other's lives. Then I needed a job, and he offered me this research position. It was a stab at reconciliation, I guess. And it pays well."

"You're working on DNA sensors?"

"My dad's a biotech guy, so, yes, that's one thing on the radar."

"Good answer. Look," Cody said, "Makah and I believe people can change. You've built a get-it-done reputation in the Valley. This is a startup, so it won't pay like PC, but there'll be a wide range of duties. I'd need my lawyer to read your nondisclosure. Your background could be quite helpful. But it's dicey, given the technology overlap between what you're working on and what I'm developing. I'm open to trusting you, but I don't trust your father. We have history—he was on the board of my last company."

"Another thing I didn't know." She hesitated. "You know, this seems pretty hard. Maybe it's not a good idea."

"Let's not give up right away. I need to talk to Makah about it. If you send me your nondisclosure, I'll get back to you next week."

On her way home, Wanda called Roseanne. "He wants me to send him the NDA. I have to reread it. It might be confidential itself, the way they write those things. But there's something acting here that's bigger than me—I just don't know what it is."

"Okay, okay," said Roseanne. "But you're going to need a lawyer. Do you know Janet Philips? She could do this. She's not afraid of PC."

"I need to sleep on it, but thanks."

"Keep me updated. Maybe you should think about it in Cancun!"

• • •

Later, that August, on one of those fickle Northern California days that decides to feel warm but only in the sun, Wanda was following her practice of visiting the Bear Creek Preserve and sitting in the same spot as on her first visit. She would hike the two-mile loop, sit for a half hour, and walk it again in the opposite direction. She liked the repetition and the way each part of the routine revealed something new about what was outside and inside.

She dropped into contemplation as she trod the familiar path. Cody had offered her a trial period, and everything seemed to be going well. She liked the variety, and he seemed to believe in her, though she wasn't sure why. She could tell he respected her competency and work ethic. Her insider knowledge of the financing side provided perspective on how they made decisions, supplementing his personal experiences with Opti-Drip. But what was this redemption thing he and Makah had? Was Makah forgiving her? Could she trust that?

She liked that Kelp Ecology was based on ethical principles. They were working to get it certified as a B Corp, meaning it achieved standards for social sustainability, environmental performance, accountability to stakeholders, and transparency. Capitalism with social values—what a concept.

How would her father take it? Cody told her he'd seen him last year at Half Moon Bay, looking drunk. *Dissolute*, he'd said. She wondered where her father's head was these days. There was tension with PC's lawyers about the NDA. Cody had engaged Janet Philips to read it. Wanda liked Janet, clear and strong in her advice. Her legal opinion was that the most egregious clauses were unenforceable but that Clemens could make life expensive and difficult if he sued. Janet had talked to PC's general counsel, a law school classmate from Cal. They agreed it would be in the interests of both parties to avoid litigation. The counsel said Clemens wasn't happy, but he didn't want to further alienate his daughter. The lawyers set a schedule of quarterly attorney disclosure conferences. So far, that was going okay.

Her head felt like a conference table crammed with personalities, different parts of her own psyche. The needy child. The selfish teenager. The sexy blonde. The smartass. The arrogant bitch. The hurt lover. The excellent student. The determined manager. Sometimes they got noisy, the voices, shouting at each other, at her. And who is it who hears the chatter? It's not like she heard them out loud. More like colors or flavors. Waves of feeling. Bewildering.

Wanda jumped off her hamster wheel of self-doubt. She studied the forest canopy from her bench. A deep silence welled up inside her. What was appearing? It wasn't new—it had always been there inside her. How could she not have noticed? It didn't seem to have a name. A touchstone to test ideas, even actions, against. Deeper than a conscience, without the guilt and judgment.

The silence channeled through her with the park's seasonal changes—the fog and the rain, the sudden snow and the dew. She knew that the redwoods had something to do with it—their shaggy russet bark with its deep crenelations thrilling her touch, their roots that stretched out the width of the canopy, interlocking with those of their neighbors, stabilizing the whole community. When she was with them, her ego seemed to fall away, into a larger pool of consciousness. Sometimes, when an uncomfortable feeling arose, she tried letting it wash through. Don't block it—don't act it out. All her voices, held by this new awareness. Fascinating. Grounding.

Then there were the people she encountered on the trail. More, coming from Silicon Valley. Perhaps they were feeling something similar, some draw to the natural environment. Most of them were quietly respectful. Others talked loudly about anything you could imagine, like they were in Starbucks. At those moments, they seemed oblivious to the beauty she was perceiving. They left marks of their activity, like the litter that she had taken to collecting. Like the poop bags they left beside the trail. C'mon, people, finish the job. Your mother doesn't work here!

Often, when she drove down to Monterey for her weekly in-person with Cody, she'd walk along the ocean afterward. The coast's beauty made her feel the same way, only wetter, with bigger sound. The same things inside her too, the painful and the hopeful all tangled together. Those energies lived not only in the park. She wouldn't have minded leaving some of the painful ones there, along with the poop bags.

How had this happened? She tried talking to Roseanne, who called it "woo-woo." But it wasn't. It was as real as anything else. More real in some ways. It wasn't like she was levitating. Not even on weed. It was something strong she couldn't deny. She'd heard this happened sometimes, the beginner's mind.

She hadn't talked to her father since she'd left PC. The holidays were coming up, but she was still afraid of him. The hurt. She focused on the moment. Hard enough.

23

SCHOOL WAS BACK IN SESSION. The text from Suzanne came while Makah was teaching. When class was over she read—"Does Luz do TikTok?" Odd of Suzanne to be so cryptic.

Makah called her from her office. "What's up with your text? In any case, the answer is no, or at least I don't think so, and I'm pretty sure I'd know."

"I didn't find an account that looked like hers. But she's on there, and it's not great."

"*You* are on TikTok?"

"My niece is on it. She's thirteen, and my brother and his wife keep close tabs. I was watching her show about farm animal sounds, and the app served up a post titled 'Indian Chicken Dance,' and there was Luz."

Makah rose from her chair. "What do you mean?"

"I'll send you the link. It's kind of cute, actually. She's in the school playground doing these little chicken moves, her head bobbing back and forth, and clucking. But some boy recorded her and posted it with rude comments. And now there's piling on. I'm worried she's going to see it."

"Okay, I'll try to find it. What are the comments?"

"I don't want to repeat them, but they start out racist against Indians and people of color and go downhill from there, saying she's fat or ugly or stupid or retarded. Some of the comments might be from her classmates—that often happens."

"She so doesn't need this." Makah sighed. "She's only recently been socializing more at school. This might drive her back into her shell."

◆ ◆ ◆

When Makah picked her up from school, Luz was silently impenetrable, the other after-school option being rapt enthusiasm about something she'd learned. "How was your day?" met with no response. "Everything okay with your classmates?" produced scrunching down in the back seat. She was on the edge.

At home, Luz ditched her book bag and hurried out to the chickens. From the window, Makah watched her talking to them and walking around the yard holding her precious Princess Lay-a. Makah used the time to figure out how to get on TikTok and watch the ten-second clip. She shuddered. Her daughter's isolation. Brains are never enough. As she shut her laptop, Luz came in, her face impassive, hard.

"Mom," she said, "what's *acoustic*?"

"Hmm . . . it relates to sound and hearing—dogs have a greater acoustic range than humans. They can hear sounds we can't. Why do you ask?" If only Cody was around.

"A couple kids at school called me acoustic today. They were teasing me. I didn't like it—felt mean."

"Has this happened before?"

"One of them was my new friend Glenda. You know, the one I told you whose dad plays guitar for her, and she sings on YouTube?"

"Wait, are you sure it was insulting? Maybe she was saying you can sing."

"You know I can't sing, Mom. I just do animal calls, right? And the other girls . . . One of them called me a *crazy Indian,* and there were other things too." She hugged herself.

"Words can hurt, Luz. I'm so sorry. I'll talk to Mrs. White about it right away. You want to tell me more about what they said?" Makah reached out for a hug, but Luz shook it off.

"Leave me alone!" she shouted. "I'm going to my room."

• • •

"Where's Luz?" Cody asked when he got home.

"She hasn't come down for dinner. She's okay, but she doesn't want company."

"Oof!" Cody said after Makah told the story. "I remember when some kid called Andrés *acoustic.* It's mean slang for *autistic.*"

"She's not autistic. She's fine." Not going there.

"I'm not an expert, but I checked into the condition when that happened to Andrés. It's just that some people's brains work differently from so-called neurotypical people."

"Ah, psycho-jargon. We've had faculty training on it. Sure, she's different in some ways, or people might think so, anyway. But she's okay, even when she gets like this. Kids can be so mean." She'll grow out of it.

"Do you want me to talk to Mrs. White?"

"We both should," Makah said. "I'll set something up for tomorrow."

"Yeah, okay, we don't want bullying. It can really be destructive."

"You want to tell *me* about it?"

• • •

"I really appreciate your bringing this to my attention," said Mrs. White, facing Cody and Makah in her cramped principal's office. "We have zero tolerance for bullying here. But of course, we can't jump to conclusions. The TikTok belongs to one of the boys, and I have already called his mom. It's a long story, but the posting should be down by now. I haven't checked lately."

"Thank you for acting so quickly," Makah said. "But what's going to prevent this from happening again?"

"We're talking with the boy's parents, and we're sending out a reminder to all parents—you'll get the email this week. We're putting up new posters in the classrooms. And we're reminding the playground monitors to be watchful and to intervene if they see it happening. The cyber side is more difficult. We reported the posting to TikTok, but the boy's mom is taking it down anyway, which will be faster. The video's still out there, reposted, but in theory, the algorithms should catch it and clean it off. That's not completely dependable. We need you to keep us informed."

"Luz was quite upset," Cody said. "We're not litigious folks, but it's important that this be addressed. It seems plenty of lawyers are out there wanting to help stop bullying."

Mrs. White's gaze darkened. "Mr. Wilson," she said, "I don't respond well to threats. What you *can* do is join the committee the PTA has formed to address this issue. Your daughter's recent experience will help energize the group."

"Wait. How long has this been going on here?" Makah asked.

"The national PTA has been addressing this issue for years. And the school has an anti-bullying policy, as required by California law since 2012. As you should know as a teacher, state funding depends on us having our act together. But most important are the kids."

"Thank you, Mrs. White," Makah said.

"One more thing, Dr. Andrews. It's our policy that the child visit our in-school counselor for at least one session, just to take stock of the impact of the incident. I'm sure you understand." She raised her eyebrows at Cody. "Is that agreeable with you both?"

Makah and Cody traded melancholy glances. Cody regarded the principal with a shrug. "Of course, Mrs. White. We'll talk to Luz about it."

"Luz didn't come in today. How is she doing?"

"I'm sensing this isn't the first time she's been bullied," Makah said. "But now she's resisting school, which is unlike her. Maybe the counselor can reassure her that she'll be safe here."

Mrs. White smiled. "Please don't worry. We're committed to her safety, believe me. I going to keep my eye on her personally."

• • •

That afternoon, Makah found Luz in her room, huddled under heavy blankets.

"Hello, honey," Makah said. "How are you doing?"

Luz poked her head out. "A little better. I still feel sad. It hurts when they make fun of me. I'm tired of it."

"Your father and I talked with Mrs. White—she's on your side. She wants you to talk to the school counselor about it. Is that okay?"

"Do I have to go back to school to talk to her?"

Makah smiled. "You have to go back to school in any case. But I think this might help. Will you be a brave girl and give it a try?"

"Our ancestors were brave, Mom."

"Yes, they were. And you are too. Can I get you anything? Sometimes you like me to brush your hair." It needed it.

"No." She scooched back under the blankets. "Leave me alone."

Her daughter's muffled reply pierced her heart. "I'll check on you later, Luz. I love you." She crept out, leaving the door cracked. Later she told Cody, "This is hard. She reminds me of myself when things were bleak on the rez. I'd feel trapped and just curl up into a ball. I was in high school before I broke through."

Cody held her tight.

• • •

When Cody dropped her off the next morning, Luz spotted her friend Glenda walking toward the school. Luz hurried away, but Glenda called to her, saying, "Luz! Wait, wait for me!"

Glenda ran to catch her. "I'm sorry, Luz. I'm sorry I was mean to you. The other girls started it, and I didn't think. I didn't remember how to behave."

Luz studied the ground, twisting her hands. She remembered about being brave. She looked up at her schoolmate. "It felt bad, Glenda. I thought we were friends."

"I know how it feels, Luz. Sometimes kids make fun of me on YouTube when I post my music videos. It makes my dad furious. He's scary when he's angry." Her voice trailed off. "Anyway, can we be friends again?"

"Okay," Luz answered. "Let's be friends again. You're a great singer."

"And you're so good with animals. I love how the birds respond to you. It's like magic."

"Thanks," said Luz. "Like that Alphabet Rockers song we learned in Ms. Fernandez's class: *Everyone's different, no one's the same.*"

"*I'm-a stand up for you*, Luz."

• • •

After Luz talked to the counselor, she said she felt safer, and the bullying seemed to subside. Makah got an email from the counselor a few days later, asking to meet with her and Cody.

After greeting them, the counselor asked, "Has Luz ever had a psychiatric evaluation?"

"No," Makah answered. "Are you saying something is wrong with her?"

"I don't think there's anything wrong. She's an amazing girl—smart, brave, and so intuitive. But some of her behaviors suggest to me that it might be good to evaluate her for ASD."

"What's that?" asked Cody.

"Sorry, it stands for autism spectrum disorder. But it's not so much a disorder as differences in the way some people process information and interact—"

"I know that," Cody said. "My son has some of the behaviors. I just didn't know the acronym."

Makah fidgeted. "You heard about the 'acoustic' comment, right? It was on TikTok, too." This was getting out of hand.

"I did, but that's not the reason I'm suggesting an evaluation," the counselor said. "I'm not qualified to do a diagnosis—it's more my gut feeling. There's one more thing. The word *spectrum* can be misleading. People tend to think of it as linear, like more or less severe. It's more like a circle of behaviors and characteristics, and some are very powerful in a positive way."

"Greta Thunberg is autistic," Makah said. "She's one of Luz's heroes."

The counselor smiled. "She refers to her autism as a superpower. Luz has great potential, especially if she understands better who she is and how she may be different from other kids in some ways."

As they drove home, Cody's reaction was positive. He told Makah, "You know, the animal behaviorist Temple Grandin is autistic. She writes about how being with animals got her through her childhood—animals, and her 'squeeze chute,' something she built for herself after watching cattle calm down when they were held tightly in a big clamp. The deep pressure."

"It's like Luz under her heavy blankets," said Makah. "She's taking care of herself."

"Dr. Grandin says, 'The world needs all kinds of minds.' We just have to help Luz embrace her differences. What do you think, shouldn't we get her evaluated?"

"I need to think about it, Cody. Give me some space. It's too much right now." Way too much.

24

LIFE AS A CROW HAS ITS JOYS AND SORROWS, like anyone's. Just a few weeks ago, my dear Anjo and I were perched calmly in a Doug Fir, preening each other. Well, we got the call to go harass a Cooper's Hawk that was hunting in a patch that our peeps considered their territory. We joined the posse and found the Hawk in an old snag, surveying the marsh below. About a dozen of us flew around it cawing and fluttering, but she refused to move. After a while, most everyone left and Anjo and I went back to what we had been doing, this time in a Fir not too far from the intruder. But I guess our posse had gotten under her feathers, for she came after us. We leaped into the air, and she chased us. Then Anjo tried one of his favorite acrowbatic moves, a double barrel roll—like the sky dancing he did when he was courting me—trying to shake her. I'd kept on going and, as I wheeled around, I saw that the move had slowed Anjo down, and the Hawk was hurtling down at him, her fearsome yellow legs extended, talons out. I dropped to the ground and tried to divert her with my best injured Crow imitation, but she hit him hard and they fell together. She mantled over him, shifting her talons to bleed him out while tearing at him. He was yelling for mercy. I cawed loudly for backup and three or four friends showed up. We slammed into her multiple times, and she finally abandoned him and flew into the north.

Anjo was hurt bad, his chest all open. There was nothing we could do. I said my goodbye and stood beside him for hours until a Coyote came by and looked like trouble. My mates comforted me in the roost. I can't put that scene out of my mind—it wakes me up at night. Life's just not the same. He haunts my dreams.

When I ran into Tania, I told her about it and she consoled me. After that, she told me of a dream she had, and its consequences.

Tania the Cougar dreamed she was small, still a cub. A Coyote stalked her, found her in a tight spot, cornered. He killed her. What she most remembered from the dream was the Coyote's words: "Not on my own account. Cat's not my thing." Sometimes she puzzled over the vision when she crouched in ambush, waiting for the right moment to pounce on some unwary Rabbit.

Over the weeks, as the dream worked its way into her psyche, a feeling came into her, an energy not entirely her own. She found herself working her way up the hills closer to human settlements. Late one night, she was attracted by a noisy outdoor gathering behind an enormous house. She stole into a tree above the house and watched the humans come and go. Later, it got quiet. She dropped onto the roof and crouched, with intimations of what the Coyote dream had meant.

25

FOR A YEAR SINCE HIS RUN-IN WITH THE FAWN, a recurrent nightmare had tortured Jack Clemens. He was walking in a jungle when he heard growling, stalking him from above. In haste, he stumbled over roots. Macaws screeched. He fell. The pursuer dropped from the canopy. He felt a heavy paw on his back, hot, wet breath on his neck. Then he was looking down at the scene. A panther was standing over a dying gazelle. He awoke.

He tried various remedies. If he took enough Ambien to sleep through, he was groggy in the morning. The more so if he'd been drinking—too often the case. He considered going back to that pushy therapist he'd seen briefly after the divorce.

One Thursday, he was at the Rosewood's bar when one of his buddies, a combat veteran, mentioned having "weird dreams about animals."

"What dreams?" Clemens asked.

"They're like pursuit dreams. I feel like I am back in Afghanistan. There's a pack of striped hyenas following me at a distance. It's threatening, but not immediately dangerous. I turn and fire at them, and they back off. I never hit one. I keep moving and they keep following me. The dream usually just fades away, but I remember it." The vet sipped his

Chivas. "Hyenas rarely attack people, you know. But the Pakhtuns kill the females and cut out the vulva. They believe it will attract women."

"Wow. That one I hadn't heard. My daughter might say your dreams are channeling the hyenas' anger."

"Whatever."

Their server came by. "How are you gentlemen doing?"

"Fine," said Clemens.

"I couldn't help but overhear you. Other customers have been talking about scary animal dreams. Kind of creepy."

"Strange times," Clemens observed.

• • •

Later that September, Clemens made an appearance at a party at Peder Lieth's sprawling property off Skyline Drive. The estate, which had cost Lieth $40 million, comprised a 14,000-square-foot, five-floor, Tudor-style home sitting on an eighteen-acre lot, planted and manicured to feature the mansion and its oversize pool and yielding to a buffer of firs and redwoods that created an atmosphere of privileged privacy. The party ran into the wee hours, the booze flowing freely, lubricating the rumors of IPOs and mergers and affairs. Eventually everyone had enough and left.

Lieth was moving slowly, absentminded, a scotch in hand. He was unsettled, having argued with Jennifer about business strategy earlier in the evening. The annoying part was that Clemens could see, and might have heard, the whole thing. Their profitable partnership at PC had become grudging. Clemens was dragging his feet on the creative schemes he and Jennifer cooked up. Lieth was of two minds, but when she told him, "Just can the fucker, he's dead weight," he told her to shut up.

"We'll see who shuts up!" She'd stormed off toward the bar.

Now Lieth was naked, ready for bed, when he heard a thump on the roof. Curious, wary, he struggled into his bathrobe and opened the sliding door onto the patio. All quiet. He walked out toward the practice green, the smooth flagstone cold under his bare feet. He stumbled over a putter that some idiot guest had left. "God dammit," he muttered. His toe was throbbing. He peered up at the roof. A large cougar gazed down upon him, intent, calm. Lieth froze.

On the security video, Lieth appeared quite comical, his bathrobe opening, his mouth working feverishly. You could watch him turn his back and bend down to pick up the club. That was right before the cat entered the frame from the top, landing on him, 130 pounds of muscle stretched on a tough, lightweight skeleton. She decked him.

Dazed, groggy, Lieth cursed and tried to get up. He turned over, but she held him, swatting his face with her claws. He grabbed her leg, but she pulled it away easily. She let him struggle in terror for a few endless moments before sinking her canines into his neck and ripping his throat out in a fountain of blood. The form convulsed and was still. Tania stepped off, licking the blood off her face and paws. She surveyed the scene around her and leaped over the fence, vanishing into the woods, on moccasins no one can hear.

Lieth's groundskeeper found the body the next morning and called the private security company, who contacted the police. Someone leaked the video, and it went viral. One comment read, "Whoever Lieth with a beast shall be put to death." Another mocked Lieth's zero handicap, giving the cougar credit for a hole in one. Wildlife experts were at a loss to explain why a normally reclusive animal would attack a human without provocation. Trackers came out with dogs. They followed the scent over the ridge and south toward Santa Cruz for about six miles through dense timber until they lost the track. No sightings, although the Buddhist monks at the nearby Taungpulu Kaba Aye Monastery observed large paw prints a few days later, keeping, like cougars, such mysteries to themselves.

The attack was the talk of the Valley for weeks, a major disturbance in the investor ecosystem. To his amazement, Clemens stopped having the dreams. Weird. Such a brutal, effective kill. And maybe appropriate—living by the sword. The thoughts scared him enough to tell people he'd be taking some time to reflect, organize his business, his thoughts, and himself. As he reevaluated his life, he considered taking up aikido. He was attracted to its primary goal of "overcoming oneself" and to its path to self-defense that avoided injury to one's attacker. He knew that if he stayed in the finance business, he would have to protect himself better. At the same time, he was becoming sympathetic to the idea of compassion toward those who might seek to harm him. He found a dojo in Mountain View. The sensei was skeptical of the middle-aged capitalist and rode him. But Clemens persisted and won his teacher's respect. He started to progress and grew in composure and self-confidence.

On the business side, he was courted by associates of Lieth who knew and admired his ability to get things done. But the rank cynicism and frank self-interest he had previously taken for granted now repelled him—that dog-eat-dog, every-man-for-himself milieu, so veiled and vindictive, that he'd made his career in.

His ex-wife's slide into depression's sinkhole, the deer incident, his animal dreams, the continued distance from Wanda—yet there'd been a brief opening—all tumbled in his mind. His head felt like a front-loading clothes dryer with no off switch.

He began using Fridays to walk in the parks west and south of his house. The fresh air, the greenery, the sounds of birdsong cleared his head. This was the off switch he had been searching for. He slept better. He didn't have an answer, but he was calmer about it. He diverted himself by reading about the habits of the cougar.

One Friday, he happened into the Bear Creek preserve. A car in the parking lot looked like Wanda's, and, as he approached it, he recognized the dream catcher hanging from the mirror, the one her mother had given her. His heart skittered. He took a deep breath and started down the path. In about twenty minutes, he saw Wanda coming toward him. He stopped, waited.

"Wanda," he said, as she came closer.

"Dad! What are you doing here?"

Uncomfortable, eight feet apart.

"I'm taking walks in nature on Fridays to help clear my head. This is my first time here—it's very nice. Have you been here before?"

"Ahhh, yeah. It's my . . . refuge. Of course, it's not really mine, but I usually have it pretty much to myself on a weekday."

Neither moved.

Then she stepped toward him with a kind smile. "How are you doing?"

"A bit lost, though not here on the trail—I mean, not yet." He sucked his breath. "Do you have time to talk?"

She hesitated. The birdsong was reassuring. "Okay. There's a bench that encompasses the valley. It's about equidistant either way on the path. Follow me." She turned around and started walking.

They walked in silence. The trail widened, and she let herself lag back to where he was. She named the calls of Steller's jay and western raven, the melodies of song sparrows. They made small talk until they arrived at the bench.

"I'm trying to figure out what to do next," Clemens said. "That Lieth thing hit me. Maybe I'm burned out on the VC world."

She turned her head sharply. "Really, Dad? It doesn't sound like you."

"I guess I want to turn over a new leaf." He stretched his arms and torso in a slow aikido move. "We'll see how long it lasts. But I've cut down my drinking, so that's a step in the right direction. How are you doing? I hear good things about Kelp Ecology."

"I still like it. Cody is a great boss, and our skill sets complement each other. I'm still learning, and the company's growing, so I'm not in a hurry to do anything different. We're engaging with the Rumsen and Esselen communities to get their perspectives on the aquatic ecosystem. It's a unique approach that the science labs have not fully valued. It's exciting."

Wisps of cloud began to veil the sun. Clemens felt uneasy, unsure. "Maybe it's getting late. I should get going."

"It was good to see you, Dad." She buttoned her jacket. "I'm glad you're doing better."

They walked back to the cars and headed down the hill into the Valley. On their ways home they were of the same mind—surprised and a little hopeful.

• • •

A few weeks later, Clemens got a call from his ex-wife's brother. She'd been in a head-on with a drunk driver. Brain injuries. She'd already been depressed, borderline suicidal. Now she was in a psychiatric facility. The docs thought she could recover over time, that it might help her find a way out.

Clemens's own head was pounding. He felt something like remorse. He texted Wanda and asked her to call him "about your mother."

Wanda called him later that day. "What is it?"

"Your mother's been in a serious accident." He gave a rough outline. "You should call her brother for the details, but she's not doing well."

"Shit. Anything else?" She was surprised how her armor was up. Was he possibly feeling guilty about the divorce? As if.

"Well, yeah," he said, "one other thing. I've been thinking of you and our relationship. It's broken, and that's mostly my fault. Anyway, I've told our lawyers to lay off on the NDA. Lotta reasons but anyway, I've decided, well, you're trustworthy, that's all." He could barely get the words out of his mouth, and they surprised him. He needed to tell the lawyers ASAP.

"Okay . . . and thanks." What was he up to? Could she find out—and did she even care? Anyway, it was different. "As far as me," she said, "I'm doing fine, actually. I still like the company and the variety of duties. And the people are nice." Her numbness was wearing off. "What are you going to do about Mom?"

"I asked her brother to let me know if she needs any help. I'm not Mr. Popular around there." A nervous laugh. "You think you might go?"

"I'll have to talk to him. It's hard to process."

"I know. Keep in touch."

• • •

Cougars fascinated Clemens. He joked to himself that the allure of an animal considered a symbol of primal feminine awareness was because there were no women in his life. Yet the catalyst was Lieth's murder. He wondered what ever happened to that cat. Had it fared better than that LA hills celebrity cougar they euthanized after it killed a dog tied up in a yard? As he got into the animals' habits and their mythology, he developed insights—leading without insisting that others follow, using one's gifts responsibly, exercising "power with" instead of "power over," and recognizing leadership potential in everyone. It was far from what he was used to in the Valley, where "great leadership" was seen as blind optimism, fearless agility, and a fanatical work ethic. At the end, some would mention humility—"aw shucks" signaling—but it was usually fake. Respectful listening rarely made the list.

He visited three cougars—all rescues—at the Oakland Zoo. They displayed agility and adaptability, a canny stealthiness, and a penchant for secrecy. He began supporting organizations like the Center for Conservation Peacebuilding. He recalled his animal dreams and how they'd ended when Lieth died. He needed to return to where he had killed the fawn—a crime of arrogance, unfinished business.

One afternoon he retraced his path, driving up past Lieth's old place to the ridge at Skyline. He stopped for coffee at Alice's Restaurant before beginning the curvy descent down the west side. When he reached the spot, he recognized it right away. He'd avoided the place for a year. He walked into the woods to where he remembered the doe standing. It was muddy, and his loafers made a sucking sound. He found a patch of dry ground. His khakis were all spotty. He saw a paw print in the mud, four inches wide. It had to be cougar. So lucky! Then a low, throaty growl behind him. He twisted around slowly, tried to look big, made eye contact.

The cougar seemed amused. She changed her tune to a shrill call, like a child's scream at play. Clemens flinched. She sat on her haunches and watched him. "So," she seemed to say, "you may remember me from your partner's famous video. Thank you for being part of my fan club."

How much of this was he imagining? He tried to master his panic. The cat was between him and the car. "Velvet paws! Velvet paws!" he said in his strongest voice. "He had it coming!"

The animal tilted her head, gave a terse growl, and waited.

Clemens waited as well.

They watched the light fade. The animal seemed in no hurry.

Clemens grew tired of looking big. "How about if you look at it this way? I have nothing but respect for you. If you want to take me out, that's your business, I suppose. But I can be worth more to you and yours alive than dead." He moved toward the cougar in a calm, concentrated manner, without animosity, the way his sensei had taught him, avoiding the escalation of violence, projecting internal power.

The cougar scrutinized him. "I see you. We can make a deal. I'm getting a bit long in the tooth. It's been a great life, but we felines wear out quicker than you do. I'm not complaining, mind you. Oh, a few aches and pains, but I got my licks in. I used to be a Domestic Cat, so it's been a blast. Here's what I propose. You take the baton from me—to pay close attention to the Divine Feminine—without losing the best of your maleness, and I let you go about your business. Isn't that the direction you were already heading, if not in so many words?"

Clemens received the transmission roughly but clearly. It felt like a deft blow from his sensei, more admonition than injury. He wanted more.

"What are you talking about?" he asked.

This next came to him as in a dreamsong, as if sung by the best voices of the women he'd loved, his grandmothers, his mother, Wanda, his ex when they were young, even Jennifer. *When the powers of the Feminine are engaged—heartfelt sincerity, deep listening, clear speech, unmovable centeredness, playful humor, an irresistible spirit—the world changes. The Masculine has the opportunity to welcome its best self, the possibilities of fellowship and solidarity, of cheerful frugality and conservation, of courage and sacrifice.*

"Okay. I'll do it," he said, projecting confidence over his confusion and fear. But how?

Tania growled softly. "Done and done," she said. "One last thing. When you see Cody, tell him Tara sends love. Now, move along."

Clemens sidled around her, keeping the cat's yellow-green eyes in his gaze. He hustled across the road and hopped into the car. He wiped his forehead with a gym towel.

Tania turned away with a soft rumble and disappeared into the woods. *Humans.* She looked back through time, to Rome, when killing large animals had become spectacle, the emperor Trajan slaughtering over ten thousand to celebrate a military victory. Velvet paws, indeed. She sharpened her claws on a fallen log. It was near dusk, and she was hungry.

26

IN EARLY OCTOBER, Cody and Makah joined Suzanne and Kipp for dinner on the veranda. His well-trimmed hair and graying beard gave Kipp a distinguished mien. An excellent cook, he attributed his skill to his French mother but admitted having taken classes at the Culinary Institute of America. "It's the CIA of cooking," he liked to say in his best Roger Moore affectation. He prided himself on being careful with the food. "The first rule of cooking is 'Do no harm,' particularly given the abundance of fresh ingredients here in California." They feasted on locally raised organic chicken (Luz being at a sleepover at Glenda's), organic brown rice, bok choi lightly sautéed in toasted sesame oil with garlic and raisins, and, in Cody's honor, a delicious seaweed salad with rice vinegar, rice wine, ginger, and cayenne. The accompaniment was a medium-bodied red blend from Paso Robles.

After dinner, Cody asked, "Do you guys know anything about EarthCraft?"

Kipp closed the veranda door behind him, his other hand calmly gripping four small crystal glasses and a bottle of Amaro on a tray. "You mean the video game Suzanne's been regaling me with stories about—the game you're playing while you're supposed to be working? I hear it's all the rage at the research institute."

Makah snorted. "He's not just playing it at work. I've had to forbid him from sharing it with Luz, or she'd stop doing her homework altogether. It's addictive."

"I told Makah it has applicability for Indigenous networks, but she's skeptical."

"Cody may be right," Suzanne said. "It's not just a game. It's also a set of communities, including a network of ecologists who are using the game infrastructure to model outcomes—perturbing an environment and seeing what happens. An intern at the lab turned us on to it."

"A couple of my Korean students were talking about it after class one day," Makah said. "I guess one of them was playing it during my lecture. 'Am I boring you?' I wanted to ask."

"So, what's the relevance to Indigenous?" Kipp asked.

"Maybe EarthCraft could become a platform for Indigenous communities to organize across national borders and identities," Cody answered. "One advantage is that the game is legal in repressive countries. Unlike Facebook."

"Most Indigenous communities don't have high-bandwidth internet access," Makah said. "The networks I'm in do well to make email and WhatsApp work."

"That's a good point," said Cody. "There would have to be a low-bandwidth option."

"It reminds me of the so-called metaverse," said Kipp. "Did you know the term was coined in Neal Stephenson's *Snow Crash*? That novel came out in 1994. People in that world spent their time jacked into the metaverse via a cable connecting their brain into an immersive display console with a keyboard and other controls. From there they went to school or work, made music, everything. It was a three-dimensional, multisensory virtual reality."

"The metaverse is still vaporware today," said Cody. "Hype."

Kipp pounced. "The internet spawned virtual communities of scientists from its inception in the 1970s. No commercial activities were permitted before 1989. Scientists around the world created work groups using curated email lists to share and collaborate on research. The possibility of a virtual community that transcends national borders and identities, made up of decentralized autonomous groups that form into a politically oriented confederation, has long been a dream of internet visionaries."

Suzanne laughed. "Thank you, Dr. Hughes, for that exposition." She rolled her eyes. "He thinks he can get away with a history lecture because of his English accent."

"And thank *you*, Dr. Suze, for indulging me," he said, giving his habitual response.

"The January 6 insurrection showed us what your 'decentralized autonomous groups' can do," said Makah. "That whole thing was organized using social media and messaging apps. Not an encouraging prediction of where the technology is taking us. Social media is the principal platform for disinformation, exploited by the enemies of democracy worldwide."

"Not to mention the TikTok incident with Luz—that was a peek into the toxicity that's out there," said Cody.

"Technology is a tool. Like any tool, it can be used for good or bad." Kipp was in his zone—the political history of technology—and finishing up his tenure as chair of the history department. "It's up to people to make the right decisions. Technology gets out in front of policy, and law brings up the rear. Today, technology is evolving faster than ever while governance systems are less responsive than ever. That's why decentralized organizations, confederated in an agile way and aided by high-speed, high-bandwidth communications interest me. They might build consensus faster than the current top-heavy political systems that are relics of the industrial age."

"Luz would say we need to learn from the animals," Makah said. "Or *planimals*, I've heard them called. Like elephant herds, bee colonies, and redwood groves—communities where individuals work together on behalf of the group."

"How's it going with Luz and Anna?" Kipp asked. "The sense of connection those two have with nature is uncanny. I don't know what to make of it."

"We haven't heard much from Anna lately," Cody said. "I think she might be taking an extended break. She does that—she calls it *centering*."

"She and Luz are in touch on email, but Luz was saying she misses seeing her," Makah said. "So, I wonder about the planimals and whether they're working together—"

"As if that's even a thing," Cody said, trying to obscure Makah's reference to the still-secret planimal gatherings. "We'll have to wait until someone builds a safe, commercial platform for that kind of new-age governance. Maybe some VC will figure out a way to make money on it."

"Right," said Makah. "They'll sell ads, and it will be free to the users—the standard e-business model—'If the product is free, you are the product.'"

"Ooh," said Suzanne, turning to Makah. "I forgot to tell you the juicy rumor I heard today. It's about your promotion. I was in the dean's suite—I'm friendly with his secretary, Donna—when the dean emerges from his office, clearly exasperated. 'That Clemens,' he says, 'he's still on the warpath about Wanda.' Then he notices me, flushes red, and scurries back into his office. Well, I asked Donna what was going on. 'Makah,' she whispered."

"Omigod," Makah said, "Clemens is still mad about my firing Wanda nine years ago? Unbelievable. He must not even talk with her—for god's sake, she's working for Cody."

"Clemens is a take-no-prisoners kind of guy," Cody said.

"So *that's* the reason for the dean's hesitation," Makah said. "Clemens must be threatening to pull his donation. How much is it, anyway?"

"It's hard to tell from the IRS 990s," Suzanne answered. "They list multiple companies as donors, but I've heard it's about a million a year."

"Whoa," said Makah. "I can see why the dean would hesitate. If Clemens is holding the donation hostage against my promotion, well, this could get interesting. Right now we're still waiting for the reference letters to come in, so it's not ripe yet."

"It should come to a head soon," Suzanne said. "They'll want to be done in time for contracts in the spring. I hate to say this, but you may need a lawyer. What's your take, Kipp?"

"You Americans love to litigate. But I should think this could be resolved quietly, internally. The dean just has to, as you Americans like to say, 'man up.' A little faculty pressure might help him do that. Why don't I give your department chair a call, Makah, and see what he knows? I need to talk to him about a faculty senate matter anyway."

"Okay, Kipp," Makah said, "but be careful. I don't want to be seen as a complainer."

"Don't take that attitude, Makah," Suzanne said. "You have to stand up for yourself."

"I know, you're right. It's too easy for me to slip back into the system's view of how women and minorities should act—'Know your place and stay in it.'"

"You're so done with that, Makah," Cody said. "Your body knows it, and you live it every day. Your brain just forgets sometimes. Mine does that too, especially if I'm tired or stressed."

"Eternal vigilance is the price of liberty," said Kipp.

27

LUZ HAD BEEN PONDERING the connection between the TikTok incident and her chickens. Imitating them at school had turned into a problem. She decided it might be a good idea to have a talk with her egg-laying friends, and when a sunny, late October evening came along, she told Makah, "I'm going out to feed the chickens and give the coop a good cleaning. It might take a while."

"Fine, Luz," Makah said. "Dad's going to be late today, so we won't eat for a couple of hours. Have fun."

Luz scooped a portion of grain and some scratch from the tightly sealed bins and opened the gate into the chicken yard, calling her hens, as she always did, with a *tuck-tuck-tuck*. They came quickly—Princess Lay-a, Yoko Ono, Big Bird, Chicken Little, Hen Solo, and Esmerelda, in honor of her Grandma Toni's oldest. She set to cleaning the coop while they ate, collecting three eggs and adding fresh hay to the nesting boxes, chatting casually about the weather and humming tunes in her singsong way.

By the time they finished eating, Luz was done with her chores. She sat on the ground near Lay-a and picked her up, stroking her. "I want to talk with you and your sisters," she began. "I love you all—so much that sometimes I think I might be part chicken. You've seen me out here clucking and imitating your chicken walk. It makes me feel happy. I've read about how all chickens may have come from a single flock of junglefowl in Thailand, thousands of years ago. But I don't really know what that feels like to you all—if you have stories about the past that you tell each other, about how you came to the important place you have in human society."

Princess Lay-a made a clucking sound and Yoko Ono, who was second in the pecking order, came toward them. Luz let go of Lay-a, who began gently preening Yoko, clucking to her gently.

"Yoko," clucked Lay-a, "do you want to start the old story for Luz?"

"Yes, Lay-a," Yoko clucked. "She already understands us for ordinary conversation, but for this—shall we do the magic?"

Lay-a nodded, and the pair uttered a series of sharp cries, like squeaky car horns, a call-and-response. The tempo increased, became more legato, and ended on a long, dissonant chord, which appealed to Luz's nature and she joined them. For a moment the three creatures called together. Luz stopped to take a breath, and the hens fell silent.

Yoko clucked at Luz. "Now you can hear us fully. Our story begins, as you said, several thousand years ago in a land far away. The people there worshipped the Red Junglefowl—exquisite birds with red, gold, and black plumage. The people began to keep them in their temples, and, over time, they domesticated them for their eggs. Soon into that experiment, there was born a chick who grew into a stately hen, her scarlet and indigo plumage the match for any of the great many roosters who favored her in her time. The people called her Kaypah Rachiní—Queen Forest Hen. She was the progenitor of the most prolific and productive line of domesticated fowl, hatching and co-mothering hundreds of chicks during her seven-year life. Over centuries, the people hybridized her offspring with other Junglefowl, and then, as the breeds differentiated, produced the many billions of Chickens alive today comprising over a thousand breeds. We Orpingtons are direct descendants of Queen Kaypah."

"You have royal blood in you," said Luz. "I am honored to meet you in this way."

"There is more," said Lay-a. "We learned this all from our mothers, who learned it from their mothers, all the way back. As Yoko mentioned, Queen Kaypah had many roosters. But her mother, Queen Mae, was different in that way. Red Junglefowl can be monogamous, and Queen Mae was. Sadly, her longtime mate was eaten by a Panther, after which she hid for a year. Her sisters worried about her, but they became used to her absence. One night, toward the end of her exile, it is told that a great wind spirit came through the forest, taking the form of an iridescent blue, male Fireback—a Pheasant revered in that part of the world. The jaunty Fireback had long, curved indigo tail feathers, bright red head and legs, and a glossy black plume behind his head. His panting squawk could be heard throughout the forest that night. Within a few weeks, Queen Mae laid a single, large, reddish-brown egg, which she incubated until our beautiful Queen Kaypah hatched and began her life."

"That reminds me of *Chicken Big*," said Luz. "But where did your exotic ancestors come from originally?" Luz asked. "I learned that birds are related to reptiles."

"All birds are reptiles," Yoko answered. "But only the ground-dwellers survived the asteroid. The flying birds went the way of the dinosaurs. In those days, our ancestors were predators, with sharp spurs and hard, scaly legs."

"Technically, we birds *are* dinosaurs," said Lay-a. "Our history is nearly as long as life on the planet. You already know that we want respect in addition to a comfortable and productive life. Now you can understand why."

"This is so interesting," Luz said. "I want to hear more about Queen Kaypah and what you think about stories like 'Chicken Little' and 'Little Red Hen,' and why there are chickens on the top of French churches."

"Perhaps another time," Lay-a said, "for we have some questions for you. Why do you imitate our walk and talk?"

"It makes me happy," said Luz, "or at least it used to. Then something bad happened to me, and it took the fun out of it. Some kids bullied me."

"We have bully stories too," Lay-a said. "They often involve foul roosters, but it happens with hens too. Fortunately, we all get along fine here, right Yoko?"

"Princess Lay-a is a good mother hen—she's well-named," Yoko said. "It's too bad you stopped, Luz. We liked watching you. You were getting good at it. We discussed it quite a bit and decided you did it because you like us. That made us happy."

"I do love you all. I love how serious you are—like the Little Red Hen. When the other animals wouldn't help her, she just did it herself. And I don't think you're at all like Chicken Little, scared of the sky falling."

"One thing we *are* scared of is a Hawk plummeting upon us from the sky. We keep a watch and warn each other loudly if we spy one. That's the true origin of that story," Yoko said.

"But it's safer here because of the way the Crows guard us," added Lay-a. "That's pretty unusual. We're also lucky. Unlike nearly all our kin, we don't live in egg factories, nor are we headed for your dinner table."

"I didn't realize the crows were protecting you from hawks. I guess Koro has something to do with that—it's part of our partnership that I didn't appreciate. Thanks for telling me. She used to tell Skah to protect me, but I guess she's taken that on herself for the last two years." Luz sighed.

"We feel his spirit out here in the yard. From the top of the coop, we can see the place where he is sleeping the long sleep," said Yoko. "We believe it is his spirit that protects us from Coyotes."

"Going back to the Little Red Hen," said Lay-a, "you remind us of her sometimes—doing it yourself."

"I'm kind of isolated in school," Luz said. "My chicken dance didn't help with that. Some kids have been nice, but others stay away from me more than ever. I thought if I called in some animal spirits they would protect me. You gals are my closest animal friends, so I thought I'd start with you."

"Humans have some strange ideas about animals," Lay-a said. "It's kind of like how some white people try to pretend they are Indians. It can be offensive and disrespectful. We knew you weren't being disrespectful. But it's not by imitation that you get the Spirit."

"Wait," Luz said. "The Spirit? It sounds like it's just one spirit, not, like, chicken spirits or coyote spirits."

"That's exactly what Lay-a is saying," Yoko said. "Sure, every species has its own traits, every individual her own personality. But all life, all existence, is part of one Spirit, and one Spirit is part of all existence."

"So how do I get the Spirit that you animals have?"

"You can start by not thinking of us as *you animals*," Yoko said. "You are part of nature, a big part."

"The next step is to spend some time with yourself," Lay-a added. "You will find the Spirit inside you."

"I spend a lot of time by myself already. It feels scary wild in here."

"That's what we're talking about," said Yoko. "It's the you you already know, that you've always known. There's a quiet place, a stillness, a vastness inside you that is always available."

"Letting that be," said Lay-a, "letting that be you. For it is who you are."

"I'm afraid," Luz said. "I'm afraid of myself. When I feel crazy I don't know what I might do. Sometimes I get out of control, like really angry. It scares my mom."

"If you get scared, you can always come to us," Yoko said. "Just remember that we're part of the same, but we're not the same. You're you and I'm me and Princess is . . . well, Princess is special. But even she gets scared sometimes. Being scared is part of being alive."

From the house, Makah called. "Loo-ooz. Your dad's gonna be home in ten minutes. Can you come set the table?"

"I gotta go now. I love you gals," Luz said. "Sure, Mom, I'm coming!" she yelled.

Luz stood up to her full height. She walked through the gate with new confidence, eager to meet the Spirit she already knew, again, for the first time.

PART FOUR

28

YEP, LAY-A SPOKE THE TRUTH—we did set up a security perimeter around Luz's Chickens. It's part of our direct action campaign to protect the humans on Team Grandmother. We tend to keep these security arrangements quiet. I mean, no need to ruffle the Hawks' feathers. They can get a bit tetchy. Deviousness has been known to serve the greater good. There's an old story, about a Raven, or perhaps a spectacular Crow—it doesn't matter so much; we're like sisters and brothers. Anyway, long ago, the world was dark. All the animals and people moved in darkness, the world lit only by fires, except for a selfish chief who kept Sun, Moon, and the Stars inside his roundhouse, each in a beautifully carved box.

Raven, whose feathers in those days were, as you know, snowy white, was irritated by the chief's thoughtlessness and vowed to liberate the light for the world. But how could he get into the chief's house? Raven thought about this over many long nights. He decided on a plan. The chief's beautiful daughter came to the stream every day to drink. One day, when the princess arrived at the stream, Raven—a shapeshifter—turned himself into a speck of dirt and threw himself into the water. When the princess's helpers dipped a ladle into the stream, he floated into the ladle. But the helpers noticed the dark fleck and poured the water out.

Now, Raven is clever and does not give up easily. When he was in the ladle, he noticed it was green. He decided to turn himself into a hemlock needle. When again he cast himself upon the water, the helpers did not see him, and the princess swallowed the needle.

In a few weeks it became known that the princess was pregnant. Her father was upset at first, but she was of age, and he was excited about a grandchild. After the months passed, a son was born to the princess. Elated, the chief doted on the child.

But the boy was noisy and fussy. Although he played with the toys in the house, he kept asking for the beautiful box that held the Stars. The chief could not deny his grandson and brought the box down from its shelf. When the chief was preoccupied, the child opened the box, letting the Stars out. They flew into the sky. This upset the chief, but the child was happy.

This peaceful time did not last, however, for the child became fussy again and demanded the box containing Moon. The chief relented, and soon, Moon was released and adorned the night sky with her many faces. This time the chief was quite angry and gave the child a stern scolding. Peace returned for a few weeks. The child insisted on the last box. In desperation and affection, the chief surrendered, warning the child severely. Of course, the child opened the box, and Sun escaped into the world.

The chief flew into a rage. But before he could punish his grandson, the boy transformed himself back into Raven. The chief was furious at Raven's deception. He closed the door of his house tight and chased after Raven with a canoe paddle. The only way out was the smoke hole in the ceiling. Raven squeezed through it—escaping certain death—and blackening his features from beak to toenail.

A Raven gave this story to the Tlingit Tribe on the Northwest Coast. And it's true: The light cannot be kept hidden forever. But sometimes its release requires a sacrifice. We Crows tell that tale of courage to our youngsters, with its mix of desire, heroism, and treachery. Yes, Raven saved the world, but he violated the trust of his loving grandfather. If we Crows had a Talmud, there'd be commentaries on the ethics. Nothing good comes without a cost. Sometimes trickery is necessary. Even I have been known to hide Piñon nuts from my kin in preparation for winter.

29

MAKAH'S EXPERIENCE WITH THE GOLDFINCH continued to worm its way into her psyche and attitude. She worked at being cheerful, and the practice changed her. The spring's tender foliage once again delighted her. Cody and Luz welcomed her revival. Her focus on community felt different to Cody than after Chanson died, when she dove into her work as an escape. She had more energy for him and for family. Luz warmed to the attention and to Makah's help with her homework, and enjoyed their jokey chats in the kitchen as she learned how to chop vegetables. Makah showed her how to hold the vegetable on the cutting board with her knuckles closed to protect her fingers if the knife slipped. She taught that a sharp knife is safer than a dull one, and how to check the edge safely. Sometimes Makah thought about her life in New Town, when she was a year or two older than Luz, learning the same tricks from her mother, but in an edgier way, the conversations becoming argumentative about trivial things like the size of a carrot chunk for the Three Sisters stew. She wondered when Luz would turn into a typical teenager.

But Luz was focused on other things.

Cody had mentioned Luz's school incident to Andrés, who reached out to his half sister. "Dad told me about the TikTok stuff, and the counselor," he said over the phone as he walked in a wooded part of the college after class. "I know about that. I get grief about my fixation with birds. 'Hey, bird boy,' the guys say. 'What's that crow saying?' But they're not really interested in knowing. Most of them anyway. I ignore them and go over to the ornithology lab. It's friendlier there, but a little lonely. How are you doing, anyway?"

Luz was in her room finishing up her homework. "Oh, Andrés, thanks. It's hard. I love the animals, and they seem to love me back. But it's hard to talk about to most people, and though the bullying has stopped, I'm still being cautious. I don't need that right now. Things are changing for me in other ways."

"I remember when Rosa was your age," he said. "She was definitely going through stuff I didn't understand. She and my mom would have these secret meetings."

"Yeah, well, my mom's only so much help."

"How about Anna?"

"She's cool, but it's more, you know, formal." Luz paused. "Did you, like, get treatment for ASD?"

"Not so much, just a couple of sessions with a counselor. I'd rather talk to the crows."

"Yeah, I know. My mom's not that into the counseling part. I guess it's okay. It was good to learn about neurodiversity, but it doesn't seem like mine's that severe. It goes in waves. Sometimes I just have to cover up. Other times I can get outside—like in the woods—and things feel better. I've been walking more down in the park by the house, where I have friends. I'm trying to think of Greta as a model."

"Greta's example helped me a lot, Luz. Rosa admires her too, but she's more neurotypical than I am. There's not much correlation in fraternal twins. Call me anytime, Luz. It's nice to have a sister who's a bird woman."

• • •

Sometimes on her walks, Luz would think back to the first congress, when the mom coyote Shakti threatened direct action against humans. Now there was the boy coyote who she sensed was living near her, in her woodsy refuge. Shakti had scared her with her threatening *wowoooo-woo* at the congress. Did the planimals carry through on the threats they made? She resolved to be careful on her ninja walks.

Some had. One coordinated vigilante campaign targeted fossil-fueled air conditioning systems in Atlanta, focusing on commercial and industrial facilities and megamansions. Natterings of starlings landed on refinery roofs and constructed dense, nest-like structures that blocked air intakes; mud daubers fouled cooling coils while spiders gummed up air filters; house mice damaged sensors; and an unusual pathogen got into the food at a private dinner of CEOs at an air conditioning expo.

Planimal saboteurs also disabled facilities serving private jets, and factories making single-use plastics. A swine flu variant swept through China's pork factories—high-rise pig warehouses—requiring the slaughter of a quarter of China's 400 million pigs and turning an area of Sichuan Province where the carcasses were buried into a "national sacrifice zone."

After noticing several such incidents, an enterprising reporter at *Forbes* imagined a pattern. When she called the Environmental Protection Agency, a young division chief in the Climate Change Division confirmed a dozen incidents—not for attribution, of course. The reporter's story grew legs. Memes of snarling wolves and fierce hawks trended.

People in tune with the natural world worked to amplify the narrative, but it was hard to get mainstream science to believe that "Nature" or "the Earth" was actually speaking to humans. The idea that plants and animals could interact across species for mutual benefit had not been researched beyond a few studies of symbiotic and mutualistic species—like the traveling pods of whales and sharks who hunt together, the same individuals reuniting year after year. Even those interactions stretched the limits of scientific orthodoxy.

On the other hand, the planimal actions became a hot topic in Indigenous conversations. Makah found herself in global Zooms with biologists, philosophers, and social scientists. There was interest in having a small, in-person workshop. Monterey would be a fine location after tourist season.

Professor Chase mentioned it to Dean Denny, who was interested in the reputational cred it would bring the school. "I'd like to support that," the dean said, "but I'm short on cash these days."

"Well, I'll keep looking," said the chair. "On a related matter, Dean, I think you're going to have to bite the bullet and approve Makah's promotion. I heard from Kipp Hughes the other day, and there's concern among the faculty about the precedent. Kipp mentioned 'academic freedom.' He didn't say how he heard about it, and I'm not sure I see it that way, but he told me something else you might be interested in."

"Oh, lovely," Denny said. "What else?"

"You remember that graduate assistant Makah fired after she first got tenure—Wendy or something?"

The dean dissembled. "Vaguely. What about her?"

"There seems to have been some kind of reconciliation between the two women. That Wendy woman is now working for Makah's husband's company."

Denny whistled softly. "Now *that's* interesting," he said. "Thanks, Chase. Thanks for calling."

They hung up and the dean came out of his office. "Donna," he said, "please get me a call with Clemens."

At the appointed time, the dean was prepared. He opened the negotiation with, "Jack, I'm getting pressure from the faculty on this professorship matter. You've supported the school for a long time, and I'm wondering if you've reconsidered your opposition."

"Not exactly," Clemens said. "That's your problem."

"Of course," the dean said, "but there's a wrinkle. It involves your daughter's employment situation."

"What business is that of yours?" Clemens maneuvered, prevaricating. "She left my company, and I haven't heard from her since. It's a sore point, and I don't appreciate your bringing it up. You're not helping your cause."

"You might want to look into the family behind a company called Kelp Ecology, Jack. Just saying."

"Damn. Let's suppose I did that. Then what?" He used his surly voice.

"Then," said the dean, "you might have an issue—that is, if news of your position got around to Wanda, that's what. That could happen anytime." He took a deep breath. "On the other hand, I need your help with an international workshop we're trying to organize. It will be great for our reputation, and your support might help smooth over any possible misunderstanding."

"Wait. Is this a Makah workshop?"

"That's the idea."

"Goddammit, Dean. This isn't any way to act with a longtime donor."

"Jack, look. I have to promote her, and I'm going to. I'm trying to give you a way out here. But you've got to let me know. Time is of the essence."

"No, you look." Clemens shook his head. "I'm willing to put this matter behind us if you are."

Denny paused, smiling to himself. "Jack, you have always been a wonderful supporter of our work here. I knew I could count on you. You are a true friend of the university."

"Yeah. You bet, Dean. And by the way—"

"Yes?"

"Nice job. I didn't think you had it in you."

Dean Denny thanked him again and hung up. "The games people play—with other people's lives," he muttered and came out of his office. "I feel like I need to take a shower," he told Donna, "but I guess I'll just go for coffee. Can I bring you anything?"

• • •

Galvanized by her promotion, Makah sprang into organizing a workshop on "Cross-Species Mutualism." She felt light inside when she imagined sharing her deepening appreciation of the connections across species with her Indigenous colleagues working on the climate crisis around the world. She enlisted Anna to help with the agenda. Anna advised her to open the meeting by speaking of "beginning the healing," echoing Ursula's call. Twenty of her Zoom partners—Indigenous biologists, political scientists, and medicine people from North and South America and Southeast Asia—spent two and a half days together, talking around a big table and walking in small groups in the woods or along the beach, watching and listening to the birds and mammals, caressing the plants, enjoying their common Pacific Ocean.

The meeting was off the record. There was no formal consensus, but Makah's summary report, by quoting remarks without attribution, gave a sense of the workshop's energy.

> Everyone here has described local examples of what appears to be collective action by plants and animals to draw attention to the damage the industrial lifestyle is causing to the planet.
>
> We are discovering new channels of communication between species. We do not know exactly how they work, but some organisms are responding to signals from other organisms at a distance. Movement of one species seems to bring others to the same place at the same time, for purposes that remain unclear. The combination of species and behaviors we have seen, including predators forbearing from attacking traditional prey, is unprecedented in our traditions or the literature.

> It is like the elders have told, how during the First Times the animals and plants were active in the formation of the world and the creation of humans.
>
> A few people in my community seem to be able to predict these events before they happen. They say they come to them in visions or dreams. But we cannot get the authorities to listen to them.
>
> The political system in my country has no ability to respond intelligently to this phenomenon. It is outside their knowing. Government is acting in random, uncoordinated ways.

Makah was inspired to close the meeting with a simple question: "If the planimals can work together, why can't we?"

30

I HAD HOPED THE FOILED ATTACK on Ursula was a cosmic sign of the turnaround. Not so, it seems. It's been a year since the last Congress, and the slow pace of progress drove some of my fiercer planimal relatives to collective action. *Ecotage!*

Somehow I can't blame them. Another early, sweltering summer is making everyone grouchy, except for reptiles enjoying the heat and hot-weather species expanding their habitats at the expense of temperate flora and fauna. Fire season started in January after only a few weeks' respite, hard on the forests and the firefighters. Glacier melt is accelerating—much of the massive Thwaites ice shelf in Antarctica collapsed into the ocean. Severe drought in northeast India killed millions of Cattle, creating a public health crisis. Pitiable, angry climate refugees from the Middle East and Northern Africa streamed toward Europe in increasing numbers.

Low-lying coastal and island nations continued raising the alarm. A tsunami tore through the South Pacific on the anniversary of the last big one, displacing fifty million Bangladeshi and Indonesian people and killing half a million across Southeast Asia. Singapore's naturally protected location saved it from the worst, but powerful typhoons strained its flood preparedness and emergency drainage systems. Singapore real estate slipped by a third. Recognizing that tidal surges were near a low point of the moon's nodal cycle, which would peak in less than ten years, the country doubled down on building sea walls and creating regional climate action alliances. Meanwhile, temperatures kept rising—land temperatures by five-hundredths of a degree centigrade each year, oceans closer to three-hundredths. A slow, inexorable burn.

Governments and companies had reversed course on climate, dismissing it as a "side effect" of economic growth. Fossil fuel was back in style. War spread and escalated, wasting scarce political attention, financial resources, and carbon rations.

Although popular unrest was increasingly visible online and in the streets, breaking with the old ways of living was proving arduous for most humans, not to mention changing or replacing the old institutions that held the old ways in place. The world remained far from reaching agreed climate targets.

Against this backdrop, we held a third planimal Congress at a remote Mendocino cove, a place far from Monterey, where the scraggly Redwoods rooted into the cliffs. No humans were present. After an arduous journey, Ursula stood weary on the rocky beach. I perched on her shoulder under a cold, persistent drizzle. At least the trees liked the weather.

Only a few other animals attended in the flesh. Maybe no one actually showed up, it's hard to say, for interspecies communications were functioning at full capacity, as they did in the Old Times, before the noise of technology disrupted them. In any case, here's what the Congress looked like from my perch.

"We are together again, having passed through a hard year since our last meeting," Ursula began. "Thank you for joining and for your wonderful energy and activity during this trying period. I am accompanied once again by Koro, our astute Crow messenger and intermediary. Please welcome her in your hearts, for I am sorry to report that her dear friend

Anjo took his flight into Grandfather Sun earlier this year. We will miss his rowdy good humor."

"Thank you, Ursula." I suppressed a sob at the mention of my Anjo. "And thank you to the other members of our core group—Scree, Zarapito, Snave, Vespa, the ubiquitous Lichen—for holding me. Thanks also to Tania for her continued attention to our security needs. Our agenda today reflects the gravity of our situation. As you know, our meeting is being transmitted throughout the region via the Network."

"We will begin," said Ursula, "by reviewing the effects of actions taken by parties on both sides of the divide. Vespa will speak first about human actions, followed by Snave who will recount planimal activity. Vespa?"

"Thanks, Ursula," Vespa buzzed. "Humans are, as ever, a mixed bag. Some seem to have declared war on the rest of life, while others are doing their best to support the turnaround. Here in our region, there is division across the two sides of the mountains that run north–south. Close to the coast, humans tend to support climate goals, whereas east of the mountains, it's more about going back to when resources seemed unlimited and people believed they were the Masters of Nature. We all know that doesn't work with eight billion humans. One possibility is that they take each other out, but the scale of death sufficient to make an ecological difference is way beyond anything the species has experienced, even in war. Meanwhile, their efforts to learn from and collaborate with Nature are isolated and disorganized. Their own electronic networks are being used to harden their divisions." She lit wearily on a twig. "The establishment is not supportive of working with Nature. In sum, we find little cause for optimism. There are lots of grassroots efforts—political protests and changes in schools, including even teaching about the Elephant Code. Good people everywhere are doing their best. There are glimmerings of a popular movement that could transform societies—although not always in positive ways. I'm afraid it will take dramatic events to change people's perspective on a scale that will reverse the present trajectory."

"My turn now," rattled Snave. "Following along what Vespa said, our own collective actions to change humans' minds have had limited impact. Humans are still in denial that they can, and must, work synergistically with us for the common good. They cling to their theology of dominion over all life, of domination based on patriarchy. They have forgotten that we all come from our Grandmother and will return to her in time. On another paw, fewer and fewer planimals are advocating for continuing the actions against humans. There was great interest in the brave deed of a certain head of security against a wealthy capitalist, but the impact was short-lived. The overriding sense is that, while attacks may educate a few, the costs may soon outweigh the benefits."

"Please elaborate," I said. "Do you mean that our brave vigilantes are concerned the destruction is not worth the animal lives lost?"

"No," said Snave. "It's deeper than that. We have recognized that the better approach is to 'be the change we want to see.' If we want humans to respect the planimals, we need to model good behavior. Or at least avoid bad behavior. It gets back to the Code—that last sentence about the effects for seven generations." Snave paused, coiling herself as tall as a Cobra so that all could see her. "It's the broken arrow, the end to unending war."

While this serious talk proceeded, an exhilaration of Whimbrels, tipsy from the rain, stopped by on its annual migration to feast on juvenile Dungeness Crabs burrowed in the tidal sand. Ranging along the shore, plunging their long, curved beaks deep into the muddy beach, their heads washed by receding waves, they'd pull a Crab out and shake it, cracking the brittle legs in their beaks before swallowing the juicy thing. I watched Zarapito slip away from the meeting to greet his cousins and exchange weather reports. "Try the Crabs," smacked a Whimbrel. "They're delicious." But Zarapito scurried back.

“Thank you, Vespa and Snave,” I said. “Now, Scree, give us an update on the Elephant Code in our region.”

“In the western region, the Elephant Code, under the title ‘Draft Code of Conduct for Human Survival,’ has been receiving considerable attention among humans, particularly west of the mountains. There is a ballot initiative in California next fall that would direct the state government to evaluate all major decisions using the principles set out in the Code. This is progress. But one must remember that, even if it passes, it will take years to implement. Groups of people are discussing how it would affect their lifestyles. This, too, is positive. Yet most animals, including humans, rarely limit themselves in the absence of pressure from outside forces, local norms, or their peers. So, as they like to say, the jury is still out.”

That pretty much sums it up, except that Ursula, who has become rather philosophical, gave a nice farewell message:

“From the discussions and reports, the sense of the meeting seems to be a mix of discouragement and determination, with a dash of optimism. I, for one, share these feelings. We have no choice but to live. It is *how* we live that matters. The fact of this meeting, in the face of great hardship to come, is testament to the collective urge for life. Our dear Grandmother blesses us and reminds us that she is there for us whenever we are ready to take her into our heart.”

“Safe travels to you all,” I added. “I do not know when we shall meet again. In the meantime, may all living beings live in peace with our Grandmother.”

“Amen,” intoned Lichen.

31

LATER THAT SUMMER, Tatiki achieved full maturity, awakening a keener hunting energy. The scents of other Coyotes became pungent. He felt more alert, more wild. He extended his range, traversing a variety of female and male territories. He tracked one female into a hollow, where he sensed there might be a den. As he came around a corner, a snarling older male confronted him. Tatiki barked. As the male bared his teeth, Tatiki observed the female emerging from the den behind the male. She watched the two animals calmly. The male advanced toward Tatiki, who decided he might have better things to do. He pivoted warily, slinking away, when the male charged. He chased Tatiki to the edge of the clearing. Tatiki kept running until he was well away from the pair. There was always more to learn.

A few weeks later, he detected Kali's familiar scent, which had taken on an alluring tang. He picked up his pace. When she saw him approaching, she growled at him. He slowed and she ran at him, snarling with a mix of playfulness and aggression he had not seen from her since their first Ground Squirrel.

The courtship lasted several days. At one point, a stray male passed through, but Kali displayed no interest. Tatiki dispatched him with the bravado he'd recently learned. At dusk, he brought Kali a Rabbit.

The ensuing tryst was a festival of nuzzling, nipping, yapping, and, at last, the long tie between them. She shook herself, and they touched muzzles.

Downhill from the Chicken house, the pair found a large, abandoned Weasel den, its lingering mustiness weaving fancies of hunting one together. From the new lair, they could sneak under a fence into unexplored hunting grounds. Nine weeks later, Kali whelped a litter of five. Their lives became very busy.

⬩ ⬩ ⬩

Tatiki and Kali spent that year keeping their pups fat and schooling them in the tricks of urban Coyotes. One evening, as Tatiki returned to the den, a fat Rabbit carcass swinging from his jaws as he loped along, he wondered about his trickster side, a part he was aware of but had never cultivated. His father didn't speak of it, but an old auntie had told him that Trickster took many forms, all linked to Coyote's role as co-creator of the world. Full of his worthy lineage, he trotted across Veterans Drive as a matte green Tesla Model S hurtled around the corner, swift and silent. The Tesla sounded its horn—tuned to a Hyena's cackle. Tatiki leaped into the ditch, bruising his snout. The Rabbit flew from his jaws into the thicket. Ignominious. Tatiki shook himself and retrieved his catch from the briars, scratching his face in haste. He limped back to Kali and the pups, reminding himself of pride's double edge.

Up the hill, he heard a commotion in the Chicken house. It seemed the horn had rousted the hens from their evening laying. He caught the girl's voice calming them, her voice sounding older than before. He thought about the girl, her black hair and luminous skin, about growing up and dealing with the world and its dangers and beauty. Perhaps he could connect with his inner trickster and be of some use. What he didn't know was that his trickster had already captured him.

Now Trickster does take many forms in legend and myths, and Tatiki's auntie was right, at least when it came to Coyotes. All animal tricksters have divine powers and are unpredictable. Some are merely mischievous, playful—jokesters. Other incarnations cause trouble, tempting humans down the road to hell. In some stories, Trickster generously brings fire to humans, the way Prometheus did. Some can escape from dangerous situations without harm. Tatiki's was a shapeshifter, like Raven in the Tlingit story. And, like Raven, he had a certain affection for humans, more so than the ordinary Coyote.

⬩ ⬩ ⬩

Although no humans observed the third congress, the Network carried the news throughout the region. People sensitive to such things caught the planimals' pessimism and resolve. Anna felt the change in her gut for several weeks, fasting and meditating to process it, to integrate it into her sense of the world, attempting to discern its implications for her own life. One day, over tea in Makah's garden, Anna brought it up.

"The plant and animal spirits are unhappy," she said, her words heavy. "It's affecting me. I see them in dreams. I saw a long line of ants trudging over a hill. When I drew closer, they turned into black bears. They seemed weary, even though in the dream it was the height of berry season, and they should have been happy. I followed them. They were heading toward the sea. When they arrived at the beach, they just kept going, into the water. Some of them drowned. Others turned into salmon, who swam out to sea. Then I saw many of them in a fishing net, hauled up onto a boat and cleaned and frozen for market. I have not found a place to put this vision."

They listened to birdsong, the drone of a neighbor's leaf blower, and the hens' clucking. Makah brought the calumet from its shelf and filled it with bearberry. She raised it to Anna, who nodded. They lit the pipe and passed it back and forth.

Anna continued, uncharacteristically candid. She felt vulnerable, yet it was safe here with the spirit of the pipe and her friend. "The unhappy visions reflect something inside me—restlessness and self-doubt. The bear connection last year left me unsettled. People see me as this insightful healer. Yet I feel disturbed, lost, wandering in the wilderness. I'm too old for this." She spat on the ground in rebuke. What a mess.

"Thank you, dear Anna. I see you. I regret your pain and suffering." Makah reached over and touched her friend's hand. "We're in a time of tremendous change. Maybe now is the moment for you to step deeper into your cross-species voice. I can feel it in you, and in Luz. It's so important."

"Thank you, dear one. Being seen is healing. I hear you and take your words to heart. And you are also right about Luz—she has such a strong inner sense of that voice in her core. It will be important that we help her protect that, especially as she is maturing. She is becoming a young woman."

"You're right there. I have been wondering, did the Rumsen have a coming-of-age ritual for girls?"

"I have heard about it, but it has fallen away from use. How about among the Nueta?"

"A similar story. The boarding schools suppressed it and then it was forgotten. Anyway, what if we had one for Luz?"

From down the hill, a coyote yipped, its call answered by another nearby.

"We could do that," Anna said. "It is important to involve the men. That was traditional, but especially now. Time to restore the balance."

When Luz came home, Makah told her about the idea. The timing would depend on when she had her first bleeding.

"That'd be great, Mom. We could invite some of my friends from school. The Jewish girls have a ceremony, so why can't we?"

"Your dad will like this, I think."

"I like it, and Mom will too," Cody said when Makah told him. "My sister Clara had had a *quinceañera*, which was part rite of passage, part debutante ball. I'm not sure about Dad. Luz is younger, and this would more explicitly recognize her biological femaleness. But I can work on him. In any case, we should definitely include some males. Maybe Andrés will be interested."

An exuberant Anna returned a few days later. "Karuk people just south of Oregon on the Klamath River revived the ceremony in 1996, after over a hundred years. They call it the 'Flower Dance,' and their practices track well with Rumsen stories. The Karuk believe that when the government outlawed and suppressed the ceremony, the Spirit People continued to conduct it from the Other World. A Karuk woman who lives near me in Salinas told me, and she will help us. There was even a film about it, *Long Line of Ladies*, that was featured at Sundance."

Over the next few weeks, the family talked with Toni and Blake, Mandy and Robert, and Suzanne and Kipp. Cody mentioned it to Wanda and discussed it with Andrés and Rosa. Anna brought her Karuk neighbor over from Salinas to talk with Makah and Cody. Makah spoke of it to Luz's teacher. And Luz talked to Glenda.

Now Luz felt nervous, embarrassed. "Everyone will know I've started!" she told Makah.

"Yes. And it's about so much more than that. It's about community—your role in the community as a woman and a leader, and about the community's responsibilities toward you. In the future, your daughters will look forward to their Flower Dance. You will see."

Following tradition, the ceremony would begin with an ordeal of seclusion for Luz, her eyes covered for several days as she discovered a conversation with herself, connecting to herself as a spiritual being and person, fasting, with only acorn water to drink. Afterward, to welcome her womanhood, there would be ceremony and dancing, for which the men would arrange the site, practice their music—inviting Andrés to add his birdsong—and prepare to cease their normal life activities for a day.

• • •

When Luz's first period came in August, they set a September date. Mandy and Robert came in from Bismarck. Cody pitched a tent in the backyard, overlooking the valley, its flap facing away from the house. Makah tied a deerskin blindfold over Luz's eyes and led her to the tent. She kissed her. "We will come get you in three days," Makah said. "We love you very much."

Luz wasn't sure she could stand it. The novelty wore off the first day. She was frightened at night. The familiar sounds of the valley animals seemed more acute, more urgent, than she was used to. Her thoughts scattered. Deep breathing helped, but she would lose concentration, distracted by the chickens' gentle conversations or the drone of an airplane. Violent images—men and women fighting, of people whom she loved dying, and of her brother Chanson—brought her to tears. She felt like crying out, giving up.

Somewhere during the second day, she exhausted these strategies and stories. She surrendered in despair. It was at that point she felt the Earth Spirit come into her in a different way than before. It surpassed the wonder for life that made it a source of joy for a girl. Now it included a sense of suffering, of sorrow. The two, sorrow and joy, revolving like yin and yang figures—*taijitu*—the wholeness of the absolute. She saw her mother, her grandmothers, and a long train of women stretching out behind them into the distance: women of all ages, colors, and shapes, many carrying books, tools, bandages, food, water, or children, made strong through adversity. She saw Ursula sitting up, placid, watchful, in a forest, two hungry cubs nursing at her breasts. She felt her own body's confounding changes move in her bones, firing her nerve ends. The smell of pine and scrub grass grounded her.

On the third day, she woke to the soft huff of a coyote. She heard the chickens chattering nervously in the coop behind her. In the half space between the dark and the daylight, one foot still in dream, she sat up.

Luz spoke silently from her heart. "Coyote, welcome here. I thank you for sharing your land, your presence with me."

"My name is Tatiki," said a clear voice. "You met me with my mother, Shakti, at the Congress several years ago." He felt out of body, as in a vision. He was channeling that buried canine. Skah—his *name.*

Luz could not be sure if the sound was real or in her mind. "Yes, I remember you. Why are you here?"

Then, a light wind. "Skah."

Luz considered this. "I miss him."

"He is here," said Tatiki from his kind trickster. "He has a message for you."

She heard a rustle in the grass and moved to the tent door. She pulled the flap aside, letting Sun's light hit her face. Taking a sip of acorn water, she waited.

"Skah asked me to tell you three things," Tatiki said. "The first one is as follows. You have been given powers as a girl, and more will come into you as a woman. You must use these powers wisely on behalf of all living things."

Luz maintained an excited silence, her every sense tuned.

"Second, in particular, your mind has a keen edge, honed by your sharp eyes and ears. But your dear heart is the most reliable pathway to the truth."

"Ho," acknowledged Luz silently, feeling her powers rise within her.

"Third," he said, "there are many ways to get things done, and the shortest distance between two points is not always a straight line. Your single-mindedness can shut out other voices that would help you. *Listen.*"

Luz considered this last point, feeling it was rather a complicated message. She wanted to ask about it.

Again the light wind stirred the grasses. She sensed the redwood behind her. Sun warmed her. "Thank you, Skah and Tatiki," she communicated. "Thank you for this visit."

"We are right here beside you. Wherever you need us, we will be there." Tatiki followed the deer path down the hill to his den. Trickster was overpowering. He told it all to Kali.

"Well, you had your own coming-of-age this year, my dear," she said, licking his face. "I'm very proud of my mate and his powerful trickster. We shall see where that energy leads you."

• • •

Makah came to fetch Luz at dusk, when the light was soft, so as not to blind her when they untied the deerskin. They broke her fast with a simple Three Sisters stew. Now the women of the community came to her, each having considered what she would say in private to Luz after she emerged a woman—what they believed in, what was important to them, and about medicine and magic.

Her Grandma Mandy was the first to come into Luz's tent. The two women sat on cushions as Mandy told Luz how lucky she was to have such a supportive environment for this transition, how wonderful it was to see the old ways returning, how her Great-Grandmother White Owl would be so proud to see her young descendant becoming such a smart and beautiful woman. She told about rituals she remembered from her mother and shared her perspectives of being an Indian woman in America.

"Do you still remember the story about Spider and Beaver-girl?" Mandy asked. "It was the first one you learned by heart. You were only four."

"Of course," said Luz. "Spider was a handsome hunter. The young women liked him because he brought home plenty of food. His Grandmother Woodpecker helped him test the maidens to find out if one was good enough to be his wife. They would build a fire in Spider's lodge. The girl went inside, and Woodpecker would close the smoke flap, making it smoky inside. None of the maidens could stay in the lodge as long as Spider. Then Beaver-girl came. Spider liked her and wanted her to win. He made a weak fire with little smoke. Beaver-girl laughed at him. She used Beaver medicine to make a very smoky fire, so smoky that Spider couldn't stand it. He called out to her, but she did not answer. Maybe she had left or was dead!

"Spider felt his way around the smoky lodge until he ran into Beaver-girl's foot. Again, she laughed at him. He felt bad. A woman was stronger than he was! He kicked Beaver-girl three times very hard. That made her mad, and she grabbed one of Spider's legs and pulled and pulled. She pulled all the legs. When Woodpecker opened the flap, she saw an ugly grandson with a small body and very long legs. But Beaver-girl loved him anyway, and she knew he would still be a powerful hunter. Spider forgave her for treating him so roughly, and they got married."

"Well told!" said Mandy. "I always wondered why you liked that story so much."

"Because Beaver-girl was smarter than Spider but still loved him."

Mandy laughed. "Beaver-girl was also stronger than Spider."

"Spider must have really loved Beaver-girl if he married her after she pulled his legs," said Luz.

"Maybe Spider thought the women would find him less attractive and he would have trouble finding a wife."

"I don't think it's about sympathy," Luz said. "The story's about seeing beyond appearances, seeing someone as who they truly are. And about making up after a fight."

Mandy paused. "That makes me think about the Wounded Knee occupation in 1973. There was this incredible group energy. You remember when Obi-Wan felt a 'great disturbance in the Force?' The connection was like that at Wounded Knee. There was hatred, between the Indians and the Marshals Service, and also among the various Indian factions.

And there was solidarity, for it was a symbolic place to remember the 1890 massacre. I went down there from the rez, from New Town, where your grandfather's clinic was. I had to see it with my own eyes, the feeling was so strong. But everyone could have learned from the story of Spider and Beaver-girl. We have not made as much progress as one might hope. There's still too much animosity. It's now your time to make a difference. And I know you will succeed."

After Mandy, Grandma Toni pulled aside the flap and told a story about her father, Galeno. "When your great-grandfather was eight," she said, "his family came to California from Puebla, Mexico. The family of a boyhood friend, Albert Baez, helped him get established and into medical school. Albert later became a famous physicist. My older brother was born during the war, while my father was the doctor at the internment camp. They named him Baez in gratitude to Albert's family. After the war, they moved to Salinas, where I was born. My dad still practiced medicine, which is how I became a nurse. My brother, who would have been your great-uncle, was killed in '75. That's how your dad got his middle name. I'm telling you this, Luz dear, because it shows how you come from a long line of people who persevered in the face of adversity. It's like that song Albert's daughter Joan used to sing, 'Carry It On.'" Toni sung the lines lightly. Then she said, "Luz, you will encounter challenges you don't think you can handle, but you can. I know how strong you are already, and you will be even stronger as you mature as a woman."

Wanda visited next. "It's great you have come of age, Luz. And I am honored to be here. But I must warn you—about men. They'll ogle you, with thoughts on their minds, sexual thoughts."

Luz squirmed, then sipped her water. "I have started to notice those looks already."

"I don't think much of men in general. I mean, Cody's great, but my dad . . . .He was mean to my mom—they fought a lot—and then he cheated on her. Plus, he was mean in business, always looking out for himself, to heck with anyone else."

"We need both men and women to make things better," Luz said softly.

"He's better now," Wanda continued. "He seems to be changing. I guess I am too. I must have gotten some of his hardness, growing up in that household. Both of us have been connecting with nature these days. He's into cougars, and I'm into redwoods. I guess that's appropriate. But for me, sometimes I just feel peace, you know?"

Luz smiled. "Anna calls that the Earth Spirit."

"You can trust it, Luz. It's totally reliable."

Rosa was delighted to be part of the ritual and the chance to spend time with her Grandmother Toni. "This is so awesome, Luz. I've never been in anything like it. I thought a lot about what I'd say. All these older women are so much wiser than me. So I'll be practical." She offered some sisterly advice, including about ways she'd learned to manage her periods, physically and emotionally, about PMS. "It can definitely not be the best time to make big decisions," Rosa warned, "but you have to maintain. You've got to own it—not let anyone make you feel bad about it. If you stay strong, you can have a big effect. Remember, Greta was fifteen when she started her first protest.You remind me of her."

Luz's heart fluttered as she hugged her. "Thank you, Rosa. You're not only my sister; you're my friend."

Anna and Luz sat together in silence for a long time. Luz could feel Anna's energy inside her, filling her with strength and resolve, with hope. At the end of their time together, Anna said, "Are there questions I can answer?"

"Thank you for taking such good care of me. I have one question."

"Yes, my child?"

"The magic we experience between us, and with the animals and plants, so present at this celebration—why is it not something that is talked about in everyday life?"

"Human societies evolve according to their histories," said Anna. "The culture of the modern world, which has long dominated Turtle Island, favors individual action and control over nature. It relies primarily on empirical means. Magic requires yielding to forces beyond one's control. Love is like that—sublime yet frightening. You will see, my young friend. Meanwhile, do not fear."

After Anna departed, Makah entered with a big bundle. The two sat in silence, for in the weeks of preparation, much had passed between them, and they were in harmony.

"Are you ready to put on the regalia?" Makah said.

"Yes, Mom. Can you help me? All these fringes, and the wraparound skirt . . . I'm not used to them."

Makah unwrapped the colorful, ornamented fabric, a bright beaded necklace, a shiny crow pin, and soft moccasins. Helping Luz with each piece, her heart filled as she told the story of its origin and meaning.

"Do I look okay, Mom? I'm nervous."

"You look magnificent. The ancestors would be so proud."

They pulled the flaps aside for the last time. Shouts went up, and as the drums began and the singing, Luz swirled among her family and friends, including Andrés and Glenda and Sharone, who she was thrilled to see after a long time. Makah watched through moist eyes, her hand warm in Cody's. Luz would remember those days as a harbor, a place of courage, of strength and endurance, where she met herself and found out what she was capable of, knowledge that would prove to be of great use in the years to come.

32

ONE UNEXPECTED BENEFIT FOR WANDA from the negotiations with her father was a friendship with her lawyer, Janet. They were the same age and discovered they both enjoyed hiking in the redwoods. After matters with Clemens were settled, the two women found they were becoming fond of each other, and soon they were dating.

When Clemens heard about it, he was surprised, uncomfortable. If Wanda was happy, at least that was good. He wondered about kids and reminded himself that anything was possible. There was so much change, though—he felt lost again. But she *was* his only child.

Cautious, father and daughter settled into a rhythm of monthly calls, supplemented by the random coffee. They mostly talked about their business lives, but sometimes the conversation lurched into the personal. Clemens would mention his friends' grandchildren. Wanda was intrigued. He seemed . . . softer, less of a Neanderthal.

He told her he was exploring the idea of a crowdfunded, participatory platform to support climate justice. The app would enable the creation of decentralized, autonomous organizations, or DAOs. "DAOs are already being used to organize and manage cryptocurrency companies. These would be a variant, known as a DisCOs—distributed cooperative organizations—which leverage technology to create inclusive, locally grounded, internationally networked cooperatives to coordinate social, environmental, and other commons-oriented work."

"That's a lot of jargon, Dad. What would it actually do?"

"Bring people together who have common goals—like pointing out greenwashing by fossil fuel companies or developing new ways of communicating climate risks at the local level—and enable them to coordinate their actions. It would incorporate trust through transparency. Kind of like 'know your customer' in the finance industry. That's how we'd keep the trolls out. It's still in the idea stage."

"You mention crowdfunding," Wanda said. "Are you thinking of, like, GoFundIt?"

"I talked to their CEO," Clemens replied. "They might be interested in a partnership where I would match the crowdfunding with private equity. They like the synergy of using their distributed-funding mechanism to build a distributed platform. But I need to find a hook that connects to their broader global vision of making a positive difference before they would put the company behind the idea."

"What about mentioning the latest addition to the endangered species list?"

"What do you mean?"

"Humans, Dad."

"What?" Clemens asked. "Now *we're* endangered? It seems a stretch to me."

"The idea's been around since at least 2012, but it doesn't seem to have caught fire."

"Maybe," said Clemens. "Maybe this is our chance. Maybe this will inspire GoFundIt."

• • •

The next time Wanda was in Monterey to meet with Cody, she brought it up.

"My dad's interested in the 'humans as endangered species' idea. He's thinking about building a crowdfunded platform that would allow local climate activists to collaborate across borders."

"Luz is already active with Fridays for Future," Cody said. "And there's also Extinction Rebellion. Both those sites have maps of planned events. Makah has her international networks. Is there a need for another platform?"

"I guess it could be a utility to support organizations like those. A powerful collaboration tool—you know, using AI and VR."

"That's ambitious, but then so is he. He'd need to collaborate with those organizations before launching," Cody said. "And he'd need a diverse set of advisors to keep him tuned into local needs, diversity issues, and youth leadership."

"Those are good thoughts. I'll pass them on."

Cody sat back in his chair. "That would be ironic, wouldn't it? I mean, you and me helping Jack Clemens with a business idea? I need a walk. Want to come?"

Cody and Wanda ambled along the shore, discussing the idea, buffeted by chill gusts from the sea.

He turned to her to make a comment and was caught off balance. She struck him as different, more mature, the way her curls protested the wind from under the edges of her ballcap. He glimpsed a younger, blonder version of Makah. He shook himself out. "How's it going with Janet?" Seven pelicans flew low above the waves, swooping and wheeling like fire.

"All's well, Cody. Thanks."

The pair passed a rocky cove, where a sea otter floated serenely, her pup on her tummy.

His trickster calmed, Cody said, "I guess the question is, do you have the stomach to work with Jack?"

"Right? But, honestly, I think he's trying to reform himself. He's continued to work out since Lieth was killed, even taking a brown belt in aikido. He says he likes the discipline and its emphasis on diffusing conflict. He jokes that it 'empowers clemency.' He's even mentioned 'cleansing his spirit.' Anyway, he's been able to maintain his cred with the VC community while his heart is taking him to another place. It could be an opportunity." She paused. "And he's my only family."

"What will Janet say? She saw the sordid underbelly of Peterman-Clemens."

"It's a new idea, but she's an adventurer." She stretched languidly. "Look, I want you to know how much I appreciate all you and Makah have done for me. I'm not leaving Kelp Ecology anytime soon. Just thinking things over."

"I know you'll keep me posted. I'm not opposed to the idea—actually, Makah and Luz might want to get involved. We'll work it out."

They stood in the wind of Monterey Bay. The world seemed open with hope, with the possibility that people could find their ways without stepping on each other or trampling the planet. The two colleagues sensed it, the energy strong between them.

• • •

Jack Clemens pursued his idea of a trusted, bottom-up, change support app. He found a 2020 report from the Organization for Economic Cooperation and Development that documented three hundred experiments in facilitated community deliberation to produce solutions in urban planning, zoning laws, health and environmental policy, and infrastructure priorities. Clemens put his own money in, and GoFundIt hosted a campaign with its brand behind it, a departure from its usual business model. Enough money came in to hire a couple of software engineers, recruit some community climate advisors, and pay Wanda to manage the stand-up. The company, Network Action, adopted the slogan, "See Beyond the Horizon."

The plan had gelled at a dinner meeting at Cody and Makah's house. Wanda, by now a familiar face in the household, arrived with her father. It was the first time Cody had seen Jack in person since leaving Opti-Drip.

Cody saw a different Clemens than he'd known years before. He appeared chastened, more mature, more careful. He'd heard that Clemens was resisting self-indulgent, tech bro politics, promoting something he called "rightsizing." The idea was that the wealthy would voluntarily limit their assets to $50 million and put the rest into arms-length, community-managed charitable organizations vetted for transparency and efficiency. Apparently, he had convinced the manager at the Rosewood bar to give rightsizers a free drink if they went public with their commitment. So far, there were only three of them, but he continued to push the idea. It seemed to Cody that Wanda was on to something about her father's changes of heart.

The get-together began in the backyard, sipping good California wine under the redwood. Clemens seated himself in a comfortable chair and raised his glass. "Cody, I bring you greetings from an old friend. She said to send you her love, actually."

Cody eyed Clemens, who wore an impish grin. Wanda seemed in the dark as well. "Love is always welcome in this house, Jack. Who is this mystery woman?"

"Did I say it was a woman? No, this female was of the feline persuasion. Tara. My source implied you'd know who I meant."

Cody and Makah exchanged glances. "That was Cody's Burmese cat," Makah said. "She died years ago. Cody, er, *we* were both so fond of her. A coyote killed her after they moved down here from San Jose."

Luz piped up. "Remember when the goldfinch told me Tara had gotten an upgrade? And that she might be working on climate?"

Clemens was intrigued. "I don't know about any goldfinches, but if that so-called upgrade involved a cougar, then I guess you could say she's working on climate."

"Wait, what?" Wanda asked. "What are you talking about?"

As Clemens unrolled the tale of his encounter with Tania and her involvement in the Lieth murder, his listeners were astonished that this no-nonsense capitalist was talking to animals, curious that Tara's spirit had continued as a huntress, and hopeful that his apparent changes boded well for others of his kind.

"I'm surrounded by people who talk to animals," said Cody. "Or in Wanda's case, plants—namely redwoods. Sometimes my science mind blocks me from the connection that runs in my blood. Maybe in all people's blood."

Clemens peered at Wanda. "Redwoods?"

"Cougars?" she kidded.

The dinner conversation ended up sketching out the transition for Wanda from Kelp Ecology to Network Action over the following three months.

Wanda's move engaged the interest of Makah and Luz in the new platform—Makah for her Indigenous network and Luz with her continued involvement in the school strikes. Makah used the new tool to power a several-month conversation to synchronize local community climate actions across borders. The tool's features, including a low-bandwidth wiki, also helped communities of action develop standards of conduct for discussions and decisions, reducing acrimony around disagreements. In California, it promoted conversations about the Elephant Code ballot initiative. Built-in accountability and transparency, tweaked to local preferences, enhanced trust. The software complemented in-person connections, enabling trust to be built the old-fashioned way—relying on someone and having them come through for you.

33

IN THE MID-2020s, a series of strong tremors occurred along the San Andreas Fault. The shocks reminded seismologists of the months before the 1989 Loma Prieta quake. They warned that a larger quake might be coming. The locked fault northwest of San Juan heightened concern, for when one slips, it can release tremendous energy in a short time.

"These shakes are making me nervous," Cody told Makah one late fall day. "Let's make sure things are tied down and our emergency supplies are up to date."

"Do you think it's different this time?" But she already believed it.

"The animals seem restless," he said. "Luz says the chickens are off their feed. It seems different, somehow."

Meanwhile, the California drought that began in the early '20s persisted. The American West was drier than it had been in one thousand years. Even the most senior water rights holders, longtime California farm families and companies, were suffering mandated cuts of over 80 percent. The attitude in the Central Valley, which produced 8 percent of US farm output on 1 percent of total farmland, was angry, restless. A tractor caravan disrupted Sacramento in July, driving by the state capitol building, blasting air horns and creating a rowdy vibe. Climate activists harassed the edges of the parade with sarcastic street theater.

The governor met with a delegation. It was not a successful meeting. There was talk of a blockade.

Although the tone was tense, large protest events in Sacramento had devolved into nonviolent set pieces since the armed occupation led by the Jefferson Militia a few years earlier. The militia's attack on the capital escalated when antifa and eco-militants took them on using guerrilla tactics. Washington, watching the state police and the National Guard failing to restore order and instead exacerbating the situation, sensed things might have gone too far in the rebellion camp. Fearing a loss of governmental legitimacy, economic chaos, and civil war, the president, with rare bipartisan support, ordered in regular army and Special Forces units. Two dozen people died; hospitals treated hundreds for gunshot wounds and chemical poisoning. After that, things cooled off all around.

The real heat did not abate. For the past three summers, consecutive weeks of temperatures over 110 afflicted the Central Valley, with some days hitting 119, breaking the previous high of 115. Demand for air conditioning caused brownouts. During fire season, safety dictated power cuts on windy days to avoid downed lines and spark-caused fires. Emergency generators added to the heat, noise, and reduced air quality.

By early December, there was a chill in the morning air. One Saturday morning, Luz and Makah were in the house reading while Makah finished her coffee. Luz was reading Andrew Krivak's *The Bear*, about a girl who develops a friendship with a bear after her father dies. Makah was rereading a ten-year-old report by her colleague Will Steffen—"Trajectories of the Earth System in the Anthropocene"—which observed that "the rapid trajectory of the climate system over the past half-century along with technological lock-in and socioeconomic inertia in human systems commit the climate system to conditions beyond the envelope of past interglacial conditions." Heading for hell in a handbasket, irrecoverable for millennia.

A few minutes after eight, Luz was startled to spy her friend Tatiki through the glass doors leading into the garden. He appeared to be in distress, lying on the ground twitching and looking very sorry for himself.

"Mom! It's the coyote I met during my fast. He's hurt." Luz rose to go outside.

"Wait, honey. He might have rabies. That can make them unpredictable." She picked up a stout walking stick from their hiking stash. "Let's go see."

Luz opened the glass carefully and spoke to the animal. "Tatiki, dear Tatiki, are you okay?"

Tatiki whimpered, continuing to quiver. The two women emerged from the house and stood in the yard, a few feet from the animal, Makah trying to emanate calm while maintaining a firm grip on her cudgel.

Suddenly, Tatiki leaped to his feet and trotted off nonchalantly, glancing backward with a laughing bark. They watched him descend into the valley as if nothing had happened. At that moment, 8:17 am Pacific Daylight Time, a magnitude 7.5 earthquake raced along the San Andreas Fault at seven thousand miles per hour. Near the epicenter, San Juan Bautista, buildings pancaked, gas and water mains broke, and roads fell into the seam opened up along the fault. Very strong shaking and significant damage occurred in the Salinas Valley, Silicon Valley, San Francisco, San Jose, Oakland, and Berkeley, with strong shakes causing lesser damage in Napa Valley, Sacramento, Santa Cruz, and Monterey. Makah and Luz turned toward the house just in time to watch through the window as the heavy, new kitchen chandelier swayed and ripped from the ceiling, crashing upon the place they had been sitting just minutes before.

Staggered by the unimagined shift in their circumstances, they waited outside as aftershocks rolled through, dislodging debris hanging from the ceiling inside.

Makah hugged Luz. "Many thanks to your friend, Tatiki, for saving us from injury."

"It was Skah, too—*your* old friend. His spirit." *Whenever you need us, we will be there.*

"I hope someone's looking out for Cody!"

Across the region, crumbling buildings killed those inside them. Fallen electric lines and broken natural gas pipes started fires. A strong aftershock took out two critical electrical substations, causing automated-control software to respond unexpectedly and shut down the grid throughout the Bay Area. No cell service. Only the billions of dollars in government and private investments to reinforce buildings and increase resilience after Loma Prieta kept the damage from being much worse.

Emergency crews were paralyzed, unable to communicate or move. The FAA ordered a nationwide ground stop. Stock exchanges halted trading. The internet slowed to a crawl. Officials along the coast did their best to get people off the beach in anticipation of a tsunami.

Cody was driving home from an overnight visit with his parents. Blake's health was declining, and Toni was having difficulty caring for him. He'd left San Jose early that morning. Traffic was light. He had just crossed the Salinas River when the first shock hit. Terrified, Cody watched as, in his rearview mirror, the southbound span he'd just crossed buckled into the creek. A slow-moving truck full of chickens behind him hit a gash in the highway and blew out its front tires. Many factory chickens were liberated, only to learn the hard way about the local coyotes. The driver stepped out, apparently uninjured.

Spotting only brake lights ahead, Cody pulled off the highway at the next exit and parked in a Walmart lot. Chaos. A section of the building had collapsed. What was happening with Makah and Luz? No bars on his phone. His text to Makah failed. A dozen people sat or lay injured on the pavement. Cries came from the rubble. People were pulling frantically at the concrete and rebar. He was half a mile in from the beach and ten miles from home. He should help. No. Gotta go home. Time to hoof it. Grabbing his knapsack and water, he took off, keeping his distance from shore. Using back streets, he worked his way around the perimeter of the eerily calm Monterey airport and made it home just after noon.

Luz ran toward him. "Dad! Yay!" She grabbed him, starting to cry.

"She's been a brave young woman," Makah said. "I'm proud of her. Are you okay? How did you get here?"

"I'm fine. I walked. The roads are jammed. I'm so glad you were outside when it happened."

"Luz can tell you about that. It was a miracle."

The house seemed safe enough for the moment—the "quake-proof" retrofit during the remodel a prudent investment. Cody found a hard hat left from the construction and ventured inside. He came out with their go bag and camping equipment. "It's a mess, especially the kitchen. Major cleanup ahead. But there's no reason to leave, I don't think. There's nowhere to go, anyway. I think we just camp out for a few days."

They connected with the neighbors and helped where they could. In three days, they began tackling the mess inside the house, listening to sirens and hustling outdoors during the aftershocks, which would continue to cause damage in the region for two years.

• • •

Fifteen minutes after the quake, a twenty-foot wall of tsunami hit the coast, destroying coastal marine habitat and flooding the lower level of the aquarium, the damage exacerbated by a wash of petroleum and chemicals from compromised storage tanks near the estuary. Fires destroyed a fifth of California's remaining forests. The state burned like an inferno until six days of early rain put out the fires. Like many areas, Monterey remained isolated, although power and most water were back after two weeks. Schools and many businesses were closed.

It was as if the United States suffered a massive stroke. California offline meant that nothing worked right nationally or internationally.

There were shortages of critical materials, food rotted in the Central Valley, the seafood industry was disrupted, the internet slow and unpredictable. Markets dropped 20 percent. In California, over four thousand people died, with tens of thousands more suffering from interrupted health services.

In the aftermath of the quake, Blake had a heart attack that proved fatal in the absence of medical help. Andrés, hiking in the woods with friends near Santa Cruz, survived a fire by following an intrepid crow who led him and some friends on a narrow escape route. He was recovering from burns with his mother and stepfather in Fremont.

The devastation exacerbated the effects of extreme weather. Beyond the stifling drought and scorching temperatures, the landscape itself was transformed. Forests became stands of burned matchsticks. Chunks of coast fell into the sea. Mudslides closed roads and buried structures. Stream beds became dry canyons, the life along their banks withering away, the animals desperate for habitat. Fish stocks shrunk in the disturbed coastal waters. Orchards withered. High prices brought hunger. The "Trajectories" paper Makah had been reading predicted larger effects—"In some terrestrial cases, such as widespread wildfires, there could be a pulse of carbon to the atmosphere, which if large enough, could influence the trajectory of the Earth System."

The post-quake fires added to the feeling that the planet was out of control, on a runaway path to Hothouse Earth—the catastrophic, self-reinforcing overheating that would take thousands of years to recover from, resulting in worldwide drought, flooding, refugees, and climate conflict.

• • •

A week after the quake, Cody, Makah, and Luz sat with neighbors around a makeshift barbecue pit, smoking various meats folks had stored in their freezers before the power went out. "Now we will see what happens,"

Cody said. "Whether people realize how we're all in this together, humans with each other, and with nature too. We can do more together here, I know."

"Luz told me how that coyote called you out of the house, Makah," said one neighbor. "I had read that dogs sometimes get restless before an earthquake, so I guess it's not too amazing, but you guys were so lucky. It makes me think about animals with more respect."

"The Earth herself has shifted, releasing a century of geologic tension," said Makah, studying the pit, its smoldering embers. "Maybe this will serve as the final wake-up call."

"At a minimum," said Cody, "it should be favorable for the Elephant Code ballot initiative this November."

⬩ ⬩ ⬩

As Thanksgiving approached, Cody walked the shoreline. The trail had crumbled in places, and there was debris on the beaches and in the surf. Yet the ocean seemed not to be paying attention. Sea otters still played in the powerful waves. Kelp fronds floated lazily in the spume. Cody sat on the rocks and pondered the aftermath, the way it had affected Luz and Makah. His wife seemed resolute, centered, focused. "This all reminds me how fragile our way of living is. I'm thrown back to more primitive times, the hardscrabble lives of my ancestors on the reservation and before. We got through that, and we'll get through this," she had told Cody.

The usually hopeful Luz was less sanguine. She was jumpy, fearful. When an aftershock came, she would run outside and curl up in a ball. She'd started sleeping outdoors in the tent she'd used for her Flower Dance. Cody and Makah tried to reassure her, hoping that time would heal the trauma. They traded stories and suggestions with other parents and drew on post-trauma healing techniques—tapping, clearing dark energies.

On the rocky shore, Cody thought he heard voices in the crashing surf. He found it unnerving. One particular spot drew him, where a brilliant yellow sea lichen colony hugged a rock, bathed in intermittent surf. As he clambered over the wet rocks, it seemed the voices became more intelligible. Suddenly, he lost his footing.

He sprawled into the snarling sea, into a deep and turbulent hole, where swells knocked him against the sharp rocks, the breakers crashing upon him like rafts of icy slush. Sea water choked him. He flailed, his boots pulling him down. A heavy piece of driftwood floated before him between swells, and he grabbed it, pulling himself up enough to get purchase on the bank. Another wave drenched him, sucking him back, his head grazing the yellow rock. He grabbed its lichen-crusted surface and pulled himself out and lay spent on the riprap. In his painful daze he imagined he heard the rock say, "Be careful, man. We need you."

Cody lay on the rock until he caught his breath. He got up—nothing broken!—and shook it off. He was freezing, his mind foggy. *Scrotumtightening—you got that right, Jimmy.* He grimaced. As he limped home, he wondered about the voice from the rock. It was probably shock. Makah was upset enough about the fall that he resisted telling her about the voice. Instead, returning in a few days, still off balance, he sat beside the rock and asked, gently, "All right. What is it you need me for?"

"Good question," said the voice, which was now distinct and seemed to be coming from the lichen. "When we said, 'Be careful, man,' we did not mean you specifically, nor men in general. You humans are not 'a little lower than the angels, crowned with glory, with dominion over the fowls of the air and the fish of the sea and every creeping thing.' That story is over. You may be the crown of creation, but you've backed yourself into a corner."

Cody felt the way he had on acid.

The voice continued. "We lichens believe that life on Earth is at a beautiful crescendo. So, why should you humans kill it off? You understand that, which is why we're asking you, a descendant of Buffalo Bill

Cody, to step back from the day-to-day and embody a longer view. You'll be drawn into conflicts where everyone is in a frenzy. Help them take a breath. Help them see the big picture—our every action, our every thought, reverberates through the Cosmos. What each of us does, how each of us lives, matters."

At those words, Cody was blown apart by a realization of how well and deeply he loved the world—the fluff of the chickens as a boy, the sunsets from Skyline Drive when he was at Stanford, the damp earth smell of Makah's gardens, the cries of gulls in the wet sea air, Luz's playful chatter and enchanting smile, his accomplished twins. It wasn't about "saving" the planet—it was about living. Like the lichen, in partnership and harmony. He'd always tried to make that happen in his work and marriage. Now a greater force called his heart to partner with his head and lead life lightly, with serious intention.

Wave spume bubbled over the rocks like champagne. "Que bueno," Cody said, spontaneously recalling a song his mother loved, sung by her favorite musician El Potrillo, whose open heart let him love a woman who loved another man. Cody'd always wondered why she'd loved that song, for her faithfulness to Blake had been unswerving. But perhaps there was something else she had always loved even more than her dear husband, some energy of sensuality that enlivened her, enriched her life, in ways that he and his father didn't see. He remembered her working as a nurse-midwife before she retired, how she knew things from her curandera mother, who grew herbs in her window and made them into a salve that helped stop bleeding when Cody cut himself as a boy, and how she would talk quietly with the chickens and how they loved her. That crazy word—*ecosexuality*— "thinking of nature as lover." The wordless connection, resonating in his bones.

"Que bueno," he repeated. The sea, its infinite expanse, its unchanging changeability, its deep capacity for nurturing life. He shivered and wondered about Buffalo Bill's distant gaze in the photo with the two chiefs.

His ancestor had served as an Indian scout for the cavalry, seen firsthand the destruction of the old ways, yet worked intimately with animals in his show. Was the old showman's mind's eye lost in the origins of man's natural connections?

PART FIVE

34

THAT EARTHQUAKE JOGGED MY MEMORY of ancient times, stretching back to the early days of our dear Grandmother, back when the first life forms were emerging. Not my personal memory, of course, but through the Society, there's reachback into forever.

As life became more diverse and intricate, the beauty of creation was made manifest. Humans were the natural next step. Bright and inquisitive, you love beauty and are blessed with empathetic spirits. That's why I wonder sometimes how your species got so crosswise with the rest of creation. Relations used to be so much better. As the chronicles relate—

Not so very long ago,
Animals and people were closer.
The wild things would approach
In peace and curiosity. Dancing!
Some say the animals
Would come into the foyer,
Pose for portraits. We have seen them,
Lion and lamb, and heard
Their stories in fables.

Images of such meetings can be found on shards of ancient stoneware, sold until recently only in secret, the faded glaze of pots and friezes confirming a softer boundary, a common tongue. Your Saint Francis lived that way. Moreover—

Women were particularly adept
Connectors, life's flowing energies
Native, the protection of life alive
Deep within, the old spirits made present
In moonlight communion.
Their grace aligned with the creatures' own
Magnificence, exuberance in life,
Uncontainable in any frame,
The curve of the swan's wing
Like a mournful lyre.

Many are the stories of our connections with you, in children's books and creation stories from people around the world, a handful of which I have already related. Maybe these stories aren't scientifically accurate—you may call them *myths*—but they say something about how you once thought of us planimals.

So it happened that, when human beings first appeared on Earth, as the latest and most complex evolutionary introduction to the natural world, they lived intimately with plants and other animals of every description, from the tiniest one-celled Diatoms to the greatest Whales. Some call that era the Old Times, when every species played its part in the symphony of life. Those Diatoms produced up to half of the planet's oxygen, while Whales' gigantic bodies fed hundreds of other species.

At some point, the story goes, the creatures of the Earth convened in a Great Powwow. Some details are lost in the mists of time, but it is possible to piece it together by studying the creation myths of human cultures and, equally, by listening to the voices of all creation. For the symphony continues, varying its themes, becoming more complex, the mix of instruments changing. Life on Earth remains an amazing, exquisite dance.

By the time of the Great Powwow, it had become evident that humans were unlike any animal seen before. Human ingenuity and skill had the potential to outstrip the capabilities of even the cleverest vertebrates, the most well-protected insects, the most resilient lichen. As the human population organized itself into clans and tribes and villages, concentrating its effects, some creatures became concerned that things could get out of balance.

Mastodon, a ten-foot tall, eleven-ton precursor of the Woolly Mammoth and today's Elephants, was known to be the wisest creature on the planet. She was standing with her mate in the forest, pleasantly digesting the fruits of her recent browsing, when she felt the vibration of the footsteps of a large and surprising delegation approaching from across the savannah. For one thing, Cave Lion and Giant Deer led the motley parade, two species not usually on friendly terms. Insects and birds, reptiles and amphibians, worms and bacteria and fungi—dozens of species—joined them. The plants of the forest and the grasses of the veld, connected through a variety of networks, stood as witness. A man and a woman were there too.

"To what do I owe the honor of this great visit from such an improbable cross section of creation?" Mastodon raised her trunk to its full height while casting a wary eye at Lion.

Lion spoke. "We seek your wisdom as to the future of our relations with our human brothers and sisters. We are afraid of their power and where it will take our Grandmother in the times ahead."

"Let us give thanks to our Grandmother Earth and to her lover the Sun, and to all of our planimal sisters and brothers who make each of our lives here possible." Mastodon made a regal and surprisingly graceful bow. "It is you who are the wise ones for bringing this question forward. Indeed, I share your concern." She nudged her mate, who was staring sternly at Lion. "But surely you have already discussed this with our human siblings, for otherwise they wouldn't be here with you. Thank you for trusting the power of connection." She turned to the humans. "Dear friends, welcome here. You have heard the concerns of the rest of creation. What say you to this?"

Woman spoke first. "For many generations, we have lived in harmony with our sibling creatures, taking only what we need to feed our families and observing our rituals that honor them. We speak with them frequently, and they teach us the ways of the world. We wish to continue to live in harmony."

Man then spoke. "We are sad that our siblings are worried about our ways. We do not understand why they feel this way. We are merely trying to live our lives. The separation they are creating between us and them makes us feel angry and insulted. It's like we are being driven from the Garden." He glanced briefly at Lion and Deer. "That is why we are glad to have this Powwow with you."

Mastodon addressed Deer. "When I saw you walking peacefully next to Lion, I thought, I am dreaming? Am I in Paradise? Do you have anything to add?"

Seven feet at the withers, with magnificent, moose-like antlers, Deer towered over even the majestic Lion. "We are sorry that some of our sister and brother humans feel rejected. We appreciate their rituals and honor the many beautiful times we have spent with them. Speaking as a prey animal, I can say that being killed by a human is no worse or better than being killed by a Lion." She smiled ironically at her toothy companion, who flexed his claws discreetly. "But there is one difference: Humans' brains are too big for their own good. And for ours."

"Tell me more," Mastodon said, deftly swatting a Fly with her excellent tail and hip-bumping her mate—who rumbled quietly, "Be serious."

"They are just too damn smart!" came a voice from on high. "I should know!"

Some animals cowered at the powerful sound, but Mastodon flicked her trunk reassuringly. "Leave it to you, Roc, to tell it like it is!"

The noble bird laughed. "I have considerable ability to see into the future, where I will be transformed by human myth into a great Eagle. But now, I am simply a very large Crow." She jumped down to the ground with a mighty thump, fully eight feet high and brilliant white. "Like humans, I am intelligent and imaginative. Why, if you gave me writing and thumbs, well, y'all look out!" She paused. "But seriously, it's the passing on of knowledge from generation to generation through language and symbol, and then building on it. That is the breakaway innovation that humans, for the moment, have a monopoly on. This is why we need them to agree to curb their appetites, just slow it down a bit, this progress thing." Roc burped loudly. "Sorry! I just ate the most delicious Rabbit carcass, but it *was* a little ripe."

Tittering scattered through the gathering, and then, silent anticipation.

"All right, look," Mastodon said. "No one's in charge here except our Grandmother. You have recognized that, on a good day, I can speak for her. What She would say is that Roc is right. So let me ask you, dear humans, do you agree to curb your appetites, to slow down the pace of progress so that the rest of us can adapt, and we can all live together in relative harmony?"

The two humans considered each other. He nodded to her, and she spoke. "We have learned a great deal at this Powwow, and we thank all of our siblings for including us. It is a miracle to be standing unafraid among such fierce predators as Lion and Wolf. We humans may be smart, but some of you are so much bigger and stronger and faster than we are that we have had to band together to protect ourselves. We will continue to push back against the wild, for our own survival."

Man said, "Thank you all for this meeting. We will take this question back to our people. Your arguments for restraint and moderation are compelling, and we will make them clearly. We will tell this story. It will go down through the ages and be adapted and interpreted and changed according to culture and circumstance. Some of us will heed your request through our actions and others will model it in the societies we build. Hopefully, that will be enough. However, humans are a very independent lot, and we are not able to provide any guarantees."

The two-leggeds bowed low to the multitude, and they went out of that land, returning unto their dwelling places, where these envoys transmitted Mastodon's request, and history proceeded as they had foretold, with some walking in the way of the Spirit, and the world itself moving on, in the ways it has, until today.

But wait, I notice that Ursula has been listening to my story. Do you have anything to say, my dear?

Thank you, Koro. In addition to noting that the delegation included a beautiful Cave Bear, I have a philosophical observation. There are many theories about why humans are separated from nature and from each other. Philosophers, social scientists, and religious figures all have their opinions. Perhaps it was "progress" that allowed humans to isolate themselves—whether by moving the livestock out of the house and into a barn or by being able to kill at increasing distances and scales—and so the connections, the sympathies, were weakened but for a few favored pets.

However, such distancing is not irreversible. There is the "old language" with which humans could once speak directly to other animals. Koro knows humans who speak passable Crow. Some of you probably speak, or whisper, Horse, Cat, or Dog. These spoken languages are beautiful. When sister Kimmerer was young, a Cheyenne elder, Bill Tall Bull, told her that the plants and animals "love to hear the old language—it's true." Putting his fingers to his lips, he said, "But you don't have to speak it here. If you speak it here," he touched his heart, "they will hear you." Maybe some people will try it—it takes time, like learning any language—but it will help.

You have such a way with words, my dear. May our human relatives heed your call and help us all begin the healing in honor of our beautiful Grandmother.

35

ONE MORNING IN JANUARY, having fed and thanked the chickens, Luz came upon the dear goldfinch who foreshadowed Skah's reincarnation. He lay peacefully under the redwood. She felt a painful nostalgia, another loss amid the general devastation, compounding the feeling of absence that hit her in waves when she thought of Anna, whom she'd not seen since the earthquake. She sat down under the tree beside the little bird, talking to it softly, thanking it, wishing it a safe flight into Sun.

Makah watched from the window. She had learned to leave Luz alone in such moments. She had never told Luz of her own conversation with the goldfinch. Now she regretted that. Makah felt blocked, missing being there for Goldfinch.

Feeling the bird's deep connection to her brother, Luz decided to bury the goldfinch beside Chanson. As she turned the soil over, a familiar affection washed over her. Skah. The coyotes were barking. Luz caught the vibe. She tuned into the coyote energy, and Skah's presence increased, opening her heart in her desolation. *Bring together the good parts of the old and the new ways. Discard what no longer serves.* Skah's voice came to her from within, from a resonance in her consciousness, the Skah–Tatiki spirit merged with her own, embedded and available forever. She shivered, wondering. Destruction? Rebuilding?

Imagination. Adaptation. Together.

Amid this all—Luz mourning, Makah fretting, Tatiki and Kali hunting the hillside below the house, and the favored Princess Lay-a taking a dust bath—a wise crow offered three sonorous caws.

Luz looked up. "Thank you, Koro." She returned to the house, where Makah clattered pots in the kitchen, generating a fog of worldly busy-ness, a jarring racket. "Mom! I need to visit Anna. Dad can get the bikes ready. You can ask Suzanne if she'll watch the chickens." She headed for her room.

"Just a minute," said Makah, her tone sharp. "You're getting too big for your boots, young lady. I have a relationship with Goldfinch too. He came to me when your dad and I were on retreat. He has helped me release my inner light. And Chanson's site is sacred to me. You could have asked me to join you. Sometimes your willful single-mindedness gets to be too much."

Luz recalled Skah's words to her during her fast. Reluctantly, she could see her mother's point. But something inside protested. "Mom. Enough. He was my brother. Anyway, I'm growing up. You say the goldfinch released your inner light. Well, maybe in some areas, but I'm not seeing it." She grabbed her book bag and stomped out

Makah considered her options. Grounding her made little sense amid the chaos. She remembered her own fights with her mother. Just give her some space. She took some kinnikinnick from its carved box. Outside, she knelt beside the new grave and placed the herbs on it. Standing, she twirled in a slow circle, her right index finger in the air, her eyes closed. She shook off the conflict.

When she told Cody about the exchange, he simply said, "Congratulations for taking a deep breath. Storms rage inside Luz, and inside you. You saw the big picture on this one, and I admire you for that. Let's see how we can make this expedition a successful and fun adventure." He hustled out to get the bikes ready.

Early the next day, the threesome made the twenty-mile trek over the hills to Anna's, their bikes packed with essentials still scarce in Salinas since the quake, plus some fresh rockfish in an ice pack. The way was rough, narrow, but open, with debris piled up on the sides. They could smell the evidence of earlier sewer breaks between Salinas and the Marina treatment plant. The trip took three hours.

Parts of Anna's house—closer to the epicenter—had collapsed, destroying some treasured memories, but she had intermittent water and power. The remaining structure was unsafe, and the roof leaked. She was living outdoors most of the time. It would be months before anything but the most basic repairs would be possible. There was no lumber to be had.

Their arrival heartened Anna. In the backyard, they traded stories of the past months' trials. Makah mentioned Luz's insistence that they make the trip. They shared smoke medicine. Cody sautéed the fish with garden garlic and zucchini. Anna resurrected a sauvignon blanc she'd stashed for a special occasion.

"The forced isolation reminds me of the Covid days," Anna said. "It's a meditation for me, so I don't really mind. I'd rather stay here than go somewhere else and abandon all the work I've done in the garden over the years. The continuation of that life is meaningful to me."

"I'm happy that my classes are mostly back in person," said Luz. "I get to see my friends, at least until I start high school this fall. My friend Glenda's family is doing okay, though her father's not working right now."

"The economy will take time to come back," said Cody.

"It can't," Anna said. "Not in the same way."

Luz scratched her head. Skah—*discarding what no longer serves.*

Makah swept the air with her arm. "As Cody knows, I agree. We have to live differently, with greater reliance on local resources. We're lucky to be here."

Anna nodded. "Yes. And others will come. We're receiving refugees from San Juan and even the Central Valley."

"We are too," Cody said. "It's putting pressure on fragile infrastructure. There's increasing crime, primarily theft."

"But many people are being generous," said Anna. "In some places, the eco-people and the separatists are talking to each other. It seems more people are hearing—and heeding—the wake-up."

The night was cool, and the foursome fell asleep to the calls of owls and coyotes. As the parents left the next morning, Cody told Luz he'd be back to get her in a few days. "Be well and be peaceful, my young one," he said, giving her a one-arm hug. "We need you harmonious in the turnaround."

• • •

She and Anna made tea and warmed tortillas. They sat in the sunshine. "So, you were insistent about coming. Your mother seemed unsettled when she spoke of it. What's up?"

The pair gazed admiringly at an imposing crow sitting comfortably on a scarecrow in Anna's neighbor's garden as Luz said, "I'm just afraid we're not moving fast enough to change the way we live. People here seem to understand it's a real emergency. But it took an earthquake to make that happen."

"Wait," said Anna. "That doesn't make sense. Why would that upset Makah? I mean, more than we all are?"

Luz flushed. "You're right. We had a fight about a dead goldfinch, and I felt like I needed to see you. I miss you."

"I've missed you too, and I'm sorry to hear about your fight with Makah. It sounds like you are becoming a normal teenager. These things usually work themselves out over time, so maybe try not to take it too much to heart." She regarded the scarecrow. "Luz, is that Koro, who we saw at the last congress? It looks like her, but I can't be sure."

Luz smiled. "Why don't you ask her?"

At that moment, Anna's neighbor came out of his house waving a rake at the crow.

"¡Largarse! ¡Vete!" the man hollered. "The cries—graznidos—I'm sick of them."

The saucy crow had hopped over the fence and perched on Anna's apple tree.

"We like crows, Señor Alvarez," said Anna. "This is my goddaughter, Luz, who is visiting."

"Luz?" he said. "When I look at you, I *feel* light. A good name for this ahijada."

"Gracias, Señor Alvarez," said Luz.

"Hablas español, chica?"

"Bastante bien, Señor."

"Que bueno. Disfruta el dia, amigas," he replied, going back into his house.

"What's a *goddaughter*?" asked Luz.

"It means that I am partly responsible for your moral and spiritual development, my love. Do you like the word?"

"Are you my godmother?"

"If you like, yes."

"I like that a lot, Anna."

• • •

A FEMA helicopter passed rapidly overhead at low elevation, the staccato din of its engines cutting the morning air.

Then Luz turned to me. "Well? What is it, Koro? I sense you have something on your mind. Tell us." I froze. The Society warns against direct public conversations with humans in their own language. Only *in extremis* should a planimal pierce the veil, though I admit I've been sloppy at times. Yet now, our dear Luz had asked me directly. I cleared my throat.

"I'm here to say that we planimals have adopted a fresh approach to working with humans. Things are getting desperate. You both know what we're already doing—Anna, your connection to Black Bears through Ursula's son, and Luz's to Coyotes through Tatiki, and even Jack Clemens's to Cougars through Tania. We're becoming more systematic, adopting specific people, hoping some of our better traits will shine through, or at least that humans will be more able to see the world through planimal eyes. But even more is needed."

"The Crow have long been allies of my people," Luz said. "We're grateful for the partnership with all planimals. Koro, you encourage me to be insistent, clear, and caring in my communications." She looked down. "Except for the other day with Mom."

"This is great news," broke in Anna. "We so welcome this shift among the planimals. I hope we humans can be worthy of it. But may I ask a question? The other day—"

"Wait. I wasn't finished." I hopped to a lower branch. "I'm here to ask you to help me organize a meeting between planimals and humans to discuss how we can work together. It will be one of the first such meetings on the planet."

"Wow," said Luz. "That's a big deal. Of course we'd like to help."

Anna nodded. "What can we do?"

"We need a site, one that's easier for people to get to than where we held the Congresses. What about that circle of rocks, about five miles east of here, as we Crows fly?"

"The Rockpile," said Anna. "That's what they call it around here. It's an abandoned Indian ceremonial site. An Ohlone elder once told me it had been desecrated by a mining company. It's accessible enough, I suppose, but it might require some healing."

I nodded. "Perhaps you could attend to that. We'll take care of the rest. We hope there will be maybe twenty people. You will have connections to some."

"We can do that, can't we, Luz?" Anna asked. "And now for my question. I was walking to get food in Salinas and a man was sitting beside the road with vegetables for sale. As I walked by, he looked hard at me and rubbed his left ear, his eyes expectant. Your mentioning Ursula reminded me of that habit of hers. I'm wondering—"

I was starting to get antsy. "If he knows her? Yes, that's Modesto Corazón. He's your neighbor's nephew, and he was present with a friend at the first and second Congresses. You can talk to him about anything—including the upcoming meeting. His totem animal is a Western Rattlesnake, like Snave, if you remember her. But enough—I should move on."

As I left, I remembered one more thing and turned around. "Luz, you remember the shawoman, with the bow and arrow. She will come to you in dreams. She will help you in your work, but only if you protect her. Thank you for what you're doing and for what you will do."

"Wait," Luz said. "Before you go. Have *you* adopted anyone?"

"That—is a secret." And into the west I flew.

36

AFTER I CONFERRED WITH ANNA AND LUZ, we planimals set to work organizing the meeting with the humans. It was a hazardous undertaking, but as Scree observed, "We've got to do something—the ocean's getting way too hot."

We chose the summer solstice as the date and watched as Anna, Luz, and Modesto, with the blessing of Ohlone leaders, worked many spring weekends to heal the Rockpile from its depredations and prepare it for our ceremony. They cleaned up discarded machine parts and beer cans, trimmed away the Poison Oak that had invaded, burned smoke medicine and sage, and meditated and chanted. In the end they realized that the meeting with the planimals—assuming it went well—would itself be part of the healing.

Our idea was to invite all the human observers from the Congresses. If they brought their friends and families, it could be enough for a start. They might have ideas about how to grow the movement. We connected with the five other observers from the first Congress—Modesto's pal Juan and the four others—folks who held more mainstream views about human–planimal relationships but still cared deeply about "nature" and "God's creation." Then we created "coincidences" to help our guests answer our call, physical events that freed up their time and shifts in their virtual worlds—like on their GPS navigation—courtesy of the virtual, silicon-based cousins of Worm and Virus.

On the morning of the solstice, we assembled and waited at the Rockpile. Modesto and Juan showed up with a couple of their *compañeros*, followed by Luz, Makah, Cody, and Anna—who was taking advantage of one of Cody's stout walking sticks to get around, feeling rather stiff after moving rocks several weekends in a row. Soon after that, a pair of Pheasant-hunting brothers from the Central Valley—falconers—arrived with their bird respectfully hooded, followed by four well-muscled women who made it down from the north coast wearing California Women in Timber sweatshirts.

Everyone was pretty disoriented by the ways we got them there, but the locals—Anna and Modesto—welcomed everyone with a sumptuous buffet of Mexican, Asian, and Western-style vegetables and meats, honorably harvested. The falconer brothers and the two loggers who'd been at the first Congress were delighted to be with all of us planimals together again, for Ursula and I had a brought along the whole gang. Scree, Zarapito, Snave, Vespa, and the intrepid Tania joined the ubiquitous Lichen and half a dozen sparse Redwoods in that dry place. Other invited participants included the stalwart Orres, clever Tatiki, and seven Goldfinches.

A few random guests showed up as well—Jack Clemens and Wanda, Kipp and Suzanne Hughes, some local Rabbits and Squirrels, and two special beings I'll tell you about later. It's hard to control the emanations, so some folks got wind of the event without our intention.

Not all the humans had a clue why they were here, so they got to know each other over the delicious spread while picking up the what's-going-on. I overheard Makah mentioning the Elephant Code and was reassured by a sense that all the humans present were familiar with it and, for the most part, comfortable with its spirit.

While the people socialized, we planimals had a quick huddle to review our plan for the opening ceremony and the agenda. We had one simple outcome in mind: Create the basis for a planimal–human alliance of mutual respect— for each other and for our Grandmother.

• • •

When the moment seemed auspicious, Ursula stood up and, with a soft growl, got everyone's attention. Then, as arranged, the two special beings strode into the center of the Rockpile. One was a majestic Tule Elk, one of six thousand living in California. (There were half a million in 1800.) This old fellow stood five feet high at the shoulder and weighed in at eight hundred pounds. He sported a massive, four-foot-long rack, and, in his present incarnation, could stand on his hind feet for several minutes at a time. The other was the shawoman, magnificent in her deerskin regalia. Ursula retreated and gave them the stage.

The two spirit creatures began a slow, rhythmic dance, circling each other, ceremonious yet wary, chanting in a transcendent tongue. As the wonder at their presence subsided, a pair of Woodpeckers, perched on tall snags in the east and west ends of the arena, began call-and-response drumming. The logger women picked up the beat, and soon there was a regular concert, with people clapping and birds twittering. I even croaked a beautiful riff in classic *rococrow* style.

When the dance ended, the two figures stood back-to-back, surrounded by the gathered crowd—the medicine woman facing the humans and the Elk facing the planimals. In unison they chanted—

Welcome all wonders, welcome. We bring word
From Grandmother Earth and her incandescent lover
Grandfather Sun, the ultimate sources and
Protectors of all life. You who have come here now

Manifest your love for them and for each other
And foster the healing of this place.
For each of us here stands or perches or lies upon
Sacred ground, occupied from before memory
By our common ancestors, species
Who lived for millennia and disappeared,
The First Planimals—the original
Living inhabitants of this territory,
Their niches now settled by others.

In recent times, the First Peoples lived here
In harmony with the land and waters
For countless generations. We honor them and their
Ongoing fight to restore and make known their ways
Of seeing themselves—like all of us—
As guests at our Grandmother's table.
Now we gather here to find common ground
Across the chasm that has come to separate us,
So that we might thrive together and build
A new world based on mutual respect,
And respect for our life-giving planet.

"Welcome, indeed," Ursula said. "May we hold silence and let this prophetic offering find its place in our hearts."

At this moment, the falconer brothers chose to remove the hood from their bird. The American Goshawk—bigger than me—was bug-eyed at the variety of fauna arrayed before her. She began a study of the Rabbits, who were twitching nervously. The fearsome blood lust in her bones perturbed my equanimity. Meetings across the great divide can trigger instinctive responses.

"Speaking of respect," one falconer said, "my friend Gos and I would like to show some respect for those rabbits. She'll remain here on my glove. But I'm making a point. Some of us here are not interested in a no-violence, vegan future. The truth is, some beings must die so others may live. Humans are the apex predator, and there is no one else—not even some wily virus—that's going to displace us anytime soon. You all need to get that straight if we're going to have a conversation."

A logger woman chimed in. "The same goes for harvesting forest. Sustainability can be improved, but some trees need to come down to supply materials for human life to continue. And, given the way humans live today, we need to work with fire to manage the undergrowth and prevent wildfires."

Tania, as the fiercest nonhuman predator present, responded. "Brother Falconer, Sister Gos, Sister Logger, thank you. Death and life are a circle, and some killing is necessary. I won't be tucking into Ursula's berry bushes, no matter how hungry I get. No one on our side is talking about ending killing. We're talking about balance—and, as you have acknowledged, respect—mutual respect."

A maracas-like rattle from Snave got everyone's attention. "For the record, I have long advocated what we call 'let Nature take her course,' meaning that if you humans are destined to kill yourselves off and take a bunch of the rest of us with you, then we planimals should try to adapt—not fight the larger arc of history. While I'm here to see if we can work together, I'm skeptical. Tania mentioned balance, but it seems clear humans have to move first. So, let me ask you: What have you got?"

Clemens spoke. "The biggest imbalances come from the rich—I should know. That's why I am busy recruiting other wealthy people to rightsizing. Originally, that meant limiting your assets to $50 million, but now we've added a limit on consumption—$1 million a year. I know this seems like a lot of money to most of you. But if we could get the very wealthy—the top 1 percent worldwide—to adopt these limits, global carbon emissions would drop more than 10 percent, about equal to the total emissions of the United States."

The logger woman spat on the ground. "You rich guys better get your act together soon, or the rest of us will be coming after you." She looked at the falconer, who nodded, his mouth a taut line, his eyes grave.

Cody was standing under a lichen-covered oak. "Let's calm down here, people. We humans need to work out the issues of fairness and justice among our species, that's clear. But we're here to talk things through with our relations in the natural world and come closer to living by the Elephant Code—honor the Earth, respect each other, minimize harm to other lives, and be mindful of the future consequences of our actions. All of us here are comfortable with those values."

Luz looked across the divide at Tatiki and said, "How about we talk about what we already agree on?" When no one responded, she pushed on. "We all love the beauty and majesty of creation."

Tatiki spoke. "We also love our families and will defend them against danger."

"You two make it seem so simple," Makah said. "We love the planet, and we love our families. Climate change is threatening them both. We know what humans need to do—change our lifestyles so they are sustainable for everyone, and change the ways we farm and fish and log to recognize the natural cycles and synergies. Cooperate like the Three Sisters. What can you planimals do that will help us make that change?"

Lichen responded. "We will support you in changing the ways you manage the natural environment. If you protect natural systems like forests and fisheries, farm in ways that take carbon out of the air, and restore damaged systems, we will meet you halfway. We will partner with you by adapting and, for those of us who are endangered, staying alive. A thriving natural world is to the benefit of all life."

Lichen's positive energy was the moment we had been waiting for. From a tall fir behind me, an acrowbatic volée began an arabesque. Soon they were joined by whirling Starlings, Pigeons, Gulls, and Hawks tracing intricate patterns in the dusky sky. Sun cast an orange glow on the scattered clouds. Then a band of Coyotes, led by Tatiki, began a melodious howl. After a few rounds, Gulls and Jays added their cries to the melody, the Woodpeckers threw down a double-stroke roll, Snave did her rain stick thing, while Vespa and the Hornets played kazoos.

The show brought Elk and his dance partner back into the center in a passionate rondo. Luz was the first to join them on the dance floor, followed soon by Modesto and Juan, a fluffle of Rabbits, two of the logger women, Wanda, and others. Many participants fell into contented wonderment at the beauty, the hearts of the planimals and humans falling into harmony and peace.

Ursula couldn't resist going out into the mix. She swayed and growled softly to the beat, enticing Orres to join her.

The two Bears shuffling together reminded Kipp of the dancing Bears he'd seen when visiting Eastern Europe as a boy. He mentioned this to Anna, who was standing next to him.

"That was a sad practice," she said. "I'm glad it's in decline."

"England outlawed it in 1911," Kipp said. "But you're the bear woman. You should be out there with them."

"I had been thinking that." She moved into the swirling throng, striding forward with her stick. She bowed to the two Bears and moved with them in a graceful sway.

Suddenly, a rogue aftershock rumbled through, distracting the dancers. Off balance on her hind legs, Ursula toppled over onto Anna, two hundred furry pounds pinning the woman to the dusty earth. The Bear rolled off quickly and began gently snuffling Anna, who remained still but awake. Seeing the Bear's mouth so close to Anna, an alarmed logger rushed over, joined by a falconer who had grabbed Anna's walking stick. They yelled at Ursula, jabbing her with the stick. Ursula backed away, confused. As the rescuers helped Anna to her feet, the Goshawk pulled free from her fine, black elkhide glove, no longer disposed to contain her natural instincts. She fell like an arrow upon the plumpest dancing Rabbit, her talons deep in its shoulders as she lifted it into the sky, landing with it on a branch above the gathering.

The falconer called his bird, and she came, bringing the Rabbit, who was gravely wounded. Knowing the bird's next move would be to tear open her still-wriggling prey, the man deftly broke the Rabbit's neck.

Everything stopped. The birds fell silent to their perches. The planimals and humans retreated to their sides, each tending to their wounded.

"This was to be a place of peace," yelled Scree. "Leave it to the humans to start the killing."

"Hey, chill out, loudmouth," the falconer replied, "or I'll send her after you."

I could feel anger radiating from the planimals and feared it would blow the gathering apart. But it didn't matter, for participants from both sides had already turned their backs on each other and were leaving the Rockpile.

"Wait!" I cried. "We can work this out!"

But it was too late.

Elk came over to me. "Keep the faith," he said. "As soon as I saw that elkhide gauntlet, I feared there'd be trouble. Nevertheless, the meeting was a bold stroke, if only a beginning."

The shawoman was more direct. She advanced toward Luz, Anna, Makah, Suzanne, and the loggers. "You women have to get your act together. It's your time now, but you must seize it. Mark my words."

Returning to the center, the two beings bowed to each other and evanesced. As the rest of the participants dispersed, Ursula and I remained, along with some of our core group, as did Anna, Luz, Modesto, and their companions.

"We will have to try again," Modesto said. "We're sorry that a simple misunderstanding escalated into a conflict. The falconer should not have lost control of his bird."

"These things happen," Ursula said, "but we'll get nowhere by claw-pointing. Let us each talk to the others on our side. We will be in touch."

"May all beings live in peace," said Anna. "Everyone was changed today."

37

IN SEPTEMBER, Luz entered high school at Andrew Lang, a private K–12 institution in Pacific Beach. One attraction was the student radio station, where she imagined being a DJ and hosting her own talk show. Her parents liked the racial and international diversity, the academic rigor, the safety when compared with the public high school, and its lower, post-earthquake fees.

The fifty freshmen traveled to a two-day overnight retreat at a camp in the Santa Cruz mountains near where the congresses had been, which made Luz feel at home. She kept her planimal experiences to herself as she scoped out her classmates, meeting several dozen of them in the various bonding exercises the teachers put them through. Many of the students already knew each other, having been together in the middle school and even the elementary school, but there were enough newbies and enough curiosity among the longtimers for Luz not to feel alone. The ethnic diversity also made it easier. There didn't seem to be any other Native Americans, but she had seen the shawoman in her dreams, and ferocity was growing within her.

As the school year progressed, she made friends with a few of the other girls. A junior named Siena DJ'd at the radio station, co-hosting a talk show with a senior, Chas. Luz admired Siena and confided her desire to host a weekly talk show about environmental issues. Siena talked to her co-host, and they agreed to let Luz hang out with them in the studio during the show. Luz's faculty advisor approved.

The show was random, focusing on the teen perspective, student life, and eclectic music. Luz liked the vibe. As she talked more with Siena about her own ideas, Siena suggested that maybe next year they could air an all-female show with an environmental angle. The possibility thrilled Luz.

A boarder from Reno, Siena went home in November for a few days because her mother was sick. Chas invited Luz to sit in for Siena. Luz jumped on the opportunity. That Thursday afternoon, they did a show featuring Indigenous music they had collected from websites around the world. The format proved popular with the international students, who called in to recommend other Indigenous artists.

When they were off-air, Chas suggested they go to nearby Pebble Beach and get a coffee. Luz was nervous, but she admired Chas, a school longtimer who played varsity soccer. A hefty guy, he played center back, organizing the backline and defending the goal. Chas's divorced mom, whom Makah met at a parents' day event, was a manager at the Pebble Beach golf course. She told Makah that Chas admired Luz for her independent spirit. Makah had smiled at that.

Luz texted her mother to tell her that Chas was going to give her a ride home after they got coffee. The shift in plans unsettled Makah, but Cody was out of town, and she had run into an issue at a late school meeting. She felt relieved not to have to pick up Luz.

Chas was driving a mint-green electric Audi convertible, an advance graduation present from his father. They drove down to the Pebble Beach Market, near the coastal overlook and its rough shore. They talked about the show, which they agreed had gone well.

As they entered the shop, Chas said, "You know, you're a natural at radio. You were great tonight. Your voice is really strong."

"Thanks, Chas." Luz felt proud. Several listeners had sent in favorable comments during the show, and Chas had not dominated the conversation.

"Want anything to eat?" Chas asked.

The paninis looked tasty, and she was hungry. They ordered some, and coffees. At the shore, the air was brisk, the clouds hinting rain. They wandered along the gravel beach, admiring the flat, round stones that people had stacked into little towers. The sea lapped lazily on the sand as they finished their paninis and coffees.

Chas slowed down and kicked at the sand. "This is very nice," he said. "I'm enjoying being here with you. Maybe you can come visit me at Cal next year. They have a great radio station up there, KALX."

"I love KALX," Luz said. "They play everything. They've got enough DJs that they don't have to fill schedule with BBC and NPR."

Chas stopped and turned toward her. "I like you, Luz," he said. "Can I kiss you?"

"No! No, I don't want to. Let's just be friends."

Chas put his hand on her arm and pulled her toward him.

She resisted, but he maintained his grip. "No! I said no. Let go!"

He grabbed her other arm and pulled her in.

It was happening too fast. She remembered Wanda's warning at her Flower Dance. She felt Tatiki's protection. Suddenly, the shawoman's energy surged through her body. She stepped hard on Chas's instep, pushing him backward, off balance, breaking his grip. He stumbled but caught himself. They faced each other, two arms' lengths apart on the sand.

"What was that?" she snarled. "I thought we were friends."

"You're strong. You surprised me. I thought you Indian girls were easy."

She kicked sand at him. "We had enough of that in the old days. You are such a jerk! I can't believe it." She'd been a fool. No way she could tell Mom, who hated this kind of stuff.

"I'm sorry." He grimaced as he massaged his knee. "I was out of line. I do like you, Luz. I don't want to lose you as a friend."

Luz considered his words, the fearful look on his face. She sighed. "You were *way* out of line. I should report you, but I don't want to start out at this school by making a big deal. And it would totally freak my mom out. But I *will* tell Siena."

"I'm really sorry, Luz. I don't know what came over me. I'm feeling kind of crazy lately. I'm nervous about college, and my dad's on my mom's case and—"

"This is not about you, Chas."

"Right. I hope you'll forgive me." He bent down to inspect his knee, which seemed to have been twisted in the tussle. He worried about the upcoming playoffs. "How did you do that?"

"Let's go. Take me home." In the car, she, grey rocking in cold silence. Why did she say she wouldn't report him? Mom again.

They arrived. Luz saw Makah standing in the kitchen. She burst in.

"How was the show?" Makah asked.

"It was fine—great, actually. Mom, I have to finish a paper. We ate paninis, so I'm not hungry." She flew out of the kitchen.

Makah knew something was off. She parked the feeling for now.

Luz *did* have a paper due, a report for the school's Student Environment Council, having volunteered to review the most recent local activities of Extinction Rebellion and Fridays for Future. She'd been taking part in the school strikes for years and was recognized as a leader in the wider Monterey student environmental movement. She was drawn to Extinction Rebellion, finding its more militant stance exciting, perhaps more dangerous. Her schoolmates found her exotic amid the button-down school culture, this activist young woman of color and mystery.

Yet she felt isolated. Glenda had moved away after the quake. Siena was her only real friend, and when she returned and Luz told her what had happened, Siena was angry.

"I should have warned you: He has a reputation. Don't let him get away with it—that's the old way. We've got to stand up for ourselves against the arrogance and entitlement."

"I know," said Luz, "but I'm more focused on standing up for climate. I don't want to spread myself too thin." It would be too embarrassing. "I got even, though—he couldn't make the playoffs."

"I heard he told the coach that he'd slipped on a rock. How'd he fall, anyway? He's twice as big as you."

"I don't know," Luz said. "Something happened and he tripped backward, I guess." She'd promised to protect the shawoman.

Siena smirked. "Right. Anyway, people loved your show, and you're acing your classes, I hear."

"That's all going fine. But I don't have friends. Except you, I mean. People seem to keep their distance. Most of the time it doesn't bother me. I like being by myself. But sometimes I get lonely."

"Don't your animal friends keep you company?"

Luz flushed. "Uh, well, sure, they're nice and helpful and all. They help me cope. But I *am* human—it's not like I can date a coyote."

"You could do worse, I suppose, but I hear you. My mom always says, 'Being a teenage girl is life's hardest passage.'"

"How's your mom doing?" Luz asked.

"She's okay. She has stomach issues, but maybe it's stress. Ever since my dad died."

"I'm sorry. My great-grandmother was sick a lot, but that's how my grandmother met my grandfather. He was the doctor."

"That's a good story," Siena said. "You know, thinking about Chas, it might be a chance for us to do our own show this year."

"What do you mean?" Luz asked. "He's locked into it now, especially since he can't play ball."

"But what if he thought you were going to report him?"

"I told him I wouldn't."

"Maybe you changed your mind. I could tell him you were thinking about it. That you wouldn't feel comfortable in the studio with him and that neither would I. Which is true—he creeps me out."

"I don't know. What if he says no? Then what do we do? Do I have to report him?" Luz asked.

"He doesn't want you to report him," Siena answered. "So the question is, does he think we're bluffing? The way you must have fought back—I'll bet he's afraid of you now. He's such a typical bully."

Luz scowled. "Do it." Being brave works.

Siena's foray was successful. Chas would quit the show before Christmas.

"Let's celebrate!" Siena said when they heard the news from the station director in the studio. "It's a victory."

"I know how," Luz said. "Can we take your car?"

From the Pebble Beach Market, the young women took their coffees and, retracing the path of Luz's triumph, rematriated the shoreline.

38

BEFORE THE QUAKE—now known as "the San Juan"—before all plans were put aside, Wanda and Janet had talked about getting married. Now it was November, and they hurried forward, with new respect for life's brief run. Anna officiated at a small ceremony in a sacred grove of redwoods, after which the wedding party joined a large gathering at Jack Clemens's Atherton house, which he had converted to all solar and used as the offices for Network Action.

Late in the festivities, Cody and Jack found themselves on a couch together, sampling a rather fine scotch from Jack's extensive stock.

"I was thinking about the Rockpile, Jack," said Cody. "I hated for it to end that way."

"There are always setbacks, Cody—you know that. Change is hard, and you rarely get it right the first time."

"My grandfather Ethan used to say, 'If you're winning more than 51 percent of your fights, you're in the wrong league.' It's the tough things that are worth striving for. Speaking of which, it's very cool that you hosted this wedding. I imagine that might have been tough for you."

"Agility is critical these days," Jack said. "There's no normality. That freaks people out, but there's no use denying it. It's only going to get more so in the years ahead."

"Well, this is some party—so many people here from the tech and finance communities; some I hadn't seen in years and others I'd long been wanting to meet."

"Thanks. I'm happy the way it's going. Yeah, looking at this crowd, you'd think tech had become gender diverse. There's progress for sure—it's not just straight, single men coding our future anymore." He shrugged. "Finance is another story, but even there we're making progress. In both cases, executive levels are thin. Same goes for ethnic diversity, which I guess we did okay on—today, anyway. Some of my old colleagues think I've gone off the deep end, pushing for more balanced leadership. They don't want to let go of control."

"I've found that women coders experience the world more holistically than many men," Cody said. "They tend to take a systems approach and a longer-term view. They don't park their values at the door. Take my daughter Rosa—her coder friends can't even imagine the old 'move fast and break things' mentality. Now it's all about global collaboration and creating resilient systems that interact positively with each other."

"I hope it's changing," said Jack. "There are still too many stories of women who feel they had to conform to the male systems to get anywhere, and even then, weren't taken seriously."

"Makah still runs into that assumption every day in academia—men expecting women to say yes and women trying to please. The younger ones are the change agents, but there's a big pile of history to slog through to get there." Cody paused. "You're an older guy, Jack. How did you become open to women's workplace challenges?"

"Sixty-two this year," Jack said. "Yeah, I have to say that my ex-wife's accident was a bit of a wake-up call. Then after Lieth's death, I got into cougars, and they kinda got into me. The cougar represents the primal feminine awareness in some traditions. It was all confusing for me at first. But then Wanda fell in love with Janet, and here I am. I have to admit it was a challenge, that last part. But that's just between us guys."

"The connection between Tania and Tara still amazes me. You know what Tara means, right? It's the *divine feminine* in Buddhism."

"I know about that," said Jack. "But these cats are not all about compassionate love—they're killers."

Cody laughed. "True. That could be their Kali side."

"These cats are no collies."

"Of course not, Jack. I was referring to Kali, the fierce Mother Goddess of the Hindus, who wears a garland of skulls to remind us of time's unbending cycle."

"Oh, now that's *nice*. Well, we need more fierce women. Say, Cody, you like poetry, don't you?"

"I do, I do, Jack. What about it?"

Jack got up and walked over to the bookcase. "Wanda gave me this collection for my birthday last year. There's a poem by Susan Griffin in it—'I Like to Think of Harriet Tubman.' Tubman was fierce, and so is Griffin." He handed Cody the book.

"Tubman is such a hero, Jack." He took the book. "I live with a fierce woman—it works well for me. But there's something else. I don't think I ever told you about my encounter with a sea lichen colony. Lichens are hybrid plant–animal organisms. They're a harmonious, collective living arrangement. Anyway, we had a talk, me and these sea lichens, sort of like your talk with Tania. The outcome was to really tune myself into my heart's call, besides what my head says. I'd always thought of the heart as feminine, and maybe it is my feminine side, but anyway . . . .This conversation is making me see that my heart's call can be fierce even in the service of harmony. It's like a fire in my belly."

The two men sipped their whiskeys and watched the crowd. People began coming up to thank Jack before leaving.

"I guess I better go back to being the host," Jack said. "Cody, thanks for the chat. To be continued, I hope."

"Likewise," Cody said and went off to find Makah and Luz.

• • •

Wanda and Janet made their exit under a festive shower of sunflower chips. A variety of corvids called loud congratulations, not least to stake claims for the fatty seeds lying scattered on the ground. The newlyweds were off to camp and hike in the California wilds.

After the crowd dispersed, Clemens wandered around, collecting glasses for the caterers, who left him, at last, with a clean and orderly house. He opened a secret door in the liquor cabinet behind which hid some fine old scotch. As he considered his choice of a final drink, he spotted something colorful in the back of the cabinet. He reached back and retrieved a lavender envelope. It was addressed to him in Wanda's hand.

He poured a short whiskey and sat down on the couch in front of the picture window that reached to the bay. It was a cloudy fall day, softening the light on the water. A single container ship, unlike years before when six thousand of them plied the seas dumping diesel crude and worse.

The envelope felt heavy. He opened it carefully and pulled out the matching card. There was a heart on the front. He opened it, tremulous, and read:

> Dear Dad,
>
> This is just a little thank-you note for everything you have done and lately, become. I never thought I'd say this, but it's great being your daughter.
>
> The other thing is that I have some news. Janet is pregnant. The donor's a friend of ours. You'll meet him later. I think you'll like him. Anyway, I know it's not exactly what you hoped for, but we're really looking forward to having a child in our life. It's thrilling. We hope you agree.
>
> Much love, see you when we get back.
>
> —Wanda

For Clemens, it was bittersweet. He felt old and out of touch. He'd given up hope for Wanda's motherhood, and now here it was, only different. Confusing but good. Good news on a good day. He lay down on the couch and took a little nap, the whiskey sitting untouched on the table.

• • •

Historians pondering the shift in attitudes that began in the mid-twenties would ask, Why did people all over the world step back from tribalism? Fear of living in an uninhabitable world? That played a part, pushed along by disasters and conflicts. But disaster and fear can also cause people to react in anger and hostility, to fall back and defend themselves, their own.

The need for systemic change had become obvious. Although investments in Meltdown Prevention, Adaptation, and Remediation were clearly the highest and best use of capital and labor, the market was not delivering that outcome. Those in power feared the economic, social, and political dislocations that abandoning Earth-killing technologies and activities would bring. Yet, without investments in a climate-friendly future, the dislocations would be orders of magnitude greater and longer lasting.

The global shift toward a more communal worldview grew up like the spring tendrils of ferns from the forest floor of everyday life. Beginning at the most personal level, it spread in kitchens and at dinner tables, around smoky cooking fires and in family sleeping quarters, in extended families, in churches, temples, sanghas, classrooms, coffee shops, affinity groups, online networks, and salons. Millions of honest conversations about what to do and how to work with others.

The tone and terms of these conversations were myriad—exposing the dysfunction of old prejudices, building bridges across polarities, opening up to unconscious bias against the other and to apology and reconciliation. These inner shifts led to crucial changes in behavior—a willingness to risk trusting someone else, and to forgive them, when possible, for failure. To glory in the beauty and the blessings of Grandmother Earth.

While divisions remained, a provisional ceasefire was emerging among the people, a willingness to try something new. In other ways, it was old—the ideal of community, of mutual aid, of the common good. The détente was fragile, but promising.

PART SIX

39

ONE OF THOSE CONVERSATIONS began in Makah and Cody's kitchen the following spring. Makah heard Luz parking her bike. She continued prepping vegetables for dinner. Now to try her own brand of bridging divides, at home.

As Luz came in, damp from the March drizzle, Makah asked the question she'd been preparing. "Wasn't your environmental committee meeting today? Are they liking your radio show with Siena?"

Luz brightened, shaking the rain off her poncho as she hung it on the hook by the door. "Pretty much, Mom. We've been using the show to float ideas out there on the ether. That's an old radio word Chas taught me last semester."

"I thought the show was fantastic this week," said Makah. "It's nice that Chas moved aside to let you and Siena do it on your own. I've been meaning to thank his mom."

"Mmm, I'm not sure she was that happy about it, Mom. What did you like in today's show?"

And why was that? No, stick to the plan. "I liked the part about how we have much to do. I recorded it. Here, I'll play it. I'd like to send it to my network, if that's okay." Makah found the excerpt and Luz's bright voice said—

> "Although there is significant progress, there is still a lot to do. Two degrees centigrade above pre-industrial levels is a certainty. The questions we face now are harder—
>
> - Can Earth's temperature be stabilized at that hot level?
> - If so, how many people living sustainably can She support?
> - How do we cushion the unavoidable suffering that is coming—especially for those less fortunate?
> - What is the path—aided by technology, and grounded in partnership and mutual respect among all living beings—to a true turnaround, a new way of being?"

"I just think that's so profound," Makah said. "How did you come up with it?"

"We came up with it at the environmental committee. Some science majors are really into future scenarios, and the more political students are keyed into the social justice aspects. I seem to be the one speaking for the planimals. It's not always easy."

"What kind of responses have you been getting?"

"People text in during the show, and I share the comments with the committee."

"Like what?" A conversation!

"One student proposed that the school should turn the athletic fields into community gardens. Some people thought it was dumb, would be a waste of time, or just make people mad, but others said, what about half the fields? We're going to turn it into a proposal for the school. Along with what we're calling 'extreme gardening'—like ultimate in intensity." She paused. "It lines right up with the Elephant Code, Mom—honoring the sanctity of the Earth."

"The Code has become great teaching material. And it survived the legal challenges after voters adopted it. Who thought the Supreme Court would vote for climate? You know, you make me think of Anna. It was wonderful to be with her at Wanda's wedding. But I feel like we've all gotten so busy on our individual projects we're losing touch. I talk to my international colleagues more than I talk to anyone here."

Luz considered that. "Maybe you're a balance to Dad and me—we're focused more on local action. But we need to build a world where love shines through in all our actions—love for each other, for all living things, for the planet. We need to be the changes we want to see."

"That's such an interesting insight, Luz, and a beautiful sentiment. Something to live up to. But I was wondering what you meant when you said, 'It's not always easy'? I mean about talking for the planimals."

"We've been here before, Mom—some kids think I'm a freak. I've gotten tough, though. I can handle it. I'm even mentoring some younger students in getting in touch with their natural connections." Luz paused. "I guess Anna's taught me more than I realized."

"It can be tough to be different." She's fidgeting—slow down. "How about helping me make a salad?"

"Okay."

The two fell silent in their tasks for a few minutes.

"I'm sorry," offered Makah. "I wish we could talk more easily. But I guess this happens when girls become teenagers."

"So it seems, Mom," Luz said. "But thanks for trying." She paused, then, feeling her strength, took the leap. "Mom, how can you tell if a boy likes you?"

Makah looked straight ahead, trying not to blunder. "It's not always obvious," she said. "Sometimes they don't know themselves. They might be nice to you or tease you. The real question is, how do you know if you like them."

"Hmm," said Luz. "So, there's this junior on the environment committee, a day student who lives in Seaside. His mom's Rumsen. He hangs around me after the meetings. We're in World Lit together, and he kind of tries to sit next to me. He never says much. Siena kidded me about it. I hadn't even noticed."

"What's he like?"

"He's a good committee member, always shows up and does what he says he'll do. He's not in the popular crowd. He's a wonderful swimmer, but not varsity. He's got brown hair, not too tall. I like the comments he makes in lit class—he likes the old-world stuff, you know, like Rumi and Hafiz. And he's cool with my talking with the planimals."

"That sounds nice." Softly now, keep the channel open. "That's the first time you've mentioned a boy, Luz." Damn. She was shrinking back.

Not without relief, they heard Cody arriving. He sauntered in, grinning. "How are my beautiful ladies this fine afternoon?" he asked, smelling of fish and kelp.

"Nothing like bringing the outside in," said Makah, drying her hands and giving him a squeeze. "You were definitely in it today, I can tell."

"We had a great time on the water, and our software's already making a difference in calibrating harvest rates for the kelp. We have enough data to publish a solid article in *Aquaculture Journal*." He stomped his boots. "What are you guys up to? But let me get these clothes off and wash up."

"That'll be good, Dad."

Over dinner, Makah said, "Luz and I were wondering what else we can do on climate. I've been reading how citizen action groups are stepping in where government or corporate action is lacking. That's what your groups are doing, Luz. It's the spirit of 'Think globally, act locally.' I guess if a lot of people do a lot of small things, it can add up to big changes."

Luz put down her fork. "What's the alternative? We can't wait forever for the power structure to deconstruct itself. It's got to come from below."

Cody said, "In our neighborhood community of action—our own version of Families for Future—we're ridesharing, tool-lending, taking joint responsibility for those in need, maintaining and reusing electronics and other hardware rather than replacing them, and expanding community gardens. Fridays for Future is helping. Your friends have been out there planting, weeding, harvesting, and distributing food."

"I agree," said Luz. "The movement's gotten more practical. At last week's climate meeting here, I heard about a group that's working to restore overgrazed stream beds. And many are pushing back as consumers, avoiding polyester, joining Buy Nothing New, and redefining status in our peer groups away from material wealth."

Makah said, "I've been reading about the move to a 'circular economy,' with its watchwords 'Eliminate waste, circulate goods, regenerate nature.' It's a shift from an extractive relationship to the Earth. In ag science now, they're emphasizing learning from and using the forces being unleashed by climate change to positive effect—planting wheat where it's too hot for corn, intercropping agave with mesquite in dry areas to create drought-tolerant animal fodder—"

"Your mom's borrowing from our joint paper about adaptive bioecology, rooted in the ways animals and plants are adapting to rapid change. People are even working cooperatively with the planimals. After consulting through animal whisperers, they're fitting migratory birds and fishes with lightweight environmental sensors to monitor patterns of change in the weather, the atmosphere, the oceans, and the planimals' own adaptations. It's like what the lichen said at the Rockpile—adapt and thrive."

Luz sighed. "What about the planimals' culture? We need something new, some new structures, some partnership where all life gets a say in what happens to the planet."

"Aren't those structures already in place?" Makah asked. "The natural world speaks to us if we observe its behavior, its cycles and variations. Certainly, the Earth is speaking to us, through extreme weather and even earthquake and volcano activity. Are we willing to listen and act on what She is saying? The natural world will get the last word, for sure." She stood up to clean the dishes. "Speaking of natural voices, Luz and I were talking about the Elephant Code."

"At least we got parts of it into law, and it's posted on the wall at the office," Cody said. "The hardest one is the last clause, 'We will be mindful of the effects that our actions have for seven generations.' It's hard to think of even two generations, to Luz's kids, for example."

"Dad! Please. I'm not even sixteen. Don't be talking to me about grandchildren. Besides, is it right for people to have more kids right now?"

"Sorry, I didn't mean it that way. You know I support you in your budding climate career. You hardly have time to eat and sleep anyway. So, no pressure!"

Makah rolled her eyes at Luz. They were close to the intimacy of the Flower Dance.

• • •

Solitary since Wanda's wedding, devoting herself ascetically to contemplation and writing, Anna missed her Monterey friends. Occasionally she would spot Modesto Corazón visiting his uncle across the fence. They would exchange the ear-rubbing sign as an affirmation of the energies becoming ever more present on the planet.

Sensing that her long isolation was coming to its natural end, she planned a visit with Makah and Luz. Cody would be in SoCal assessing the damaging impact of rising temperatures on local kelp ecologies in anticipation of what was coming to Monterey. She fasted for two days. The next morning, wearing her bear claw necklace under her shirt, and having given up her car like so many, she walked out to the road and waited. Heat shimmered off the potholed asphalt track that led over the coastal range. She stood in the shade of California oaks, their pointy acorns scattered underfoot in the dry October morning. One or another Crow would land on its hopping legs, grab a nut, and prance with it before taking off to hide it for winter, wary of the watchful eyes of its fellows, lest the tidbit become another's prize.

I stopped by, dropping a sprig of White Sage at Anna's feet. We communed briefly, and I blessed her journey. "We'll talk later," I assured her.

An hour passed. Anna remained patient, still. She sipped her water bottle and closed her eyes, listening to the birdsong, the Crickets, the random breeze in the Oak branches, the thuds of ripe acorns, the groan of a truck straining to climb the hill. The engine's whine grew louder, then abated as its source seemed to come to a halt not far past her. She opened her eyes. It was a farm truck full of vegetables. Two men got out and started walking toward her. The driver rubbed his left ear, and she recognized Modesto.

"Anna," he said, "necesitas paseo?"

Anna nodded, returning the sign. "Muchas gracias."

"This is Juan Matus," said Modesto, "un gran amigo indio de México. You may remember him from the Rockpile, that crazy day."

A thin, grizzled man with weathered skin approached. Vigor shone through his aging frame. His eyes sparkled, glinting in the mottled sun as he came under the oak canopy.

"Con gusto, honorada," said the man. "Reconozco vuestro conexión," he continued, nodding at the other two.

In the ancient truck, Anna sitting between the men on the bench seat, they rode without speaking, enveloped in the engine drone, the gears growling over the pass.

As they ascended, a sentience came into the space, the awareness that abides in the shadows beyond the light of our feeble campfires, filling the cab and its occupants with the eternal moment of gratitude and beneficence. The facade of everyday existence crumbled away, inviting the pilgrims into unity with their ancestors and the land.

"Espíritu de la tierra," Juan said.

"Del corazón," Modesto whispered.

"Siempre bienvenida," Anna said. "She is always welcome."

Time waited for them, only Modesto's muscle memory guiding them down the hilly curves.

Presently, the road straightened out, so as to deliver them tenderly into the King's Mountain, the city known as Monterey. And the ancestors of that place retreated into memory, leaving only the land, so that the trio would be present in their ordinary forms at the time of their arrival.

"Eso fue grande," said Modesto.

"For sure. Such a blessing. Thank you," Anna said, as they let her off at Makah's.

• • •

The occasion for Anna's visit was a harvest ceremony and a reunion with Mandy, in from Bismarck for an extended stay. Luz and her foremothers had also fasted for two days, staying quiet, tending mindfully to the garden and the house. The garden was at the peak of late summer maturity—the corn high, its ripe husks near bursting; the beans festooned with pregnant pods and entwined in firm embrace of the cornstalks; the rambunctious squash hugging the ground, its gourds growing stealthily through the night to surprise the morning gardener. The hens feasted on discarded greens. It was a time of culmination.

When Anna arrived, they rested, sipping water and talking quietly, catching up on Luz's school and her climate work, Makah's networks and feelings of reconnection, Cody's calm energy since the sea lichen, Anna's current contemplations, and life back in the hills and plains of North Dakota. When sundown came, they broke their fast with sacrament and song.

• • •

They spent the next morning in the garden, talking with the Three Sisters as they moved carefully among them, humming harvest songs from their traditions.

I arrived amid their preparations, followed shortly by a flirtation of Goldfinches. We birds took up residence in the redwood. The Coyotes in the canyon sang a morning chorus. Anna touched her Bear claw and blessed the gathering of three generations of Nueta women. She then joined us in a silent planimal vigil.

When all was ready, Makah began by thanking the squash for protecting the soil and holding space for the beans and corn. On hands and knees, she clipped the heavy gourds, handing them to Luz, who brushed the soil off before passing them to Mandy, who sat with a large basket to receive them. As she worked, Makah cleared space around the stalks, preparing the way for Luz.

Now, the young woman thanked the squash and corn for protecting and supporting the beans. She thanked the beans for adding nitrogen to the soil. She moved lightly among them, handing the plump pods to Mandy and leaving the thin ones for a later day. Where their leaves blocked access to the fat corn, she pushed them aside. Mandy passed the beans to Makah, who sorted them by size and quality.

It was Mandy's turn. She sang a Nueta corn song she had been given by her mother. She took a corn knife among the rows, slicing off the big ears, handing them to Makah to inspect and pass to Luz.

By noon they had finished. They rested in the shade and surveyed the bounty of cooperative horticulture.

"The Three Sisters remind me of Cody's lichens," Makah said. "Three species living in harmony."

"Three is a good number for that—two can produce opposition," Anna said.

"Or bliss," blurted Luz. "I mean, so the poets say. Like Hafiz!"

The older women watched Luz's discomfort with amusement.

"*Some* people are growing up." Mandy smiled.

• • •

When Cody returned that evening, he felt the love in the house. "You're like the *four* sisters," he said, "just like the way the sunflowers in the garden attract the pollinators for the vegetables."

"That metaphor is a stretch, Dad." Sisters . . . so awesome.

Now the quintet set to cleaning the vegetables, getting them ready to carry over to the food bank. They sliced the squash into rings, which they hung to dry in Nueta fashion. They feasted on an excellent stew the women had toiled and troubled over during the afternoon hours, wild in their attire and their minds' eyes, joking among themselves of a sailor's wife with chestnuts in her lap and other play, foul and fair.

"What are you ladies snickering about?" Cody asked as he tucked into the stew, a homemade rusk in hand.

"Poetry," said Makah. "Luz was speaking of Hafiz and bliss this afternoon."

"There was an adolescent edge to it," Anna said. "See, she's coloring."

"What was that poem you used to quote to me, my favorite Hafiz—'The Woman I Love'?"

"Perhaps it was this," Cody said.

"The Beautiful One whom I adore
Has pitched His royal tent inside you,
So I will always lean my heart
As close to your soul as I can."

After Cody cleaned the kitchen and they were sitting around with fresh apple pie, Mandy said, "Anna was saying she is about due for an important birthday."

Anna nodded. "Hard for me to believe, but yes. I'll be seventy-five in October."

"We should celebrate *your* coming-of-age!" Makah said. "We can have a big do, a festival of gratitude for your life of service."

"I'm down with that," said Cody. "I'll be responsible for seafood—animal and vegetable."

Luz smiled. "I will consult with the planimal spirits and propose a gift for you, Anna, if that's all right."

"You all are gift enough," Anna said.

40

ANNA'S SEVENTY-FIFTH BIRTHDAY was the occasion for a two-day circus of gratitude, retreat, banquet, ceremony, celebration, Powwow, conference, and party. Held over the weekend of Indigenous Peoples' Day, it sprawled out of Makah and Cody's house onto the street. There were performances and seminars at the American Legion Hall in Veterans Park, recently refurbished with community assistance. The wooded lot and labyrinth at St. James Episcopal Church served as resting and meditation space.

The preparations were their own adventure—tracking down Anna's old friends, engaging the Ohlone communities she had worked with for many years, recruiting dancers live and virtual, making decorations, and organizing the feast. The mainstay Three Sisters stew simmering in a giant pot now included tomatoes, peppers, garlic, various chilis, and plenty of cumin. Luz and Andrés, guided by consultations with the planimals, worked with noted Rumsen artist and elder Linda Yamane to create a painted redwood box, to replace Anna's medicine box crushed during the quake. Sun, Moon, and Stars covered three sides, with Raven on the fourth. The top featured a broken arrow. A Black Bear peered down from inside the lid. The effect was luminous and profound.

The festivities began with a Grand March, followed by a Bear Dance performed by a mixed-gender intertribal group and led by an all-woman drum circle. Luz and Makah, wizards at creating immersive hybrid meetings, activated Network Action's virtual reality version, now in beta. It powered a twenty-four-hour meeting space, enabling global participation in an open-ended set of concerts, sacred ritual, speeches, debates, dance, graphic art, and conversation. The rotating emcees—Luz, Makah, and Suzanne, supported by Cody, Kipp, and Rosa—went with the flow. Anna connected with her friends in person and remotely, giving and receiving blessings. She looked forward to watching the replay and to taking part in a special Rumsen Nation ceremony at Indian Canyon two weeks later. It was there that the medicine box would be presented formally. By special invitation, Luz would carry it in. "After all," said Anna, "it *is* a box of light."

Planimal spirits were present in great numbers. I led a volée of my cronies in aerial displays and chanting. A charm of Goldfinches performed a madrigal, supported by a Raven bass line. In the evenings, there were Coyote serenades, which chilled a few spines. Andrés interpreted our Crow calling, reporting that we had voiced the planimals' appreciation for the combined cooperative human energies swirling around the event. It was a shimmering sliver of the Old Times, the wild things approaching in peace and curiosity, singing, if not dancing, for no one was quite ready for us to come into the foyer and pose for portraits.

Late the first day, however, we heard yelling down at the Veterans Hall. I flew down to check it out and found Clemens in a standoff with a vet in his early fifties.

"The Iraq War was based on a lie," Clemens was saying. "You guys had no business being there. Several hundred thousand Iraqis died, most of them civilians. It was criminal."

"Thousands of American soldiers died, and tens of thousands were injured," said the vet. "I lost several buddies in a firefight in Mosul and came home with bad PTSD. My wife left me. People like you just trigger me. Here you are enjoying the hospitality of our hall and dissing your hosts. What an asshole."

The vet moved toward Clemens, who took a deep breath and adopted a relaxed, alert stance.

"Bring it on," he said evenly.

The post commander, a retired marine colonel, inserted himself between them. "You know the rules, Tommy—no fighting on the property. And as for you—I suggest you take your leave."

I watched Clemens shaking his head as he returned to the main party, where he made excuses for leaving early and headed off.

• • •

On Monday, the neighbors, glad of tranquility's return, helped with cleanup. Later that day, the core group was resting in the backyard.

"I only wish Blake had been here to experience it all." Toni sipped a cool glass of peppermint tea. "And it was wonderful to see Robert and Mandy online, even if they couldn't make it in person."

"Mandy did such a great job of organizing that Nueta Corn Dance videoed from New Town," Suzanne said. "You must have been so proud of your mom, Makah."

"Your international network was also outstanding, Makah," Anna said. "It has expanded and matured since your workshop. People are making change happen at every level. And how I loved that Malaysian Orang Asli adoption ceremony! Such an honor for me. What glorious regalia, such captivating language and music. With all this love, I don't feel a day over seventy."

Kipp and Cody came out, bearing hors d'oeuvres. "Anyone hungry?" Kipp asked.

"Where did you get these shrimp?" Toni asked. "Amazing."

"A rare and special gift from a fishery adopted by the aquarium," Suzanne answered.

Cody paused, holding a tamale. "Say, Jack. Sounds like things got a little tense there down in the Veterans Hall."

"Yeah, what was that about?" Makah asked. "I heard you almost came to blows with some guy."

Clemens was sitting with his daughter and her wife, holding his grandson, Adam. "Yeah, I got a little hot under the collar. Sometimes, the recently converted are their own worst enemies. It was a discussion about ethics, and I said something about the immorality of war. One veteran took offense." He shook his head. "I made a fool of myself. But it reminded me that change doesn't happen overnight, even with the best of intentions. Humbling for me."

⋄ ⋄ ⋄

The dusk crept across the sky, tinting the eastern clouds. The hens began their evening rituals. Tatiki and Kali, thankful the crowds had dispersed, prepared for the evening's hunt with their new litter. A stillness fell over the little gathering.

"You know, sometimes out here I really feel the presence of Chanson," Makah said. "It would be nearly time for his coming-of-age. But life is thorny. As the Lakota Tȟáȟča Hušté (Lame Deer) said, 'Nature, the Great Spirit—they are not perfect. The world couldn't stand that perfection. The Spirit has a good side and a bad side.'"

Anna touched her necklace. "Yes. I've had this bear claw forever. Bear Medicine is dark and powerful—it must be used with care. I learned that after Luz and I watched as the marvelous Ursula told a story about the arrogance of one of her cubs. A year later I met that bear—Orres—now much older, near Indian Canyon. He reminded me of what his mother said after she faced death from an angry human—'May the Universe now begin the healing. Let each stand in their place.' Powerful ancient energies were released that day, energies that drive me forward in my efforts to be a healer and a voice for other species."

Luz smiled at Anna. "The way you use your gifts continues to inspire me. I mention you often in our youth network, and you saw this weekend the support you have." In the distance, they heard Coyotes yapping. "Even the coyotes. That's Tatiki's litter. He and Kali must be training them."

"Thank you, Luz, for reminding us of Skah," said Makah. "We remember him fondly, not least because he brought me together with Cody." At this, a treasury of Goldfinches—staunch holdovers from the fall harvest ceremony—billowed out, glittering in the fading sunbeams and chattering over and around where Makah was sitting.

The evening breeze subsided with the sun as Wanda, holding their son, led Janet over to the Redwood and whispered to it, honoring it for its towering witness, its resilience, and its generosity as part of the carbon cycle.

Cody stood up, gazing into the distance, where a Gull hung in the sky. "For me it's about the sea lichen, calm but wild, with their profound connection to the planet, their explicit coexistence of species in one organism, a simple model of biodesign that can be attempted everywhere, at every scale. They're an original community in action, like the one that has emerged here in our multispecies neighborhood and habitat and, more deeply, with all of you here this evening." He turned toward the group, his hands at his sides. "May we live and love our Grandmother from this place of communion and mutual respect in the years to come."

But Luz was disturbed by a great feeling of something unfinished. She rose and walked into the garden, its vibrancy, its fragrances. Passing into the Chicken yard, she let herself be engulfed by the soft chatter of her flock, the vista beyond the hill where Tatiki and his family were hunting, and the resting places of Skah, Chanson, and Goldfinch. All this beauty, this sadness.

Luz's musings touched me—her embodiment of the planimal spirit—and I flew down and landed on the coop beside her.

And then, we turned toward you, dear reader.

I began. "We thank you all for taking this journey with us, a journey that has just begun. We look forward to your efforts to heal relations with our dear Grandmother and with each other, for there is nothing more valuable any of us can be doing."

Now filled with Earth Spirit, Luz spoke. "Thank you, Koro. I offer my gratitude especially to my mother, Makah, to dear Anna, and to the 'long line of ladies' who have nurtured me, most especially our Grandmother. And to many men as well, my dear father, Cody, and the other compassionate men who have worked, and are working, on behalf of all life. Thank you to my multicultural ancestors and all First Peoples of this land for their way-showing and to all my precious relations past and present—Skah, Tatiki, the hens, and the communion of planimal spirits that is ready to welcome humans.

"We are guests upon this crust of earth where everything—the sea, the sky, the rocks and streams, the planimals, the cosmic dust—is alive, as humans are, with heart, mind, history, and spirit. Across the glorious seasons, we seek the path that we, living beings, must find together as kin. That way does not lead back to the land or to some Edenic ideal. Rather, we must make our way as any family—with our conflicts and instincts, triggers and sharp elbows—learning from the best traditions of our past and embracing the most promising possibilities of the future, taking, as Snave once said, the *long view*.

"We will navigate the road ahead by living responsibly, assisted by the sensible use of climate-positive technologies. There will be suffering, but we shall not lose faith in the fundamental goodness of creation, nor in the prospect of healing.

"This is what I have learned so far, dear Koro. I give it back to you."

"Wow," I said. "Thank you, Luz. I will be keeping in touch as you step into your own future as part of Team Grandmother. Speaking for the planimals, we'll be there for you."

And for you, dear reader. We hope our tale has provided insight and inspiration and has opened your heart to the Earth and all who live here, to partnership with all life. We can do it, believe me, with love . . . and a little help from our friends.

THE END

The Elephant Code

Code of Conduct for Human Survival

We will honor the sanctity of the Earth, and all Her life.

We will treat each being with respect for what and who they are.

We will harm other life only to the minimum necessary for survival.

We will be mindful of the effects that our actions have for seven generations.

Acknowledgments

I AM GRATEFUL FOR THE ABUNDANT help I have been given by loving friends and relations, whose contributions go beyond measure; by artists, writers, and musicians, who have taken me into their worlds with compassion and skill; by many "planimal" teachers—friends, acquaintances, and sometime adversaries; and, by the Universe itself, and its embodiment in and through our dear Grandmother.

To the scientists, poets, and other creators I have drawn from, I hope I have been true to your intentions. I offer special gratitude for the generosity and courage of the Native American authors, artists, and readers who provided comments and insights, helping me identify and correct unintentional stereotyping and unconscious bias. Each of us has the responsibility to treat these precious lands, skies, and waters with respect and care, and to steward them in partnership for the coming generations. Half of any profits from the sale of *Crows Calling* will be used to support actions such as the Indigenous Environmental Network.

The following people deserve special thanks for their help with the manuscript: Destiny Allison, Mary Anderson, Carl Anderson, Robert Anderson, Dick Ashford, Illana Berger, Daniel Clapper, Cely Constanza, Davis Hake, Jim Gilkeson, Allen Levin, Aaron Ortega, Banks Pecht,

Nicole Phillips, Kathryn Rauhut, Charles Reynolds, Christina Forbes Reynolds, Simone Rich, Paul Richards, Michael Scanlon, Anna Schoenbach, Seongmin Song, Diane Tegtmeier, Brad Volpi, Cynthia Volpi, Trey Walker, Beth Weise, and Linda Yamane. Thanks as well to the fun, hardworking team at Greenleaf Book Group, especially Dee Kerr and Maxine Marshall, and to my fearless query coach Mark Malatesta.

Finally, to my beautiful and creative wife, Mara Anderson, who enthusiastically read dozens of drafts, providing incisive and welcome commentary and unforgettable emotional support, go my deepest appreciation and heartfelt love.

The Climate Crisis

"MOM," SAID LUZ, sitting at the dinner table during her junior year. "I want to do a radio show that's only about climate change and habitat loss. It's like there's too much info out there, and it's confusing everyone. But I don't know where to start. I need an introduction that summarizes the situation in less than ten minutes. Then my listeners will start discussing it, and we'll have an interesting show. I can also play recordings from various experts, and of course, there's lots of music these days—like the latest Wyngs release 'Shrouded Sky.'"

"I remember Wings, McCartney's band—their album *Wild Life*. My dad loved it. But what do you think, Cody, what should she say in her ten minutes? I feel like I'm too much in the weeds to know where to start on a summary."

"It's not McCartney, Mom. It's just an all-bird band."

"Nice," Cody said. "Okay, so I like talks that have three parts. You could start by describing how climate change affects people's lives. Then you could discuss habitat and biodiversity. You could end with what's being done now and the urgency of more action."

Luz tried Cody's outline, and it worked pretty well. That weekend, Kipp and Suzanne came over and she read the script to the four adults.

She also read it to Andrés and Rosa and to her friends. Here's what she came up with after all the comments.

Hello everyone, and welcome to another episode of *Luz on the Loose*, coming to you live from Pebble Beach at andrewlang.edu/radio. Today we're talking climate change—beginning with how it's affecting our lives and what's causing it—so for sure the show's going to heat up. We'll also talk about habitat loss and biodiversity. We'll end with what is being done globally and locally—and what more we can do.

Every year, the planet is getting hotter, and we're all seeing the results. Yesterday's high tides are becoming tomorrow's average sea level, submerging our beaches and low-lying roads and putting airports like SFO out of service for days at a time. Hotter, bigger wildfires are killing people and planimals, destroying property, and making insurance unaffordable. Catastrophic floods are driving people from their homes. Longer periods of hot, dry weather are causing droughts, reducing water for drinking, changing the crops farmers can grow, and turning some lands into deserts. Some parts of the Middle East are already too hot for people to survive outdoors.

Climate change presents a fundamental threat to human health. It affects natural and human systems, including health systems. It's called a threat multiplier, reversing decades of health progress. Climate change is leading to death and illness from heat waves, storms and floods, the disruption of food systems, more severe disease, and mental health issues. It is undermining livelihoods, equality, and access to health care and social support. These climate-driven health impacts hit harder on women, children, minorities, migrants, and older people. *Pause here.*

What caused this crisis? By now, everyone agrees human activity since 1850—the dawn of the industrial age—is the primary cause of global warming, primarily from fossil fuel burning and other sources, like even cattle burping. Modern lifestyles release greenhouse gases—carbon dioxide and methane in particular. They're called "greenhouse gases" because they keep the Earth's heat from escaping through the atmosphere and warm things up, just like a greenhouse. The greenhouse heats up the air and the land, and also the sea. The warming oceans expand in volume, and melting glaciers and ice sheets add more water, leading to more violent storms and rising sea levels. Never in the last million years have these gases been so concentrated in the atmosphere. *Pause here.*

Back in 2015, the nations of the world signed a binding climate treaty. It aimed to limit global overheating to less than two degrees centigrade, or *c*, and preferably to 1.5 degrees c, compared with 1850. Meeting these targets would have required a 45 percent decrease in greenhouse gas emissions from 2010 to 2030. Today, however, human activities are emitting more greenhouse gas than ever. The world has given up on 1.5 c, which will lead to major consequences—unbearable heat, drought, flooding, refugees, extinctions, and climate wars—worldwide.

Even these predictions assume that we don't hit any of the major "tipping points"—events that could blow the problem out of the water (haha) in unpredictable ways. These include the melting of the Greenland or West Antarctic ice sheets, the collapse of the Gulf Stream that warms the Atlantic Ocean and Northern Europe, runaway thawing of the permafrost that blocks carbon emissions from the northern lands it covers, and mass die-offs of warm-water coral reefs that protect coastal areas and are critical to the global food chain.

Speaking of die-offs, let's talk about habitat loss. What *is* it, anyway? It's when changes to the natural environment make it hard or impossible for the species who live there to survive. They have to adapt or move, or they will die. Take our closest relatives—the vertebrates—including elephants, penguins, turtles, and fish of all kinds. These wildlife populations have plunged, on average, by three-quarters in the last fifty years. For example, in 2015, in the mountains of Kazakhstan, 200,000 saiga antelope—60 percent of the world's population—died in just three weeks when abnormal heat and humidity turned harmless bacteria into killers.

A lot of people think, *So what if some animals or plants die off?* We'll still be okay, right? What you have to remember is that humans and planimals are interdependent.

When species disappear, humans suffer. Of course we'll miss our planimal friends, including having fresh fish for dinner and feeling sad at the eerie silence in the woods where birdcalls used to be heard. I can tell you: Being in nature is good for your mental health.

And there are scarier losses. When no bees pollinate, no apples or corn will grow. Most cancer drugs come from bio sources, many from remote places where Indigenous peoples' knowledge of plant and animal curative powers come into play. As natural habitats are destroyed by human activity, some animals move closer to humans, increasing our chances of getting infected by animal diseases, like swine flu and Covid.

Finally, the loss of trees—deforestation—means that our leafy relations are no longer there to take carbon out of the atmosphere, creating a vicious cycle of heating and destruction.

So, what is being done and what can we do?

Climate change is a global problem, and the United Nations is trying to address it. I already mentioned the goals set for carbon reduction—goals we are not meeting. A similar situation exists with biodiversity—lots of talk but no real commitments of resources. The implementation is left up to national governments and politics.

To me, overall, it seems unlikely that governments will lead the way to sustainable climate solutions in time. There are promising developments—vision and innovation—underway from private sector leaders. We are starting to get big payoffs from moving to solar and wind energy, but we also need to stop turning natural ecosystems into malls and data centers. AI can help us, but it also uses a lot of additional electricity.

More and more people are trying to do the right things—reduce consumption in their individual lives, bring back native ecologies, innovate to reduce carbon emissions, and work with others to change the systems. My mom and dad are both working hard on it. The big factor is the clock. The extent to which we and future generations will suffer in a hotter, different world depends on the choices we make now.

We need to continue working to slow down global warming. The experts call that mitigation. But we also need adaptation—admitting that a very different future is coming and preparing to live in it. For example, as my dad says about the ag sector, old-fashioned methods like rotating animals through the pastures, composting, not transporting food all over the world, not using oil to make fertilizer, and moving from grain-fed to grass-fed meat can really make a difference. Walking and cycling and shifting to sustainable, healthy diets help everyone.

On a more global perspective, nearly three billion people still burn kerosene, coal, wood, or other biomass for cooking. Getting them on clean energy will increase their quality of life while reducing global heating, air pollution, and lung disease.

Behavior and lifestyle changes can inspire others to shift to low-emissions consumption. If we share the benefits and burdens, more people will support such big changes. Low-cost options for mitigation and adaptation are already available. There are so many great things we can do together. We'll talk about this more on the show, but for sure check out www.regeneration.org for ideas.

Okay, I see I've already got some questions and comments coming in through the chat. . . .

Selected References

I. Climate and the Environment

Boulton, Chris, Timothy Lenton, and Niklas Boers. "Pronounced Loss of Amazon Rainforest Resilience Since the Early 2000s." *Nature Climate Change* 12, no. 3 (March 2022): 271–78. https://www.nature.com/articles/s41558-022-01287-8.

Branford, Sue. "Mexico Devises Revolutionary Method to Reverse Semiarid Land Degradation." Mongabay. August 11, 2021. https://news.mongabay.com/2021/08/mexico-devises-revolutionary-method-to-reverse-semiarid-land-degradation.

Campbell, Iona, Adrian Macleod, Christian Sahlmann, Luiza Neves, Jon Funderud, et al. "The Environmental Risks Associated with the Development of Seaweed Farming in Europe—Prioritizing Key Knowledge Gaps." *Frontiers in Marine Science* 6 (March 2019). https://www.frontiersin.org/journals/marine-science/articles/10.3389/fmars.2019.00107/full.

Diffenbaugh, Noah, and Elizabeth Barnes. "Data-Driven Predictions of the Time Remaining Until Critical Global Warming Thresholds Are Reached." *Proceedings of the National Academy of Sciences of the United States of America* 120, no. 6 (January 2023). https://pubmed.ncbi.nlm.nih.gov/36716375/.

Ehrlich, Paul. *The Machinery of Nature*. Touchstone, 1987.

Fereidouni, Sasan, Graham Freimanis, Mukhit Orynbayev, Paolo Ribeca, John Flannery, et al. "Mass Die-Off of Saiga Antelopes, Kazakhstan, 2015." *Emerging Infectious Diseases* 25, no. 6 (June 2019): 1169–76. https://pubmed.ncbi.nlm.nih.gov/31107235/.

Finney, Mark, and Robert Martin. "Short Fire Intervals Recorded By Redwoods At Annadel State Park, California." *Madroño* 39, no. 4 (October–December 1992): 251–62. https://www.jstor.org/stable/41424920.

Hall, Dale, and Nic Lutsey. "Effects of Battery Manufacturing on Electric Vehicle Life-Cycle Greenhouse Gas Emissions." The International Council on Clean Transportation. February 9, 2018. https://theicct.org/publication/effects-of-battery-manufacturing-on-electric-vehicle-life-cycle-greenhouse-gas-emissions/.

Hawken, Paul. *Regeneration: Ending the Climate Crisis in One Generation*. Penguin, 2021.

———. *Carbon: The Book of Life*. Viking, 2025.

Hickman, Caroline, Elizabeth Marks, Panu Pihkala, Susan Clayton, Eric Lewandowski, et al. "Climate Anxiety in Children and Young People and Their Beliefs About Government Responses to Climate Change: A Global Survey." *The Lancet Planetary Health* 5, no. 12 (December 2021): e863–73 https://www.thelancet.com/journals/lanplh/article/PIIS2542-5196(21)00278-3/fulltext.

Hill, Alice. *The Fight for Climate After Covid-19*. Oxford University Press, 2021.

IPCC. *Climate Change and Land: An IPCC Special Report on Climate Change, Desertification, Land Degradation, Sustainable Land Management, Food Security, and Greenhouse Gas Fluxes in Terrestrial Ecosystems*. Intergovernmental Panel on Climate Change, 2019. https://www.ipcc.ch/srccl/.

IPCC. *Climate Change 2021: The Physical Science Basis—Summary for Policymakers*. Intergovernmental Panel on Climate Change, 2021. https://www.ipcc.ch/report/sixth-assessment-report-working-group-i/.

IPCC. *Climate Change 2022: Impacts, Adaptation and Vulnerability—Summary for Policymakers*. Intergovernmental Panel on Climate Change, 2022. https://www.ipcc.ch/report/sixth-assessment-report-working-group-ii/.

IPCC. *Climate Change 2023: Synthesis Report. Contribution of Working Groups I, II, and III to the Sixth Assessment Report*. Intergovernmental Panel on Climate Change, 2023. https://www.ipcc.ch/report/sixth-assessment-report-cycle/.

Jägermeyr, Jonas, Christoph Müller, Alex C. Ruane, Joshua Elliott, Juraj Balkovic, et al. "Climate Impacts on Global Agriculture Emerge Earlier in New Generation of Climate and Crop Models." *Nature Food* 2, no. 11 (November 2021): 873–85. https://www.nature.com/articles/s43016-021-00400-y.

Johnston, James, R. Keala Hagmann, S. Trent Seager, Andrew Merschel, Jerry Franklin, and K. Norman Johnson. "Commentary: Large Trees Dominate Carbon Storage in Forests East of the Cascade Crest in the United States Pacific Northwest." *Frontiers in Forests and Global Change* 4 (March 2021) https://www.frontiersin.org/journals/forests-and-global-change/articles/10.3389/ffgc.2021.653774/full.

Kemp, Luke, Chi Xu, Joanna Depledge, Kristie Ebi, Goodwin Gibbons, et al. "Climate Endgame: Exploring Catastrophic Climate Change Scenarios." *Proceedings of the National Academy of Sciences of the United States of America* 119, no. 34 e2108146119 (August 2022). https://doi.org/10.1073/pnas.2108146119.

Kilgore, Bruce, and Dan Taylor. "Fire History of a Sequoia-Mixed Conifer Forest." *Ecology* 60, no. 1 (February 1979): 129–42. https://doi.org/10.2307/1936475.

Kimmerer, Robin Wall. *Braiding Sweetgrass: Indigenous Wisdom, Scientific Knowledge and the Teachings of Plants*. Milkweed Editions, 2013.

Laybourn Laurie, Henry Throp, and Suzannah Sherman. *1.5°c—Dead or Alive?: The Risks to Transformational Change From Reaching and Breaching the Paris Agreement Goal*. IPPR and Chatham House, 2023.

Lopez-Ridaura, Santiago, Luis Barba-Escoto, Cristian Reyna-Ramirez, Carlos Sum, Natalia Palacios-Rojas, et al. "Maize Intercropping in the Milpa System. Diversity, Extent and Importance for Nutritional Security in the Western Highlands of Guatemala." *Scientific Reports* 11 (2021). https://doi.org/10.1038/s41598-021-82784-2.

McKibben, Bill. *Eaarth: Making a Life on a Tough New Planet*. Macmillan, 2010.

———. *Falter: Has the Human Game Begun to Play Itself Out?* Henry Holt and Company, 2019.

Mearns, Robin. *Social Dimensions of Climate Change: Workshop Report 2008*. World Bank, 2008. https://www.semanticscholar.org/paper/Social-dimensions-of-climate-change-%3A-workshop-2008-Mearns/7df10a5447b389ee6c267b58bf5c7b56b3f0a476 .

Mildrexler, David, Logan Berner, Beverly Law, Richard Birdsey, and William Moomaw. "Large Trees Dominate Carbon Storage in Forests East of the Cascade Crest in the United States Pacific Northwest." *Frontiers in Forests and Global Change* 3 (November 2020). https://www.frontiersin.org/journals/forests-and-global-change/articles/10.3389/ffgc.2020.594274/full.

Pathak, Tapan, Mahesh Maskey, Jeffery Dahlberg, Faith Kearns, Khaled Bali, et al. "Climate Change Trends and Impacts on California Agriculture: A Detailed Review." *Agronomy* 8, no. 3 (2018): 25. https://doi.org/10.3390/agronomy8030025.

Pollan, Michael. *The Omnivore's Dilemma: A Natural History of Four Meals*. Penguin, 2006.

Radovich, John. "The Collapse of the California Sardine Fishery: What Have We Learned?" In *Resource Management and Environmental Uncertainty: Lessons From Coastal Upwelling Fisheries*, edited by Michael H. Glantz and J. Dana Thompson, John Wiley & Sons, 1981: 56–78. https://calcofi.org/downloads/publications/calcofireports/v23/Vol_23_Radovich.pdf.

Ripple, William, Christopher Wolf, Michael Phillips, Robert Beschta, John Vucetich, et al. "Rewilding the American West." *BioScience* 72, no. 10 (October 2022): 931–35. https://academic.oup.com/bioscience/article/72/10/931/6651305.

Sáenz Arroyo, Andrea, Callum Roberts, Jorge Torre, Micheline Cariño-Olvera, and Julie Hawkins. "The Value of Evidence About Past Abundance: Marine Fauna of the Gulf of California Through the Eyes of 16th to 19th Century Travellers." *Fish and Fisheries* 7, no. 2 (May 2006): 128–46. https://onlinelibrary.wiley.com/doi/abs/10.1111/j.1467-2979.2006.00214.x.

Seed, John. *Thinking Like a Mountain: Towards a Council of All Beings*. New Society Pub, 1988.

Steffen, Will, Johan Rockström, Katherine Richardson, Timothy Lenton, Carl Folke, et al. "Trajectories of the Earth System in the Anthropocene." *Proceedings of the National Academy of Sciences of the United States of America* 115, no. 33 (August 2018): 8252–59. https://pubmed.ncbi.nlm.nih.gov/30082409/.

Stephens, Scott, and Danny Fry. *Fire History in Coast Redwood Stands in San Mateo County Parks and Jasper Ridge, Santa Cruz Mountains*. US Forest Service, 2007. https://research.fs.usda.gov/treesearch/28263.

Stoms, David. "Energy Infrastructure Risks from Climate Change." California Energy Commission, Energy Research and Development Division, 2014 Workshop on SF Emission Reduction Strategies, Long Beach, CA, May 6, 2014, https://www.epa.gov/sites/default/files/2016-02/documents/stoms-infrastructure-risks-presentation-2014-wkshp.pdf.

United Nations Environmental Program. *Emissions Gap Report 2021*. 2021. https://www.unep.org/resources/emissions-gap-report-2021.

United Nations Environmental Program. "Convention on International Trade in Endangered Species of Wild Fauna and Flora, Appendices I, II, and III." 2021. https://cites.org/eng/app/appendices.php.

World Meteorological Organization. *2024 State of Climate Services: Five-Year Progress Report (2019–2024)*. WMO, 2024. https://library.wmo.int/viewer/69061.

World Bank Group. *Green, Resilient, and Inclusive Development*. 2021. WBG, 2021. https://hdl.handle.net/10986/36322.

World Wide Fund for Nature. *Living Planet Report 2024*. World Wide Fund For Nature, 2024. https://files.worldwildlife.org/wwfcmsprod/files/Publication/file/5gc2qerb1v_2024_living_planet_report_a_system_in_peril.pdf.

II. PLANIMAL STORIES

Beier, Paul. "Cougar Attacks on Humans in the United States and Canada." *Wildlife Society Bulletin* 19, no. 4 (January 1991): 403–12. https://www.jstor.org/stable/3782149.

Clark, Joseph. *Beastly Folklore*. Scarecrow Press, 1968.

Clutton-Brock, Juliet. *A Natural History of Domesticated Mammals*. Cambridge University Press, 1999.

Coldwell, Will. "Queen of the Corvids: The Scientist Fighting to Save the World's Brainiest Birds." *The Guardian*. June 19, 2022. https://www.theguardian.com/environment/2022/jun/19/queen-of-corvids-the-scientist-fighting-to-save-the-worlds-brainiest-birds.

Collin, Yvette Running Horse. "The Relationship Between the Indigenous Peoples of the Americas and the Horse: Deconstructing a Eurocentric Myth." PhD diss., University of Alaska, 2017. https://scholarworks.alaska.edu/handle/11122/7592.

Doyle, Brian. *Mink River: A Novel*. Oregon State University Press, 2010.

———. *Martin Marten: A Novel*. Macmillan, 2015.

Dunayer, Jane. "Sexist Words, Speciesist Roots." In *Animals and Women: Feminist Theoretical Explorations*, edited by Carol J. Adams, and Josephine Donovan, 381. Duke University Press, 1995.

Feher-Elston, Catherine. *Ravensong: A Natural and Fabulous History of Ravens and Crows*. TarcherPerigee, 2005.

Flores, Dan. *Wild New World: The Epic Story of Animals and People in America*. National Geographic Books, 2022.

Frembgen, Jürgen W. "The Magicality of the Hyena: Beliefs and Practices in West and South Asia." *Asian Folklore Studies* 57, no. 2 (1998): 331–44. https://www.jstor.org/stable/1178757.

Graves, Keith. *Chicken Big*. Chronicle Books, 2010.

Hansen, Kevin, and Mountain Lion Foundation. *Cougar: The American Lion*. Northland Pub, 1992.

Harriman, Arthur, and Robert Berger. "Olfactory Acuity in the Common Raven (Corvus Corax)." *Physiology & Behavior* 36, no. 2 (1986): 257–62. https://pubmed.ncbi.nlm.nih.gov/3960998/.

Henderson, Claire. *The Aboriginal North American Horse*. Testimony in support of Senate Bill 2278 (North Dakota), February 1, 1991. https://returntofreedom.org/PDFs/AboriginalNorthAmericanHorse.pdf.

Kalof, Linda. *Looking at Animals in Human History*. Reaktion Books, 2007.

Kopf, R. Keller, Sam Banks, Lauren Brent, Paul Humphries, Chris Jolly, et al. "Loss of Earth's Old, Wise, and Large animals." *Science*. November 21, 2024. https://doi.org/10.1126/science.ado2705.

Krivak, Andrew. *The Bear*. Bellevue Literary Press, 2020.

Larson, Gary, Robert Timm, and Scott Hygnstrom. *Prevention and Control of Wildlife Damage: A Handbook for People Who Deal with Wildlife Damage Problems*. Diane Pub Co, 1994.

Louv, Richard. *Our Wild Calling: How Connecting with Animals Can Transform Our Lives—and Save Theirs*. Algonquin Books, 2020.

Minta, Steven, Kathryn Minta, and Dale Lott. "Hunting Associations Between Badgers (*Taxidea Taxus*) and Coyotes (*Canis Latrans*)." *Journal of Mammalogy* 73, no. 4 (November 1992): 814–20. https://doi.org/10.2307/1382201.

Moss, Cynthia. *Elephant Memories: Thirteen Years in the Life of an Elephant Family*. William Morrow & Company, 1988.

Mustill, Tom. *How to Speak Whale: A Voyage into the Future of Animal Communication*. Hachette Book Group, 2022.

Ryden, Hope. *God's Dog: A Celebration of the North American Coyote*. iUniverse, 2005.

Shaw, George Bernard. *Androcles and the Lion*. Penguin Books, 1962.

Sheldrake, Merlin. *Entangled Life: How Fungi Make Our Worlds, Change Our Minds & Shape Our Futures*. Random House, 2020.

Toynbee, Jocelyn. *Animals in Roman Life and Art*. Cornell University Press, 1996.

Trimble, Lawrence. *Strongheart: The Story of a Wonder Dog*. Whitman Publishing Company, 1926.

Wohlleben, Peter. *The Power of Trees: How Ancient Forests Can Save Us if We Let Them*. Greystone Books Ltd., 2023.

III. INDIGENOUS CULTURES

Allen, Paula Gunn. *Grandmothers of the Light: A Medicine Woman's Sourcebook*. Beacon Press, 1992.

Berman, Tressa. *Circle of Goods: Women, Work, and Welfare in a Reservation Community*. SUNY Press, 2003.

California Environmental Protection Agency. "2013 Tribal Consultative Listening Sessions Summary." July 2013. https://calepa.ca.gov/wp-content/uploads/sites/6/2016/10/Tribal-Documents-2013yr-ListSessions.pdf.

Cameron, Anne. *Daughters of Copper Woman*. Press Gang Pub, 1981.

Curtis, Edward S. *The Mandan, The Arikara, The Atsina*. Vol. 5, *The North American Indian*. The University Press, 1909.

Dove, Mourning. *Coyote Stories*. University of Nebraska Press, 1990.

Dundes, Alan, and C. Fayne Porter. "American Indian Student Slang." *American Speech* 38, no. 4 (December 1963): 270–77. https://www.jstor.org/stable/453225.

Fenn, Elizabeth. *Encounters at the Heart of the World: A History of the Mandan People*. Hill and Wang, 2015.

Fire, John (Lame Deer), and Richard Erdoes. *Lame Deer, Seeker of Visions: The Life of a Sioux Medicine Man*. Simon and Schuster, 1972.

Gimbutas, Marija, and Miriam Robbins Dexter. *The Living Goddesses*. University of California Press, 1999.

Graeber, David, and David Wengrow. *The Dawn of Everything: A New History of Humanity*. Farrar, Straus and Giroux, 2021.

Hanson, Erin. "Oral Traditions." Indigenous Foundations. First Nations Studies Program, The University of British Columbia. https://indigenousfoundations.arts.ubc.ca/oral_traditions/.

Hernandez, Jessica. *Fresh Banana Leaves: Healing Indigenous Landscapes Through Indigenous Science*. North Atlantic Books, 2022.

Hollow, Robert Charles, Jr. "A Mandan Dictionary." PhD diss., University of California Berkeley, 1971.

Hyde, Lewis. *Trickster Makes This World: Mischief, Myth, and Art*. Farrar Straus & Giroux, 1998.

Jamail, Dahr, and Stan Rushworth. *We Are the Middle of Forever: Indigenous Voices from Turtle Island on the Changing Earth*. The New Press, 2022.

Jones, David. *Poison Arrows: North American Indian Hunting and Warfare*. University of Texas Press, 2009.

Kelly, Isabel. "Ethnography of the Surprise Valley Paiute." *University of California Publications in American Archaeology and Ethnology* 31, no. 3 (1932): 67–210 https://digicoll.lib.berkeley.edu/record/82933/files/ucp037-004.pdf.

Kroeber, A. L. *The Chumash and Costanoan Languages*. The University Press, 1910.

Kroeber, Alfred Louis. *Indian Myths of South Central California*, 1907.

Margolin, Malcolm. *The Ohlone Way: Indian Life in the San Francisco-Monterey Bay Area*. Heyday, 1978.

———. *Deep Hanging Out: Wanderings and Wonderment in Native California*. Heyday, 2021.

Martin, Calvin. *Keepers of the Game: Indian-Animal Relationships and the Fur Trade*. University of California Press, 1978.

Matthews, Washington. *Grammar and Dictionary of the Language of the Hidatsa*. Cramoisy Press, 1873.

Mayfield, Thomas Jefferson. *Indian Summer: Traditional Life Among the Choinumne Indians of California's San Joaquin Valley*. Heyday Books, 1993.

Meyer, Roy. "Fort Berthold and the Garrison Dam." *North Dakota History* 35, no 3–4 (1968): 220–355.

Mixco, Mauricio. 1997. "Mandan Switch Reference: A Preliminary View." *Anthropological Linguistics* 39, no. 2 (Summer 1997): 220–98. https://www.jstor.org/stable/30028466.

NAMI. *Donde Vivemos: Libro De Rompecabezas De Arte Indigena Americano*. National Museum of the American Indian, 2012.

Nelson, Richard. *Make Prayers to the Raven: A Koyukon View of the Northern Forest*. The University of Chicago Press, 1986.

Neihardt, John. *Black Elk Speaks: Being the Life Story of a Holy Man of the Oglala Sioux*. Bison Books, 2000.

Pritchard, Evan. *Native American Stories of the Sacred: Annotated & Explained*. SkyLight Paths Publishing, 2005.

Ramirez, Renya. *Standing Up to Colonial Power: The Lives of Henry Roe and Elizabeth Bender Cloud*. University of Nebraska Press, 2018.

Redvers, Nicole. *The Science of the Sacred: Bridging Global Indigenous Medicine Systems and Modern Scientific Principles*. National Geographic Books, 2019.

Risling-Baldy, Cutcha, Lyn Risling, Lois Risling, Melodie George-Moore, Tayshu Bommelyn, and Geneva Shaw. "Revitalizing Flower Dance Ceremonies in Northwest California." Two Feathers NAFS. June 12, 2020. YouTube video, 1:44:45, https://www.youtube.com/watch?v=369ni8tUBlU.

Suzuki, David, and Peter Knudtson. *Wisdom of the Elders: Honoring Sacred Native Visions of Nature*. Bantam, 1992.

Treuer, David. "'A Sadness I Can't Carry': The Story of the Drum." *The New York Times*, August 31, 2021. https://www.nytimes.com/2021/08/31/magazine/ojibwe-big-drum.html.

Wiegand, Phil, and Jay Fikes. "Sensacionalismo Y Etnografía: El Caso de Los Huicholes de Jalisco." *Relaciones: Estudios de Historia y Sociedad* 98 (2004): 49–68. https://www.redalyc.org/articulo.oa?id=13709803.

Will, George Francis, and Herbert Joseph Spinden. *The Mandans: A Study of Their Culture, Archaeology and Language*. Peabody Museum Press, 1906.

Williams, Maria, and Felix Vigil. *How Raven Stole the Sun*. Abbeville Kids, 2000.

Yamane, Linda. *When the World Ended; How Hummingbird Got Fire; How People Were Made: Rumsien Ohlone Stories*. Oyate, 1995.

Younging, Gregory. *Elements of Indigenous Style: A Guide for Writing By and About Indigenous Peoples*. Brush Education, 2018.

Zehtabchi, Rayka, and Shaandiin Tome, dir. *Long Line of Ladies*. 2022: *New York Times* Op-Docs. https://www.nytimes.com/video/opinion/100000008461725/long-line-of-ladies.html.

IV. CONSCIOUSNESS AND KINSHIP

Baldwin, James. *Notes of a Native Son*. Beacon Press, 1988.

Boone, John Allen. *Kinship with All Life*. Harper & Row, 1954.

Buhner, Stephen Harrod. *Plant Intelligence and the Imaginal Realm: Beyond the Doors of Perception Into the Dreaming of Earth*. Bear & Company, 2014.

Einstein, Albert, and Michael Amrine. 1946. "'The Real Problem Is in the Hearts of Men'; Professor Einstein Says a New Type of Thinking Is Needed to Meet the Challenge of the Atomic Bomb." *The New York Times*. June 23, 1946. https://www.nytimes.com/1946/06/23/archives/the-real-problem-is-in-the-hearts-of-men-professor-einstein-says-a.html.

Feiten, Tim. "Mind After Uexküll: A Foray into the Worlds of Ecological Psychologists and Enactivists." *Frontiers in Psychology* 11 (2020): 480.

Freire, Paulo. *Pedagogy of the Oppressed*. The Seabury Press, 1970.

Godfrey-Smith, Peter. *Metazoa: Animal Life and the Birth of the Mind*. Farrar, Straus and Giroux, 2020.

Grandin, Temple, and Catherine Johnson. *Animals in Translation: Using the Mysteries of Autism to Decode Animal Behavior*. Houghton Mifflin Harcourt, 2006.

Harvey, Andrew, and Carolyn Baker. *Saving Animals from Ourselves: A Manifesto for Healing the Divine Animal Within*. iUniverse, 2019.

Hermanns, William. *Einstein and the Poet: In Search of the Cosmic Man*. Branden Publishing Company, 1983.

Holgate, Ben. *Climate and Crises: Magical Realism as Environmental Discourse*. Routledge, 2019.

Low, Philip. "The Cambridge Declaration on Consciousness." Edited by Jaak Panksepp, Diana Reiss, David Edelman, Bruno Van Swinderen, Philip Low, et al. Proceedings of the Francis Crick Memorial Conference, Churchill College, Cambridge University, Cambridge, England, July 7, 2012. https://fcmconference.org/img/CambridgeDeclarationOnConsciousness.pdf.

Maufort, Jessica. "Book Review of Climate and Crises: Magical Realism as Environmental Discourse." *Ecozon@* 11, no. 1 (Spring 2020): 204–6. https://ecozona.eu/article/view/3265.

Nagel, Thomas. 1974. "What Is It like to Be a Bat." *The Philosophical Review* 83, no. 4 (October 1974): 435–50. https://www.jstor.org/stable/2183914.

Penrose, Roger. *The Large, the Small and the Human Mind.* Cambridge University Press, 1997.

Powers, Richard. *The Overstory: A Novel.* W.W. Norton, 2018.

———. *Bewilderment: A Novel.* W. W. Norton, 2021.

Sheldrake, Rupert. *Science Set Free: 10 Paths to New Discovery.* Crown Pub, 2012.

Shepard, Paul. *Thinking Animals: Animals and the Development of Human Intelligence.* Viking, 1978.

Smolin, Lee. *The Life of the Cosmos.* Oxford University Press, 1997.

Soga, Masashi, and Kevin Gaston. "Extinction of Experience: The Loss of Human-Nature Interactions." *Frontiers in Ecology and the Environment* 14, no. 2 (March 2016): 94–101. https://esajournals.onlinelibrary.wiley.com/doi/10.1002/fee.1225.

Sonea, Sorin, and Leo Mathieu. "Evolution of the Genomic Systems of Prokaryotes and Its Momentous Consequences." *International Microbiology* 4, no. 2 (June 2001): 67–71. https://esajournals.onlinelibrary.wiley.com/journal/15409309.

Sperry, Roger. "The Riddle of Consciousness and the Changing Scientific Worldview." *Journal of Humanistic Psychology* 35, no. 2 (Spring 1995): 7–33. https://journals.sagepub.com/doi/10.1177/00221678950352002.

Uexküll, Jakob von. *A Foray into the Worlds of Animals and Humans: With a Theory of Meaning.* University of Minnesota Press, 2013.

Williams, David. *The Trickster Brain: Neuroscience, Evolution, and Narrative.* Lexington Books, 2012.

Yong, Ed. *An Immense World: How Animal Senses Reveal the Hidden Realms Around Us.* Random House, 2022.

V. SCIENCE, HISTORY, AND GOVERNANCE

Bell, Tom, Kyle Cavanaugh, Vienna Saccomanno, Catherine Cavanaugh, Henry Houskeeper, et al. "Kelpwatch: A New Visualization and Analysis Tool to Explore Kelp Canopy Dynamics Reveals Variable Response to and Recovery from Marine Heatwaves." *PLoS One* 18, no. 3 (March 2023). https://pubmed.ncbi.nlm.nih.gov/36952444/.

Brancato, Mary Sue, L. Milonas, Ed Bowlby, and Ronald Jameson. "Chemical Contaminants, Pathogen Exposure and General Health Status of Live and Beach-Cast Washington Sea Otters (Enhydra Lutris Kenyoni)." Marine Sanctuaries Conservation Series ONMS-08-08, Silverspring, Maryland, February 2009. https://nmssanctuaries.blob.core.windows.net/sanctuaries-prod/media/archive/science/conservation/pdfs/brancato.pdf.

Brown, Daniel James. *Facing the Mountain: A True Story of Japanese American Heroes in World War II*. Penguin, 2021.

Detweiler, Shane, and Anne Wein, ed. *The HayWired Earthquake Scenario: Societal Consequences*. US Geological Survey Scientific Investigations Report 2017-5013-R–W. October 2021. https://doi.org/10.3133/sir20175013V3.

DisCO.coop, Transnational Institute, and Guerilla Media Collective. *If I Only Had a Heart: A Disco Manifesto*. 2019. https://www.tni.org/files/profiles-downloads/disco_manifesto_v.1.pdf.

Fink, Augusta. *Monterey: The Presence of the Past*. Chronicle Books, 1972.

Hackl, Cathy. "What Are DAOs and Why You Should Pay Attention." *Forbes*. June 1, 2021. https://www.forbes.com/sites/cathyhackl/2021/06/01/what-are-daos-and-why-you-should-pay-attention/.

Hansen, Brian, Magnus Jacobsen, Anne Lise Middelboe, Christina Preston, Roman Marin III, et al. "Remote, Autonomous Real-Time Monitoring of Environmental DNA from Commercial Fish." *Scientific Reports* 10, no. 1 (August 2020). https://pubmed.ncbi.nlm.nih.gov/32764624/.

Luhung, Irvan, Yan Wu, Siyu Xu, Naomichi Yamamoto, Victor Wei-Chung Chang, and William Nazaroff. "DNA Accumulation on Ventilation System Filters in University Buildings in Singapore." *PLoS One* 12, no. 10 (October 2017). https://pubmed.ncbi.nlm.nih.gov/29023520/.

Lynggaard, Christina, Mads Bertelsen, Casper Jensen, Matthew Johnson, Tobias Frøslev, et al. "Airborne Environmental DNA for Terrestrial Vertebrate Community Monitoring." *Current Biology* 32, no. 3: 701–7. https://www.sciencedirect.com/science/article/pii/S0960982221016900.

Mathieu, Léo, and Sorin Sonea. "A Powerful Bacterial World." *Endeavour* 19, no. 3 (1995): 112–17. https://doi.org/10.1016/0160-9327(95)97496-U.

Organization for Economic Cooperation and Development. *Innovative Citizen Participation and New Democratic Institutions*. June 10, 2020. https://www.oecd.org/en/publications/innovative-citizen-participation-and-new-democratic-institutions_339306da-en.html.

Palumbi, Stephen, and Carolyn Sotka. *The Death and Life of Monterey Bay: A Story of Revival*. Island Press, 2011.

Ramirez, Alexia. "Police Need a Warrant to Collect DNA We Inevitably Leave Behind." American Civil Liberties Union. March 10, 2020. https://www.aclu.org/news/privacy-technology/police-need-a-warrant-to-collect-dna-we-inevitably-leave-behind.

Rogers-Bennett, Laura, and Cynthia Catton. "Marine Heat Wave and Multiple Stressors Tip Bull Kelp Forest to Sea Urchin Barrens." *Scientific Reports* 9, no. 1 (October 2019): 15050. https://pubmed.ncbi.nlm.nih.gov/31636286/.

Seok, Youngung, Joonseok Lee, and Min-Gon Kim. "Paper-Based Airborne Bacteria Collection and DNA Extraction Kit." *Biosensors (Basel)* 11, no. 10 (October 2021): 375. https://pubmed.ncbi.nlm.nih.gov/34677331/.

Shirasu, Mika, and Kazushige Touhara. "The Scent of Disease: Volatile Organic Compounds of the Human Body Related to Disease and Disorder." *The Journal of Biochemistry* 150, no. 3 (July 2011): 257–66. https://doi.org/10.1093/jb/mvr090.

Smith, Linda. "High-Rise Piggeries: What China's Pork Industry Transformation Means to U.S. Farmers." *Ag Web Farm Journal.* August 2, 2021. https://www.agweb.com/news/livestock/pork/high-rise-piggeries-what-chinas-pork-industry-transformation-means-u-s-farmers.

Stefos, Theodor, Dimitrios Lolis, Alexander Sotiriadis, and George Ziakas. "Embryonic Heart Rate in Early Pregnancy." *Journal of Clinical Ultrasound* 26, no. 1 (December 1998): 33–36. https://doi.org/10.1002/(SICI)1097-0096(199801)26:1<33::AID-JCU7>3.0.CO;2-K.

Stephenson, Neal. *Snow Crash: A Novel.* Spectra, 2003.

Strand, Nicolle. "Shedding Privacy Along with Our Genetic Material: What Constitutes Adequate Legal Protection Against Surreptitious Genetic Testing." *AMA Journal of Ethics* 18, no. 3 (March 2016): 264–71. https://doi.org/10.1001/journalofethics.2016.18.3.pfor2-1603.

Taira, Taka'aki, Roland Bürgmann, Robert M. Nadeau, and Douglas Dreger. "Variability of Fault Slip Behavior Along the San Andreas Fault in the San Juan Bautista Region." *Journal of Geophysical Research: Solid Earth* 119, no. 12 (October 2014): 8827–44. https://doi.org/10.1002/2014JB011427.

Toppozada, T., D. Branum, M. Peterson, C. Hallstrom, C. Cramer, et al. "Map Sheet 49: Epicenters of and Areas Damaged By M≥5 California Earthquakes, 1800–1999." California Division of Mines and Geology, Department of Conservation. 2000. https://www.conservation.ca.gov/cgs/Documents/Publications/Map-Sheets/MS_049.pdf.

U.S. Fish & Wildlife Service. "FWS-Listed U.S. Species by Taxonomic Group." 2022. https://ecos.fws.gov/ecp/report/species-listings-by-tax-group-totals.

Whitmore, Liam, Mark McCauley, Jessica Farrell, Maximilian Stammnitz, Samantha Koda, et al. "Inadvertent Human Genomic Bycatch and Intentional Capture Raise Beneficial Applications and Ethical Concerns with Environmental DNA." *Nature Ecology & Evolution* 7 (2023): 873–88. https://www.nature.com/articles/s41559-023-02056-2.

Yoshida, Shosuke, Kazumi Hiraga, Toshihiko Takehana, Ikuo Taniguchi, Hironao Yamaji, et al. "A Bacterium That Degrades and Assimilates Poly (ethylene Terephthalate)." *Science* 351, no. 6278 (March 2016): 1196–99. https://doi.org/10.1126/science.aad6359.

Zhang, Rongpeng, and Tianzhen Hong. "Modeling of HVAC Operational Faults in Building Performance Simulation." *Applied Energy* 202 (September 2017): 178–88. https://doi.org/10.1016/j.apenergy.2017.05.153.

A Conversation with the Author

How did you come to write *Crows Calling*?

I was taking a walk in a redwood forest near Oakland, California. It's a place I've visited often, so peaceful and restorative. I was standing in a quiet grove of redwoods, their brown-red trunks reaching to the sky. Suddenly, crows were calling from the emerald canopy above me. It was unlike any call I'd heard, insistent and serious, but not an alarm warning of an approaching hawk. It had a deeper resonance—more considered, if you will. I felt they were telling me how angry and upset they were at the destruction of the natural world around them. *This is our home*, they said, *and it's your home too.* You humans need to get your act together. And YOU need to be part of that. YOU need to convey OUR message to your fellow humans. We have GOT to live together in harmony. We'll be watching you, they said. That's when I started writing *Crows Calling.*

So that explains why Koro, the crow, plays such an important part in the story. But why did you decide to make her the narrator?

Actually, I hesitated about it. Some readers find it challenging. But the crows reminded me that it was their voice that was behind the story, so I had to. I've come to think of planimals as underrepresented voices in our modern society.

What do you want readers to take away from *Crows Calling*?

I hope my readers start to think differently about how they relate to the rest of the natural world. I want them to tap into their own experiences relating to other life forms. Almost all of us have had some kind of communication with other plants and animals—planimals. Dogs and cats are most common for many of us. We know how they sense our thoughts and moods, how they communicate their wishes and their love. By giving the planimals voice, I make explicit those nonverbal communications. It's as if we could read their minds. When we remember that other animals and plants are like us, we can start to treat them with love and respect. If we do that, maybe we can all work together in love to heal the grave injuries of climate change.

What do you mean when you say "when we remember"?

I believe each of us knows, deep down inside, that we are part of the flesh and bone of nature, that we're of a piece with the world, that we all come from the same stuff, that we are all made of stars. This recognition is prevalent among traditional cultures. Fortunately, in America we have many Indigenous people still living here in our communities. Some of them can help us remember our place in the universe. Yes, we are the most powerful animal, the top of the food chain. But in the words of John F. Kennedy, "To those to whom much is given, much is required." This is the message of *Crows Calling*.

How did you establish your own deep connection with nature?

My father and mother both loved the great outdoors. When we went on vacation, it was often to a rural or natural spot where we would hike, and they would fish. When I got into the Boy Scouts, I had the opportunity to be out in nature quite a bit, and I think that deepened my connection. We always had dogs and other animals in the house when I was growing up, and I felt a certain kinship with them, perhaps because, being in the military, we moved houses regularly and so I didn't necessarily have a lot of old friends. Finally, there's my religious and spiritual upbringing, which taught me to revere life and to honor and care for the beauty of creation. As my friend Illana Berger writes, "To walk on this Earth is to walk in the presence of the sacred."

You had a long and successful career working in international security. Why write a novel?

Crows Calling addresses the gravest threat to human security—climate change—so in this way, the book follows the arc of my life. After a long sojourn in the corridors of power, I grew impatient with the formal processes of business and government that societies use to advance their goals. I came to appreciate how the weight of human history constrains the paths of change. My longstanding reverence for the natural world and its vibrancy came into the foreground, unsealing the ancient origins of art and beauty. I was drawn to rekindle the fires of the pen, first through poetry and now in fiction, with a focus on the nature of the human experience and our connection with the larger forces alive in the universe. Art can reach the human heart in ways nothing else can.

***Crows Calling* has a lot of climate science and politics, much of which doesn't seem so optimistic about where we are headed. Is that your view?**

I'm an optimist by nature, and *Crows Calling* has an optimistic ending. But I *am* concerned. We humans tend to think short term, and climate change is a long-term process. Even if we stopped every destructive thing we're doing tomorrow, air and ocean temperatures would continue to rise for several decades, given the amount of carbon already in the atmosphere. We also tend to think we can engineer our way out of any problem.

Technology is critical to carbon reduction and climate adaptation, but it's not enough. We need to change our lifestyles in a big way, or our dear Grandmother Earth will change them for us.

Why should people believe the climate science in *Crows Calling*? You're not a climate scientist.

You don't have to be a climate scientist to understand climate change. The United Nations Intergovernmental Panel on Climate Change (IPCC) has produced clear and unambiguous reports for the last fifteen years. They're available online, and there are executive summaries that are digestible by the readers of *Crows Calling.*

You write about Indigenous customs and about women's issues in *Crows Calling*. Does it worry you that some readers may find it arrogant to hear a white male voicing those perspectives?

Some readers may be offended by one or another part of the book. That comes with the territory. I've done my best to consult with Indigenous people and with women about the scenes and depictions that are in the book. *Crows Calling* stands on its own, and I'll leave it to the readers to decide if its perspectives merit their attention. But I think it's important sometimes for white males to give respectful voice to those who are typically underrepresented in our society's conversations.

What do you mean when you talk about the "Old Times"?

By the Old Times, I mean the time before widespread writing, when people passed on knowledge from generation to generation through songs and stories. Oral tradition is at the foundation of all cultures, and as scholar Erin Hanson writes, that collective community enterprise kept the social order intact. It also reinforced our connection to the natural world by using the landscape and its planimals as grounding for the stories' lessons. One

Canadian Indigenous response to early settler claims that they owned the land in what is now British Columbia, is said to have been "If this is your land, where are your stories?" Of course, we cannot go back to the Old Times. But remembering them with affection can remind us of who we are and where we live—one species among millions alive on the face of our beautiful planet.

Who is your favorite character in *Crows Calling*?

I have to say I have two favorite human characters. Of course I love Luz, the main character whom we follow from the age of ten until she's fifteen and in high school. She's really my hero in terms of the way she deals with the challenges of growing up in a scary world. My other favorite is Jack Clemens, the selfish venture capitalist who has his own struggles and learns a few things in the course of the story that make me hopeful about the future. Of course, when it comes to animal characters, I have to favor Koro, the crow narrator. I love how she takes her mission, but not herself, so seriously.

Why did you capitalize the names of some planimals? It's not conventional style.

It's one way to underscore the equality among species—humans included. We humans capitalize words like Ohlone or French, out of respect for heritage. In the book, planimals are doing something similar when they refer to a Crow or a Bear.

What have readers told you they enjoyed about the book?

Readers tell me they find the characters sympathetic and inspiring. They enjoy the social, political, and economic diversity of the people and the personality quirks of the animals. They like how the characters stretch themselves to understand each other. They say that the book changes their sense of what's possible between the species, and they welcome the optimistic tone. Many appreciate the straightforward explanations of climate change and the practical examples of what they can do.

Unlike many climate books these days, *Crows Calling* is neither dystopian nor apocalyptic. What makes this story real?

Ultimately this is a story about families—human families and the larger family of "all our relations"—our plant and animal relatives who live here with us on this fragile Earth, our island home. What makes *Crows Calling* real is that it depicts regular people and planimals living their lives while they figure out how to adapt to the coming changes in the environment and learn what we can do to make a difference.

What's next for you as an author?

Right now, the novel suits me. I have another one in the works. It's quite different, although, like *Crows Calling*, it explores the joys and challenges of our human experience as contemporary Americans.

About the Author

BRUCE MCCONNELL is an agile and accomplished shapeshifter, having flourished as a poet, roofer, artist-blacksmith, mechanical engineer, tenor, business consultant, national security official, non-profit executive, and peacemaker. A collection of his poems, *Living from Here*, was published by Anvil Press (US). He recently moved to Ashland, Oregon, to feel closer to his relations in the natural world. *Crows Calling* is his first novel.